Michael Wood is a freelance journali
Newcastle. As a journalist he co
throughout Sheffield, gaining first-h
procedure. He also reviews books fo. ....quaa, a website
dedicated to crime fiction.

      X x.com/MichaelHWood
      f facebook.com/MichaelWoodBooks
      ◯ instagram.com/MichaelWoodBooks
      BB bookbub.com/authors/MichaelWood

Also by Michael Wood

DCI Matilda Darke series
For Reasons Unknown

Outside Looking In

A Room Full of Killers

The Hangman's Hold

The Murder House

Stolen Children

Time Is Running Out

Survivor's Guilt

The Lost Children

Silent Victim

Below Ground

Standalone
The Seventh Victim

Vengeance is Mine

Short Stories
The Fallen

Victim of Innocence

Making of a Murderer

THE MIND OF A MURDERER

A Dr Olivia Winter Thriller

MICHAEL WOOD

One More Chapter
a division of HarperCollins*Publishers*
1 London Bridge Street
London SE1 9GF
www.harpercollins.co.uk
HarperCollins*Publishers*
Macken House, 39/40 Mayor Street Upper,
Dublin 1, D01 C9W8, Ireland

This paperback edition 2024

1

First published in Great Britain in ebook format
by HarperCollins*Publishers* 2024

Copyright © Michael Wood 2024
Michael Wood asserts the moral right to
be identified as the author of this work

A catalogue record of this book
is available from the British Library

ISBN: 978-0-00-861886-5

This novel is entirely a work of fiction.
The names, characters and incidents portrayed in it are
the work of the author's imagination. Any resemblance to
actual persons, living or dead, events or localities is
entirely coincidental.

Printed and bound in the UK using 100% Renewable Electricity
by CPI Group (UK) Ltd

All rights reserved. No part of this publication may be
reproduced, stored in a retrieval system, or transmitted,
in any form or by any means, electronic, mechanical,
photocopying, recording or otherwise, without the prior
permission of the publishers.

For Mum
(Just don't read the sex scenes. Chris made me put them in.)

Prologue

Forensic psychology is the application of scientific knowledge to help answer questions in the study of criminal practice. Through analysing the history of the criminal, interviewing the killers and the friends and family of the suspects it is hoped a better understanding of the murderer and their acts can alert the authorities to the killers of the future.

You can sit opposite an incarcerated mass murderer and ask him questions and he will answer you, but how much can you trust his answers? Serial killers are, by design, great manipulators.

The theory behind the science is intricate. In my experience, the best person to fully understand a serial killer is one of his victims. Like me.

Chapter One

DOLLIS HILL, LONDON

Thursday 15th February 2024

After a double shift at the Royal Free Hospital, Phoebe Harper was hoping to get home, order a takeaway, have a long soak in the bath until the delivery arrived and spend the evening in front of the television gorging herself on spring rolls and crispy duck. As soon as she turned the corner and entered the road where she lived, she knew her quiet evening was ruined before it had even begun.

Her next-door neighbour, Donna Fletcher, was forty today and was having the party to end all parties. Phoebe had known about it for months – she'd even been invited – but had turned it down because she knew she'd be tired after work.

The road was packed with randomly parked cars. Donna's driveway was cluttered, and it wasn't difficult to spot the party house; a light was on in every room. The front door was wide open, and people were spilling out onto the street, bottles in hand. Thumping music sounded from within.

Donna, dressed in an unflattering little black dress, trotted unsteadily down the street towards Phoebe. She was wearing a plastic tiara on her head, a pink feather boa around her neck, and had an open bottle of prosecco in her left hand.

'Pheebs,' she slurred. 'You're home. Please tell me you're going to join us.'

Phoebe could smell the alcohol on her breath before she even opened her mouth. 'I'd love to, Donna, but I'm dead on my feet. I've been at the hospital for eighteen hours.'

'Pleeeeease?' Donna begged, managing to stretch the word for longer than was necessary. 'For me? Just one little drinky?'

'I can't. I've got to be back at work by eight tomorrow morning. I've got this weekend off. I'll take you out for lunch on Saturday if you're free.'

'I never say no to a free lunch,' Donna said with a smile. 'Thanks for your present. They're gorgeous.'

Donna put her arm around Phoebe and led her up the street to their homes. 'It's a shame you can't come. Roger's here. I've told you about Roger, haven't I? He's gorgeous. Six foot something, amazing body on him, and my James has seen him in the showers at the gym. I don't know any measurements but even James was impressed, and I've told you how big he is.'

'Yes, Donna, you have. Many times.'

'According to James, Roger is a sucker for a nurse's uniform too. He'd be on you in seconds.'

'As fun as that sounds, I'm really not in the mood tonight.'

'Never mind. I'll introduce you to him another time.' Donna took a swig from the bottle of prosecco and proffered it to Phoebe who waved it away. 'Listen, any chance we can park a couple of cars on your driveway? The net curtains are twitching. I don't think it'll be long before them across the way call for the police.'

'Yes, sure. No problem. Why don't you invite them over? They can't complain if they're invited.'

'I did. I went round on Saturday. He gave me a right earful about council regulations regarding loud music and occupancy levels. Boring old bastard.'

'Donna!' The call came from the doorway of the party HQ. They both turned to see James stood on the doorstep. 'Alice's been sick. Where's the mop?'

'She's such a lightweight,' Donna said to Phoebe. 'She only has to hear a cork popping and she's heaving.' She kissed her on the cheek. 'We'll try to keep it down,' she said, stifling a laugh and heading back to her house through the maze of cars.

'Don't worry about it,' Phoebe called.

She unlocked the door, stepped into the house and closed it behind her. From inside, all she could hear was the dull thud of music and muffled laughter. Once she had the television on, she was sure she wouldn't have her evening interrupted.

She locked the door, put the security chain on and picked up the post. She flicked through the brown envelopes as she headed into the kitchen, slapping them down on the worktop. She switched the light on with her elbow. The whole room lit up in a brilliant white light. She went to the fridge, pulled out a bottle of wine and poured herself a glass. Unconsciously, she let out a heavy sigh.

There was a loud bang on the patio door at the back of the room that made her jump. She turned and saw James standing outside. He waved to her.

Phoebe took the key from the hook on the dresser, unlocked the door and pulled it open. A blast of cool air hit her in the face.

'Jesus, James, you scared the life out of me.'

'Sorry, I thought you'd seen me. Look, I know it's an imposition, but can we borrow your patio chairs?'

'What?'

'I know it's February, but we're having a barbeque and we haven't got enough chairs. Can we nab yours?'

'Course you can,' she smiled.

'I'll bring them back round tomorrow, once I've sobered up.'

'I doubt they'll be getting used until the summer. Keep them as long as you like. They might be a bit damp though. Do you want the cushions?' she asked as he began grabbing the wooden seats.

'Please. I'll have them cleaned if anything gets spilled on them.'

'Hang on.' Phoebe went back to the dresser. She opened a drawer and took out a key. 'Here you go. They're in the shed. Just pop them back in when you're done with them.'

'You sure?'

'Yes.'

'Thanks. Are you sure you can't pop round for a quick drink?'

'I'd better not. Once I get started, I don't know when to stop.'

'Donna's the same. I hope this is the only time she plans on turning forty. She was thirty about five times. See you later.'

Phoebe smiled and closed the door. She watched as James took the four chairs and squeezed through the gap in the fence between the two houses.

Phoebe refilled her glass of wine and took it upstairs.

The house was warm, the heating having come on as timed at six o'clock. She started running the bath, poured in a large amount of bubble bath, then went into her bedroom to change. Before stripping off her nurse's uniform, she looked out of the window into the garden next door. The party was in full swing. She could see the silhouettes of people dancing inside cast onto the lawn. She would love to be with them but didn't dare risk being late for work tomorrow. The hospital was struggling to cope as it was, being understaffed and with extra patients following the harsh winter.

She closed the curtains and tried to block out all sounds of the party. If she couldn't hear it or see it, she wouldn't feel so bad about missing it.

Phoebe wrapped a pink towelling dressing gown around her. She went back to the bathroom and removed her make-up in the mirror above the sink. She couldn't believe Donna was forty. She certainly didn't look it. As she wiped away the foundation and eye shadow, the lines and wrinkles were revealed. It would be another three years before Phoebe hit the big four-oh, and she wasn't looking forward to it. Donna was married and had two children, a good job, holidays twice a year and a new car every eighteen months. Phoebe was single, childless, had a demanding job and no money for a holiday or a car. Things would have to change this year. She'd been thinking about entering private practice, but that would mean turning her back on helping real people at the heart of the NHS, something she loved doing.

She sighed and turned away from her tired reflection. She pulled out the hair tie and allowed her dull hair to fall down her shoulders. The bath was full, the room had filled with steam and a relaxing aroma rose from the bubble bath. She turned off the tap and threw the dressing gown to the floor. She was just about to step into it when the doorbell rang.

Phoebe sighed. She put her dressing gown back on and headed for the stairs. She opened the door, expecting it to be Donna or James or maybe even the hunk from the gym.

'Sorry to interrupt,' a man of average height with neat dark hair and staring blue eyes said. 'I've come from next door. I've been sent round to ask if you can spare any wine glasses. There seems to be more people here than expected.'

Phoebe looked out at the madness of the party. The other neighbours wouldn't be as accommodating as her. She doubted it would be long before the police turned up.

'Sure, come on in,' she smiled, opening the door wider.

'Sorry, I haven't woken you up or anything, have I?' the man asked, noticing her dressing gown.

'No. I've just got home from work. I was about to take a bath. How many glasses do you want?'

'I'm not sure. How many can you spare?' he asked from the hallway.

She opened the doors to the dresser and began to reach up for a glass. As she did, her shoulders were grabbed, and she was pulled backwards from behind. She felt a kick to the back of her knees, and she buckled to the floor. Shocked, she looked up and saw the man standing over her, a sweet smile on his face and a twinkle dancing in his eyes. From behind his back, he pulled out a large carving knife.

He held the knife aloft. He was about to bring it down when Phoebe swiftly kicked him hard between the legs. He let out a shout and doubled up in pain. She pushed him to one side and ran out of the kitchen and into the hallway. She pulled at the front door, but it was locked, and the chain had been replaced. In her panic, she grabbed at the security chain, but her shaking fingers couldn't get any purchase on it.

'You fucking bitch.'

She turned to where the voice was coming from and ducked just in time as the large knife slammed into the wooden door. She scrambled to her feet and headed for the stairs, quickly crawling up them on her hands and feet. She could hear the intruder following behind her.

She ran into the bedroom and slammed the door closed behind her, but she was too slow. The man had managed to get to it before it closed and was forcing it open. He pushed as she struggled to keep him at bay.

As loudly as she could, Phoebe screamed, hoping someone, *anyone*, would hear and come to save her. The noise from Donna's party was getting louder. There was no way anyone would hear her cries.

The bedroom door was forced open and Phoebe fell backwards onto the carpet. The man entered and stood over her, knife aloft in his right hand.

Phoebe was crying. Her breathing was erratic as he came towards her.

'Please. Please don't kill me,' she pleaded.

He brought the knife down quickly, but Phoebe's reactions were quicker. She kicked him hard in the shins. His knees buckled and he fell, but not before the knife had pierced the skin on her exposed leg. She screamed out in pain, and looked down at the blood seeping out of the wound.

She tried to stand up. She pushed her attacker out of the way. He fell backwards again and hit his head hard against the fitted wardrobe door. She pulled herself to her feet and stumbled out of the bedroom, limping towards the top of the stairs, half running, half falling down them.

Out of breath, panicking, frightened and bleeding, Phoebe struggled with the front door. Her fingers were shaking so violently she couldn't find any grip on the Yale lock. She pulled the door open, but the security chain was still on.

'Fuck!' she cried.

She closed the door, ripped off the chain and opened it once again.

It was pitch-black outside. All she could hear was thumping music and raucous laughter coming from next door. Ahead, three people made their way up the cul-de-sac, heading for Donna's house. Two had a bottle in hand and the third was carrying a large present with a red bow on it.

She stepped out into the cold air.

Phoebe opened her mouth and let out a piercing scream as her intruder grabbed her by the collar of her dressing gown and pulled her back inside, slamming the front door closed.

She fell to the ground, but was able to look up and watch as the attacker leaned down towards her.

'I knew you'd be a fighter the moment I first saw you,' he said calmly into her ear. 'I love a woman who likes to play.'

Chapter Two

Friday 16th February 2024

Detective Inspector Jessica Sheffield was sitting behind the wheel of the Vauxhall Astra. Something caught her eye. She looked up and saw her partner heading towards her. She took a deep breath and slowly let it out. She knew how this conversation was going to play out.

The door opened and Detective Inspector Foley climbed in, bringing with him a blast of cold air. He slammed the door closed.

They sat in silence while they both looked outside at the scene of organised chaos going on around them. White-suited forensic officers were busy entering and leaving the house at the top of the cul-de-sac. Uniformed officers were knocking on neighbouring doors, notebooks in hand, talking to sombre-faced residents on the doorsteps.

'You know what I'm going to ask you, don't you?' Foley asked.

'I do,' Jessica replied.

'And...?'

'I can't.'

'Why not?'

'I promised.'

'It's the same bloke, Jessica. No witnesses, very little forensic evidence from what we can tell so far, and he's escalating. You've seen the body. You've seen how she suffered. Nobody knows serial killers better than she does.'

'She doesn't work active cases. You know that. I know that. I promised I'd never ask her.'

Foley turned in his seat to look at the DI. 'There's a woman in that house who's been stabbed to death. He's used her as a fucking pin-cushion, for crying out loud. She was only young, mid-thirties, worked as a nurse at the Royal Free. She was doing good work, helping the sick, and this bastard comes along and decides to use her as his plaything. He's laughing at us, Jess.'

'Don't call me Jess,' she said, still staring out of the windscreen.

'Sorry. But he is. All I'm asking is for you to talk to her.'

The silence took over once again. Jessica chewed on her bottom lip as she thought. She could feel her partner's cold stare burning into her. She knew he was in a difficult position. Once the press found out there was a serial killer trawling the streets of London, killing women who lived alone, they'd have a field day and Foley's life would be made more complicated than it was now.

'Fine,' she said quietly. 'I'll ask. Just this once. And if she says no, I'm not going to keep hounding her. She's my friend. One of the few I've got.'

Foley's relief was evident by the huge grin on his face. His ice-blue eyes lit up. 'I understand. Thank you, Jessica. I'd kiss you if we didn't have an audience.'

'Just... don't get your hopes up, all right?'

It was too late for that. Foley left the car and headed back to the crime scene. She watched as his head was held high and there was a spring in his step. He was putting all his faith in Jessica being able to convince a notoriously private person to help with what was bound to become a very public investigation. There were times when she really hated her job.

By the end of a difficult working day, Jessica's usual smart appearance had changed. She looked at her reflection in the black mirror of her computer screen and rolled her eyes. Her ponytail had come loose at some point and strands of mousy hair stuck up in all directions. The small amount of lipstick she'd put on had smudged and she had a dry fleck of mayonnaise at the corner of her mouth from the disappointing tuna salad sandwich she'd eaten in a rush.

She put on her jacket, sneaked the copied files into her bag and headed for the door.

'Jessica?'

She turned at the sound of her name being called. DI Foley was standing in the doorway to his office.

'You won't forget, will you?'

'I'd love to forget,' she replied. She turned and left the office.

Driving in London was no easy task. It didn't seem to matter what the time of day was, there was always a traffic jam to wait in. When it came to the evening rush hour, it was every man for himself.

Jessica was tempted to put the blue flashing lights on to upset her fellow commuters even more, but what was the point? She wasn't exactly in a rush to ruin her friendship, and what plans did she have for this evening anyway? All she had to look forward to was a tub of Ben and Jerry's and a crap film on Netflix to watch, with Stanley on the sofa next to her licking his balls.

It took her the best part of an hour to drive to Modbury Gardens in Camden. She found a parking space and looked up at the stylish terraced property. It was the only house in the street that was in darkness. There was no point in ringing the bell.

Nobody was home and her scooter wasn't parked in its usual place. Jessica turned off the engine and settled down in her seat to wait.

Jessica closed her eyes. It had been a long day and a challenging week. She was shattered. She was working on a serial murder case and had four other cases that required her input. She was due in court next week to give evidence against a rapist, which would mean hours of hanging around waiting to be called when there were other things she could be doing.

Her phone vibrated in her pocket. She pulled it out and saw it was a text from DI Foley. She rolled her eyes and opened the message: 'I really do appreciate what you're doing. Fish and chips on me tomorrow.' It made her smile. She was about to reply when her car was lit up by the single headlight of an approaching scooter. Show time.

Olivia Winter was a short, very slim woman in her mid-thirties. Her dark-brown hair was sensibly cut into the neck and her eyes were large and dark. She preferred travelling by scooter as she could zip her way through the heavy London traffic. If she was in a car, she'd have to sit and wait, and that wasn't good for Olivia. She always needed to keep moving. Always.

She parked on the pavement outside her house and headed up the steps to the front door as she removed her gloves and hunted for her keys in the deep pockets of her jacket.

'Olivia.'

She turned abruptly at the sound of her name. It wasn't late but it was already dark. Living in a cul-de-sac meant there was only one way in or out. Whoever was calling her had been lying in wait. A figure approached her steps. It wasn't until they passed a lamp post that she recognised her caller and visibly relaxed.

'Jessica? What are you doing here?'

'I've come for a visit. It's been a while,' she said, holding up a bottle of wine in each hand.

'It's Friday night. Aren't you usually out on the town?'

'The last time I went into a nightclub the music was so loud it gave me toothache. Sadly, my party days are over. I'm now officially middle-aged. I've even invested in carpet slippers. Save me, Olivia,' she pleaded.

Olivia smiled. 'Come on then. I'm afraid I haven't got much food in. I only arrived back yesterday.'

Olivia unlocked the door and stepped inside. She waved the fob on her keyring over the security alarm then typed in a four-digit number.

'How was the big American adventure?' Jessica asked, following her into the spacious hallway.

Olivia headed for the kitchen, turning on lights as she went.

'It was good.'

They entered the brightly lit kitchen and Olivia picked two glasses from the shelf and placed them on the solid oak-topped island in the centre of the room.

'You're not very tanned.'

'I spent fourteen days lecturing. I went from university to university and hotel room to hotel room. The only time I caught any sun was when I stepped out of a taxi.'

Jessica opened a bottle of chardonnay and poured them both a healthy glassful. 'You must have had some time for fun.'

Olivia shook off her jacket and hitched herself up on one of the stools. She took a large gulp of wine and her features softened.

'I was invited out to a stunning five-star restaurant in Atlanta by this professor who looked like a cross between Hugh Jackman and Chris Pratt.'

'Ooh, gorgeous,' Jessica smiled.

'The meal was out of this world. I've never tasted food like it. We had a good chat too, and there was some serious flirting going on.'

'Don't stop.'

'Then the dessert arrived. Dark-chocolate mousse with raspberries and champagne ice-cream. I'd already had a few drinks and was feeling light-headed...'

'I know where this is going,' Jessica said, getting excited.

'Then his wife came to the table, picked up my pudding, slammed it in his face and walked out.'

'Oh. OK, so I didn't know where it was going. Did you know he was married?'

'Of course I didn't.'

'Oh well, you win some, you lose some.'

'I was more disappointed at not getting to eat my dessert,' she smiled.

'But apart from that it was a successful trip?'

'Yes. I enjoyed it. The lectures went down a storm. I signed plenty of books and if I never have to answer another question about whether or not I know the royal family personally, it'll still be too soon.'

Jessica laughed. 'Why do Americans think we all know the royal family?'

'I've no idea. One of these days I'm going to tell them I've got William and Kate on speed dial.'

They both giggled, visibly relaxing in each other's company. The wine was flowing freely, and Jessica topped up both glasses as Olivia found a bag of Kettle Chips in the back of the cupboard.

'I had the most hellacious date a couple of weeks ago,' Jessica began. 'Now, you know my rule about dating people I work with, but this new DC has joined child protection and I'm not kidding you, he is seriously fit. He's straight off the box of Calvin Klein underwear. He's so beautiful I want to cry when I see him.'

'Oh my God,' Olivia smiled, taking a handful of crisps.

'I decided to be modern and asked him out for a bite to eat.'

'In the hope that he'd say he'd like to eat you.'

'Of course,' Jessica smiled. 'Anyway, we went to this Chinese close to work and he spent the entire meal talking about himself. Everything we talked about, he turned the subject back to himself. He kept checking his reflection out in the window and constantly looking around to see if anyone was looking at him. Talk about conceited. I actually got more satisfaction out of getting out of the taxi alone than inviting him in. I didn't think it was possible for a man to be too good-looking, but he's definitely it.'

'I thought women were supposed to be high maintenance?' Olivia asked.

'The tables have turned. I don't want to go out with a man who spends more time in the bathroom than I do.'

'Have you got anyone else lined up?'

'No. I'm that busy at the moment, I haven't got time. Besides…' She waved the comment away. 'Still, on the plus side, by working myself to a frazzle, I'm not spending any money and my holiday fund is growing nicely. July cannot come soon enough. Italy is not going to know what's hit it when you and I get there,' Jessica said with a huge smile. 'I plan on doing lots of the three Ws.'

'Do I dare ask what they are?'

'Walking, wine and waiters.'

'I really hope we don't have adjoining rooms.'

'Olivia, sweetheart, when was your last holiday?'

Olivia thought for a moment. 'I… I can't remember.'

'Exactly. Whenever you do go abroad it's for work. You need to let your hair down, let your guard down and let your knickers down.'

'You are incorrigible.'

'And proud of it. Speaking of which, dare I ask if anything more has happened with you and The Handsome Stranger at the swimming pool?'

'I haven't been since before Christmas.'

'Olivia, how long have you known him?'

'I don't know him.' She stifled a laugh.

'Exactly. You've been going to that pool for over fifty years…'

'Slight exaggeration,' Olivia interrupted.

'You're letting life, and opportunities, pass you by. Now, take some advice from someone more carefree. Next time you see him, grab him by the trunks, drag him to the nearest disabled toilets and ride him like a cowboy at a rodeo.'

'Oh my God, Jessica. I think I'm blushing,' Olivia said, almost shocked. 'I'm guessing you've had experience of a disabled toilet.'

'Only once. But my goodness, it was hot.' She upended the bottle of wine over her glass, but only a few drops came out. 'Wow, this one must have had a hole in it.' She began opening the other bottle. 'So, what are you working on at the moment?'

'Well, Sebastian and I have been granted funding to look into the nature versus nurture debate.'

'Sebastian? Isn't that a cat's name?' Jessica interrupted.

Olivia tried to stifle her laughter. 'Sebastian Lister. I've worked with him for ever. You've met him God knows how many times. Are you sure that's your first bottle?'

'I know who he is. He's just… well, he's quite easily forgettable, isn't he?'

'He's got a lot on his plate. He works and looks after his kids. That's all he's got since his wife died last year, bless him. Anyway, we've identified fifty killers around the world who were adopted either at birth or soon after. We're going to look extensively into their backgrounds and those of their birth and adoptive parents and see if upbringing versus genetics plays a part in shaping the future life of a killer. I think we've spent longer on the questionnaires than we have trying to find people to take part.'

'Sounds interesting,' Jessica said, half-heartedly.

'It's going to be a long time before the results are in. We need to sort out translators for those non-English-speaking volunteers, arrange video interviews et cetera. It's a long project. However, it's something that— Sorry, is everything all right?' Olivia asked.

'What? Yes. Why do you ask?'

'You look distracted all of a sudden.'

'Do I?'

'Yes. Something on your mind?'

'No.'

'Yes there is. Come on, out with it.'

'Shit,' Jessica uttered under her breath. She took another sip of wine. 'Before I say anything, I want you to know that this isn't my idea.'

'You want my help?' Olivia asked. Her voice had dropped, and she looked down into her own now empty glass.

Jessica took a deep, shaky breath. 'Three women have been murdered. When I say murdered, I don't just mean strangled or a single stab wound to the chest, I'm talking butchered. They all share similar character traits, and they were all killed in their own homes. However, there's no sign of forced entry. We've looked into their backgrounds but none of the victims knew each other. We have no witnesses and very little forensic evidence.'

'Jessica, you know I don't work on active cases,' Olivia said, jumping down from her stool and going over to the bi-fold doors that looked out onto her large expanse of back garden.

It was pitch-black outside and all she could see was her tired reflection looking back at her, which was just as well considering the battering her garden had taken over the winter.

'I know. I'm aware of that. I didn't want to ask you, but, my partner – DI Foley – he's under some serious pressure here. The press hasn't made the connection between the three victims so far, but it's only a matter of time before they do.'

'I'm sorry. I can't help you,' Olivia said, matter-of-factly, without turning back.

'I'm not asking you to work full time on this. I know you're busy with research and you've got a new book out later this year, but if you could just glance at the case files.'

Olivia heard rustling coming from behind her. She turned and saw Jessica had her bag on her lap and was struggling to pull the thick files out.

'You came prepared,' Olivia said drily.

'I know it's a cheek. I know we said we'd never ask each other to help when it came to work matters, but, Olivia, if you saw these women, you'd see how much they need you.'

'I don't want to see them,' Olivia almost snapped. 'I can't look at an active case. You know all this, Jessica. You know what I went through.' She scratched at her left shoulder unconsciously.

'I'm aware of your past—'

'Are you?' Olivia interrupted. Her voice was raised. Her face had reddened and a sheen of sweat appeared on her forehead. 'I know you were around when it all happened, but sometimes it feels like...' she trailed off. 'If you really understood, you wouldn't be asking me to look at those files.'

'It's because of what you went through that I'm asking,' Jessica pleaded.

Olivia made her way back to the kitchen island. In the corner was a neat stack of mail she'd accumulated while she'd been away in America but hadn't got around to opening yet. With shaking fingers, she rummaged through the pile until she came to one she was looking for. She knew it would be there. Without fail. She barely looked at the scrawled handwriting on the white envelope before throwing it at Jessica.

'Open this.'

'What is it?'

'Just open it.'

Jessica frowned as she picked up the cheap envelope. She didn't recognise the writing and the postmark was smudged. She opened it and pulled out a folded sheet of plain white paper. On the front was a big red heart. Inside, a simple message: *Happy Valentine's Day, my love.* It was signed with a single kiss.

'Is it from him?'

Olivia nodded. Her bottom lip wobbled.

The atmosphere in the room had intensified.

'Does he send you one every year?' Jessica asked.

'Valentine's Day, birthday and Christmas.'

'Why didn't you say anything? We could have put a stop to this.'

'He'd have found a way. That's what people like him do,' Olivia said. 'If I get involved in an active case, the press will find out. They'll dig into my background, they'll find him and it'll start all over again.'

'You don't know that.'

'I do know that. Look, I'm sorry about those three women, I really am, but I cannot help you.'

Jessica looked down at the childish card in her hands. 'How long has this been going on?'

'Years.'

'Why haven't you told me about them?' Olivia didn't reply. 'Olivia, I'm your oldest friend, yet there are times when I feel like I don't know you at all. You should have told me about this. Not as a detective, but as a friend.'

'I don't want any… I don't want to think about it. About him. If I ignore them—'

'It won't go away,' Jessica interrupted. 'Ignoring him isn't making him stop.'

'If I acknowledge them, it'll add fuel to the fire and he'll start sending more. There are times when ignorance is bliss. This is one of those times.'

'You should still have told me, at least. Why do you have to go through everything on your own?'

Olivia shrugged, but she knew the answer. She couldn't open herself up to people because she knew it would leave her vulnerable.

'Olivia. Olivia, please…'

'I think you should go,' Olivia said, turning back to the large windows.

'I'm caught between a rock and a hard place here, Olivia. I didn't want to ask you, honestly, but...' Jessica fell silent. 'I'm sorry,' she eventually said, quietly. 'I really am.'

Olivia didn't say anything.

Jessica climbed down from her high stool. She picked up her bag and left the kitchen. It wasn't until she heard the front door close that Olivia turned around. She saw the crudely made Valentine's card sitting on top of the three files Jessica had left behind.

Leaning against the glass of the window, Olivia wrapped her arms tightly around herself. Her head felt heavy. She didn't blame Jessica and hated being so harsh with her, but they had an unwritten agreement never to discuss their active work life with each other, and Jessica had just broken through that wall. She could feel her heart pounding loudly in her chest and the prickly sensation coming from the scars on her shoulder, reminding her, taunting her.

Chapter Three

Olivia sat on the leather sofa in the corner of her large kitchen. Her eyes kept landing on the files Jessica had left. Why had she come here tonight? Surely the Metropolitan Police weren't so desperate that they had to request the services of a complete basket case like Olivia Winter.

She felt angry. Jessica knew about Olivia's past. She knew the torment she had been through, yet she seemed perfectly at ease about coming here and presenting her with more agony. What kind of a friend did that? It was obvious to Olivia that Jessica wasn't a real friend. Olivia should have known that someone in her position would bide her time and wait for the right case to come along to ruin what Olivia thought was a genuine relationship built on mutual respect.

Olivia's legs felt leaden as she pulled herself up from the sofa. She grabbed the Valentine's card off the countertop and stomped out of the room.

The house in Modbury Gardens was spread over four floors. It was far too big for one person, but Olivia liked the space and the solitude. Other residents in the street had converted their basements into self-contained apartments and let them out to single professionals and students. Next door had rented theirs out to a junior doctor and although Sam was a lovely young man, Olivia couldn't think of anything worse than having a perfect stranger living so close by.

She never used the lower ground floor. It was equipped with a small kitchen and bathroom and there were two good-sized rooms which could be used as a lounge and bedroom or two bedrooms. It even had its own entrance. It had remained empty since the day she moved in.

Olivia lived mostly on the raised ground floor. She loved her large contemporary black and white kitchen. When she moved in there were double swing doors leading off into the dining room, but she'd had those removed and the space sealed up to make a solid wall. She had no need for a dining room; she wasn't the entertaining type. It was now a very cosy lounge with two large Chesterfield sofas, bookcases lining the back wall and a widescreen TV on the wall above the fireplace. It was minimal, but it was comfortable.

On the same floor was a master bedroom with an en suite. The whole floor felt like a luxury hotel suite.

There was just one room on the first floor and it had been originally designed to be the reception room. Olivia used it as an office for when she worked from home. She'd had the whole room decked out with a fitted oak desk, filing cabinets for her research, shelves and whiteboards. It was her central hub. There was a fourteen-foot roof terrace leading off it, and in the summer, on the rare occasion that London was bathed in sunlight, she would open up the bi-fold doors. If it wasn't for the smell of exhaust fumes, and the constant noise of traffic, she could be in the middle of the countryside instead of one of the busiest capital cities in the world.

The top floor was somewhere Olivia rarely ventured. The space in the roof of the house had been designed as a bedroom with en suite. It was Olivia's secret office. She went up occasionally, when her mood was low, and she needed answers to questions she didn't dare ask.

Other identical houses in the street were home to families, successful couples with three or four children, whereas Olivia's was the only one with a single occupant. That was how she liked it. Olivia needed space. She needed to be alone. If it wasn't for work, she'd spend her whole time here, so she wanted to spread out. There had to be designated areas for relaxing, sleeping and working. When the front door was closed and secured, when the windows were alarmed, that was when Olivia could settle and breathe.

She went into her bedroom at the front of the house, opened the floor-to-ceiling doors of the fitted wardrobe and dropped to her knees. She rummaged around the shoe boxes and discarded handbags for what she was looking for. Right at the back was a handmade oak box she'd found in a second-hand shop in Greenwich many years ago. It had an intricate architrave design on the lid and a dark-green velvet inlay. The key to the lock was missing and it was worthless, but Olivia loved it. The plan had been to keep her knick-knacks in it, the precious keepsakes she had gathered over the years. Instead, it had become the place where the cards and letters she received at various points throughout the year were hidden. The Valentine, birthday and Christmas cards, the letters on the anniversary, the random pleas for her to visit. She wanted to destroy them, but Sebastian begged her to keep them. They'd come in handy, he'd said. She had no idea why.

She stuffed the latest card in the box, closed the lid and put it back in its usual place, covering it up with old scarves and a pair of sandals she hadn't worn for years.

She looked up and found her eyes were blurred with tears. She lay down on her king-size bed, snatching up the blue soft toy she kept on her pillow. Its colour was fading, bleached by the sunlight, it was tatty and had a fusty smell about it, but it would remain on her bed until the day she died.

On the bedside table was a small framed photograph of her mother and sister. They were sitting in the back garden of their home; the sun was beating down on them, the sky was a stunning deep blue and they were both grinning at the camera, full of life. Her younger sister, Claire, was holding a blue dog which she took everywhere with her.

'What dogs are blue?'

Olivia gave a pained smile at the memory of her sister asking the obvious question when she first saw the dog. It didn't matter that he was a strange colour; Claire had loved him. He'd slept in her bed every night. Now he slept with Olivia.

She placed the frame back on the table next to a well-thumbed paperback copy of *Little Women*. It had been her mother's favourite book. The bookmark was still on page seventy-six where her mother had last been reading and it would remain there.

Olivia climbed under the duvet and wrapped it tightly around her. She closed her eyes, but sleep refused to come. Her body might be tired, but her mind was wide awake. It was always wide awake. Her haunted thoughts whirled around twenty-four hours a day. They frightened her, they held her prisoner, but she continued to hold onto them, and add to them.

Chapter Four

Saturday 17th February 2024

Olivia rarely remembered her dreams, only the nightmares. She woke on the Saturday morning and her head felt much lighter. A bright light tried to enter the room by the gaps at the sides of the curtains. Spring was on its way. The tough winter was slowly losing its stranglehold on nature, and despite the nights still being cool, the days were getting longer, and the sun was warming up. Soon, there would be no need for scarves and hats and gloves when leaving the house. Olivia hated the summer. She wore high-neck tops and long sleeves to cover her scars, which attracted more attention. Who wore jumpers during a heatwave?

She climbed out of bed, neatened the duvet and looked at her shattered reflection in the wardrobe mirror. She loathed what she saw looking back at her.

Olivia didn't have a plan for today. She needed to fill her fridge and cupboards with food following her return from America, and after the copious amount of food and drink she'd consumed over there, she should perhaps think about—

She stopped dead in her tracks as she entered the kitchen. The files. She had forgotten all about them. She edged towards them and held the very corner of one between the tips of her finger and thumb. She lifted it slowly and angled her head to take a sneaky peek. She let go the moment she glimpsed the first photograph.

'Fuck,' she said to herself.

Olivia stormed back into her bedroom, struggled to get into a pair of tight-fitting jeans, threw on a T-shirt and jumper, grabbed her rucksack from behind the corner and headed for the front door. She swiped her mobile to life and made a call while she hunted around for her keys. After five rings, the voicemail kicked in.

'Jessica, it's Olivia. You need to come back and collect these files at some point over the weekend, or they'll be in the bin on Monday morning.'

Olivia drove a black Honda PCX125 scooter. It was perfect for the London streets. One of her pet hates was being stuck in traffic. Her mind tended to wander when she had nothing to do and if you drove a car and lived in London, you could spend ninety per cent of your commuting time waiting to move. That would be hazardous to Olivia's state of mind. The scooter helped her to weave through the traffic.

The swimming pool was a fifteen-minute drive from her home. She parked close to the entrance and headed straight for the changing rooms. As usual on a Saturday morning, it was busy, but she found a quiet corner for her to quickly change into the specially designed and very expensive costume. It had a high neck and long sleeves and looked more like a surfer's suit than something to swim a few lengths in. Even though she was a regular at the pool, Olivia still garnered strange looks because of the costume.

She lowered herself into the pool and allowed the warm water to envelop her. She loved the smell of chlorine; it was clean and fresh. She watched other swimmers as they did their laps slowly and gracefully.

She set off, parting the water with her hands and feet in the breaststroke. She reached the end of the pool and came to a stop. She was breathing heavily already. A man came to a stop beside her. Olivia felt herself redden and looked away. Jessica's words from last night came back to taunt her as The Handsome Stranger stopped and ran his fingers through his dark-brown wavy hair.

'Hello. Haven't seen you here for a while,' he said between pants.

Olivia smiled at him. 'No. I've been away.'

'Holiday?'

'I wish. Work.'

'Anywhere nice?'

'America.'

'Lovely. Shame you didn't bring the sun back with you.'

'I couldn't get it through customs.'

He smiled. 'Ah. You up for a challenge?' he asked with a glint in his eye.

'You'd have me beat by the end of the first lap. I'm shattered already.'

'Spoilsport.'

He pulled his goggles over his eyes and set off again, purposely splashing Olivia as he went. She laughed. She watched as he swam with all the speed and dexterity of an Olympic athlete. As Olivia was about to set off for her more sedate lap, she noticed a woman looking her up and down, frowning at the strange swimsuit she was wearing.

Olivia had seen the man often when she came for a swim. They had started out by smiling and nodding at each other. After a couple of weeks, he had made the first move by saying hello. A month after that they had their first chat at the edge of the pool while resting. Since then, they'd challenged each other to the odd race, talked about other people in the pool and their strange changing-room habits, even had a coffee together in the café afterwards. Yet, Olivia still had no idea what his name was. Did he know hers? Had they even formally introduced themselves? Olivia couldn't remember, and it was far too late in their 'relationship' now to ask him what his name was without looking ridiculous. Whenever she thought of him outside of the sports centre, he was The Handsome Stranger. He had dark hair and smiling blue eyes, a firm, slightly stubbled jawline and a hairy chest. His stomach was flat and firm. She didn't like to look any lower, as much as she wanted to.

She remembered Jessica's words when she had told her friend about The Handsome Stranger after their first meeting, and she hadn't been able to get him out of her mind for some reason.

'Budgie-smugglers can be very deceiving,' she'd said. 'They squeeze everything in so tightly and once they're off you can sometimes get a real eyeful. Mind you, anything more than a mouthful's a waste, in my opinion.'

Olivia laughed at the memory and went back to her swimming.

After six more laps, Olivia climbed out of the pool. She was knackered. Her fitness levels had slumped in the past couple of months. She felt better in mind, body and soul when she swam twenty laps without breaking a sweat. It helped to clear her mind. When she was swimming, her dark thoughts evaporated. She had no idea what was occupying her brain while she was in the middle of exercise, but when it was over, she always had some kind of answer to whatever had been troubling her.

She headed for the changing room, running her fingers through her short, wet hair, wiping the drops from her face. She turned the corner and literally bumped into The Handsome Stranger. He stood on her foot with his huge size twelves. Olivia squealed.

'Shit, I'm so sorry. Completely my fault. I wasn't looking where I was going,' he said. 'Are you all right?'

'Yes, I'm fine,' she smiled through the pain.

'Can you walk?'

'I think so.' She hobbled, and he caught her arm.

'You can swear at me if you like.'

She looked up at him and laughed.

'Come over here. Rest your foot for a bit.'

With his strong, wet arms around her, he led her over to the benches outside the changing rooms and sat her down. He lifted her leg up and held her foot in his hands. The touch of his huge hands was soft, almost delicate.

'Is this tender?' he asked, pressing on the top of her foot.

'Yes. It's probably just bruised. Don't worry about it,' she said, trying to take her foot back.

He placed her foot in his lap and began to rub it gently. She swallowed hard and looked up at him. Their eyes met.

'How's that?' he asked softly.

'Perfect,' she said. She pressed her foot against his crotch and felt him harden.

She looked away and her eyes fell on the door of the disabled toilet. Suddenly, Jessica was screaming at her in her head to take this opportunity and run with it. She looked back at him and bit her bottom lip. He raised a questioning eyebrow and smiled.

Olivia quickly looked over her shoulder to make sure nobody was watching before she stood up and limped to the toilet. She pulled open the door and disappeared inside. He followed.

He locked the door behind them then turned to look at her. At well over six foot, he towered over her. He placed his hands on her face and bent down, kissing her softly on the lips. She reached for the light switch and turned it off.

They didn't have time for passion. Olivia grabbed the zip at the back of her costume and pulled it down. It was always difficult to remove when she was wet, but she yanked it off with ease.

The Handsome Stranger stepped out of his swimming shorts. He grabbed Olivia, picked her up and pushed her up against the wall and began kissing her neck. She turned her head quickly and banged it hard against the hand drier.

'Fuck,' she said.

'Are you all right?' he whispered.

'I'm fine.'

She wrapped her legs around his waist, and he lifted her further. She held onto him tightly, arms around his neck. He placed his hands on the wall to steady himself and the automatic drier came on, blasting them both with warm air.

Olivia bit her bottom lip to stop herself from laughing.

The Handsome Stranger moved her further along the wall, away from the drier, not noticing he'd pulled the red cord hanging from the corner of the room. Within moments the door was forced open by two staff members. The looks of concern dropped when they were confronted not with a disabled person needing help, but two very able-bodied adults misusing the facilities.

'Not again,' sighed one of the staff members. 'I don't know why we don't just put a condom machine in here and have done with it.'

Olivia closed her eyes and squeezed them tightly shut. She could feel herself reddening with embarrassment. She released her hold of The Handsome Stranger and quickly pulled on her swimming costume.

'Excuse me,' she said to the staff member blocking her exit, keeping her head down to avoid eye contact.

As she made her way to the female changing rooms, she heard the man in the background try to explain their situation.

'It's our wedding anniversary,' The Handsome Stranger said. 'We're spicing things up, you know, something to tell the kids one day.'

Olivia couldn't help but smile. *Well played*, she thought.

Olivia spent a good half an hour in the showers. The water wasn't hot enough and no amount of hair scrubbing and scratching at her skin with an exfoliating body scrub would remove the shame and guilt she felt. When the light had been turned on and the small room lit up, all Olivia could think of was everyone seeing her scars.

Olivia had lost all sense of time when she left the sports centre. It was almost lunchtime and she hadn't eaten since yesterday afternoon. When she arrived at her scooter she noticed a heavy stone in the footwell. She picked it up. It was acting as a paperweight for a business card. She looked around but there was nobody watching.

The card belonged to an Ethan Miller who was a freelance photo-journalist. She turned the white card over. Written in a scrawl was the message, *You're gorgeous. Call me.*

She stuffed the card into her jacket pocket. She could feel herself smiling. A very fit, very handsome and very sexy man was attracted to her. That never happened. He obviously hadn't noticed her scars in the toilet. Olivia had no intention of calling him, but for a brief moment, it felt amazing to be wanted.

Chapter Five

Olivia stopped at a café on her way home. Her growling stomach was crying out for food. She ordered a bowl of soup and a coffee strong enough for the spoon to stand up in. She sat at the window, dipping artisan bread into the homemade vegetable soup, looking up occasionally to watch the world pass her by.

She could feel her tensions ebbing away and her shoulders begin to relax. She lived for moments like this. As much as Olivia enjoyed her work, taking time away from thinking about serial killers and trying to work out what the hell was going through their minds for just half an hour or so was bliss.

'I thought it was you.'

Olivia looked up to see Jessica standing next to her.

'Are you following me?'

'Of course not. I was doing some shopping.' She held up two paper bags as evidence. 'I was calling in here for some beans and saw you through the window; thought I'd come over and say hello. Can I join you?'

'Sure.'

Jessica sat opposite her and Olivia went back to eating her soup.

'I'm sorry about last night,' Jessica said after a silence had developed.

'It's OK.'

'We're under a lot of pressure at work and Foley... You know what? You don't need to hear this. Are we all right?'

Olivia smiled. 'Of course we are.'

'Still going to Italy in July?'

'Definitely.'

'Good. Can I buy you a carrot cake muffin as a peace offering?'

'You most certainly can.'

Within a minute, the atmosphere between the two had thawed. Olivia told Jessica about her interrupted fumble with The Handsome Stranger in the disabled toilet, which caused Jessica to spit out her latte.

'Oh my God, Olivia, I can't believe you did that. What gym do you go to? All the blokes at mine are horrible.'

'I'm not telling you,' she said with a sly grin.

'Blimey, I can't believe it,' Jessica smiled. 'I know I said it last night, but I don't think I'd ever dare do anything as risky as that.'

'No. You just prefer to have sex in front of five thousand people at Glastonbury.'

Jessica visibly blushed. 'I was young. It was my first weekend away without my parents. I was finding myself.'

'All you needed to do was look for the nearest bloke.'

'I think we can both say we've had our fair share of embarrassing encounters.'

'They get the blood pumping, though.' Olivia sat back in her seat and sipped her black coffee. 'It's the excitement, the rush, the thrill; it makes you feel alive.'

'You are aware you could get arrested if caught having sex in a public place.'

'You make it sound like I trawl the parks looking for men to drag into the woods. It's not a regular thing.'

'I know. I'm just teasing you.'

'Are you sure you're all right, Jessica? You look... different, somehow.'

'I'm fine. Just tired,' she said, looking forlorn. 'I'm at work more than I'm at home. I was called out on Christmas Day and Boxing Day and still expected to work New Year. I was thinking about this yesterday. Do you know the last time you and I went out for a meal? March. Almost a year. How did that happen?' She took a deep breath. 'Don't tell anyone, but I'm thinking of quitting.'

'What? But you love being in the police.'

'I know. But I love having low blood pressure more. I'm only thinking about it at the moment. I've not made any firm decisions.'

'What would you do?'

'That's the thing. I've no idea. All I've ever wanted is to be a detective.'

'You could teach,' Olivia suggested.

'I can't think of anything worse.'

'I teach. It's not that bad.'

'Standing up in front of a group of gormless students? No thank you.' She shuddered. 'I'm probably just going through a mood. The weather doesn't help either, does it? This winter seems to be never-ending. I'll be fine once we get a bit of sun.' She looked out of the window and up at the grey sky.

Olivia leaned forward and placed her hand on top of Jessica's. 'There's nothing else, is there?'

'I'm fine,' she said. An obvious lie, judging by the tears welling up in her eyes. 'Look, I'd better go. Stanley will be wanting a walk. The fresh air will do us both a power of good.' She stood up and reached for her coat on the back of the chair. 'I got your voicemail. I'll come round for those files on Monday after work, if that's OK?'

'Of course. I tell you what, come by around six and I'll make us something. We'll have a night in.'

Jessica smiled, but it didn't reach her eyes. 'I'd like that.'

Olivia stood up. They embraced and Jessica left the coffee shop quickly, and without looking back.

Olivia slumped back in her seat and looked down at her half-drunk coffee. She'd been enjoying the chat and her lunch, but now it was lying heavy on her.

Why did life have to be so difficult?

Olivia had a second shower as soon as she arrived home. When she stepped out, she could still sense the smell and feel of The Handsome Stranger on her. She'd have to try and get used to calling him Ethan now she knew his name. She loathed herself for giving in to her basic animal urges, but it was the excitement and the thrill that reminded her she was still alive.

In the kitchen, Olivia set about making herself a cup of tea. While the kettle boiled, her gaze was drawn to the files on the side. It was as if they were giving off some kind of radar. She could feel a great surge of energy emanating from them. She closed her eyes tight and tried to think of something else to block them out from calling to her.

She played with the teabag in the mug with a spoon, allowing the water to swim in and out of the leaves. She turned away from the files, but knew they were there. She thought of Jessica in the coffee shop and her heart sank. She was a strong and intelligent woman; to break down like that, and in public, was not like her at all. The strain she was under must be overwhelming.

Olivia turned around and faced the files. She breathed deeply in and out, weighing up her options before realising she was simply delaying the inevitable.

'You're bloody killing me here, Jessica,' she muttered to herself.

Olivia's office on the first floor was spacious and neat. In the middle of the room was an empty oak refectory table. It was where she usually sat when she needed to spread her notes and photographs out while she pondered the deep aspects of her work. She headed straight for it.

Victim number one was Sarah Millington, a thirty-year-old proofreader in North Wembley. She had dark-blonde hair, blue eyes, a small button nose and a row of freckles running beneath her eyes. She was five foot six inches tall and slightly overweight. She had a bright, beautiful smile that lit up her face and made her eyes sparkle for the camera. Olivia found herself smiling at the picture. She was pretty. On the back of the picture, the information told her it had been taken three months before she was killed on December 17th last year.

The crime scene photographs showed a trail of destruction throughout the house. There was evidence of a struggle in the living room, kitchen, hallway and landing, and the master bedroom. Blood spatters were found on the walls of the staircase, on the carpet on the landing and stairs, and in the bedroom where she was found. The last few photos were of the body in situ. She was face down on the floor in the bedroom. She was fully clothed and barefoot. Her white shirt was saturated in blood, as were her jeans.

From a drawer beneath the desk, Olivia took out a powerful magnifying glass and had a closer look at the body. The knife wounds were wide and deep. They were also erratic. There appeared to be no set pattern to the stabbings: back of the legs, buttocks, the shoulders, the left hand, even the sole of her right foot. Another photograph showed Sarah after she had been turned over by scene of crime officers. Her white shirt was still buttoned up. There was no evidence of any form of sexual attack, so this had not been a sexually motivated crime. There were stab wounds to her chest and stomach, one to her neck and face. This attack was barbaric savagery.

Olivia put the photographs to one side and lifted out the report written by the crime scene manager and the first officers on scene. Sarah had been found by her mother on the morning of December 18th. Sarah had set aside that day to go Christmas shopping with her mum. When Sarah didn't answer her phone that morning, Judith Millington went around to the house her daughter rented in Spencer Road. When her knocks went unanswered, she used the key she had been given for emergencies and entered the house. She knew there was something wrong when she saw the drops of blood on the stair carpet. She carefully made her way up the stairs and when she entered the bedroom, her screams were heard around the block.

Police officers had conducted themselves with their usual professionalism, securing the scene and allowing only scene of crime officers into the house until they were satisfied they had collected sufficient evidence. Then, detectives were allowed in to conduct their own search and become closely acquainted with the victim to try and understand who would want to enact such a violent crime against her.

The post-mortem report told Olivia that the victim had been stabbed twelve times, and ultimately this was the cause of death. Stab wounds ranged from one to three centimetres wide and from eight millimetres deep on the sole of her foot to going right through the palm of her hand and to seven centimetres deep into her stomach.

The time of death couldn't be established by the pathologist, but police interviews with neighbours and the analysis of Sarah's computer and phone records helped to put together a rough estimate of when she had been killed. Her next-door neighbour, Rebecca Babcock, had spoken to her briefly around twelve o'clock when she was returning home and Sarah was signing for a parcel on the doorstep. She had sent an email at three o'clock on the afternoon of her death and a text message at fourteen minutes past three to a friend in Birmingham who had recently had a baby. Estimated time of death was put at around four o'clock that afternoon.

The delivery man had been tracked down and interviewed and ruled out from having had any part in Sarah's death.

The first thing that puzzled Olivia was how the killer had gained entry to the house. There was no sign of forced entry and the front and back doors had been locked. The front door only had a Yale lock so the killer could have closed and locked the door behind him as he left, but that was very risky. Even though it had been winter, and got dark early, there would still have been enough people around to notice him leave by the front door.

Olivia picked up a pad and pen and made a note. Yes, Sarah had been killed in the late afternoon, but there was no evidence to suggest the killer left the house straight away. None of the neighbours interviewed saw anything suspicious. He could have remained in the property until the small hours of the morning and left quietly while everyone was asleep. If that was the case, this was a very confident and clever killer.

According to police reports there were no items taken from Sarah's house and, looking at the crime scene photographs, there were plenty of expensive items worth stealing. Sarah was still wearing the diamond earrings she had been given by her mother on her thirtieth birthday seven months ago. This was not a burglary gone wrong. This wasn't a crime of chance. The killer had chosen this house and this victim specifically. The question was, why?

Chapter Six

Olivia leaned back in her chair and stretched. She had been poring over the crime scene photographs, autopsy reports and witness statements for over an hour. She ached and needed to get blood pumping around her body again.

Sarah Millington had been stabbed in the front and back. At some point, she had been lying on her back when the killer had stood over her and stabbed her in the chest and stomach. Yet she'd managed to break free, and had tried to escape. Her fingernails had broken, showing signs of a struggle. The stab wound straight through her left hand was evidence she had tried to defend herself. She wasn't tall, and she had been barefoot, yet she had still managed to outmanoeuvre her killer on more than one occasion. What did that say about who her killer was? Was he taller or shorter? Slight or heavily built? Confident or scared?

How frightened must Sarah have been when she was lying on her back and watching the man standing over her with a knife in his hand?

Olivia was taken back in time to when she was nine years old. She had been chased out of her house, over the garden fence and into the woods beyond. She'd slipped or tripped on something and fallen flat on her face. She turned around and there was her would-be killer, her father. He loomed over her. He looked like a complete stranger as his eyes bulged with rage. His clothes were wet with blood. In his red right hand, he held a large carving knife.

Paralysed by fear, she couldn't move. She didn't even try to move.

The first stab wound hit her in the centre of her left shoulder. The pain was immense, and she let out an ear-piercing scream. She felt something wet land on her face. It had started snowing again. She loved the snow. It was so peaceful and relaxing.

The pain from the knife being pulled out of her was more painful than when it went in. She screamed again at the second stab. She didn't feel the third. She was unconscious by the fourth.

Why hadn't she struggled like Sarah Millington had with her killer? Had Olivia resigned herself to being killed, even though she was only nine years old and had her whole life ahead of her? Perhaps Sarah had fought back because she had wanted to live. Maybe she had enjoyed life and had wanted to continue her journey. Whereas Olivia Button, aged nine, had been more than happy for it to end. Why was that? Her life had gone a complete one-eighty so quickly. She'd been looking forward to a happy family Christmas. Now, her family was gone; her father had wiped them out. Was life really worth living with everything ruined?

Olivia turned to look out of the large bi-fold doors overlooking the back garden. It was mid-afternoon and dusk was starting to set in. Another day almost over. Another day during which her interaction with people had been kept to a minimum, although there was that fumble with The Handsome Stranger. Ethan, she corrected herself. She frowned. He must have seen her scars. The light in that small toilet cubicle was very bright. So why did he want to see her again when she was so physically damaged? She didn't know anything about Ethan but their interactions over the months made him someone she wouldn't mind getting to know better. Maybe she should give him a call and see where things went. What was the worst that could happen? She sniggered. She knew the answer to that one, and had the scars to prove it, both mental and physical. She wouldn't call Ethan. There was no point. He'd only end things once he discovered who she really was.

The self-induced isolation Olivia had going on was not good for her, but being around people confused her. Even having had coffee with Jessica in the café, although pleasant at the time, left her going over the entire conversation, looking for signs of having lowered her guard and revealed more about herself than she felt comfortable with.

'For God's sake, Olivia, shake it off,' she chastised herself. Jessica was her best friend. Her only friend. Jessica knew everything about her there was to know. She turned back to her desk. Best friends helped each other out, and Jessica needed her help.

Victim number two was twenty-eight-year-old Joanne Douglas, who lived in Stilecroft Gardens. It wasn't far from Spencer Street, where Sarah Millington had been murdered. In fact, it was within walking distance.

Joanne had been a pharmacist. She had taken a week off work to decorate the house she had recently bought, when she was killed on January 18th, just thirty-two days after Sarah. Joanne was five feet seven inches tall, of slim build and had shoulder-length dark wavy hair. She had a thin face, green eyes and a small mouth.

Although she had only recently moved in, and the house was empty of furniture, the crime scene photographs looked similar to those taken in Sarah's house. There were signs of a disturbance in every room on the ground floor: paint cans overturned and spilled onto the bare floorboards, glass in the kitchen door smashed, a curtain torn from the living-room window. There had been a violent tussle between killer and victim.

Blood spatters adorned the wall in the living room and a spray of blood arched on the wall of the staircase, giving Olivia the impression that Joanne had tried to run upstairs, and the killer had stabbed her deep and quickly whipped out the knife, causing the spray. It had been a frenzied attack.

Joanne was found early the next morning by a neighbour who noticed the back door to the house was slightly ajar. However, there was no forced entry to the property; no broken locks on the doors or windows. Whoever had killed her had been invited into the house, or wormed his way in somehow, just like with Sarah Millington.

The crime scene photographs showed Joanne lying on the floor in the old-fashioned bathroom on the first floor. She was on her side, blood pooled around her. She'd been wearing old baggy clothes – tracksuit bottoms and an outdated England football shirt. Both were splattered with various colours of paint and both were saturated in blood. The post-mortem examination revealed she had been stabbed sixteen times (four more than Sarah) in the legs, right arm, back, chest, shoulder, stomach and neck. The stab to her neck proved the fatal one. From a close-up look with her magnifying glass, Olivia could see the knife had entered the right side of her neck and the blade had been pulled across, as if, during the struggle, the killer had tried to slash her throat open. Behind Joanne was the bath; there was no way the killer could have stood behind her when he inflicted this injury, making Olivia believe he had been standing in front of her. If this was the case, he would have been covered in the blood that would have shot out of her ruptured arteries. How had he managed to flee the scene without being noticed, especially if he was covered in blood? Unless he had waited in the house with the victim until the cover of darkness allowed him the perfect getaway.

There were similarities with Sarah Millington – they both lived alone, for example. But who knew about that? Family and friends, colleagues and possibly neighbours, but who else? Was this the link between the victims? Did they both know the same person who knew they lived alone and would be able to wait in their homes until darkness without fear of interruption?

Olivia compared the photographs of the victims in happier times. They didn't look alike. One was short and slightly overweight where the other was tall and slim. One had dark-blonde hair while the other was just dark. The killer wasn't targeting them because they reminded him of anyone, so what was it? Why these two people? Was it simply the fact they lived alone? But Joanne hadn't technically been living at the house in Stilecroft Gardens. She had been decorating it while staying at her mother's house. Occasionally she had stayed overnight if she was painting until late, but she hadn't been living there.

Olivia was starting to get a headache. She pushed her chair back from the desk and stood up. She stretched to loosen her tightened limbs. It was fully dark outside now, so Olivia turned on the banker's lamp on her desk. It lit up her working space, but not the whole room. She was fine with that. She preferred to live in the shadows.

The view from the window overlooking the street at the front of the house wasn't inspiring. Across the narrow road were houses identical to hers. She watched as different lifestyles played out before her like scenes from a soap opera. She knew the Blackstocks directly opposite, sort of, but only because they'd taken in parcels for each other and Mr Blackstock – she couldn't remember his first name – had helped to get her scooter started one morning last summer when it had seemed to want the day off.

There was an elderly couple to the left of the Blackstocks who kept themselves to themselves and often had a small grandchild come to stay. The other houses were filled with families – boisterous children who didn't have any volume control. She'd seen them often going on trips out carrying copious bags and plastic boxes filled with whatever it was children needed to keep them occupied. The thought of domesticity made Olivia shudder. She could think of nothing worse than spending a Bank Holiday weekend stuck in a traffic jam on the motorway with disgruntled children in the back.

She turned back to her desk. The two files containing information on Sarah Millington and Joanne Douglas were open and their contents scattered about. One file to go. Olivia decided to continue her tortuous task before closing the door on her office, calling for a pizza and spending what was left of the evening on the sofa watching a box set of whatever she had in her collection.

Phoebe Harper had been stabbed twenty-three times. The killer was escalating in his frenzy. The crime scene photos were frighteningly similar to Sarah's and Joanne's. Once again, there was no sign of forced entry, there was a disturbance in almost every room and there was blood on the stairs.

Phoebe was found by her neighbour the following morning. Donna Fletcher, who had been celebrating her fortieth birthday the night before, had been woken by the constant knocking on Phoebe's front door. She opened her bedroom window to find two women in nurses' uniforms knocking and shouting through the letterbox. Donna, who had a spare key, unlocked the door and went to investigate. She found Phoebe on the floor of her bedroom. She had been wearing only a dressing gown and the room was a scene of carnage with blood splatter everywhere.

The intensity of the killings was growing. There had been thirty-two days between Sarah's and Joanne's murders, yet only twenty-three days between Joanne's and Phoebe's murders. These were not sexually motivated killings, of that Olivia had no doubt, despite the fact Phoebe had been wearing only a dressing gown which had fallen slightly open, exposing her bare skin. However, the violence in each killing had intensified, showing that the murderer was growing in confidence.

Olivia frowned as she went back to the crime scene photos taken at Sarah Millington's house. The killer had managed to gain entry to the property while the owner was at home without rousing suspicion. So, the women weren't known to each other, but it seemed they were comfortable in letting the killer into their house. Was the killer the common denominator? Was he the link between the victims, and, if so, how? Or maybe he didn't know them at all. Maybe there was no link. Maybe the killer was merely able to talk his way into their confidence. The type of person who would do that was someone smart, someone confident, someone calculating, and someone who had done this before.

As Olivia lined up the pictures taken of the three victims before they were killed, the realisation dawned on her. These were not the first three victims. The killer had to have practised his trick of gaining entry before. Maybe it had failed and that was why the police didn't know about it. Unless…

'Of course,' Olivia said out loud. The first known murder was too perfect. There had to have been a victim before Sarah, and the reason why the police didn't know about it was… 'Because the victim was a man,' she said.

She sat back on her seat and smiled to herself. Sarah's murder was too well executed to have been a first murder. A person doesn't decide to become a murderer and instantly know how he's going to enter a victim's house and leave without being noticed or leaving behind trace evidence. He has to practise. He has to build up to his first kill.

Olivia grabbed her pad and quickly wrote down where Jessica and her team needed to focus their investigation:

1. *Has there been an increase in burglaries in the area recently?*
2. *Have there been reports of bogus people calling at houses trying to gain entry?*
3. *Has anyone been attacked in their own home lately?*

4. *Are there any unsolved murders within the area where the victim has been male and living alone?*

Olivia would bet the advance on her next book that there was at least one more victim out there, and, judging by what type of killer he seemed to be, it was more than likely that there would be more to come, too.

Chapter Seven

Olivia had known this would happen. That was why she didn't get involved with active murder investigations. Her training, her search for answers, only kicked in once the killer was caught and was safely locked behind bars. Then, she wanted to know everything about them from the moment they were born until they were arrested. She needed to know their whole life inside and out.

Jessica had known that Olivia would be sucked in from the moment she first opened the file and would have no choice but to help. She was counting on Olivia's desire to uncover the solution at any cost. It was sneaky and underhand, and Olivia smiled wryly. She would have done the same in Jessica's position.

In the hallway, she put her coat on, and checked her pockets for keys and mobile phone. She mentally went through the process of locking every window and door in the house. She looked at her reflection in the mirror and shook her head.

'You're playing right into their hands, you stupid bitch,' she chastised herself. 'What else are you going to do with your Saturday night? Eat a whole pizza to yourself and watch *Casualty*? You're really living the life of a single thirty-four-year-old.'

Olivia constantly beat herself up, berated herself for her chosen lifestyle. But that was only to be expected when you woke up every morning hating yourself for surviving through the night when those you loved hadn't; when the mental, physical and emotional scars were too deeply rooted; when, in a world of eight billion, there wasn't one single person you could love and trust. When all this was true, what else was there but self-recrimination?

She pulled open the front door and shivered. So much for spring being on the way. She typed in the four-digit code on the alarm, listened for the beeping to begin, then closed the door behind her, locking it with the mortise.

Olivia headed down the steps and looked for the key to her scooter in the darkness. She heard the sound of sniffling and sobbing. She stopped and looked around her. There was nobody in sight.

A rustling noise, a jangling of keys, and strained sobbing.

Looking back at the houses, Olivia saw the mountain bike belonging to Sam, the young man who lived in next door's basement flat, chained up to the railings. The whole house was in darkness, however. Next door was the same.

Olivia stepped forward. She leaned over the railings and looked down into the darkened entrance to the flat and saw the shadow of a young man, searching his pockets.

'Sam? Is everything all right?' Olivia asked.

The shadow stopped moving. 'I'm fine. Thanks,' came the reply.

'Are you crying?'

'No. I'm fine. Honest.'

Olivia recognised a lie when she heard one. She lied every time she was asked how she was. She scrambled in her pocket for her mobile, turned on the torch and aimed it down the steps. The whole space lit up and the young man squinted into the light.

'You're bleeding,' Olivia said.

'I'm OK. I just fell off my bike, that's all.'

Olivia glanced back at the bike. There didn't appear to be any damage. She descended the steps, holding the phone aloft. Sam shied away from the light and turned his back on her. Olivia gently pulled him around by the shoulder.

'Sam, look at me.'

Reluctantly, he looked up.

'You didn't fall off your bike, did you?'

He shook his head.

She held out her hand for him to take. 'Come on, I've got a first-aid kit in the house. Let me clean you up.'

He laughed. 'I'm a trainee doctor at the Royal Free. I can clean myself up, but thanks.'

'I'm not taking no for an answer.'

She practically had to drag him up the steps to her house. She unlocked the door, typed in the code to the alarm, making sure Sam didn't notice the number, and turned the lights on.

Sam Halliday was in his early twenties and relatively new to London. Originally from Devon, he had the soft twang of the west coast in his accent. He was around five feet eight inches tall and had strawberry-blond hair which was unruly and grew in whatever direction it felt like. He had permanently red cheeks and pale skin and his smooth complexion looked like it had never had a razor scraped across it.

Olivia's interactions with Sam consisted of them exchanging smiles as she came home from work and he left to start a nightshift. As the weeks and months had gone on, the smile became a 'good evening', and the ice had been broken when, one evening, Sam told Olivia he had taken a parcel in for her. It was a box of her latest book released in paperback. Based on the HarperCollins logo all over the box, Sam had asked if she was an author. So began the conversation that led to them being on first-name terms.

But Olivia had noticed some of herself in Sam. There was a loneliness about him in the way he held himself tense, his shoulders rigid, never quite making eye contact, and when he did look up, there was a faraway glint in his gaze that suggested he would like to be anywhere else in the world than right here, right now.

Sam sat down on one of the stools in Olivia's kitchen and removed his helmet, revealing the full extent of his injuries. There was a nasty-looking graze above his left eye full of brick debris and gravel. Blood had seeped down his face and begun to dry. The bruise colouring his right cheek was starting to swell.

Olivia took a green first-aid kit from a cupboard and turned to Sam. 'Have you been in a fight?'

He sniggered. 'Look at me. Do you honestly think I'd get into a fight?'

'What happened?' Olivia soaked a cotton pad in antiseptic and began gently cleaning the large graze on his forehead.

He looked up at her with big eyes. 'I was cycling home when suddenly I was thrown off my bike. I looked up and there's this bloke standing over me. He'd come from nowhere and just punched me in the face, knocking me off my bike. He told me to give him my wallet and phone.'

'Did you give it to him?'

'I don't take my wallet to work. I generally put a couple of notes and some loose change in my back pocket. When he asked for my phone I realised that I'd left it in my locker.'

'So what happened?'

He winced at the sting of the antiseptic. 'I told him I didn't have anything on me, but he didn't believe me. He pulled a knife out of his pocket. He asked me again for my wallet and phone. I didn't know what to do.' Tears rolled down his face.

'What *did* you do?'

'I wasn't that far from the hospital and a siren blared out from somewhere. I think that spooked him. The guy ran off. I just picked myself up and came home. I tried cycling but the front wheel's bent.'

'Would you recognise the man again if you saw him?'

'No. It was dark and he had a scarf pulled up around his mouth.'

'Young, old, tall, short, thin, fat, black, white?'

'I don't know. Look, I just want to forget about it. It's embarrassing.' He looked down at his right hand. The skin on the palm of his hands was broken; the wounds looked angry. He flexed his fingers a few times. It was obviously painful.

'You need to report it.'

'Why? Nothing was stolen. I wasn't badly hurt. A few days and the bruises will have gone.'

'That's not the point. The next person he chooses to mug might not be so lucky. Maybe he'll go down an alleyway and confront someone. He might stab the next person, kill them, even. If you report it to the police, they'll look for him.'

'No they won't. Things like this happen all the time. I've heard plenty of stories from the doctors and nurses at the hospital. Either they've been targeted or they know someone who has. Nobody reports it because nothing happens.'

'And each time nobody reports it, it feeds the confidence of the mugger and they go on to bigger and more violent crimes.'

'I appreciate what you're trying to do, and you're right, I should report it, but I'm not going to. I'll deal with this in my own way.'

Olivia put her hands up in submission. 'If that's what you want.'

'Shit,' he said quickly as he turned his face from her to wipe away a tear.

Olivia watched him for a while. 'Is something else bothering you?'

He shook his head.

She pulled out a stool and sat down. 'It can be quite scary, living on your own for the first time. You're in a strange city, you don't know anyone. It's overwhelming, isn't it?'

Eventually, Sam nodded. He turned back to look at her with tear-filled eyes. 'I'm not enjoying this as much as I thought I would. I hate London,' he choked.

'It's a hectic city. I sometimes think you need to be born here to live here.'

'Were you born here?'

She nodded. 'Much further south though. Kingston upon Thames.'

'It sounds nice.'

'It was.' She gave a hint of a smile, which quickly dropped when she thought of home and all the torment and darkness that tinged her memory. 'Where were you born?' she asked, shaking her head slightly, keeping the torture at bay.

'Holsworthy. It's in north Devon. Very rural.'

'London must be quite the culture shock for you.'

'You could say that.' He tried to laugh but this caused his split lip to bleed again.

'Do you know many people around here?'

'No. Nobody.'

'What about the people you work with at the hospital?'

He shook his head.

'Why not?'

Again, he shook his head. It seemed to be emotionally difficult for him to speak.

Olivia edged closer. She placed a hand on his shoulder. 'Sam, believe me, I know how difficult it is to try and make friends, to fit in when you feel like you're an outsider. You need to either overcome the obstacle, push yourself forward, or—' She stopped.

'Or?'

She took a deep breath before answering. 'Or you end up isolated and alone.'

He nodded. 'I'm not good at meeting new people.'

'Well, you've met me,' she smiled. 'Any time you want to chat, you know where to find me.'

His eyes lit up. 'Seriously?'

No. Absolutely not, she screamed at herself internally.

'Yes,' she said.

'I don't think my body will stand the risk of being mugged every time I want to make a new friend.'

Olivia gave a genuine laugh. 'That does seem a tad extreme. If that's the only way to make friends, I'd definitely recommend isolation. Listen, I was going to order a pizza. Would you like to join me?'

'Weren't you just on your way out?'

'Oh.' Olivia suddenly remembered she had been about to head for Jessica's. 'It was only a work thing. It can wait until Monday.'

'Are you sure?'

'I wouldn't ask if I wasn't sure.'

Sam's bottom lip wobbled as his eyes lit up. He was genuinely touched by Olivia's offer of friendship. 'I'd love to. Thank you.'

By the time Sam had left, it was almost midnight. His wounds had been patched up, he was in a much better frame of mind and as he walked to the door his head was held high and shoulders back, filled with confidence and pizza.

They'd spent a couple of hours chatting, with Olivia asking questions about where Sam wanted his career to go and what his hopes for the future were. She learned that he was an only child to Marcus and Hilary Halliday. They hadn't had the best start in life and had worked hard to make sure Sam had a good education. He wanted to be a doctor more than anything, though his sad eyes belied his words. All he really wanted was not to let his parents down.

Olivia closed the front door behind him and set the alarms before returning to the silence of the kitchen. She cleared away the empty pizza box. She looked at the clock on the microwave. It was too late to go around to Jessica's now, but knowing her, she was bound to still be awake. Olivia dug her mobile out of her pocket and made the call. It went straight to voicemail.

'Jessica, it's Olivia. I've been through those files. I really need to talk to you about them. I have a few questions and there are some areas I think you should look into. I'm around all day tomorrow. Or I'm at the office on Monday if you fancy popping in. Goodnight.'

She ended the call.

It had been a strange day. She went over it in her mind as she sat on the edge of her bed and undressed. She could still smell the chlorine on her skin from the swimming pool, which reminded her of the encounter with Ethan. When she thought of the encounter now, she didn't feel the excitement of urgent sex. She felt embarrassed; she felt regret and shame at doing something so risky and base. She tried to shake it off. She was a single woman. She could do what she wanted and was answerable to no one. But she knew the negativity would haunt her dreams.

As she looked out of the window before closing the curtains, her view of the city had changed. Sam was right to hate the place. There was a serial killer stalking the streets of London and he was out there right now, roaming freely, planning his next kill.

Chapter Eight

Monday 19th February 2024

Monday morning rush-hour traffic always seemed to be more hectic than any other day in the week. It was one of the great mysteries of life. The journey from Olivia's home in Camden to George Street in Westminster took an extra ten minutes on Monday.

Her backpack was weighed down with the files Jessica had left her. She had expected to hear from her yesterday, but unlike Olivia, Jessica had a life outside of work. She probably spent her day off with friends, out for lunch somewhere along the river, or seeing a film or recovering from a night out. Olivia couldn't remember the last time she'd even been to the cinema. All she'd done yesterday was get battered and bruised at a Krav Maga class. It had been over a month since her last class and she certainly felt the pain this morning as she struggled to climb out of bed.

She parked her scooter down the side alley next to George Street, removed her helmet and neatened her hair as she stepped up to the blue front door, taking care not to slip on the checkerboard black and white tiles.

Looking at the building, you'd be forgiven for thinking this was home to a firm of solicitors or a private dental practice. It was difficult to fathom this was the headquarters of the Behavioural Science Administration.

Set up by the National Crime Agency, and funded partly by the NCA, several universities and the Home Office, the BSA was (supposedly) entirely independent and although its existence was widely known, its location wasn't. Its remit was to understand the behaviour and mentality of the criminal, specifically serial murderers. It was hoped that by travelling the world and interviewing incarcerated killers, more could be done to understand why they committed their crimes and, possibly, detect a killer of the future before he, or she, had the chance to strike.

The office was spread over three floors, and the only members of staff were herself, Doctor Sebastian Lister, who also freelanced as a lecturer in criminology at various universities around London, and Daisy Leatherwood, their shared secretary.

Olivia entered the building, mouthed 'Hello' to Daisy, who was on the phone, and headed for the kitchen. Sebastian was in there making a mug of tea. He looked his usual shabby self. He could have a designer suit tailor-made for him on Savile Row, and within half an hour it would look like he'd slept in it. His unruly dark-brown hair was rapidly going grey, as was the permanent stubble he insisted on sporting. Since the death of his wife from breast cancer last year, he'd lost far too much weight. Looking after four children single-handedly and trying to hold down a demanding job was not an easy task. The children seemed to be doing fine, and they were well looked after, but Sebastian was hiding his emotions behind a granite exterior, and it had aged him terribly.

'Can you buy a Gruffalo costume?'

'I like how you assume I know what a Gruffalo is. Good morning, by the way,' she said, reaching for a clean mug and flicking the kettle on.

'Sorry. Good morning. I've had an email from Robert's school. He's been chosen to play the Gruffalo in a play. I've got to provide the costume.'

'In situations like this, I direct you to my two best friends: Google and Amazon. They're bound to have the answer.'

'Thank you,' he said. 'Nice weekend?'

'Not bad. Yours?'

'Tiring. I come to work for a rest, you know.'

Olivia made herself a coffee and stepped out into the open-plan office where her post sat waiting for her on a table. She flicked through the envelopes, dreading seeing anything handwritten.

'Daisy may have found us a translator. I've told her to tell them how the nature versus nurture project is a game changer in the field of criminology and how something like this has never been done before. Hopefully that will sway them and the minuscule amount we can pay them won't matter.'

'Good thinking. Any more news on funding?'

'Yes, actually. Professor Wellbeck from California State University emailed me over the weekend. He's going to see if he can get the faculty to throw some money our way but we'd need to focus more on American serial killers. I think we're going to have to adapt the questionnaires more than we originally thought, depending on who we hope to get funding from.'

Olivia thought for a moment. 'Ask Professor Wellbeck what he wants from us specifically, and we'll go from there. We really need a couple more of the bigger universities on board. How are the questionnaires coming along?'

'Fine. I was having a tinker around late last night. I was thinking that we should probably look at the political climate around when these killers grew up. We have a few on the list who were born in Iraq and Iran. If their formative years were in the middle of a battlefield, it's bound to condition them.'

'That's true,' Olivia said, turning to look up at Sebastian. 'We really need a potted history of their childhood; not just their familial surroundings, their friendships and what their favourite films were, but the environment too. I'm looking forward to this study,' she said with a smile.

'So am I. Despite the leg-work involved.'

'If there's any travelling involved, I can do that. I know how difficult it is for you. The thing we need—'

'Sorry, mind if I interrupt?' Daisy asked from the doorway. 'There's a policeman here to see you, Olivia.'

'A policeman?'

'Yes. A detective inspector. He said it's important.'

'Everything all right?' Sebastian asked Olivia.

'As far as I know. Show him through, please, Daisy.'

'Do you want me to stay?' Sebastian asked, placing a large hand on her shoulder.

'No. I'm fine.'

'I'll be out in the front office if you need me.'

Whenever she was visited by the police, Olivia always feared the worst – or perhaps it was the best, she wasn't sure. Conflicting emotions ran around her mind. Was her father dead? If so, what was it – natural causes or had someone got to him with a shiv? Or had the unthinkable happened and he had escaped?

'Doctor Winter?'

Olivia jumped at the sound of her name. She turned and saw a navy-suited man standing in the doorway of the large open-plan office.

'Detective Inspector Foley. Metropolitan Police,' he said, stepping forward. He was a slim man with ice-blue eyes and black hair with just a hint of grey at the temples. He was clean shaven and wore a sweet-smelling yet understated fragrance. His face was lined with the wrinkled knowledge of a life well lived.

Olivia offered a nervous smile. 'Can I get you a coffee or something?'

'No. Thank you. If I have any more coffee, I'll be bouncing off the walls. I'm afraid I have some bad news.'

Olivia gripped a chair in front of her, her fingernails digging hard into the fabric. 'Oh God,' she whispered.

'Perhaps you'd like to sit down.'

She pulled the chair out and perched on the edge. She took a deep breath. She knew what was coming.

DI Foley cleared his throat. 'I'm afraid Detective Inspector Jessica Sheffield was found dead yesterday morning.'

Olivia's eyes slowly widened. She had not expected that at all. 'What?'

'She… Shit, I'm sorry.' He buckled as his emotions got the better of him.

Olivia jumped up and went around to his side of the desk. She pulled out a chair and sat him down.

'I'm sorry,' he repeated. 'It's the first time I've actually said it out loud.'

'Let me get you a drink of water.' She pulled a plastic cup out of the cooler in the corner of the room and filled it up. She handed it to him, and he took a large gulp.

'What happened?' Olivia asked, sitting next to him.

He took another sip of the water. His hands were shaking. 'She was murdered.'

'Oh my goodness. I don't know why, but you don't expect officers in this country to get killed in the line of duty.'

'Jessica wasn't killed in the line of duty. It happened in her own home. Someone managed to get into her house and stabbed her.'

'Oh my God.' Olivia put her hands to her mouth. She leaned forward in her seat and rocked back and forth. This was not the first time Olivia had been presented with the murder of someone she held dear. All the old memories came flooding back. She was jumping out of the bathroom window, landing on the cold, wet ground with a thud. She was running for her life, struggling over the fence. Then the stabbings.

Olivia stood up and went over to the window. She looked out but didn't take in the view. She wiped her eyes and composed herself before turning back to DI Foley.

'Do you know who did it?'

'We have a fair idea.'

'Oh. That's good. Well, I appreciate you coming here personally to tell me. I'm guessing you're very busy at the moment.'

'Olivia— Sorry, do you mind if I call you Olivia?' She shook her head. 'We believe Jessica was murdered by the same person who killed Sarah Millington, Joanne Douglas and Phoebe Harper. I know Jessica gave you their files. In fact, it was me who encouraged her to do so.'

'I see.'

'I'm sorry.'

'Don't be.' She gave him the ghost of a smile. She could see how difficult this was for him. He'd lost a colleague, someone he obviously liked and respected. Maybe it went further than that.

She studied his taut jawline and his rapid eye movements. 'Why are you here? You didn't come here to break the news to me gently, did you? You want something.'

Foley let out an audible sigh. 'I need your help,' he said with determined honesty. 'One of our own has been killed, and I take exception to that. I need to catch this bastard… Sorry. My boss is thinking of bringing in a profiler. Now, I know you're not a profiler as such. I've called you one many times and Jessica has delighted in correcting me: you're a forensic psychologist. However, I've read some of your work and you have amazing insight into the minds of killers, and I know Jessica thought very highly of you.'

Olivia folded her arms. 'I wasn't going to help, but I couldn't stop myself reading the files. I called Jessica on Saturday. I told her we should meet.'

'I know. I've listened to her voicemail.'

'I hope she heard it. I'd hate it if she thought I turned her away when she needed me the most.'

'Olivia, we haven't released details of Jessica's death to the media yet, but they're already making assumptions about the others. My boss will be making a statement later today and as soon as they find out she was murdered, they're going to start asking questions about a serial killer in London. I don't just want your help, Olivia, I need it.'

'You've got it.' She went back over to the desk and sat down. 'The first problem you need to address is that I think you have more than these three victims. Well, four, now.'

Foley's eyes widened. 'What?'

'The first murder is too neat. It's too perfect. The killer managed to get into the house without force. He was able to charm himself in, or he knew his victim. He also left nothing of himself behind at the scene despite there being signs of a disturbance. This man knew what he was doing and the only way for him to do that is through practice.'

'But after the second murder we looked back at any cases of women being killed who lived alone. We don't have any on our books.'

'Which is why I think you should be looking for a male victim.'

'Really?' He looked confused.

'I think that when your killer first started out, the victim wasn't the most important part of his game. He's a thrill seeker. He gets his kicks out of the chase. Once they're dead, he leaves. That's why the victim is always left where they've died. He no longer has any use for them. The reason why I think his first victim – or victims – is a male, is because he doesn't want you, the police, to see him as a lust killer. He doesn't want you to think he's a rapist or a pervert. In his mind, he's just a killer.'

'So why didn't he continue with male victims?'

'Because they'll have put up more of a struggle. Targeting a woman, especially in her own home, and especially if she lives on her own – she thinks she's going to be raped, which is absolutely terrifying, and that's what gives him his kicks.'

'But he doesn't rape them.'

'But the victims don't know that.'

Foley blew out his cheeks. 'So, I'm looking for more victims, but men?'

'You're looking for either one or two victims. There'll be signs of disturbance, and I wouldn't be surprised if you find DNA traces at the scene. You also need to check to see if there have been any break-ins or attempted break-ins at people's homes, or if they've had people knocking on the door and trying, somehow, to gain entry. If your killer knew all four victims, there would be another link between them which you would have found. As you haven't, I'm guessing these are all random, so he needs a patter to enter their homes without raising suspicion. He'll have tried this out on other people, changing his story until he found one that worked. You need to get your officers knocking on a lot of doors.'

Foley had taken a notepad out of his pocket and was frantically scribbling down notes. He looked up when Olivia stopped talking. 'This is going to be big, isn't it?'

'It already is.'

'Jesus Christ,' he muttered. 'Can I ask you a favour?'

'Another one?' She smiled slightly.

'Will you come to Jessica's house with me? Forensics have finished but I'd like you to walk through the house with me, tell me what you see. Photographs are useful, but there's nothing better than the real thing.'

Olivia went white. 'I'm not sure. I don't think I can.'

'Please. I need your help, and I really admire your work.'

She chuckled. 'Does this kind of flattery always work?'

'I'm getting better at it.'

'No offence, but you've struck out here. Flattery will literally get you nowhere.'

'Olivia...'

'I can't see a crime scene,' she said slowly, taking herself back in time to when she stood at the entrance of her parents' bedroom, seeing her mother, clinging to life, cradling her dead sister. All that blood.

'I will be by your side the whole time. The second you want to leave, we'll leave.'

He sounded convincing but she didn't trust him. She didn't know him. He wanted answers and he saw her as his only chance to get them. He was hurting at the brutal murder of a colleague, possibly a friend, and he would do anything to catch Jessica's killer. She looked at him and saw the raw pain in his eyes. She probably had the same look when she was nine, and she had no one to help her then, either.

She took a deep breath. 'I'll get my coat.'

Chapter Nine

DI Foley waited in the car while Olivia went to tell Sebastian where she was going. He tried to talk her out of it. Visiting the crime scene where a good friend had been murdered was not something anyone should have to do, but for someone like Olivia, it would be dangerous to her fragile mental state.

'Sebastian, I am fine,' she reassured him. Standing toe to toe, she strained her neck to look up to him. 'Jessica wanted my help on this, and I turned her down. If I can do this, it'll stop me beating myself up for the rest of my life that I didn't do more to help a friend in need.'

'Olivia, you can't blame yourself for what happened to Jessica.'

'I'm not blaming myself. I want her killer caught, and I'll do everything in my power to ensure that happens.'

'Nothing I can say will change your mind, will it?'

She shook her head.

'OK,' he reluctantly agreed. 'Promise me that you'll call if you need me, or if you want to talk, or… anything?'

'I will,' she smiled.

Olivia buttoned up her coat and turned to leave the building. In the doorway, she glanced back over her shoulder to Sebastian.

He looked worried. There was a reason Olivia didn't work on active crimes, and he knew it. She tried to offer him a reassuring smile, but she was fooling no one. She was scared to death of what she was about to open herself up to. As she walked to the car, she could already feel the iron grip of horror and grief squeeze tightly around her heart.

Foley drove a dark-red Toyota Auris that was in desperate need of a wash. The back and sides were splattered with mud. Inside was marginally cleaner but there was an underlying smell of wet dog. He noticed Olivia pull a face.

'Sorry about the smell. I've got two German shepherds. I took them to the beach for a run yesterday. I'll open the window a crack, but it might be a bit cold.'

'That's fine. I don't mind the smell,' she said unconvincingly. 'Oh my God, Stanley!' Olivia suddenly remembered Jessica's beloved dachshund.

'Don't worry, he's fine. He's in the kennels at the station.'

'Was he hurt?'

'No. We found him curled up next to Jessica,' he replied with a catch in his throat.

'Poor thing.' She turned to look out of the window. Her eyes were filling with tears, but she refused to let them fall.

'So,' Foley said after they'd been driving for five minutes in silence. 'Jessica told me you've been in America for the past couple of weeks.'

'Yes. I was on a lecturing tour.'

'How did it go?'

'Very well, thanks.'

'Is that something you do often?'

'Not really. I lecture at various universities around London on a freelance basis, but I decided to do this tour as my last book was published in America at the back end of last year. This was sort of a cheeky publicity thing too.'

'Sneaky. I'm sure it helped sales.'

'Well, I certainly signed a lot of copies.'

'You sound like a celebrity.'

'I can't think of anything worse.'

'Me neither. We had a film crew follow us around a few years ago for an obscure cable channel I'd never heard of. You should have seen how some of the officers were acting. I think they thought they'd be invited on all these crap reality shows.'

'Did you appear on TV then?'

'Fortunately, I didn't. They were covering a different team entirely.'

'So, what department are you in then? Do you— Sorry, did you work with Jessica?'

'Yes. I'm in the Major Crimes Unit. Jessica and I were leading the teams investigating the three murders, answerable to the same bosses.'

'Do you think Jessica may have been killed because she was a detective?'

He sighed. 'I really don't know. I hope not. We're looking through her laptop, tablet and mobile phone to see who she was in contact with recently; see if she was following her own line of enquiry.'

'I don't think Jessica was like that.'

'She wasn't. I've worked with many people over the years and Jessica is the only one I know who'd tell you absolutely everything she was doing. I'll never have another partner like her.'

'You're angry, aren't you?' Olivia asked, studying the DI.

'What makes your say that?'

'You're clenching your jaw. The vein in your neck is throbbing quite viciously and if you grip the steering wheel any firmer, you'll break it.'

'Wow, I've got Sherlock Holmes in the car with me.'

'My job is to study people. I've been doing it for over fifteen years. It's almost second nature.'

'My job is catching criminals. I've been doing it for over twenty years. It doesn't get any easier, though.'

'No. It really doesn't,' she said, looking out of the window at the landscape blurring by. 'Sorry, what do I call you?'

'Call me Foley – everyone else does.'

'I can't call you Foley. I'm not one of your team. What's your first name?'

He rolled his eyes.

'Oh. Is it something embarrassing?'

He took a deep breath. 'Amyas.'

'Amyas? Wow, fancy.'

'You haven't laughed.'

'Should I have?'

'Most people do.'

'No. I like it. Amyas. It's different.'

'It's certainly that. I took some ribbing at school, I can tell you.'

'Amyas Foley. It's a good name. It suits you, too.'

'Thank you. I'd still rather you called me Foley, though, especially when we're at the station surrounded by my colleagues.'

'Oh.'

'Problem?'

'You'll want me at the station?'

'Well, yes. You could tell my state of mind just by the way I'm gripping the steering wheel; you'll be invaluable at a crime scene, and I'm guessing you'll be able to put it much better to my officers than I ever could.'

'I've never addressed a room of detectives before. Well, not outside of a classroom, and I think there were only about ten there. How many are on your team?'

'At the moment about thirty. Just think of it as one of your lectures. I'd tell you to picture them naked, but I'm guessing that's frowned upon these days,' he said with a chuckle.

They pulled up outside Jessica's house in Highgate Hill. Olivia couldn't take her eyes off the building. It was a beautiful Victorian property and Olivia knew Jessica had felt lucky to live here.

'Had you visited Jessica's home before?' Olivia asked Foley.

'Occasionally,' he said hesitantly.

Olivia looked at him. She knew a lie when she heard one.

'Did you know much about her background?'

'We worked together for almost five years.'

'There's a great deal of difference between working with someone and knowing them. Did she tell you about her parents?'

'Yes. The first time I visited her at home she could tell I was itching to ask how she could afford such a house in this part of London. She told me all about her parents dying while on holiday when she was ten and being brought up by her grandmother. This was her home and she left it to Jessica after she died. I know my team, Ms Winter,' he said, an icy tone to his voice. He whipped off his seatbelt and climbed out of the car, slamming the door behind him.

Olivia followed. 'Amyas, I'm sorry. I didn't mean to…' She trailed off as he marched up the garden path.

The house was still a closed crime scene and a uniformed officer stood at the front door. He looked frozen to the bone. Foley showed his warrant card and told him who Olivia was. He then used a key to unlock the door.

'There are two entrances to the house. This one and the back door in the kitchen.'

'I have been here before,' Olivia reminded him.

'Of course. Sorry. The bolts on the back door are locked and they're very stiff. I doubt that door has been used in years.'

'So, this was the way the killer got in?'

'Yes.'

Olivia looked around her. There was a hotel across the road and a banner congratulating Chris and Kevin on their marriage was flapping in the breeze. The road was busy and there were neighbours either side.

'No sign of a forced entry?'

'No.'

'So the killer either knew Jessica, or he charmed his way in.'

'Jessica would never have allowed a complete stranger into her home,' Foley said, sounding confident.

'But he had to have said something to get into the house. There's no evidence that she opened the door and he blitz-attacked her. What have the neighbours said?'

'None of them saw or heard anything.'

'Not even while she was being attacked?' Olivia frowned. 'No screams or cries for help?'

'No. Don't forget, these are old properties. The walls are very thick. Not like modern houses where's it's basically plasterboard between each property.'

'True.'

'Are you coming in or not?'

Olivia took a deep breath and braced herself. She entered the house and Foley closed the door behind them.

Immediately, Olivia saw the massive pool of blood in the hallway. It had seeped into the lush cream carpet. She quickly turned away.

'Run!' she heard her mum say in her head. She really should listen to her mother.

'Initial reports say she was stabbed in the neck. That's where the blood came from.'

'My God.'

'Are you all right?'

'No. I've never been in an actual crime scene before.' She had to stop herself from clarifying that she'd been a *part* of a crime scene before.

'Would you like to sit down for a minute or two?'

'It would have been gentlemanly of you to ask if I wanted to leave.'

'Under normal circumstances, I would have done. But I need your help more than anything else right now.'

So much for her being able to leave whenever she wanted to. 'Right. Let's crack on then.' She took a deep breath and headed down the hallway towards the kitchen. It felt wrong being in the house without Jessica there. Usually, when she came around for a visit, and a bottle of wine or three, the atmosphere was lighter – there was always music playing and it had been warm and welcoming. Now, Olivia felt like she was trespassing. A stranger in a strange house.

'There's a dining room and living room to your right, which you obviously already know about. Again, I'm sorry. I'm used to doing a walk-through with complete strangers.'

'It's OK, Amyas. You don't have to apologise. Just act how you normally would at a crime scene.'

He nodded and took a deep breath. 'There are no signs of disturbance in those rooms. They're very neat and tidy. They've both been dusted for prints and only Jessica's are there.'

Olivia knew what was behind each of the doors. Jessica was an orderly person. Everything had a place and when she was working on a particularly troubling case, she had found she organised her thoughts better when cleaning. Her home was where she had felt most comfortable and relaxed. If her home was tidy, her mind would be too; that had always been the theory. Olivia had tried it a few times, but it didn't work. It took more than scrubbing the toilet to sort out the miasma of thoughts clogging up her head.

'OK,' Olivia said slowly as she thought. 'So, she answered the door, allowed him in, for whatever reason, and headed for the kitchen. The killer followed her in there.'

The kitchen was large and airy. White walls and a high ceiling, a pine table and chairs by the back door and a large American-style fridge. The surfaces were neat and tidy, containers and jars for things like tea, coffee, sugar and cereal. A Welsh dresser had a small blood spatter across it; a chair had been thrown and was lying in two pieces on the tiled floor. The vegetable rack had also been knocked over, and onions and peppers were strewn on the ground.

Olivia went over to the dresser and peered closely at the blood. 'Is this the only sign of blood in this room?'

'Yes,' Foley said. He remained in the doorway while Olivia looked around.

'This doesn't make any sense.'

'What do you mean?'

'We both know... *knew* Jessica. She was a strong woman, both physically and mentally. But that spray of blood there isn't from a deep stab wound. If he'd stabbed deep, or hit an artery, the spray would be on the ceiling, or the dresser would have been covered in it. It's just one single spray and the dots of blood decrease fairly quickly. It's like it was a surface wound to... I don't know... toy with her maybe, or to scare her, almost like a prelude.'

'Why would he do that?'

It was a while before Olivia answered. 'He wanted to get her attention, to show her why he was here, to let her know what was going to happen without causing her too much pain, so that she'd be aware of what was to come.'

'But she would have fought back.'

'Yes. I think she threw that chair at him. And, look, it's broken, so she threw it with some force. While he was incapacitated, she ran out of the room. I think she pulled over the vegetable rack too, to slow him down while she ran out of the house.'

Foley stepped out of the doorway while Olivia went back to

the front door. There were locks at the top and bottom of the door, a security chain in the middle and a Yale lock and a Chubb lock.

'Can you remember which of these was locked?' Olivia asked.

'Just the Yale.'

'Was the key still in the Chubb?'

'Yes. And there were no fingerprints on the key either. Not even Jessica's.'

'They'd been wiped,' she said, almost to herself. 'OK. I think once the killer had entered the house, Jessica headed for the kitchen and he quietly locked the door, pocketing the key to the Chubb. When Jessica came running out, she tried to open the door, but it was locked. The killer followed her from the kitchen and she had to run upstairs. There was nowhere else for her to go.'

'That's what I thought, too. If you look on the banister, there's a bloody handprint about a third of the way up. Shall we?' He pointed up the stairs.

Olivia tentatively led the way. She looked at the blood-stained carpet that was the same colour as the one in the hallway. She never coped well with the sight of blood. It was different in a photograph – she could turn it over – but when faced with actual blood, and so much of it, it was stomach-churning.

If Jessica was holding the banister going up, she was obviously at the right-hand side of the stairs. The small drops of blood on the steps had dripped from whatever part of her had been stabbed. On the other side of the stairs, the carpet was covered with larger patches of blood, pools of it in some places. There were also blood smears on the wall. Since Jessica had been found in the hallway, she had obviously come back down at some point, and by then she had been more severely injured.

On the spacious landing, the cream carpet was soaked in blood. There were four doors leading off, one to the main bathroom and the others to the bedrooms.

'The two smaller bedrooms were obviously guest rooms.'

'Yes. I've stayed in that one a few times after too many bottles of wine.' Olivia smiled at the memory. 'It's been a while, though. We've both been very busy,' she said regretfully.

'They don't look like they've been used for a while,' Foley continued. 'It seems as though she ran into the master bedroom.'

Olivia headed for the door with a smeared bloody handprint on it. She pushed it all the way open with her foot and almost fainted when she saw the devastation in front of her. She leaned against the door frame.

'Oh my God.' For a split second, she saw her mother and sister on the bed.

'Take a deep breath, Olivia,' Foley said, placing a comforting hand on her shoulder.

'Run!' her mother told her.

Blood sprays were high, hitting the ceiling and walls. The carpet and the duvet on the bed were saturated. The wardrobe, the chest of drawers, the bedside cabinets, all exquisite items of furniture, had been stained with blood.

On the double window, bloody fingerprints on the glass and handles showed that Jessica had tried to attract attention from the outside world. She'd pulled open the dusky pink curtains and tried to call for help that wouldn't come.

Olivia took a deep breath and composed herself. She'd seen many photographs over the years of the disturbing things killers had done to their victims, but being amongst it now, smelling the metallic stench of blood, having known the victim intimately for so long, felt abhorrent. She wanted to cry. She wanted to scream. She could do neither. She needed to remain professional.

Olivia cleared her throat. 'She must've jumped on the bed and scrambled over the top to get to the window.' She went over to the window and looked out. She could see the hotel across the road more clearly from this high up. Traffic went along the road at a steady pace.

'She tried to open the window,' she said.

'They're locked. The key is in the top drawer of the bedside table.'

'She pulled on the handles. She banged on the glass. How did nobody hear her?'

'I don't know.'

'Do you know the time of death yet?' Olivia asked, turning from the window to look back to Foley. She tried to ignore the drenched bedsheets, but it wasn't easy.

'No. You know as well as I do that it's not an accurate science.'

'True. I think the killer knew what kind of person he was up against. Let's say she's not too badly injured from what happened in the kitchen. She'll have run upstairs quickly. He'll have seen that she was fast, and strong. When he saw her trying to open the windows, I think he may have panicked slightly, or he may have just been caught up in the excitement.'

'Excitement?'

'Oh yes. He was loving this. Look at the sprays on the ceiling. He's brought the knife down from a great height, stabbed her deeply and pulled it out quickly, sending the spray shooting up. Then he's done it again, and again.'

'Yet she was still fighting for her life,' Foley said, looking down at the floor.

'She managed to escape him. I don't know how. I like to think she kicked him hard in the balls. You might want to check the local hospital for recent admissions. She headed for the stairs again. She's lost a great deal of blood and will have started to lose consciousness. She's leaning against the wall, lowering herself down the stairs when he catches up with her. He...' She couldn't continue. She swallowed hard and wiped away a tear before it had time to form. 'He stabbed her one last time in the neck. She fell, and where she landed was where you found her in the hallway. Can we go now?'

Foley nodded. 'I think we need a drink.'

Outside, as Foley was locking the door, Olivia spotted a man taking a banner down from the railings of the Lauderdale Hotel opposite. Olivia crossed the road.

'Excuse me, was this party a recent event?'

'Yes. A big wedding reception on Saturday night. Bloody hell, you should have seen the state of the place on Sunday morning,' he chuckled.

'A lot of people attended?'

'A good few hundred. There were cars double parked and everything. I don't live far away, so I heard about the commotion from the neighbours.'

'Commotion.'

'People are a bit prickly about their parking spaces around here,' he said, lowering his voice. 'Not to mention the loud music. I said to them, if you can't enjoy yourself at your wedding reception, when can you?'

Olivia smiled and said goodbye. She carefully made her way back across the road and met Foley at the car.

'That's when she was killed. Saturday night. There was a big party opposite. You can see the hotel from the bedroom window quite clearly. She was banging on the glass to get their attention, but nobody heard because the music was so loud. The perfect sound to cover up her screams.'

'I'll get a team to interview the staff,' he said, making a note in his pad. 'That couldn't have been deliberate, though, could it, knowing there was a big party going on right opposite?'

'I don't know. I mean, how long was that banner up? There were a couple of hundred guests there, so who knew about the party? Staff for a start, then the guests, and their friends. I'm guessing they'll have slapped it all over social media. The list is endless.'

'Come on, let's go and get that drink.'

Olivia frowned in thought as she lowered herself into the front passenger seat. 'You weren't surprised.'

'Sorry?'

'When I was saying how the attack took place, you didn't question it. You had already made your mind up about what happened on Saturday night, hadn't you?'

It was a while before he gave a slight nod.

'So, what was this all about then? I have to take a test now to prove my worth?'

'No. Not at all.' He looked at her. 'It wasn't a test. I just wanted it confirming. Jessica was a friend and a colleague. I don't want to get blindsided by this.'

They were silent while Foley pulled away from the kerb and joined the traffic.

'Hang on,' Olivia said. 'The third victim, Phoebe Harper – there was a party happening in the house next door to hers on the night she was killed. In her witness statement, the neighbour said it was her fortieth birthday and she was having a big celebration. Again, the killer used the noise from the music and the guests to mask his crime.'

'But there weren't parties at the other two murders.'

'But there must have been something. He's a thrill killer. He gets off on the chase, the kill. The fact that there are possibly hundreds of potential witnesses is the turn-on for him. When he killed Jessica, the curtains were wide open. He's stabbing her and stabbing her and outside he can see hundreds of people dancing the night away. That's the thrill. Forget the drink, take me back to the station. We need to search for that real first victim and we need to find out what was going on at the neighbours of the other two women.'

Olivia secured her seatbelt and rubbed her hands together. For the first time in a very long time, she felt wired and determined. She was going to catch this killer at any cost.

Chapter Ten

The Major Crime Unit at Sanderson Street Police Station in Holloway was a large open-plan office on the third floor of the six-storey building. From the doorway, the room looked a mess. Whiteboards on the walls were filled with crime scene photos and information on the unsolved cases of the missing and the dead. Desks were arranged in an unidentifiable pattern, the majority of them a confusion of paper and files. Phones rang, computer keyboards were hammered, detectives shared information, photocopiers and printers whirred into life to make a cacophony of white noise. Olivia felt out of her depth. There was a reason she shared an office with just Sebastian and Daisy and turned down a permanent residency in a university. She could only handle so many people at one time.

When giving a lecture to an auditorium of students she had the upper hand; she had the knowledge they were thirsty to hear. In this situation, she would be talking to police officers who knew how to catch criminals and murderers. She might as well stand at the top of the room and tell them how to handcuff someone under arrest.

Foley led the way through the room to his office. Olivia

The Mind of a Murderer

followed closely, her eyes darting from side to side to take in those around her. She was being stared at, judged. They all knew who she was and why she was here, and the burning sensation of dozens of pairs of eyes glaring at her informed her that she wasn't necessarily welcome.

'Leon, Holly, a moment,' Foley said without stopping as he passed the desks of two plain-clothed officers.

Olivia took in Foley's office. It was chaotic. There was no other word for it. His desk was piled high with files. Every space was cluttered with paperwork and folders. The carpet tiles were stained and bald in places and the waste-paper basket was overflowing. She would not be able to work in a room like this. She hoped the people of London never got to see it. They wouldn't feel secure in their homes knowing a man who inhabited an office like this was appointed to keep them safe. He placed his hand on a radiator and gave it a kick. It obviously wasn't working as the room had a chill to it. Olivia decided to keep her coat on.

'How's it going?' Foley asked as he surveyed the paperwork on his desk. He picked up a few message slips, glanced at them, pocketed a couple and tossed the rest under the table in the direction of the bin.

'Slowly,' Holly said.

'Too bloody slowly,' her colleague echoed.

'I'd like to introduce you to Olivia Winter. Doctor Winter, these are two of my best officers. Detective Sergeant Leon Rippner. We call him Jack – I'm sure you can guess why. And this is Detective Sergeant Holly Goodfellow.'

They shook hands and Olivia gave them her best placatory smile. Holly Goodfellow was a slim woman in her late twenties. She was taller than Olivia by a good few inches and had silky short black hair. She wore heavy make-up around her eyes and proffered a genuine smile when she took Olivia's hand in a tight grip. Her dark-grey suit was crisp and clean. This was a woman determined to make an impression, not necessarily on Olivia, but in the workplace generally. As Olivia had walked into the room, she had noticed the majority of its occupants were male. Holly obviously felt the need to look confident and powerful so she could match the bravado of her male colleagues, even if she wasn't built for the part. If her firm handshake was anything to go by, she was succeeding. Olivia took an instant liking to her.

Leon Rippner was in his thirties, and below average height, Olivia guessed, at five foot eight, maybe five-nine, judging by the thickness of the heels on his scuffed shoes. He was stocky but his bulk was muscular. He had short curly dark hair and an angry frown. He chewed his bottom lip incessantly and couldn't seem to stand still. He either had an urgent bladder condition or he was impatient. Judging by the daggered looks he was giving Olivia, she guessed the latter. Her impression was that he wanted to be out on the streets looking for the man who had murdered their colleague, not stuck in an office listening to a forensic psychologist.

'Introductions out of the way, everyone take a seat,' Foley said. He pulled his wheeled chair around and offered it to Olivia to sit on. Leon and Holly sat in the visitors' chairs and Foley perched on the edge of his desk. 'I've spent the last hour or so with Doctor Winter and she's spent the weekend going through the case files of the victims we've got so far. She has some very interesting theories. Olivia?'

She had the floor. She filled them in on her opinion that the murderer was a thrill killer and how she believed that there were one, or possibly two, additional victims before their first known victim, Sarah Millington. Holly was making notes while Leon sat with his arms tightly folded across his chest and his left leg jiggling involuntarily.

'So he's a psycho then,' Leon said. 'Typical. We catch him, he says he's bat-shit crazy and gets a cushy padded cell for a few years before some do-gooder gets him released as a reformed character who's found God.'

'He has psychopathic traits, but he knows exactly what he's doing. It's a misinterpretation that serial murderers suffer with mental illnesses,' Olivia corrected him.

'But I thought serial killers all had some kind of mental disorder?' Holly asked with a frown.

'Having a mental illness doesn't mean you're going to commit a violent crime. The majority of mental illnesses affect only that person and the way they perceive what is going on around them, their feelings, their moods. Someone with that kind of a disorder would not be able to commit these kinds of crimes and manipulate the crime scene to such an extent that he leaves no trace of himself, especially after four or more murders. You're looking for a highly intelligent individual who knows exactly what he's doing and is loving every minute of it. If he has a mental disorder, it will likely be a personality disorder, and that doesn't mean he's incapable of standing trial once you catch him.'

Leon's face softened slightly.

'I read a paper recently,' Holly said, crossing her legs, 'that suggested serial killers go after people who remind them of someone. I've being through the victimology of all four victims so far and there's nothing that you could say they have in common, other than the fact they're single white women, and that forms a large demographic in London.'

'Serial killers do tend to go for victims who remind them of an abuser or an ex or a domineering mother, but mostly they go for victims weaker than themselves or those who are vulnerable in society, such as sex workers, the homeless, children, the physically or mentally disabled or the elderly.'

'Stick a pin in the electoral register then,' Leon said.

'That's why I believe there are more victims you haven't discovered yet, and not just people he's killed. I believe he may have attacked someone who escaped, which is why he changed to killing women.'

'I thought killers didn't change their MO?' Holly asked again.

'The MO is fluid. It's the signature that never changes, and here the signature is the chase. I believe he stabbed Jessica in her kitchen, but not with the intention of killing her straight away. He wanted her scared. He wanted her to panic, to run for her life so he could chase her and catch her.'

'Who the hell is he, Michael Myers?'

Olivia nodded. 'Basically, yes. Until I meet him I can only guess about his background and his upbringing, but I wouldn't be surprised if you find every kind of slasher film in his collection. He'll be obsessed with scaring people in order to kill them. That's what gives him his power, his dominance.'

'But, surely, if you know that, then you can work out what kind of a person he is,' Holly said.

'I can try.'

'So, what do you want us to do?' Holly asked, turning to Foley. 'Are we looking for other victims?'

'Yes,' he said. 'Go back to last summer at least. We're looking for a single man or a single woman killed in their own home with a knife.'

'You also need to look for an increase in break-ins or of strangers knocking on doors and trying to talk their way into the house. By the time he came onto your radar with the murder of Sarah Millington, he'd got his patter down to a fine art, and it's worked for him on four occasions. However, he'll have needed to try that out.'

'We don't have the officers for this,' Leon said, looking at his boss.

'I know,' Foley said, running his fingers through his hair. 'But it's what we're going to have to do to find him. I'll get uniform drafted in and we'll get the community police and the specials out there knocking on doors.'

'But—' Holly began.

'Just leave the logistics to me,' he said, raising a hand to stop her asking another question.

'I'm guessing you have many unsolved murders on your books. What I need to do is work backwards,' Olivia said. 'I'll start with Jessica's murder and go back through the other three victims. Then, with the other victims you've got, I can see which ones relate to this case and which don't. There will be a pattern. I just need to find it.'

'There isn't a pattern with the victims, though, is there?' Holly asked, getting slightly agitated.

'There will be. It just hasn't been found yet.'

'But I've looked—'

'Holly, Doctor Winter has been doing this for fifteen years. She'll find it.'

Olivia looked at the floor. The weight of this whole investigation was resting on her shoulders. She had never had such a responsibility before. She could feel herself starting to sweat. From somewhere deep in her mind she remembered the breathing exercises she was given by a child therapist when she'd had panic attacks following her own attempted murder. Suddenly, she was back to being that frightened nine-year-old girl wondering what the future held. In through the nose, count to four, out through the mouth, count to four. Repeat until you were able to face the world again.

When she looked up, Leon and Holly had gone.

'Is everything all right?' Foley asked. 'You spaced out for a moment there.'

'I was just thinking,' she lied. 'Could I get a glass of water?'

'I'll grab you a bottle. Wait here.'

Foley left his office, leaving the door open. In came the noise from the incident team. Olivia could see Holly at her desk, staring at her computer screen. She was chewing the inside of her mouth and frowning. She undid the top button on her shirt and pulled at the collar. She scratched at her neck and went back to tapping on the keyboard. Her frown deepened and she went back to scratching at her neck. She was anxious. The detective was trying hard to hide the signs, but she hadn't yet mastered the art of understanding her own subconscious and her tell-tale signs were obvious to anyone who knew what to look for.

Olivia stood up and went over to her. 'Is everything all right?'

'Yes. Fine.' Holly looked up from the screen and gave Olivia a smile that did not reach her eyes.

Olivia tried to think of something to say. She wasn't good with small talk and spontaneous interaction.

'Have you had any luck finding other potential victims?' she asked. It was a ridiculous question. Holly had literally just left Foley's office to start work.

'There are many murders involving knives that haven't been solved.' She shook her head.

'The killer wouldn't have been as confident in the beginning as he is now. As much as the idea of taking another life is giving him a thrill, there's a big leap between fantasising about it and actually doing it. I believe there are more victims before Sarah Millington, and this shows he doesn't give his victims much thought; if he did, he would have gone for women straight away. It's always been about the chase and the kill. It will have been very late in the planning that he decided precisely whom to target first. I spoke about killers targeting those who are vulnerable in society – the elderly, the disabled, sex workers, et cetera – he won't go for those, as there's no chase involved, so you can discount those from your search. You're looking for young people who will put up a fight – not too much, of course, but just enough so that he still has the upper hand.'

Holly was frantically scribbling on her pad while Olivia was talking. 'If it's true that he killed a man first, do you think it's possible he was injured in some way, which is why he changed to targeting women?'

'Something happened to spook him and that caused him to change to targeting women only. Either he was almost caught, or, like you said, a victim was too powerful for him and the game was almost lost. Once we find that victim, we can check for hospital admissions around that time.'

'Can I ask you a personal question?' Holly asked, leaning forward on her desk.

Olivia had been waiting for this. Once people knew who she was they always wanted to know about how she'd managed to survive, how she coped with what her father had done. Jessica had known all the gruesome details. She imagined Foley did, too. Had the gossip spread around the whole station? Obviously it had. She had expected Leon to have been the insensitive one, not Holly. She took a deep breath.

'Sure.'

'How do you get inside the head of a serial killer?'

Olivia relaxed slightly. So Holly wasn't fishing for gossip. That was a refreshing change.

'You don't. You just try to understand them. Don't ever try to get into a murderer's head, and don't ever let them get into yours. Once you do, you're lost.'

Holly's smile dropped and her eyes widened. 'Oh.'

'Excuse me, are you Doctor Winter?'

Olivia looked up to see a uniformed officer standing in front of her.

'Yes.'

'There's a man here to see you. Sebastian Lister. He says it's important.'

Olivia looked over to the entrance to the open-plan room and saw Sebastian with an expression of horror on his face.

Chapter Eleven

Olivia walked slowly over to Sebastian. She knew something had happened by the way he held himself and the look of pure fear. He had news for her that couldn't wait, and he was not looking forward to telling her. She immediately thought of all the killers she had spoken to, all those she had interviewed in prisons over the years. She'd been the target of some unwanted attention by killers who had become fixated on her, which was why she had an unlisted phone number and wasn't on the electoral register or any social media sites. The harder it was for people to find her, the better.

'Sebastian,' she said, her mouth dry. 'How did you know where to find me?'

'You have a tracker in your phone, remember?'

'Of course,' she said. Instinct caused her to put a hand to her shoulder. 'What's happened?'

'Maybe we should talk outside,' he said.

Olivia didn't dare look back. She could feel the eyes of the strangers burning into her. She nodded.

They left the Major Crime Unit and found a quiet corner in the corridor. Olivia didn't notice DI Foley coming towards her with a bottle of water. He must have recognised something in her expression as he paused and half hid behind a beam.

'I've had a call from Belmarsh Prison,' Sebastian said.

'Oh, dear God.' Olivia looked at the floor. There was only one inmate at Belmarsh who would cause Sebastian to race across London. 'He's escaped?'

'No. He's suffered a severe heart attack. He's been taken to Queen Elizabeth Hospital. He's asking for you.'

Olivia's face was blank.

'Would you like me to drive you?' Sebastian placed a comforting hand on Olivia's arm. She flinched.

'Where?'

'To the hospital.'

'Why?'

'To see him.'

'No,' she said firmly. 'No. Absolutely not. I'm very busy. There's a man out there who has murdered four women. I'm needed here.'

'Olivia, he might not make it. He's—'

'Sebastian' – she held a hand up to stop him talking – 'I don't care. I'm not interested in what happens to him. I need to get back.' She turned and headed back to the MCU suite.

'Olivia!' Sebastian called after her, but she ignored him. The doors swung closed behind her.

Foley stepped out from behind the pillar. 'Has something happened?'

'Sorry? Yes. No. I...' Sebastian waffled.

'Can I help?'

'Erm, no, I don't think so. It's... it's incredibly complicated.'

'Someone's had a heart attack who wants to see Olivia. And I'm guessing Olivia doesn't want to see them.'

'If only it were that simple.'

'I'm guessing it's not an ex-husband, so it has to be either a parent or guardian or a brother she's estranged from.'

Sebastian was silent for a while, weighing up how much he should tell him. 'Her father.'

'Do you want me to have a word with Olivia?'

'You don't know her,' Sebastian said.

'Sometimes that's an advantage.'

Sebastian took a breath. 'She needs to go and see him. If she doesn't, and he dies, she'll regret it. I know she will.'

'I'll see if I can help.'

Sebastian nodded. 'Thank you.'

DI Foley whispered in Olivia's ear to join him in his office. She'd been standing in front of one of the whiteboards looking as if she was reading the information on Sarah Millington. Once in the office, Foley closed the door behind her and told her to take a seat.

'I've been thinking,' Olivia began. 'I'd like to visit the neighbourhoods where these women lived. I think it would—'

'Olivia,' Foley interrupted. 'I overheard you talking to your colleague in the corridor. You're seriously not going to the hospital?'

'Of course not. Why should I?'

'Because… you need to see him. He could be dying.'

Olivia sniggered. 'Do you actually know who "he" is?'

'Your father? Brother? Grandfather?'

'No offence, but it's none of your business. You've asked me here to help you identify a killer, and that's what I'm going to do.'

'Look, let me just say this and we'll move on. Take from it whatever you want. I didn't go to see my older brother in hospital when he was stabbed. We had this feud that went back to us being teenagers. We hadn't spoken for about ten years when he disturbed a burglar at his home. He was stabbed in the stomach. My mum called me and told me to go to the hospital to see him, but, being the stubborn arsehole that I am, I refused. That was twelve years ago, and there isn't a day goes by that I don't regret that decision.'

Despite her blank expression, Olivia was struggling with her emotions.

'I just... I can't... Every time I think about him, every time I see a photo of him in the papers, it all just—'

'Olivia,' Foley cut her off, 'don't tell me what happened if you don't want to. Like you said, it's none of my business, but I do have experience of regrets. My whole life is full of them. It's much better to put yourself through the pain now than regret it later when it's too late.' He looked up over Olivia's shoulder out into the main office. 'Holly wants me. I'll give you a few minutes on your own.'

He walked out, closing the door softly behind him. Olivia sat down, turning her back to the window so nobody could see the expression on her face. Whenever she thought of her father, she thought of the last time she saw her mother and sister, and that's not how she wanted to remember them. Yet, when she tried to remember the good times, the summer holidays, the birthday parties, the happy Christmases, she pictured her father laughing and smiling and joining in the fun. The two men didn't match. He couldn't be a happy family man who loved his daughters, and a butcherer of women. It wasn't possible. So, who was the man whose knee she sat on while he read her *The Secret Garden*? Who was the man who took her and Claire to Brighton at weekends to play on the beach? Who was the man who helped his daughters make such a fuss of their mum on Mother's Day?

That was what Olivia struggled to understand. How could one man have such totally contrasting personalities and nobody be able to see he was living a lie? Unless it wasn't a lie.

Olivia shook her head. She could feel a headache coming on. She picked up the bottle of water Foley had brought her, unscrewed the cap and took a lengthy swig. It was room temperature. Was it possible for one person to have two conflicting personalities running alongside each other at the same time? She'd interviewed dozens of killers in prison, and spoken to their families, friends, neighbours and work colleagues. They'd all said the same thing – that he was a happy family man. 'Though,' they always added, as an additional comment, 'looking back, there was always something strange about him.' Was that the benefit of hindsight, or were people trying to make themselves feel better, when they should have known but didn't?

The problem Olivia had with her father was that, looking back, she really didn't know. Even now, with all her qualifications and experience, she couldn't pinpoint a moment in time when her father changed from being a loving man – happy, smiling, funny – into a serial murderer who tortured his victims, cut them up and dumped them by the Thames.

And because the great Doctor Olivia Winter couldn't understand her own father, she had no intention of going to see him. He gave up the right to call himself a dad when he destroyed her family. He was a total stranger. He deserved to die alone.

'Run!'

Olivia's mother's final word to her echoed in her head. She was right. She was always right. She should run.

She picked up her bag and sneaked out of Foley's office. She didn't look up so wasn't aware if anyone saw her, but once she was out of the Major Crime Unit and reached the stairs, she took her mother's advice. She ran.

Chapter Twelve

Olivia hated travelling on the London Underground. She avoided it at all costs. There was something about the darkness, the small space, the feeling of being trapped, not being able to see a way out, that terrified her. The same could be said for planes when she travelled around the world giving guest lectures, doing book tours and interviewing serial killers, but she didn't have the same sense of underlying danger in a plane that she got from the Tube.

As she left Sanderson Street Police Station, she hitched up the collar of her coat and started walking. She didn't have her scooter with her so couldn't simply hop on it and drive back to work or home, and she wasn't within walking distance either. She needed to be on her own. She needed to sort out her thoughts and clear her mind. She almost laughed to herself. She'd spent the past twenty-five years trying to do that, unsuccessfully. What made her think a brisk walk in the cold air of London would solve all her problems now?

Maybe it would have been better if her father had collapsed in prison clutching his chest and died right there. A quick death. She wouldn't have had all this inner turmoil about whether to go and see him or not. She didn't hate him. She couldn't hate him. Hate was a very strong emotion and one you could only attribute to a person you knew. Olivia didn't know her father at all. She thought she did, but she couldn't have done. Her feelings for him, therefore, were non-existent. This man was just a body in a hospital bed.

Olivia bumped into someone. Neither of them apologised. She staggered slightly and continued on her journey to nowhere.

It didn't seem to matter how much Olivia told herself he wasn't her father. She could denounce him, avoid seeing him, refuse to acknowledge his letters and cards, but he was part of her. Half of his DNA was inside her. She was born from his make-up. She shuddered, unsure whether it was the thought of her father's dark psychology swimming around inside her or the harsh winter breeze.

Olivia had written a paper, many years ago, about the myth of the 'killer gene'. There were people who thought serial killers stood out from the rest of the population because they had a single gene that others didn't. Monoamine Oxidase A, also known as MAOA, was a common denominator in the majority of serial killers, but not all of them had it. So, was it a killer gene or not? If so, how do you explain the behaviour of the killers who don't have the gene? Then there's CDH13, an ADHA-related gene identified in 2008, strongly associated with violent criminality. Did her father have MAOA or CDH13? Did he have neither, or both? And if so, were they in her too?

'Jesus Christ!' she said to herself as reality dawned. She quickly dismissed the idea that she was anything like her father. She had never once desired to take another life. It was the polar opposite to everything she believed in. She was not her father's daughter.

She looked up and inhaled hard to get some cold air inside her. A tear fell from her eye when she saw what was across the road directly in front of her: the ugly grey concrete of the Queen

Elizabeth Hospital. Unwittingly, she'd been drawn here as if by some kind of magnetic force.

Why had her unconscious mind done this to her? She was already torturing herself about refusing to help Jessica just before she was killed. Maybe, if she'd offered to help, they would have spent Saturday night going through the files in Olivia's office, and Jessica wouldn't have been home alone for a sadistic killer to target. Now, here she was, outside the hospital that was helping to improve the health of her murdering father. She must really love self-flagellation.

She crossed the road at the lights and entered the grounds. She couldn't take her eyes from the building, and wondered which window he was behind. Could he see her from where he was? Was he unconscious? Fingers crossed, he'd been given a clean bill of health and was on his way back to prison where he belonged.

She doubted that. Life wasn't kind to her.

She approached the main entrance and stood rooted to the spot. She didn't want to go in. She didn't want to see him. She owed him nothing.

Then why was she here?

'I thought I'd find you here.'

She turned at the sound of a familiar voice. Amyas Foley was standing by his car.

'What are you doing here?' she asked. She was cold. Her teeth were chattering slightly.

'I went back to my office, and you'd gone. I was worried.'

'Worried? Why?'

'You've just received a huge shock. I wanted to make sure you were all right.'

'I'm... fine,' she said, slowly, knowing before she said it how trite it would sound. 'How did you know where to find me?'

'I called your colleague, Doctor Lister. He told me which hospital your dad has been admitted to.'

Olivia baulked at the word 'dad'.

'You going in?' He nodded towards the building.

'I haven't made my mind up yet.'

He walked over to a bench and sat down. Olivia followed.

'When did you last see your father?'

Olivia knew the answer to that straight away. She knew the day, the date, the time and what the weather was doing.

'When I was nine,' she answered.

'You haven't seen him since?'

'No.'

'Do you think that if you went in there to see him, to talk to him, you'd be betraying your mother and sister?'

'So you do know who my father is, then?'

He nodded.

'Jessica?'

'No. She refused to reveal your secret. All she said was that you had first-hand experience of a serial killer when you were a child. I used my detective skills to find out the rest. With some help from Wikipedia, too,' he said with a cheeky smile.

'I can't believe Jessica is really gone,' Olivia said, wistfully. 'I'd usually be talking to her about this kind of thing.'

'What would she say?'

'She'd probably tell me to let the bastard rot in hell. I was at Jessica's house while my father was killing my mum and sister.'

'Really?'

'Yes. She lived just around the corner.'

They fell silent as life continued around them. The hustle and bustle of a busy hospital mixed with the noise of nearby traffic. Whatever hell Olivia was going through, the world didn't stop turning, and out there a killer was at work.

'Why are you really here, when you're so busy?' She turned to Foley.

'Well, I really need your help. And I'd like to help you in return.'

'Why? When you've literally just met me.'

'Because you were Jessica's best friend. She spoke a lot about you. She cared for you and Jessica was a good person, an excellent judge of character. I feel – selfishly, I know – but I feel like I'm still chatting with Jessica when I'm chatting with you. Does that sound weird?'

'No. It's quite comforting really.'

'Would you like me to come inside with you?'

'Would you?'

'I wouldn't have asked if I didn't want to.'

'I have my mother's voice in my head telling me to run, but I have my own voice telling me to give in to curiosity and see how the last twenty-five years have treated him.'

'Who are you going to listen to?'

'I should listen to my mum.' She didn't attempt to get up from the bench.

They walked into the hospital and were immediately surrounded by a wall of noise: the chatter of people in the waiting rooms, the sound of phones ringing and trolleys being dragged along corridors.

Foley flashed his ID to the receptionist then let Olivia take over.

'I'm here to see... Can you tell me where Richard Button is, please? I'm his daughter. I believe he's asking for me.'

It was as if the whole hospital fell silent and everyone was looking at her.

The receptionist told them where to go and Foley led her by the elbow to the lifts. They waited in silence for the stainless-steel doors to yawn open. They stepped inside and the doors closed. They were the only occupants as the lift juddered up. Neither of them spoke while the lift stopped at various floors, picking people up and dropping them off. All of them with blank looks on their faces, all of them going through their own dramas.

They stepped out into a stifling corridor and headed for the Intensive Care Unit.

'Does your colleague know?' he asked.

'Sebastian? Yes. He wrote the book on him. That's how we met. He came to interview me for it.' She smiled at the memory. 'I was horrible to him on that first meeting. I didn't want anything to do with his book or his research. My therapist said it might be cathartic if I did talk to him; if I told him my side of the story.'

'And did you?'

'Have you read the book?'

'I'm not much of a reader.' He grimaced.

'Yes, I did. It helped and it brought me and Sebastian closer.'

'Are you and he...? You know...'

'God, no,' she answered quickly. 'Sebastian is more like the brother I never had. Besides, he was devoted to Rosemary. He went to pieces when she died. Now it's just him and four kids.'

'Wow. That can't be easy.'

'It's not. But he's coping. Just about.'

It was easy to spot the room Richard Button was in, as there was an armed police officer standing outside with the door closed behind him. Olivia could feel her heart pounding in her chest as if it was trying to break out.

A doctor was walking with them. Olivia had no idea where she had come from. Her mouth was moving but Olivia couldn't hear a word she was saying.

The armed officer stepped to one side. The doctor depressed the handle and pushed the door open.

'I'll wait out here,' Foley said.

Olivia stood in the doorway. She could feel the heat coming from the room. She was sweating.

In the centre of the room was a single hospital bed. Written above it in an untidy scrawl was his innocuous-sounding name:

Richard Button. The man lying in the middle was unrecognisable. A tube was taped to his mouth, one coming out of his nose. The index finger of his left hand was hooked up to a blood-pressure monitor. Various beeps were heard at regular intervals as the surrounding machines kept him alive.

Olivia stepped closer to get a clearer look at the face. The last time she had seen him, he had been strong, with dark, wavy hair, a smooth complexion, slightly overweight and with smiling eyes. What she saw in the bed was a slim, grey-haired man with a mean jawline and a cruel expression. What surprised Olivia most was that she felt nothing for him. There was no emotional attachment. She could have been standing beside the bed of a complete stranger. She was.

Slowly, his eyes opened.

Olivia took a deep breath.

He carefully removed the mask over his mouth and proffered a cruel smile. 'Livvy, you came,' he said in a soft voice.

Olivia took another deep breath. 'Hello, Dad.'

Chapter Thirteen

KINGSTON UPON THAMES, LONDON

Tuesday 21st December 1999

Olivia Button should have been home hours ago, but she just couldn't tear herself away from her friend Jessica's house, and the amazing early Christmas present she'd received, one which her mother definitely could not hide until the big day – a dachshund puppy, so small he could fit into the palm of her hand. He didn't seem real, and his cuteness was off the scale. Olivia was as excited about playing with him as Jessica was. But when it started to get dark Jessica's mother said she should head off for home before her mum became worried.

Jessica lived in the next street from Olivia, so she didn't have far to go home. She zipped her coat up to the neck, wrapped her scarf around herself tightly and put on her gloves as she walked, all the while struggling to stop smiling after playing all afternoon with the sausage-dog puppy. She didn't notice her father's haphazardly parked car in the driveway.

She opened the front door and stepped inside.

'Mum, you'll never guess what Mrs Sheffield has bought Jessica for Christmas. She's...' Olivia stopped when she walked through the living room and into the kitchen to find the room empty. 'Mum?'

She retraced her steps and went to the bottom of the stairs. She looked up, angled her head to listen for any sound. She couldn't hear anything.

When she left, four hours ago, her youngest sister, Claire, was bounding about the house draped in tinsel, her excitement for Christmas in overdrive, while her mum was frantically in the throes of last-minute preparations.

Olivia took off her coat and hung it over the banister. She walked upstairs slowly, straining to listen for something that would indicate where her mum and sister were. She wondered if they were busy wrapping up her present, or, fingers crossed, presents.

Claire's door was closed. It was never closed. There was obviously something secretive happening in this room. She wrapped her hand around the handle, slowly pushed it down and, with a single movement, swung the door violently open. Her smile dropped when she saw it was empty.

She frowned. Where had they all gone?

She turned and went down the corridor to her parents' bedroom. Again, the door was closed. Again, it was only ever closed at night when Mum and Dad went to bed. Growing bored, Olivia swept her hair behind her ears and headed straight inside.

'Mum, Jessica's mum's bought her a puppy for Christmas. Can we have…'

Olivia stopped in her tracks when she opened the door to the master bedroom and found her mother on the bed, cradling her younger sister in her arms. It should have been a picture of happiness and normalcy, if it wasn't for the amount of blood. The bed was saturated in it. There were high sprays on the walls and ceiling. Claire, slumped in her mother's arms, had her eyes closed.

'Mum,' Olivia said, her voice barely above a whisper.

Her mum, Geraldine Button, was sitting up in bed. Her face

was pale, and blood was slowly draining out of a gash in her throat. She was taking short, sharp breaths, struggling to cling onto life. She looked at her daughter, looked her straight in the eye.

'Olivia,' she said.

Olivia's bottom lip began to wobble as she took in the scene of carnage. Tears began to fall.

'Mum,' she croaked.

'Run,' Geraldine said, breathlessly.

'What?'

'Run!'

Something caught Olivia's eye from the en suite bathroom. She turned and saw her father reflected in the mirror. He was drenched in blood and in his red hands, he was holding a knife.

She turned on her heels and ran. She slipped on a patch of blood on the carpet she hadn't seen when she came in, landing with a thud. She picked herself up and charged for the main bathroom. The only room in the house with a lock on the door. Once inside, she turned to close it just as her father slammed himself into the door. She secured the lock and stepped away from the door.

Olivia fell back against the sink.

'Olivia. Open the door,' her dad shouted from outside.

'Daddy?' she cried out.

'Olivia. Open this door right now.' He was panicking. His voice sounded angry.

In the background, Olivia could hear the sound of sirens approaching. From behind her, flashing blue lights came through the window.

Her father slammed into the door. The lock rattled and one of the loose screws fell out. Whoever was outside and coming to save her wouldn't get here in time.

She climbed up onto the toilet, pushed open the window and looked out. Below, the sloping roof of the extension was wet with sleet. She wouldn't be able to reach it from here, but if she jumped, she might be able to grab onto the guttering or something to stop her falling to the ground below. She swung her leg over the windowsill. It was so cold outside, and she'd taken her coat off. She wiped away her tears with the back of her trembling hand and looked back into the bathroom just as the door broke open and she saw her dad, covered in the blood of her mother and sister, charge into the room, knife aloft. He swung it at her. She let go of the sill and dropped.

The roof of the extension was more slippery than she expected. She flew to the bottom and didn't have time to reach for the guttering. She grabbed something that slowed down her fall slightly, but she landed on the wet grass below with a thud.

She stood up, looked back to the bathroom window. There was nobody there.

Olivia could still hear the sirens screaming into the cold air, but there was no one around to save her. She needed to run. If she jumped over the back fence and ran to the Prescotts', they'd look after her.

She reached the fence, but it was six feet tall. There was no way she could grab the top, not even if she jumped. She looked around for something to stand on, but all the plant pots had been removed and put in the shed until next spring.

Next to the back door was the recycling wheelie bin. She didn't know how much time she had, so she ran as fast as her aching legs would carry her, grabbed the bin and pulled it back to the fence. She struggled to climb onto it. She swung her legs over the fence and was about to drop down when the back door to the house burst open and her father ran out towards her.

'Olivia, get back here right now!' he screamed.

Still frozen, Olivia looked at her dad. She saw the blood on his shirt, the spatters on his face, the red droplets dripping from the knife in his red right hand. He came towards her, taking long strides. Behind him, the gate was slammed open and a man in a policeman's uniform, drenched from the sleet, came into the garden. He opened his mouth and said something, but Olivia was too far away to hear what it was. Her father screamed something back at him. It didn't sound like her dad. He sounded scared, angry, frightened and dangerous.

The man in the uniform held up his arms and stepped forward. Her dad stood his ground, refusing to move. He lunged forward, swung his arm and the man dropped to the floor. Olivia saw a spray of red shoot out of him. She screamed. Her dad turned back to her.

'Olivia, I can explain. These men, they're bad people. I'll look after you. I promise.'

Again, it might have been her dad talking, but he sounded strange.

'Help me!' she screamed as loud as she could. Her voice echoed into the night.

She let go of the fence and dropped down the other side.

She ran down the embankment and into the woods, where her cries were muffled by the thickset trees. She jumped over fallen branches, slipped on wet leaves and fell on the unstable ground. She picked herself up. She was muddy, wet and cold, but she couldn't stop. She had to keep going.

'Olivia!' She heard her father calling her name.

Olivia tried to keep her emotions in check. She told herself to stop crying but she couldn't. Less than half an hour ago she had been playing with Jessica, making a fuss over her new puppy, and now she was in the middle of a nightmare.

Olivia ran for her life in the darkness. Bare branches grazed her face and tore her clothing. She was in pain, but she knew she couldn't stop.

She slipped. She fell. She banged her head hard on the root of a mighty oak.

She turned over onto her back and looked up into the eyes of her father.

'Daddy!' she cried.

'It's all right, sweetheart. Everything's going to be all right now.'

'What's happening? Where's Claire? Where's Mummy?'

'They're safe. Nobody can harm them now.'

'I want Mummy,' she choked on her tears.

'You'll see them soon.'

Richard's tears fell from his eyes and landed on his daughter's cold face. He raised his knife-wielding hand above his head and brought it down on Olivia's shoulder. She screamed.

'I love you, Livvy,' he said before stabbing her a second time.

'I love you, too, Daddy,' she said before she was stabbed a third time.

Chapter Fourteen

Olivia winced at her father calling her Livvy. He was the only person who had ever shortened her name and she had hated it from the very first time he had used it. At the age of six, it's difficult to tell your father not to call you something. Now, Olivia still felt she couldn't speak up and she had no idea why. Sitting opposite her dad for the first time in twenty-five years, she was transported back to the moment he destroyed their family, when he stabbed her mum and sister to death and ruined any chance of her ever having a normal life.

The silence in the room was intense. Olivia had no idea what to say. She didn't want to rant, to release a quarter of a century of pent-up rage and anger. She didn't want to make pointless small talk, either, and she had no intention of asking how he was. What the hell was she doing here? Was she seeking closure or was it a perversion on her part, to see how time had affected the only surviving relative she had left? *Closure,* she told herself. That was the only solution she would accept. She needed to close the door on this part of her life. She needed to think of her mum and sister with happiness and remember the good times. The only way she could do that was by putting her father in a clearly labelled box in her mind and not having a big question mark hanging over his head. Was he a loving father or an evil killer? He couldn't be both. She refused to let him be both.

'You look so much like your mother, it's frightening,' Richard Button said. He tried to sit up, but the expression on his face made it obvious that the action caused him some pain.

Olivia didn't say anything to his predictable opening line. She remained still on the hard plastic chair, her hands clasped firmly together in her lap, her stony face staring straight ahead. She could feel her heart beating loudly in her chest and prickles of sweat dripping down her back. She wanted to leave but felt frozen to the spot.

'How are you?' he asked.

How was she? That was a difficult question to answer. She was completely and utterly alone in the world. She spent her days talking to serial killers to try to understand the motives behind someone's thirst for ending another person's life. She engaged in random, pointless sex with men she barely knew, just so she could feel a modicum of emotion. She cried herself to sleep most nights, as she missed her mother and Claire. Her closest friend had just been murdered and she was currently sitting opposite a man who had killed eight people, including her mum and sister. How was she? She had no fucking idea.

'Fine,' she croaked. Her throat was dry. She tried clearing it, but it wouldn't.

'I appreciate you coming to see me.'

'I'm not here for a social visit,' she said.

'Oh?'

'Did you honestly expect me to turn up here with a bunch of grapes?'

'No, I...' He couldn't finish his sentence. 'Well, whatever the reason, I'm glad you came. I think of you often. Do you think of me?'

'Only when forced to,' she replied. The icy disdain was evident in her voice.

'When's that?'

'When you send me letters and cards.'

'You're my daughter—'

'You gave up your right to call me that when you killed my family,' she interrupted. As much as she wanted to remain cool, it was difficult to hold onto the torrent of emotion that was building within. She tried to remember her training. She tried to replicate all the times she'd sat opposite serial killers and asked them difficult questions, and how they revelled in talking about their disturbing crimes. She had to remain emotionless. It wasn't easy.

'It wasn't supposed to end that way,' Richard said, breaking eye contact with her for the first time.

'Really? How was it supposed to end? Did you expect us to be thrilled at your change of career? Did you think we'd encourage you in your new hobby? Perhaps we could have taken up murdering as a family and gone on weekend killing sprees,' Olivia said. She was growing in confidence. The man lying in the bed opposite her was no longer a threat. He was a sad old man who could no longer hurt her.

'You were never supposed to find out. I thought I'd been careful that last time.'

'You were sloppy. You got complacent and made a stupid mistake. Like all serial killers, you believed your own self-aggrandised hype. You may have killed six women, but there was nothing special about you. You were pathetic, weak, and a habitual coward.'

He turned back to face her quickly, his face filled with fury.

'A coward?'

'You killed your wife and your daughter. You tried to kill me. You didn't want us to find out what you'd done. You didn't want us to see you crying in the dock when a whole-life tariff was passed. You're not a prolific serial predator. You're a sad, pale imitation. I don't know why I came here.' She started to get up.

'I thought Sebastian Lister did a good job in that book he wrote about me. Have you read it?' he asked before she could reach the door.

She stopped, her hand on the warm handle. 'Why would I want to read it when I lived it?' she asked, without turning back.

'There was just one minor detail that he didn't include.'

She waited.

'Motive,' Richard eventually said, causing Olivia to turn around. She could see a twinkle in his eye. 'Motive,' he repeated. 'Did you ever wonder why I killed all those women?'

'No,' she answered quickly.

'Liar. I've followed your career, Livvy. I've read your books. You have a brilliant, analytical mind, though I don't always agree with your conclusions. Surely you've wanted to know what made your own father kill so randomly and remorselessly?'

Olivia remained by the door but removed her hand from the handle. She took a deep breath, inhaling the stench of cheap disinfectant and stale sweat. Her entire body was shaking. She held herself tense.

'Come and sit down.' He nodded weakly towards the chair.

Reluctantly, she did.

The silence grew. Richard was playing for time. He wanted his daughter to ask him why. The twinkle in his eye danced and a mischievous smile spread across his lips. Olivia had no intention of pandering to his ego. She had questioned his motive for twenty-five years. Was he abused as a child? No, she knew that for a fact. He had a very idyllic childhood. Was he seeking revenge of some kind? Not that she was aware of. He'd lived a steady, middle-class life and had no reason to rail against society. Was he simply a sick, twisted, depraved individual who sought the unnecessary torture of innocent women for his own pleasure? It would seem so. But why? Why? That was the big question. Why wasn't he satisfied with what he had?

Richard sat up slowly. He reached for his plastic beaker of water and took several small sips.

'I hear there's a killer in London at the moment, breaking into single women's homes and slicing them open. Are you working on that case?'

Olivia didn't reply.

'I'll take your silence as a yes.'

'I don't work on active cases,' she said.

'No. You don't, do you? Why is that?'

'I'm not a profiler.'

'But you could help the police. You've been asked many times by detectives all over the world to help catch a serial killer and you've always turned them down. Instead, you've sat back and watched from the sidelines while the police have bumbled their way blindly in the investigation, waiting for the killer to make a mistake. That's the only way they catch them, isn't it? In the meantime, the killers notched up a few more victims and you enabled them to do that. Are their deaths on your conscience, Livvy?'

'Don't call me that!' Her voice was almost a growl. She was angry, but she was also nervous.

'Is that why you're so fucked up?'

'I am not fucked up,' she said harshly.

'You live in that big house all on your own. No friends. No family. No visitors. No lover.'

'You don't know me.'

He chuckled. 'Livvy, sweetheart, I know everything about you,' he said with a sweet smile.

'You know... nothing.'

'I know that's Detective Inspector Amyas Foley sitting outside waiting for you. I saw him in the papers a couple of days ago. He's working on this serial killer case and he's brought you here

The Mind of a Murderer

to see me, so you've obviously spent the morning together. Why has this case caused you to throw your ethics out of the window?'

'I'm not talking to you about it.'

'Tell me, Livvy, what's this guy's motive? He's not raping his victims, so he's not getting a sexual thrill out of it. He doesn't rob them, so money isn't important to him. What does that leave us with?'

Olivia didn't say anything. She looked away from her father, her eyes glancing around the room, fixing on anything other than the man in the bed. She could feel a bead of sweat running down her back.

'I didn't rape or rob my victims either. Shall I tell you why I murdered them?'

Olivia finally looked at her father. He had a smile on his face. He leaned as close to her as was comfortably possible.

'Because I fucking enjoyed it,' he said in a loud whisper.

Olivia held her breath. She felt sick.

'I was bored with life. Do you think a boy leaves school with dreams of becoming an accountant for a shitty family-run brewery, to go home at the end of the day to a mousy wife and two greedy daughters? Society dictates we do that. We think we're living in a democracy, but we're not. We're robots, automatons, programmed to go to work, get married, have a family, buy a house, pay our taxes and feed into the system so that we can lie on our deathbed and think of all the good we've done.

'But once in a while, someone breaks free. Someone sits up and realises that they're being controlled and manipulated, and they're not going to stand for it anymore. Working Monday to Friday, eight 'til five, with an hour for lunch. Sitting in the same shitty office with the same shitty people, having the same shitty conversations day in, day out, for the rest of their working life. No fucking way! It's boring. It's dull. It's oppressive. And what better way of giving the establishment a big fuck-you than putting the fear of God into them and spilling the blood of the innocent?

'You want to know why I did it, Livvy? I did it because I could. I did it because I enjoyed it. I did it because it was the biggest rush I've ever felt. Watching the lights go out in someone's eyes made me feel more alive than anything. I was a god.'

'You're sick,' Olivia said. Tears were streaming down her face. She didn't notice them.

'In your first book, you talk about killers languishing in prison with the attention of the public, the media, the police suddenly off them. They're left alone to rot in their cells, and nobody cares about them. That's why they often admit to killing people they haven't, to feel wanted again, to be the centre of attention. Have you worked it out yet, Livvy?'

She frowned. 'Worked what out?'

'Claire only received two stab wounds and died. You received four and survived. Why is that?'

Her frown deepened. She had never thought about that before. She surmised, when he cut Claire's throat, it had been enough to kill her, so he hadn't inflicted more pain on her.

'I have had more satisfaction in prison knowing that you're out there, suffering with what I've done. You were never meant to die, Livvy. I was always going to keep you alive. You were my favourite. I picture you in your big house, looking at yourself in the mirror, looking at your scars, knowing where they came from, the agony and torment that I inflicted on you. The whole world may not give me a second thought, but you do. Every. Single. Day. I live on through you and your work. You keep me alive. Four tiny little stabs and a whole lifetime of agony.' He smiled. 'All this time you've been ignoring me and refusing my visiting requests, you've thought you were making me suffer and rot in loneliness in my cell. Wrong! I'm inside your head day and night. I'm in your dreams. I'm exactly where I want to be. And you've been letting me.'

Olivia stood up and ran to the door. She pulled it open and fell out into the corridor. She could hear her father laughing as the door closed smoothly behind her.

'Olivia!' Foley jumped up from his seat and caught her before she hit the floor. 'What happened?'

'Get me out of here,' she cried through the tears.

'What?'

'Get me the fuck out of here right now.'

Chapter Fifteen

Olivia wanted to go home. She felt violated, abused. She wanted to wash off the hospital, the smell of the sick and the dying that was clinging to her hair and skin, but it didn't matter how hot she had the water, how long she stayed in the shower, she would never be able to wash away what her father had said to her.

Once through the automatic doors and into the fresh air, Olivia took huge lungfuls and began to calm down. Foley held her by the elbow and led her to a pub across the road.

The lighting was subdued. There were very few people in there. Foley walked Olivia over to the corner and sat her down. He went to the bar and returned with large whiskies for them both. She took a big sip, swallowing most of it in a single gulp.

'I hate whisky,' she eventually said.

'You looked like you needed it. I thought you were going to collapse when you came out of that room.'

'I nearly did.'

'What happened?'

'He...' She took another drink and emptied her glass.

'Would you like another?'

'No. Yes.'

Foley went to the bar and ordered two more drinks. While they were being poured, he glanced at Olivia over his shoulder. She looked incredibly fragile sat alone, as if the wrong word or phrase would cause her to shatter into a thousand pieces. She didn't need this level of stress right now. He knew it would be highly inappropriate, but he wanted so much to hug her.

He returned to the table and placed the glass gently in front of her. She looked up at him with big eyes and offered a 'thank you' smile. He sat down and prompted her to continue her story.

She took a deep breath. 'The book that Sebastian Lister wrote about my fa— About him, there was always something missing from it. I remember asking Sebastian about it while he was writing, and he said he'd asked my f— Richard... about it several times but he'd never replied. He'd never given a reason as to why he'd killed those six women.'

'And today he told you?'

'I mean, we knew he was a thrill killer. We knew he enjoyed the killing. Similar to the kind of killer you're seeking now. But there's nearly always something lacking, something missing from a person's life – that's why they become that kind of killer. I could never work out what it was with my... with Richard.'

'So, what was missing?'

'Nothing. He just said he was bored. Not necessarily bored with Mum and us, but bored with life, with society. I just... I don't think I can accept that as a motive for murder. It doesn't mean anything. It reduces his victims' lives to nothing.'

'But you've said he was a thrill killer, like the one we're seeking, and I'm guessing you've met other thrill killers around the world?'

'Yes.'

'Surely their reasons for killing were the same. They were bored with their lives. Rather than seek a change of job or move to another country, they've gone to the most depraved form they can think of and killed. Why are you so shocked that your father is like a number of killers you've interviewed?'

'I'm not. I mean, I am. I'm upset that we weren't enough for him. I've always known that, but to hear him actually say it to my face – well, it's different, isn't it?' She took another drink of her whisky. 'He told me I was his favourite. I didn't like that.'

'Understandable.'

'He told me he didn't kill me because he wanted me to live with the torment of what he'd done for the rest of my life. He wanted me, his own daughter, his favourite, apparently, to suffer. What kind of a man is he? What kind of a sick, evil man do I have for my father?'

'We don't have to turn into our parents, Olivia. We really don't. We can break the cycle. My dad was a doctor. So was my brother. So was my grandfather and so were my two uncles. I became a detective. I broke the cycle. I'm as far away from my dad as I could possibly get. We don't need to live in their shadow.'

'How can I shake him off when I have so many questions?'

'Ask him your questions,' he said, almost nonchalantly. 'The only way you can get over him is if you confront him with what you need to know. When you've done that, you have no further use for him. You can forget about him.'

'But how do I know he'll tell me the truth?'

'When you go to these prisons around the world to interview killers, do you worry about them telling you the truth?'

'Of course. They're manipulative by design.'

'So how do you tell if they're lying or not?'

'There are many ways.'

'But when you come out of the interview, do you react as you're acting now?'

'No. But then, none of them are my father.'

'Don't think of Richard as your father. He hasn't been your father for the past twenty-five years. You don't need him in your life to be a dad. Treat him as a study.'

'I've never wanted to give him the satisfaction of me studying him.'

'You'll get more out of it than he will. Use him for your own ends.'

Olivia fell silent. She looked down into her drink. She could feel the liquid burning her throat. There was no denying it had warmed her up nicely, though.

'He saw you,' she said. 'At the hospital. Through the slats in the blinds. He knows we're working together. He knows about the serial killer currently on the loose.'

'But we haven't even told the press yet. How can he know?'

'He'll have access to the internet. He's got nothing else to do with his days. He's seen the murders reported in the press and put two and two together. He's worked it out because they're exactly the same killer. Richard has seen what this man is doing and he's loving it.'

'Bloody hell,' Foley said, wiping his hand roughly over his face. 'How do you feel?'

'Sick. Angry. You know, for years he's sent me cards and letters asking me to visit him. I've always thought he wanted to explain why he killed my mum and sister, to apologise for ruining my family, make some kind of amends… I don't know, but in that hospital room, he was taunting me, torturing me with what he'd done. He was bragging about killing people to his own daughter. What kind of a sick bastard does that?'

She looked up and noticed people staring at her. She'd obviously raised her voice. She sank in her seat.

'Only you can answer that question, Olivia. You've interviewed some of the most dangerous people on the planet. You know them better than most.'

'I've always said, "Never allow a killer to get into your head", but that's what I've allowed Richard to do all these years. He's in there.'

'Is that such a bad thing?'

'Of course it is,' she frowned.

She picked up her second glass and swigged back most of her drink.

'No. I mean, the work you do, what you're working on right now, you're looking for the same kind of killer as your father was. Shouldn't that make it easier for you to find who killed Jessica and the others?'

'I can't even think of that right now,' she said. She downed the rest of her drink and stood up.

'Where are you going?'

'Home.'

'I thought you were going to talk to my officers.'

'I'm sorry, Amyas, I can't do that right now.'

She headed for the door and pulled it open. Foley grabbed a twenty-pound note out of his wallet and slapped it on the bar before following Olivia out onto the darkening streets.

'Let me drive you home.'

'No. I need to be on my own. I'll get a taxi,' she said, buttoning up her coat.

'It's miles away. It'll cost you a fortune.'

'Amyas,' she said, turning to him, 'I really don't give a fuck right now. I just want to be by myself.'

'You've had a shock. You shouldn't be alone, Olivia.'

She gave a half-smile. 'I've been alone since I was nine years old. You get used to it after a while.'

She walked away, heading God only knew where, leaving Foley behind, watching her go.

Olivia walked. It was only when she was cold, her stomach was growling with hunger and her feet were beginning to ache that she looked up and realised she was miles from home. She refused to use the Underground. Screw the cost. She hailed a taxi.

By the time she turned a corner and entered the familiar cul-de-sac where she lived, it was pitch-black. The safety of her home lay ahead. She was looking forward to a long shower, a bottle or three of wine and hopefully passing out on her bed and enjoying a peaceful, dreamless sleep.

As she walked up the steps to her front door, the security light came on. She stopped in her tracks. A bunch of yellow roses lay on the mat. Her heart sank. Yellow had been her mother's favourite colour. Whatever outfit she wore, some part of it had always been yellow. She knew her father was sick, but this was beyond evil. She picked them up by the stems and smashed them down on the steps so petals flew off in all directions, before dumping them in the wheelie bin.

Olivia fumbled with the front-door key, and eventually found the lock. She pushed open the door and fell inside. She turned off the alarm, slammed the door and locked it with the bolts at the top and bottom, putting on the security chain and the alarm. She no longer felt safe in her own home. If her father was able to get a bunch of flowers to her from his guarded hospital bedside, what else was he able to do?

Amyas Foley decided against returning to work after leaving Olivia Winter outside the pub. He felt physically and mentally drained after the past couple of days. Losing a colleague in the line of duty was one thing, that was (sort of) understandable, but at the hands of a serial killer was something else entirely. Add into the mix Doctor Winter and her troubles, and all Amyas was good for was falling asleep on the sofa with a bottle of whisky and his German shepherds for company.

On the way to his home in Barnet, he turned on his mobile phone and listened to the voicemails Goodfellow and Rippner had left him. More interviews had been conducted with Jessica's neighbours and the guests at the hotel opposite her house. No new leads had emerged, and uniformed officers were currently going door to door in and around the neighbourhoods in Brent where Sarah Millington and Joanne Douglas had been killed, to see if anyone had turned up on their doorsteps trying to gain access to their homes. So far, nothing.

Foley took a detour and headed for The Spires shopping centre. He walked through the entrance that sported the original spires from the old Methodist church either side, reaching up into the sky like turrets on a castle, and into the modern precinct. He headed for Waterstones.

Foley wasn't a great reader. In fact, he couldn't remember the last time he'd bought a book. He didn't read fiction or history books. He didn't own a cookbook and there wasn't a person who he thought was interesting enough to read their biography. His wife was a great reader. He hadn't realised how many books they'd owned until they had divorced, and she'd left taking not only her books but the bookcases too. The house had looked like it had been burgled when he'd come home from work that day. It was now four years later, and he still hadn't replaced the furniture. He preferred the sparse, minimalistic look.

He headed for the true crime section and scoured the shelves. Some of the titles were eye-catching, and the front covers of terrifying serial killers and bloodied victims were enough to give you nightmares without actually having to read the contents. He found what he was looking for: *The Riverside Killer: The Double Life of Richard Button* by Sebastian Lister. It was a thick book, around five hundred pages, and had several sections of glossy pictures. He paid for it and left.

By the time he arrived home, his two dogs were waiting for him, tails wagging enthusiastically. Before he settled down to his gruesome read over a takeaway, he grabbed their leads and took them out for their evening walk.

Foley and his ex-wife, married for twelve years, divorced

(officially) for three, had been unable to have children. They had tried for years before they sought medical help. Test results revealed Dana had a hostile womb, whatever that meant, and that had been the first nail in the coffin of their marriage. Foley had tried to tell her it didn't matter. They could live a perfectly happy and content life without a child. Dana had masked her pain by refusing to talk about it. They had stopped having sex. They had stopped conversing. Dana had used to wait until Foley came home from work before they ate, but then when he arrived home, the house would be in darkness, a plate of something keeping warm in the oven, and Dana would have gone to bed. What had finally caused Dana to leave him was when Foley came home one Sunday with two German shepherd puppies. He had seen them as companions; she had seen them as baby substitutes. A row had broken out and she had left. Two days later, the house had been stripped of her belongings and a Post-it note had been left on the door of the microwave telling him she'd started divorce proceedings. He had decided not to fight it.

Over the months and years, his dogs had grown and so had the bond between them. The divorce had been straightforward. They both went their separate ways and began new lives. Foley had his dogs and Dana met a geography teacher called Gerrard. He hoped she was happy.

Dogs asleep at his feet, stomachs full and snoring gently, Foley picked up the paperback and made himself comfortable on the sofa. The Chinese takeaway was lying heavily in his stomach. He hoped the whisky would burn it all away. He opened the cover, broke the spine straightaway, and decided to get to know what had made Richard Button kill. Hopefully, he would be able to use his findings to discover what made the killer in his current case tick.

INTRODUCTION
Picture the scene. It's eleven o'clock at night. It's dark. It's quiet.

Most people are safely tucked up in bed asleep after a hard day at work. The streets are empty. The clouds are blocking out the light of the moon and not a sound can be heard apart from the distant hum of traffic from a nearby dual carriageway.

You're about to walk down a poorly lit street when you notice someone heading in your direction on both sides of the road. To the left is a huge barrel of a man. He's wearing torn jeans and a faded T-shirt advertising a heavy metal band you've never heard of. He's balding yet has what is left of his hair tied back in a scraggly ponytail. He has a long knotted beard. Tattoos adorn his arms, a heavy chain around his neck. He's wearing biker boots and his breathing is laboured. He smells of stale alcohol and rank body odour. He oozes malevolence.

On the other side of the pavement, the man walking towards you is tall and slim. His head is held high. He has a neat haircut. He's wearing a tailored designer suit. He's carrying an expensive leather briefcase. His shoes are polished to a shine and clacking on the pavements as he walks with an air of confidence. His breath is minty fresh. He's clean shaven and he's wearing the latest designer cologne that cost £200 per bottle.

Which side of the pavement do you decide to walk down?

The chances are you'll choose the side with the man in the suit. He fits the image of the perfect family man who lives a perfect life. He represents safety, protection, and you imagine he would leap to your aid should you need it.

If you choose this path, you'll be dead before you reach the end as you'll have just crossed paths with the innocuous-looking, unassuming serial killer Richard Button.

Foley looked up from the book and let out a breath he didn't realise he'd been holding.

'Fucking hell,' he said.

Chapter Sixteen

Olivia's job wasn't one she could easily switch off from. The people she spoke to, the serial killers, the rapists, the butchers, the destroyers, they all inhabited a place in her mind and no amount of swimming, yoga and Krav Maga would silence them.

At the end of the day, she liked to try and put most of it behind her as best she could; close the door on the dark and terrifying world and spend a few hours in her beautiful home to unwind and relax. Her father had ruined that with his cheap flowers. Why was he taunting her so? Why couldn't he allow her to live her life and stop reminding her that he was still alive?

Once out of the shower, which she'd remained under for as long as she could stand the hot needles piercing her scarred skin, she wrapped her oversized white dressing gown around her and padded into the kitchen. Her head was still slightly fuzzy from the whiskies she'd drunk with Foley, and every time she burped she could still taste the burning liquid. She pulled open the door to the freezer and took out a bottle of vodka, poured herself a large measure and drank it in one gulp.

She placed her hands flat on the oak worktop and tried to

marshal her thoughts. There were so many, it was difficult to pinpoint one to concentrate on. She often felt like she was standing in the middle of a football stadium surrounded by eighty thousand fans, all of them chanting, screaming and shouting, and she was trying to listen to each and every one of them. It was a pointless and impossible task, and one that would drive her to the brink of insanity if she tried it for too long.

She heard a ping coming from the hallway. Her mobile phone was alerting her to an incoming message. She drained the glass and went to retrieve it.

Sebastian had sent her several texts over the last few hours. He was concerned for her safety and wanted her to know he was available day or night to chat. She felt warm inside, reading his message, though that could be the vodka. She fired off a quick reply telling him she was fine, and she'd fill him in on the details tomorrow at work.

When she pulled her phone out of her pocket, she'd grabbed a handful of detritus too: an empty sweet wrapper, a used tissue and a dog-eared business card. She turned it over and for a brief second wondered who the hell Ethan Miller was. She remembered the attempted urgent rough sex in the disabled toilets of the sports centre. A smile spread across Olivia's face. After the day she'd had, the thought of feeling someone on her, inside her, their masculine hands around her throat, was just what she needed to silence the demons for a little while.

Olivia made the phone call to Ethan brief. She didn't want him to think she was drunk and hoped her slurred words wouldn't put him off. When she gave him her address, he told her he'd be around in twenty minutes. He turned up in fifteen.

Olivia heard the growl of a motorbike turn into the cul-de-sac. She went up to the solid door and, on her tiptoes, peered through the spy hole. It was an all-black Ducati Monster 821 Stealth. Ethan, dressed in black biker leathers, swung his leg slowly over the bike and took off his helmet, revealing his dark floppy hair. Olivia couldn't wait for him to knock. She turned off the alarm, pulled back the bolts and opened the door.

Olivia felt herself smile. She licked her lips. She stepped back and allowed him to enter the house. Their eyes were locked on each other. They didn't speak. They didn't need to.

The door slammed closed behind him. He dropped his helmet onto the solid floor, placed his hands on either side of Olivia's face and kissed her passionately on the lips. She felt his rough stubble scratch across her face. His hands fell to her waist. He lifted her up and she wrapped her legs around him. He slammed her into the wall and kissed her harder, biting her lip, licking her neck.

She leaned into him, inhaled the peaty, animal aroma of his cold leathers. This was exactly what she wanted.

'Where's the bedroom?' he asked in a gruff, husky voice.

'Behind you.'

He kicked open the door and carried her inside, throwing her down on the bed. He stood back and began to unzip his tight leather jacket.

'Leave it on,' she said.

'Really?'

'And the boots.'

'Dirty girl.' He smiled.

He unzipped his trousers and climbed on top of her, throwing open her dressing gown to reveal her firm, naked body beneath. The lighting was deliberately low in the bedroom so Olivia wouldn't glimpse her scars as she changed. Normally she hated the thought of a man seeing them, questioning her about them, but guessed Ethan had already had an eyeful beneath the strip-lighting in the disabled toilet at the swimming pool. He hadn't mentioned them so it obviously didn't bother him. Why should it bother her? Let him see them. Let him touch them and lick them. She didn't care. If only every day could be like this.

As he entered her, her body arched. She closed her eyes and let out a gasp of pure ecstasy.

'Hello, Livvy.'

She opened her eyes wide. Her father had spoken. Ethan was pounding her hard while kissing her neck, rubbing his stubble against her. She dug her nails into his leather-clad back.

'I love you, Livvy.'

There he was again.

'Fuck,' she said under her breath. Tears formed and began to roll down her cheeks. 'Harder,' she whispered into Ethan's ear, before biting his lobe hard. He winced and let out a yelp. She needed the pain to block out her thoughts, but nothing was as powerful as her father.

She closed her eyes again and there he was, standing over her in the woods. He raised a bloody knife and brought it down into her shoulder. She felt the pain all over again as the stainless-steel blade tore at her skin and scraped against the bone. He pulled it out and she saw the blood, her blood, dripping off the tip.

'I love you, Livvy.'

'Stop.'

'What?' Ethan asked.

'No. Keep going. Harder.'

'Are you all right?' He looked concerned. 'You're crying.'

'Just fuck me.'

'Hello, Livvy.'

'Jesus Christ, no!' she screamed.

'You want me to stop?' Ethan asked.

'No. Fuck me. Harder. Hurt me.'

'Hurt you?'

'Yes. Do it. Squeeze my throat.'

'What?'

'Please.'

'I'm not into anything like that.'

Olivia began to cry. 'Please,' she begged. 'Help me forget him.'

'Forget who?'

She pushed Ethan off her and rolled out from under him. Snatching up the dressing gown from the floor, she stumbled into the en suite bathroom. She sat on the toilet in total darkness and let the tears flow.

Chapter Seventeen

Tuesday 20th February 2024

When Olivia woke up the next morning, she was on the floor of her bathroom. She didn't remember falling asleep, so must have cried herself to sleep. At first, her memory of last night was blank. For a split second she enjoyed the blissful ignorance, then her mind woke up, and it all came flooding back. *Ethan.*

She tied the belt of the dressing gown tightly around her waist, slowly opened the door and stepped into the bedroom. She doubted she'd hear from Ethan again after what had happened, but the thought of someone else out there thinking she was some kind of freak filled her with dread.

The bedroom was empty, and Olivia breathed a sigh of relief. She'd have to change swimming pools, though. She couldn't risk the embarrassment of running into him again.

Her mouth felt dry. She went into the kitchen to put the kettle on for a mug of coffee, as strong as she could take it, and saw a pink Post-it note stuck to the toaster. She tore it off and waited for her eyes to focus before she read it.

I'm guessing you'd had a bit too much to drink last night. No worries. It happens to all of us. Phone or text if you fancy going out. I really like you. Ethan, xx.

She screwed up the note and tossed it into the bin. She had no intention of calling him again. Though she knew that by the end of the day, she'd have changed her mind back and forth several dozen times.

Sebastian was waiting for Olivia in the kitchenette of their office in George Street. The whole ground floor had the familiar aroma of a strong Kenyan blend and it was just what Olivia needed to remove the rancid taste of shame from the events of the night before. A disappointing cup of instant and a slice of granary toast had done nothing to make her feel better.

They sat down in the comfortable chairs. Olivia had a pile of unopened mail on her lap while Sebastian glared at her like a therapist waiting for his client to begin their session.

'How are you feeling?' he eventually asked.

She looked up. 'I'm OK, thanks. You?'

'I didn't mean it in a general sense. I meant, after everything that happened yesterday, with Richard, how are you?'

'Oh. Fine. I think.'

'You think?'

'Well, I haven't seen him for twenty-five years. I've hardly given him much thought at all,' she lied.

'You do realise it's me you're talking to, don't you? You don't have to lie or pretend with me.'

'Sorry. I'm… I had a bad night. I didn't sleep too well.' She slapped the mail down on the small coffee table and picked up her mug, wrapping her hands around it and breathing in the soothing smell. 'To be honest, it was a shock seeing him like that. I don't know what I expected, but time hasn't been kind to him.'

'Prison affects people like that.'

'I think I had a picture of him in my head still looking how he did the last time I saw him. I don't know why I expected him to still look the same.'

'Because the last time you saw him was under dramatic and unusual circumstances. That's remained in your mind ever since. It was a huge turning point in your life.'

'I suppose. I remember asking my nan if I could go and see him while he was on trial. She said no, as it would be too upsetting for me to hear all those things. Strangely, I never asked to visit him in prison. I know he asked me to visit, though, as Grandad always told me when they received a letter from him.'

'What was different between wanting to see him in court but not wanting to see him in prison?'

'I'm not sure.' Olivia frowned. 'I think... I don't know. Maybe I assumed that while he was in court there was a slight possibility that he might be innocent. When you're nine years old you see prison as a place where bad people go.'

'And you didn't want to associate the man who was your father with a bad person?'

'Maybe.'

'Did he say anything to you yesterday?'

Olivia thought for a long moment. 'Not really. Just the usual guff about him missing me.' She quickly turned away. Sebastian knew her better than she knew herself. She didn't want him to spot her lies.

He leaned forward and placed a hand on her lap. 'Olivia' – he knew she hated being called Livvy, and he knew the reason why – 'are you sure it's a good idea to be helping the police with an active case, especially right now with everything that's happening with your father?'

'Nothing's happening with my father,' she said. 'He's had a

heart attack. I went to visit him, and when he's recovered he'll be sent back to prison, and everything will return to normal.' She gave a false smile.

'Will you go and see him again?'

'No. I've no reason to.'

'Whatever you decide to do, you know I'll back you up, right?'

'Sebastian, I know you worry about me, and it's sweet, but you don't need to. The man is a cold-blooded killer and he's where he deserves to be. I have no intention of ever seeing him again. Now,' she said, standing up. 'I have a lot of work to do today before DI Foley comes to pick me up.'

'It's made the papers,' Daisy said to Olivia as she passed her desk on the way to the stairs.

'Sorry? What has?'

'Your father having a heart attack. It's made all the papers.'

'Well, that's not surprising, is it?' she said without stopping.

Olivia walked up the carpeted stairs calmly as if she didn't have a care in the world. She could feel Daisy's eyes burning into her back.

Once in her office, she closed the door behind her and switched her computer on. As soon as it had woken up, she entered her father's name into Google and clicked news. RIVERSIDE KILLER HAS HEART ATTACK. All news outlets had the same unimaginative headline, or a variation thereof. She read the first few, but they were pretty much generic. Olivia wanted to make sure her name wasn't mentioned.

Following the arrest and conviction of her father, Olivia had gone to live with her maternal grandparents in Tower Hamlets. Button was an unusual surname and after being bullied at school, Olivia had asked if she could take on their surname and change schools. Over the course of the Easter holidays, she became Olivia

Winter. It was such a simple task to change a name, but it meant a great deal to her. She could begin her life again. She was no longer the daughter of The Riverside Killer, she was simply Olivia Winter.

However, if the press found out that renowned forensic psychologist Olivia Winter was the daughter of infamous serial killer Richard Button, they'd have a field day. The story wouldn't be tucked away on page eight of the *Daily Mail*, it would be front-page news – a banner headline and an awful picture stolen from the internet. She shuddered at the thought. The only people who knew her real identity were Sebastian and Daisy, Jessica (who was now dead) and DI Foley. She knew she could trust her colleagues, but how good was Foley at keeping his mouth shut?

Chapter Eighteen

DI Foley was on time collecting Olivia from George Street. Sebastian had told her to be careful and to call him if she needed anything. His big brother behaviour, while genuine and from the heart, was beginning to grate.

The conversation in the car on the way to North Wembley was stilted. Neither of them wanted to bring up Richard Button but it was difficult to skate around the subject, especially after how things had been left between them yesterday.

'I hope you don't mind,' Foley began. 'I bought the book.'

'Book?'

'Yes. The one your colleague wrote about your father.'

'Ah. That one. I'm sure Sebastian will be pleased with the extra sale.' She smiled to herself. 'Are you enjoying it?'

'I don't think "enjoy" is the right word. It's very... What's the word?'

'Detailed?'

'Graphic.'

'Well, when a man stabs, mutilates and hacks off the breasts of six women, it's not easy to skirt around the gruesomeness.'

'How do you cope?'

'Sorry?' she asked, looking at him for the first time.

'How do you get your head around the notion that your father was a serial killer?'

'I have no idea,' she answered honestly. 'I know what kind of a killer he was. I know he got his kicks out of murdering. Putting him into a box with all the other thrill killers is easy enough. It's what happened afterwards. It's the thought of him coming home from killing someone and sitting down at the dinner table with his family, having a laugh, a joke, smiling at us, that I struggle with.'

'When you've met other thrill killers, and you've seen how they switch off from being a murderer to being a regular member of society, do you struggle to understand how they can jump between the two personalities, or do you just have a blind spot with your dad?'

Olivia thought for a while before she answered. She thought of Benjamin Amos, a man from Boise, Idaho who was convicted of murdering five men in 2004. He stalked the gay bars, picked up single men and strangled them in their own homes, leaving them in bed to be found by friends and loved ones. At the time of the killings, Benjamin was married to Julianne. They had three children, two boys and a girl. He had a blue-collar job, coached Little League and co-ordinated pot-luck lunches at his local church every Sunday. When Olivia went to meet him, she asked him how he could strangle a man, then go home to bed with his wife.

'The pressure of being a family man, of working five days a week, keeping a wife and children living a comfortable life, the demands of a happy and safe community, they take their toll after a while. It's difficult to be permanently the go-to guy, and every time you give something up of yourself to help others, it rankles, you know? You have this little ball of stress inside you, and you keep adding to it day after day after day, and you need to reduce it somehow or you'll end up taking it out on those you love. When I killed those filthy men, I released my tension, and I went home, back to my family, a happy, contented man.'

Benjamin Amos was no different to her father. But why could she accept his motive and reasoning, but not her dad's? The answer was simple. He was her father and she looked to him as the benchmark against which all men in her life were measured. How could she do that, knowing he was a cold, sadistic killer?

'Of course it's a blind spot,' she eventually said. 'I've accepted who my dad is. It doesn't mean I have to like it or embrace it.'

'Are you worried about how others will act towards you if they find out?'

'I have too few people in my life for that to bother me. Listen, Foley, you won't tell anyone, will you?'

'No. Of course not.'

'Good. I know what the press are like. They'll love something like this.'

'You secret is perfectly safe with me.'

She turned and looked out of the window. The fewer people who knew her real identity, the better. She could trust Sebastian and Daisy and she was able to trust Jessica, too. But she had only recently met Amyas. She didn't know the first thing about him, though he seemed an easy man to chat to. There was a comfortableness about him that she was drawn to and couldn't explain why. She'd need to get to know him more. He knew so much about her yet she hardly knew anything about him. That would definitely have to change.

They pulled up on the driveway to Sarah Millington's house. Olivia remained in the car and looked up at the nondescript property.

Sarah had lived in a busy, leafy suburb, close to a primary school. Trees adorned the pavements, front gardens had been turned into driveways and the narrow road was just wide enough for single vehicles to drive down. At the times when children from

Byron Court Primary School were arriving and leaving for the day, the road must have been a nightmare; broken pieces of headlight and wing mirror strewn about the tarmac were testament to that.

'Nice area,' Olivia said as she looked around at the long road and the semi-detached houses on each side.

Foley agreed. In the background, children could be heard laughing in the school playground.

There was no car in the driveway, the garage door was closed and the coloured wheelie bins were lined up neatly. This would make a decent family home, and, close to a school, would command a high asking price when Sarah's mother came to sell it.

'Why this house?' Olivia asked, more to herself. 'We're in the middle of the road. If the killer left by the front door, he ran the risk of the neighbours from either side seeing him. Walking down to the end, he'd have to pass at least twenty houses. Someone must have seen a stranger. It was a huge gamble.'

'Maybe he knew her; that's why he was able to gain access to the house.'

'But it's so risky. And right next to a school. It's such a high-traffic area.' She noticed a couple of net curtains twitching in houses close by. 'If it was me, I'd have chosen a house closer to the end of the road for an easier getaway.'

'So, is it the house or the victim that made him come here?'

'A woman living alone, same as the other three. I'm inclined to think it's the victim.'

'So am I,' Foley agreed. 'However, she wasn't the only woman living alone in this street. So why her? Why this house?'

'What did the neighbours say in their witness statements?'

Foley opened the car door and brought out a file he'd had on the back seat. He shuddered as a gust of wind blew around him. 'Nobody saw anything suspicious.'

'And the next-door neighbour noticed a delivery guy go to the house?'

'Yes.'

'But she didn't notice anything else?'

'No.'

'Was the delivery man black or white?'

'Erm... I don't know, hang on.' He flicked through a few more pages. 'Here we are: Danny Mears, twenty-eight, from Epping, six foot, black.'

Olivia gave a rueful smile. 'I thought so.'

'Why?'

'Look around you; this is an exclusively white neighbourhood. You can tell just by looking at the nosy neighbours we've had glaring at us. The woman next door noticed the delivery guy because he was black. She wouldn't have batted an eyelid if he'd been white, which is why she didn't notice the killer.'

'You think?'

'Definitely.'

'So, the neighbour could have seen him, but she didn't clock him because he matched her demographic?'

'Exactly. People are fascinating. They'll say they're not racist, and the majority of people aren't, but we measure people by how they're different from ourselves. We see someone who is morbidly obese and the first thing we say to describe them is that they're fat. We don't say they're white or black or tall or short, but fat.'

'I suppose that's true,' Foley said hesitatingly.

'Let me do a little test. Do you live in a road with a lot of houses?'

'Yes.'

'OK. Name the first neighbour that comes to mind.'

'Alex Levin in the house two doors down.'

'Describe him.'

'Erm, well, he's tall, in his seventies, thinnish—'

'Skin colour?' Olivia interrupted.

'White.'

'Nationality.'

'Russian.'

'There you go. He's not in your demographic. He's foreign so he stands out.'

'That doesn't make me racist.'

'No. I'm not saying you're racist. I'm not saying anyone is racist. I'm saying that people pick on the one thing that stands out in a person, and it's usually their skin colour or nationality.'

'I suppose,' Foley mused.

'Come on, let's go to our next crime scene before the curtain twitchers phone the police.'

'But what makes *us* stand out from the demographic?' Foley asked as they made their way back to their vehicles.

'Well, they've just had a murder in the street, so they're obviously on their guard against people they don't recognise. Also, you do seem to be sporting a crumpled Columbo style this morning.'

Foley rubbed his stubble. 'I didn't have time to shave this morning. I was up all night reading that bloody book.'

'I'll pass on your compliments to Sebastian,' she said, smiling.

They could have walked to the house of the next victim, Joanne Douglas. It was a bright and sunny day, but chilly, and they both had plenty of time, but they were taking up valuable parking space on Spencer Road and the curtain twitchers would probably have had their car towed the moment they were out of view.

The houses in Stilecroft Gardens were almost identical to the ones in Sarah Millington's street: semi-detached, garden-turned-into-a-driveway and a garage attached. None of them stood out against the others. They all had double glazing, a burglar alarm and a satellite dish. Some were looked after better than the others, but the same could be said for every neighbourhood.

'Which one?' Olivia asked.

'That one.' He pointed. 'Near the end.'

The sky had clouded over, and the wind had picked up. Olivia buttoned her coat and lifted up the collar.

At its end the street opened up to an expansive field which was home to the Vale Farm Sports Centre and the Sudbury Court Sports Club. Various sports and events took place on these fields, which were often busy at weekends. During the week, it was quiet. The odd dog walker could be spotted here and there.

'Nice area.' Foley shivered in the open air. 'Similar neighbourhood to Sarah's.'

'Yes. Same demographic. The killer feels comfortable in this kind of neighbourhood: semi detached houses, middle class, quiet. The neighbours will be on nodding terms with each other, some may even exchange Christmas cards, but they won't be friends, as they'll be too busy with their own lives. The only way they'll know more about each other is if they have kids of the same age who go to the same school or take part in the same kind of activities. I think the killer will have grown up in an area like this.'

'But he won't live in a place like this now?'

'No.'

'Why not?'

'Your killer is single. There's no way he'll be living with a partner. After murdering four women, at least, his whole personality will have changed, and they'd have noticed. Unless…' She stopped herself.

'Unless what?'

'I was just thinking. My mother didn't guess. Or maybe she did and didn't want to believe it. To her, family life was perfect. Perhaps she didn't want that ruined, so didn't question the change in my dad's behaviour.'

Olivia turned when something caught her eye. A woman in her thirties, pushing a pram with a sleeping baby inside, a toddler trotting alongside her. She was tall and wearing a designer coat.

Her head was high, her back straight and she had a confidence in her walk. Was she married? If so, had her husband changed recently? Was he quieter than usual? Was he snapping at the children? Had his tastes in sex changed? Would she want her idyllic life ruined, or would she be happy to live in blissful ignorance?

'What are you thinking?' Foley brought her out of her reverie.

'I think he is single. He's obviously gone to a great deal of care to choose the right victim, even if it is in the middle of a busy road. He's dedicating so much time to his kills that he wouldn't be able to do that with a family, without them noticing he's missing for long periods of time. I'm guessing he'll have a job where he works unusual hours, too. Shift work, perhaps.'

'So, why is he killing people in these particular neighbourhoods? Is he jealous? Is he reverting back to a time when he was younger, perhaps his childhood?'

Olivia pulled a face. 'He's returning to what is familiar, but because something is familiar doesn't mean that it was a happy memory. Maybe when he lived in these kinds of houses he was abused; maybe he had a lovely childhood and his parents doted on him. We won't know that until you speak to him. All I can say is that there is some kind of safety connection for him to these kinds of neighbourhoods.'

'And I suppose he chose a house close to the end of the street so he could make a quick getaway by running over the field?'

'No. If he'd run, he would have stood out. The only people you see on these fields are people in sports kit or walking their dogs. I'm guessing he wasn't dressed like a football player and didn't bring his Labrador with him,' she said with a sarcastic smile. 'No, when he killed Joanne Douglas, he simply went out of the front door, walked calmly down the street and headed for home. He didn't stand out, because he knew how to act around here, because he is from this kind of environment.'

'So, the reason why he chose a house close to the field was because he'd have a longer walk to safety?' Foley asked.

'Absolutely. His confidence was growing. He was practically showing off. He's walking past the neighbours, looking in their homes at them having their dinners or watching TV, and he's thinking to himself that he's just committed a violent and brutal murder that's going to destroy their safe existence, and he loves that. That's the thrill.' She shivered when she used the word 'thrill'. An image of her father popped into her head. 'Chilly, isn't it?' she said, excusing her shudder.

'It is getting chilly. I'll treat you to a hot drink when we've finished.' Foley flicked through his file again. 'His next victim, Phoebe Harper, lived in a cul-de-sac.'

'Even better. There was only one way out for him. Also, wasn't there some kind of big party going on next door?'

'Yes.'

'He probably swaggered down that street. I wouldn't have been surprised if he'd been holding the knife aloft as he went.'

'Yes, he's growing in confidence, but that's going to lead to mistakes.'

'I don't think that's going to bother him anymore.'

'Why not?'

'He's killed four people that we know of. He's already going to be known as a prolific serial killer, and that's what he wants. He needs to be caught to get the fame and attention he desires.'

'So Sebastian can write a book about him?' Foley smirked.

'More sleepless nights for you.'

'Going back to motive, you've said he's confident, he's thumbing his nose at the neighbours as he ruins their safe existence, and he's obviously enjoying the fact the police are blind to him. Is that part of being a thrill killer?'

Olivia swallowed hard. 'Yes. He's killing because he's enjoying it.'

'Just like your dad.'

'Exactly like him.'

'Will that be his only motive?'

'We won't know until he's caught, and you can question him and dig further into his background.'

'Can I ask you a personal question?'

'Of course,' she replied, though she didn't mean it.

'You said our killer will live alone so people don't notice a change in his behaviour, yet your dad was married and had two children. You said you don't think your mother noticed a change in him, and I know you were only nine years old at the time, but did you see a difference in how your dad behaved during the time he was killing?'

Olivia stopped in her tracks and thought for a moment. 'I really didn't. Looking back – and believe me, I've done a lot of looking back over the years – I don't recall a single difference in him at the time.'

On Thursday October 5th 1999, Richard Button murdered Anna Welling, aged thirty-one. According to the post-mortem report, time of death was put somewhere between five o'clock and eleven o'clock at night. According to the book written by Sebastian Lister, Richard stated he killed Anna around six-ish.

Olivia recalled that day exactly. She'd come running home from school with a letter saying her class was going to have a Halloween competition to see which pupil could come up with the scariest costume. She wanted to go dressed as a witch, being obsessed by the film *Wizard of Oz* at the time. All through dinner, she'd spoken about her costume. Richard was home late, and his meal was warming in the oven. While he ate, Geraldine and Claire were in the living room watching television, but Olivia remained in the dining room with her father. She was sitting opposite him, elbows on the table, and they talked, animatedly, about how her costume was going to be the scariest and what they could do to make sure she won. Her father was funny, making jokes about a black wig, fake warts and teeth, and wondering if Mrs McManus next door would let Olivia borrow her black cat for the day. He was the perfect father that night, yet he'd beaten Anna Welling to death not two hours previously. She hadn't noticed. There wasn't a single hint that her father was a killer. The next day had been Claire's birthday. Olivia remembered that…

'So, how do we catch him?' Foley asked, interrupting her unplanned trip down memory lane.

'Hmm?' Olivia asked. 'Oh. I really don't know. That's your department, not mine,' she said as she turned and walked back to the car.

'There is one person we can ask.'

She stopped and looked daggers at Foley. 'By all means, ask him, but don't expect me to sit in on the interview.'

Olivia climbed into the Toyota and slammed the door behind her. She squeezed her eyes tightly shut and hoped and prayed to a God she didn't believe in that her father would have another heart attack and that it would end his life.

Chapter Nineteen

Foley held the door to the murder room open for Olivia. They walked in on a scene of carnage. A printer had been overturned, paper was strewn around the floor and toner was soaking into the already stained carpet.

'What the fuck happened here?' Foley asked.

DS Holly Goodfellow was on her hands and knees, picking up sheets of paper. 'I can explain.'

'Well, somebody better had.'

Olivia noticed there were tears in her eyes. 'Foley, maybe we should go into your office.'

Foley looked around the room. He took in the same sombre faces Olivia had noticed upon entering. 'OK,' he agreed. 'But someone had better clear this mess up. And I want to know who broke the printer. They'll be paying for a replacement.' He stormed into his small office with Holly following, head down. Olivia joined them and closed the door behind her.

'So, who's been playing around with my office equipment like they're in a creche?'

'It was Leon, sir, but he had a good reason.' Holly's voice was quiet, barely above a whisper.

'Is there a good reason for hurling a printer across a room?' Foley stood tall, hands on hips, his face full of anger.

'We've had the post-mortem results back on DI Sheffield,' she said, looking at the floor.

'And?'

She found it difficult to talk. 'Sir, she was pregnant.'

'What?' Foley gasped.

Olivia's mouth dropped open. She turned slightly to look at Foley. He took a half step back and sat down with a slump in his chair. His face was drained of colour.

'How far along was she?' Olivia asked Holly.

'A month. Maybe five weeks,' she said with tears in her eyes. 'The doctor said she may not even have known she was pregnant yet.'

'I don't think she did. She would definitely have told me,' Olivia said. 'She often spoke of wanting to have a child at some point.'

'Did she?' Foley asked.

'Did Leon throw the printer when he found out Jessica was pregnant?' Olivia asked. Holly nodded as she wiped her eyes with a torn tissue she found in her pocket. 'Why did he react in such a way? Does he often fly off the handle like that?'

'He was sort of sweet on Jessica,' Foley said, shaking his head and rummaging through the paperwork on his desk.

'Did he make his feelings known to her?'

'On many occasions,' he scoffed.

'The thing is,' Holly began, 'Jess— DI Sheffield didn't reciprocate. She liked Leon as a colleague. That was it. Nothing more.'

'Did she tell him that?'

'Yes, but he persisted. He made a bit of a fool of himself at the Christmas party.'

'You can say that again,' Foley said under his breath. 'The things people do when they've got a few drinks inside them.'

'What did he do?' Olivia asked, as she remembered what she'd done last night after having a few drinks.

'He came on to her,' Holly said. 'She rejected him, but he wouldn't stop. He tried to kiss her and she…'

'Headbutted him,' Foley said, a hint of a smile on his face.

'Jessica never suffered fools, but that's a touch extreme, isn't it?'

'Not really,' Holly said. 'He was being a bit of a letch.'

'So, what happened?'

'A couple of the sergeants took him out, put him in a taxi and told him to sleep it off. The next morning he came in, red-faced, and apologised to everyone, including DI Sheffield. She told him to forget it and put it behind them, but she reiterated that she wasn't interested in a relationship with him.'

'And did he accept it that time?'

'I think so. He wasn't happy about it, though. I mean, you don't just turn your feelings off for someone, do you?'

'Holly, did you dig out those unsolved murders for Doctor Winter?' Foley asked, getting the conversation back on point.

'Oh, er, yes. I'll go and get them.' She proffered a smile at Olivia and left the room, closing the door behind her.

Olivia frowned as she observed Foley's behaviour. She wondered why he was so keen to get off the topic of Jessica's private life.

'She's a bright woman,' Olivia said.

'Holly? Yes. She'll go far.'

'What about Leon?'

'What about him?' he asked without looking up.

'Is he bright? Will he go far?'

'If he manages to control his temper.'

'You don't like him, do you?'

'He has a bit of an attitude problem. He needs to think before he acts.'

Olivia looked around the small office, at the crime prevention posters on the walls, the charts of crime statistics and rotas.

'You're not comfortable talking about your officers' personal lives, are you?'

'Do I make it that obvious?' he said.

She smiled. 'Your office is very impersonal. You don't have any photographs.'

'I'm divorced with no kids. Who would I have a photo of?'

'Your parents, siblings. Your dogs, even.'

'I have those at home.'

'Tucked away in an album, I'm guessing,' she said, smiling.

'My office is for work. I don't want…'

'You don't want people seeing a softer side?' Olivia finished for him.

He half laughed. 'I don't think I have a softer side.'

'That's not true. I saw the way you reacted when Holly said Jessica was pregnant.'

'It came as a shock,' he said, turning away from her.

'Amyas,' Olivia said. Foley looked up when she used his first name. 'You're the father of Jessica's baby, aren't you?'

'W-what?' he stuttered, turning slightly red. 'What makes you say that?'

'A colleague would have thought it was sad that she was murdered while pregnant, but you took it personally. You also dislike Leon because of his behaviour towards Jessica. He's younger, good-looking, you probably thought he was in with a chance more than you.'

'It wasn't like that,' he said, pushing his chair away from his desk and leaning back. 'Jessica made it perfectly clear that she wasn't interested in going out with anyone from work. Who can blame her, really? She'd been there before and got burned. Huh, we all have. Leon was like a dog with a bone. Even I had to have a word with him to back off.'

'So, what happened between the two of you?'

He let out a heavy sigh. 'We had this bloke in custody. We'd been after him for a bloody long time – a notorious drug dealer. We wanted him for the murder of his girlfriend, but we couldn't find the evidence. He ended up having his car stolen. He didn't report it, obviously, but a member of the public called in about an abandoned car. We ran the registration number through the computer and when we realised who it belonged to, we sent it to forensics for a full sweep. Three droplets of blood belonging to his girlfriend were found in the boot. We finally had him. He's currently on remand awaiting trial.

'That night, I put a few quid behind the bar of the local pub and told everyone to have drinks on me. I didn't go. I never do. I stayed here and had a couple of drinks on my own. Jessica came back to see how I was. We ended up having a couple of drinks. One thing led to another and, well, you can guess the rest.'

'In the disabled toilets?' Olivia asked.

'Sorry?'

She felt herself blush. 'No. Sorry. I was… thinking of something else.' She cleared her throat to hide her embarrassment. 'How were things between you the next day?'

'Fine. We both knew it was a one-time thing. It was just… I don't know, two people letting off steam, releasing pent-up emotion.'

'Did anybody else know about it?'

'No.'

'You're sure about that?'

'Of course.'

Olivia nodded. 'What would you have done if she'd told you she was pregnant?'

'I'd have stood by her. I'm not saying I'd have proposed, but I'd have helped to raise the child as much as she wanted me to. Look, it's a moot point anyway, isn't it? She's dead. The baby is

The Mind of a Murderer

dead. What we have to do now is make sure the bastard is caught.'

He swallowed hard. Olivia watched how his face had taken on a soft, sadder look. He was hiding his grief for Jessica well, but he'd let the mask slip now he'd found out she was pregnant with his child. He was hurting.

There was a tiny knock on the glass door. Holly opened it without instruction.

'I've got the files you asked for,' she said, barely entering the room. She handed them over to Olivia.

'Thanks, Holly.'

The door was closed, and Olivia looked at Foley. He had a look of sadness on his face.

'Amyas,' she said. He snapped out of his reverie. 'I'm going to head off; go home and look through these files.'

'Right. No problem. Would you like a lift?'

'No. It's fine. Listen, don't take this the wrong way, but should you be working on this case? You're very close to one of the victims and you've just found out she was pregnant with your child.'

'I am the best person to work on this case. I will not stop until Jessica's killer is caught and rotting in a prison cell.'

'That's precisely my point,' she said. 'You're taking this too personally.'

'Any detective would take it personally. One of our own has been murdered. We all take exception to that.'

'Will you promise me something?'

'What?'

'Don't do anything… rash. If you need to talk, let off steam or anything, give me a call. You're a good detective, I can tell. I don't want you doing something that you'll regret or that will jeopardise the case when it gets to court.'

'I promise.'

Olivia gave him a smile and left the office. She'd known Jessica but she didn't know a single thing about DI Amyas Foley. She had a feeling her warning had gone in one ear and out the other. The steely look in his eye told her that he'd not rest until the killer was caught. While an admirable quality in any detective, it wasn't always a positive reaction in someone so closely connected to the case.

Chapter Twenty

It was something Foley had been toying with for the rest of the day. He kept himself locked away in his office while he mulled over whether he was doing the right thing or not. Eventually, he bit the bullet, grabbed his jacket from behind the chair, told Holly to only contact him if anything important came up and headed out.

The hospital was warm and oppressive. He exited the lift on the fourth floor and walked slowly down the corridor as if he were worried he'd notify someone of his presence by his footsteps. He nodded to the armed guard standing outside Richard Button's room, took a deep breath and went inside.

The man responsible for eight murders, two of whom were members of his own family, was lying back in bed flicking through a tabloid newspaper as if he didn't have a care in the world. His lined face was blank. His thin lips were dry and his wide eyes sparkled beneath the bright lights.

From the doorway, Foley cleared his throat to get the man's attention.

'If you're coming in then come in. You're letting all the warmth out,' Richard said as he turned the page of his newspaper.

Foley entered and took a seat. 'Mr Button, I'm—'

'Detective Inspector Amyas Foley from the Major Crime Unit of the Metropolitan Police,' Richard interrupted.

'You know me?'

He closed the newspaper, folded it in half and placed it neatly on his lap. 'The thing about being in prison is that you have a great deal of time on your hands. I watch the news, I read the papers. I'm not interested in all that political gobshite, which selfish twat is leading which country. And climate change is surely just the next step in human evolution. Ice ages come; ice ages go. But a juicy crime story gets my interest every time,' he said with a slight smile on his lips.

'You're interested in murders?'

'Of course. It's fun to see who's out there taking up where I left off. Did you know, when I was arrested and my crimes hit the news, there were four other copycat killings within the first ten days?' He leaned back in his bed, proud of the fact. 'Part of me wishes we were more like America with their mass shootings, but they've become so commonplace that they barely make the front pages. We don't have serial killers like they do, but when one pops up, it's fun to watch the story unfold.'

'Is that what you do? Scour the news for signs of a serial killer?'

'I can spot one a mile off. These murders of the four young women, they're all linked. The papers haven't cottoned on yet but I'm guessing you guys have. When are you going to alert the press? When is the fear going to start?' he asked. There was a twinkle in his eye.

'Did you get off on that when you were committing your murders?'

'I didn't get off on it, as such. It didn't excite me in the way you think when I saw my crimes in the papers, but it was nice to see my work recognised.'

'You saw it as your work?'

'More of a hobby, really. I used to see people on trains and buses reading the newspapers with my latest victim on the front page. I would have loved to have spoken to them about it. How did they feel, were they scared, were they taking any extra precautions as they went about their normal routine?'

'So it was people being scared that excited you?'

'Of course it was. I once overheard two women talking about it in a coffee shop. One of them was frightened because she lived on the river. You should have seen her face. The colour had drained from her skin, her eyes were wide, her hands were shaking, her leg was jiggling. She was bricking it. I held onto that for the rest of the day until I could find my next victim. I'm afraid I went a bit too far with her. I honestly thought the police would have caught me after that one, but they didn't.' He shrugged and smiled.

'You know, it wasn't until after my third victim, Georgina Highfield, that the press started calling me The Riverside Killer. I hadn't given the location much thought. I liked stalking my victims, walking behind them, following them, watching them go to and from work. Once the media gave me my nickname, I seemed to become more conscious of where I attacked and dumped them. I was The Riverside Killer. I'd made it. All the greats have a nickname. Do you know, people actually started to avoid walking around the Thames once that made the news. I saw fewer joggers and dog walkers around. My fear had taken hold and that was...' he took a deep breath and smiled '... the best feeling in the world. It was electric.'

'Did you enjoy seeing your victims scared?'

Richard frowned and studied Foley. 'Are you consulting me, here?'

'Sorry?'

'Are you wanting to find out why and how I carried out my crimes so you can find this bloke?' he said, opening the newspaper and pointing to a smiling photo of Jessica.

'It would be useful to understand—'

'Well, you can fuck off,' he spat. His face, soft and smiling while talking of his crimes, had turned angry and ugly in the blink of an eye.

'I'm sorry.'

'If you think I'm going to help you find this killer, you can think again. He's killed four women and you haven't a clue. The way he's going, he could become one of this country's most prolific serial killers. I'm not going to help you stop him.'

'Innocent people are dying.'

'Innocent people die all the time. How many kids have been killed in London this year due to the knife crime epidemic? How many innocent people have died in random shootings in America? How many innocent people have died in Ukraine? How many innocent people have died while you and I have been chatting?'

Foley felt uncomfortable. He swallowed hard. 'I could have a word with the governor at Belmarsh, maybe get you some extra privileges.'

Richard turned to look at Foley. His face took on a look of wide-eyed hope. 'You mean extra library time? Maybe I could tend to the flowers and vegetables in the prison garden?'

'Yes. If you like.'

'I don't like.' Richard's face dropped. 'I've no interest in gardening and I get more than enough library time because I'm a tutor helping the dicks with low IQs learn how to spell their name and send an email.' He folded his arms and gave a satisfied smile.

'Well, I've obviously wasted my time,' Foley said, standing up.

'Now, now, let's not be too hasty here. I might be able to give you a few pointers in trying to find your killer.'

Foley sat back down again.

'But I won't tell *you*.'

'Oh?'

'No. I'll only tell my daughter. You bring my Livvy here and I'll sing like a hummingbird,' he grinned.

Chapter Twenty-One

Olivia asked the taxi driver to pull up at the entrance to Modbury Gardens. Once she'd paid him, she made a play out of rummaging through her bag as if searching for her keys while the taxi reversed down the road and out of sight. She didn't want the driver seeing which door she went in.

Over the years, Olivia had interviewed hundreds of murderers and serial killers. They were all safely behind bars, but if they wanted to contact her or send her a message, they found a way to do so. She had received more than her fair share of unsolicited mail, love letters, cards, gifts, underwear and threats. Mostly they were sent to her office or via her publisher, but occasionally, someone slipped through the cracks and was able to discover where she lived.

It was slowly darkening. The day seemed to have slipped away from her and, judging by how heavy her bag now was thanks to the files Holly had pressed into her hand, her evening was going to be long too.

'Olivia.' She froze at her name being called. She was about to reach into her bag for the illegal pepper spray she'd bought on her trip to America when a bike came to a squeaking stop beside her and Sam Halliday removed his helmet.

'Hi, Sam,' she said, the relief evident in her voice. 'How are you?'

'I'm fine,' he said, giving a toothy smile.

'The bruising's faded quickly,' she said, leaning closer to look at his face in the dim light.

'Yes. Although I must have bruised my ribs too. I'm in a bit of pain when I breathe,' he said, clutching his stomach.

'Has anybody said anything at work?'

'A couple of patients asked what happened,' he shrugged.

'Not your colleagues?'

'We're too busy to notice things like that. Besides, point me out a junior doctor that doesn't have dark circles around his eyes,' he laughed.

'Well, I'm glad you're feeling better,' she said, edging away and towards the steps leading to her front door.

'I am. Listen, I want to thank you again for the other night.'

'There's no need.'

'No, seriously. I was in a bit of a mess even before I was attacked. I've not settled well into London life and I haven't made many friends. Even in a busy hospital it can get quite lonely, but what you said… you helped.'

Olivia smiled. 'I'm pleased.'

'Can I buy you a drink or something, to say thank you properly?'

'That would be lovely, Sam, but I'm really swamped with work right now. I'm going to be pulling an all-nighter.' She held up her bag as if that was proof of how much work she had.

'How about tomorrow?'

'I think I'll be having an early night tomorrow,' she half laughed.

'Well, you know, open invitation. Whenever you're free, let me know.'

'I will. Thanks.' She turned and unlocked the door. She could feel Sam's eyes burning into the back of her head. She didn't hear him move away from the bottom of her steps. She didn't turn back. She opened the door a small gap, squeezed inside and closed it firmly behind her, locking it and putting the security chain on.

Sam was a sweet boy, but that was the point; he was a boy. Young, innocent, lost in a hectic world he couldn't make sense of. Olivia had no time to play babysitter.

Olivia couldn't remember the last time she'd had anything to eat and despite her stomach growling for food, she wasn't in the mood to start cooking now. She wanted to get a head start on the files; try and find out why and where this killer had started his crimes. She poured herself a large bowl of cereal, made a strong black coffee and took it upstairs to her office where she flicked on the light with her elbow, filling the room with a warm yellow glow.

She went over to the large table in the middle of the room and set her work down. Despite her grandfather drumming into her from a young age that you should never turn the lights on in a room without closing the curtains first, as you never know who is looking in, Olivia preferred to sit in a well-lit room and see it reflected back at her through the black windows. She had no idea if anyone was looking at her – she wasn't doing anything wrong or anything she shouldn't be doing – but she didn't draw the curtains until she was ready to. She could almost hear her grandfather turning in his grave.

The first case Olivia discounted straight away, though reading what had happened to twenty-one-year-old Michelle Bryce brought a tear to her eye. On November 7th last year, Michelle returned home at eight o'clock in the evening after playing wheelchair basketball at a sports centre close to where she lived in Roxeth. She had lived in the specially adapted bungalow for only four months, finally regaining the independence she'd had before the disastrous car crash that had claimed the lives of her parents as well as leaving her paralysed from the waist down. A neighbour saw her arrive home and waved at her through the window. Two hours later, the same neighbour was going to bed when she looked out of the window and saw a man dressed in black running away from the house. When she looked up at the bungalow, she saw the front door was ajar and decided to investigate. She found Michelle dead on her bed. She'd been raped, stabbed six times and strangled.

Olivia closed the file on the photograph of the smiling Michelle, taken in happier times. The case hadn't been solved. There was no doubt in Olivia's mind that Michelle knew her killer, but he wasn't the same person responsible for murdering the four women Olivia was interested in. Michelle had been raped, and none of the other victims had.

Olivia almost dismissed the second case straight away because eighteen-year-old Calvin Ashton was killed outdoors. However, if this was an early case for the serial murderer, maybe he had been working out what was the best way to attack his victims. From the four she knew about, he enjoyed the chase, the pleasure of frightening his victims. The best way to do that was in their own homes when there was less space for them to run away. They were trapped. Outside, he didn't have that luxury. However, he wouldn't have realised that until he tried it.

She bypassed the crime scene photos and the maps of the surrounding area and went straight to the statements section of the file. Calvin was killed in Northolt Park. He had been attending a Christmas lights switch-on with his girlfriend, his brother and his brother's boyfriend. There had been a huge crowd, stalls selling burgers, hot dogs and candyfloss. A small stage had been erected where a brass band was playing Christmas carols. The atmosphere was electric as people gathered around a twelve-foot tree, waiting for the big switch-on.

Police Statement:
   CALLY JOHNSTONE, 19 Rectory Gardens, Northolt
   I've been going out with Calvin for just over a year. We go to the same college. I'm doing media and he's doing sports psychology. We didn't really want to go to the tree switch-on, but it was the first time Calvin's brother, Adam, was going out in public with his boyfriend, so Calvin thought we should show our support. That's what he was like; always doing things for other people.
   It was a really nice night, cold, but fun. Calvin was eating this huge hot dog and he handed it to me because he needed to go for a wee. Anyway, the queue for the toilets was really long so he decided to go in the woods. He was only having a wee, we didn't think anything of it. Me and Adam, and his boyfriend, Jake, stayed by the burger van and it was only noticing the hot dog had gone cold that I realised Calvin had been gone for too long. We went to look for him and while we were looking the tree was switched on and everyone cheered.
   We were shouting his name as we entered the woods. We found him straight away. He was on the ground. My God, there was so much blood.

The element of a thrill killer was there, so it was possible for Calvin Ashton to have been murdered by the same man who had killed the four women. Against the backdrop of more than a thousand people within shouting distance, he had been able to murder someone and mingle with the crowd undetected. The sense of excitement at hearing mirth and cheer behind him and screams and cries in front of him would have given him a massive thrill. The adrenaline coursing through his veins would have been as strong as an electric current.

The downside to this was, he wouldn't have been able to spend long with his victim. He would have had to flee the scene almost as soon as he'd killed him, so nobody spotted what he was doing. Calvin had been stabbed five times, and that could have been over within a matter of seconds. Had the killer been with him as he breathed his last breath? Olivia didn't think so. Very soon, the panic of being caught would have set in, especially if he'd heard Cally and Adam shouting for Calvin. He would also have been worried about any blood on his clothes, someone noticing him acting strangely, or rushing to the exit before anyone else. Later that night, while back in his own home, reliving the murder, he would have been disappointed that he hadn't been able to savour the moments as he watched the young man die.

It was a crime of opportunity, but the event would have been advertised weeks in advance. He would have known there would be a large crowd of people there, especially young people. He would have known the facilities would be overstretched as they always are at these events. With woods nearby it was obvious someone was going to use them as a toilet, so he had remained hidden until a victim presented himself. It had been opportunistic, but with a high chance of success. It also had a high degree of risk, and that was what had made him feel uncomfortable.

Olivia closed the file. The picture that went with the information was of Calvin and his girlfriend Cally dressed up at a wedding in the summer. They both looked happy and made a cute couple as they smiled into the camera. They'd had their whole lives ahead of them. Calvin's was now over. She wondered, briefly, how Cally was coping.

The next file was a stabbing in South Ruislip. Jamie Farr was twenty-four years old. He had been walking home from his night shift as a cashier at a petrol station in the early hours of Thursday 5th December when he saw a man walking towards him dressed in black. According to Jamie's statement, he didn't give the man much thought and wondered if he, too, was heading for home after a night shift. As the man approached Jamie, he placed his hand inside his jacket, pulled out a knife and stabbed Jamie twice to the left of his stomach.

Jamie fell against a car and the alarm sounded, causing the would-be murderer to flee into the night. The owner of the car had looked out of his front window, seen Jamie slumped by his BMW and called for the police and an ambulance. Jamie made a full recovery.

It was possible Jamie could have been the same killer's next victim, despite it only being four days after Calvin's murder. Had he been lusting for the thrill again already? How many nights had he spent trawling the streets of London in search of a victim? According to the files, it was around one o'clock in the morning when Jamie was stabbed. Even in London, and on a week night, it was rare to find many people out at that time. But at the end of the day, the attacker had gone out, purposely equipped with a weapon, just like with Calvin Ashton's killing.

There was no denying Jamie had had a very lucky escape. It would be worth talking to him again to try and get a better description of his attacker.

She opened the last file and was presented with the photograph of a smiling young man with stunning ice-blue eyes. He was strikingly handsome, and Olivia almost didn't want to read what had happened to him. As much as she liked to think of herself as professional and distant, she would have to be made of granite not to feel something for the victims of the killers she investigated.

On Tuesday 5th November last year, Neil Parker, twenty-four, was attending a firework display with his girlfriend, Kathryn, her parents and her four younger sisters in Clissold Park near Stoke Newington. Neil and Kathryn had been dating for three years and her parents had welcomed him into their family and treated him like the son they never had.

Kathryn had said she was hungry, so Neil was going to buy her a burger from one of the many food stalls which had temporarily been set up in the park for the occasion. He offered to buy the others something too but Kathryn's father, Dennis, had refused to hear of it. He had handed him a twenty-pound note and told him to buy everyone a burger.

Neil had set off alone and didn't return.

Twenty minutes later, around the back of the burning bonfire, a woman slipped and fell on the wet ground and came face to face with Neil's lifeless body. He'd died from a single stab wound to the heart.

Neil's death was frighteningly similar to Calvin Ashton's. They were both in very public places attending events and had become separated from their friends and family for perfectly innocent reasons. Had the killer been watching Neil and Calvin specifically, or had he been standing back from the festivities and casting his eye over the proceedings, waiting patiently for someone to be on their own?

Neil's death was quicker. A single stab wound. A direct hit. Was that deliberate or had the killer made a lucky strike? If this was the first murder in the killer's reign of terror, then he would have been nervous to begin with. Afterwards, he wouldn't have remembered much about the crime, as it would have been over with as soon as it began. Even when he was back home, alone, he wouldn't have been able to recall the murder much. He would have relied on information fed to the press.

In his mind, the killer would have been building up to this murder for a long time. He'd chosen somewhere public so he would have been able to mingle into the crowd afterwards, but the kill itself would have been disappointing. All that time thinking about it, all the planning and preparation, and it was over within seconds and the memory wasn't there. He'd not heard a scream, he'd not seen blood, he'd not witnessed the panic and horror on his victim's face as he died. That was what he wanted. That was why his second victim, Calvin Ashton, was stabbed five times. He'd seen the shock on his victim's face, he'd seen death in his eyes, and he'd loved it. When he found his third victim, Jamie Farr, the kill had been interrupted. That was when he'd realised he would have to claim his future victims in their own homes, but that would take planning, that would take careful research, and that was why his victims were women. They were the opposite from the experience he'd failed to get from Neil, Calvin and Jamie.

The doorbell rang, making Olivia jump. She looked up at the clock on the wall. It was a little after ten o'clock. It was pitch-black outside. She made her way downstairs, taking the keys out of her pocket and looked through the spy hole in the door. It was Amyas Foley. She briefly wondered how he knew where she lived, but there were many ways he could have found out. Maybe Jessica had told him. Maybe he'd taken the registration number from her scooter and looked her up. She really wasn't in the mood to see him tonight. She took a deep breath, swiped the fob over the panel on the alarm and unlocked the door.

Amyas stood on the doorstep with his hands behind his back and a huge smile on his face.

'Well, someone looks happy. Have you caught your killer?'

His face dropped slightly.

'No. Listen, I was at home, reading that book about your father, and you mentioned in your statement about how you were at Jessica's house playing with her new puppy and how much you wanted one of your own.'

'I'm sorry, Amyas, but I really don't want to go over this again,' she said, gripping the handle of the door hard.

'No. I don't want to stir up any bad memories. It's just… well, we've had this at the station for a couple of days and we don't know what to do with him, and as you mentioned always wanting a sausage dog, I thought you'd like to take care of him.' From behind his back he produced Jessica's black-and-tan miniature dachshund, Stanley.

Olivia's eyes lit up upon seeing the gorgeous bundle with large, sad, brown eyes. She held out her hands and took him from Amyas. He was so light.

'Oh my goodness, Stanley. I'm so sorry, sweetheart.' She snuggled him and tears pricked her eyes. 'I meant to ask you about him, but after everything that's happened, it just went completely out of my mind.'

She placed Stanley on the floor and allowed him to run off and explore, which he did, tail wagging and tiny legs a blur as they scurried around the house.

'This is so impractical. I'm never here,' she said.

'There's nobody else to take him. I'm sure your colleagues won't mind you taking him to work with you.'

'And how am I going to get him there on the back of a scooter?'

'Ah,' he said.

'See, I told you. So impractical.'

'I saw the look on your face when I showed him to you. You looked genuinely happy.'

'How can you not be happy with a dog?'

'Precisely. I have two German shepherds. They make going home bearable. Trust me, you'll feel so much happier, so much healthier, with a dog. These things should be available on prescription.'

From the kitchen, Stanley came trotting out with a pair of Olivia's knickers in his mouth that must have fallen off the radiator.

Foley laughed.

Olivia blushed. Already the sterile house had started to feel like a home.

Chapter Twenty-Two

'I confess that I had an ulterior motive in coming here tonight,' Foley said.

They were sitting in Olivia's rarely used living room on separate Chesterfield sofas. They both had a coffee in hand and were relaxing after chasing around after Stanley. He was currently sleeping noisily on a cushion next to Olivia.

'You went to visit Richard this evening, didn't you?'

'Bloody hell, do you read minds?'

'No. You came here and presented me with something you knew would make me happy. While I'm at my most receptive you ask me for a favour I'll find difficult to refuse. Unfortunately, I know what you're going to ask me, and the answer is no.'

'What?'

'You want me to visit my father.'

'You really are a mind reader.'

'Why?'

'I'm sorry?'

'Why do you want me to visit Richard?'

'You said it yourself, he's a thrill killer, just like the man we're after now. Who better to give us insight into how he's going to act next?'

'Who better?' Olivia asked, her eyebrows raised. 'How about the person who has travelled the world interviewing over a hundred serial killers? How about the person who has written four books on the minds of serial killers, what makes them tick, how they act, how they begin? You came to me with this. I didn't offer you my services. You sent Jessica to beg for my help and—Oh,' she said, the penny finally dropping. 'Is that what you were after all this time? You didn't want the help of a forensic psychologist; you wanted to go direct to the source. You wanted to sit down opposite a serial killer and pick his brains.'

'No. It's not like that at all.'

'Isn't it?'

'No. Your insight is invaluable. Look, in my field, we use the resources we have and we exploit what we can get our hands on in order to solve the crime. A killer will have a killer's insights, a killer's instinct. Yes, you've interviewed over a hundred serial murderers, but how many of them are manipulators? How many will have told you only what you want to hear?'

'And how do you know Richard won't tell you only what you want to hear? He's a manipulator, too, just like the rest of them.'

'I—'

'No,' she interrupted firmly. 'If you want my help, I'll gladly give it to you, but I will not be your route to get to Richard.'

A silence descended, broken only by the whining noises Stanley made in his sleep.

'I should probably be going,' Foley said, placing his mug down on the floor.

'I'll show you out.'

They walked to the front door. Neither of them said anything. Olivia unlocked the door and pulled it open. A blast of cold air entered, causing them both to shiver.

Foley slouched heavily down the steps. At the bottom he turned around.

'I'm sorry. I really am.'

'That's OK,' Olivia replied, arms tightly folded across her chest, face like thunder.

'You're still coming to the station tomorrow?'

'I wasn't aware I was needed.'

'We've lost one of our own. My team are angry. They need a direction and I think they'll listen to someone with knowledge and insight into the man they're looking for.'

She raised an eyebrow. If her best friend hadn't been one of the victims, she would probably have slammed the door in Foley's face. 'Fine. I'll be there mid-morning.'

'I appreciate it. Thanks.' He walked away, head down, hands in pockets.

Olivia remained in the doorway, a heavy frown on her face, deep in thought as she tried to work out how dark her life had suddenly become.

'Good evening.'

Olivia turned from the doorway at the greeting. Sam Halliday stood at the entrance to his basement flat, pizza box in hand.

'Oh. Good evening.' She gave a false smile.

'You look upset.'

'Difficult day.'

'Would you like to talk about it? I have pizza,' he said, holding up the box and smiling.

Olivia really needed something unhealthy and fattening right now. She walked back into the house, leaving the door open for Sam to follow.

Sam made a fuss over Stanley, who seemed to enjoy licking the young man's face. Olivia poured them both a glass of wine to go with the pepperoni pizza.

'I think he likes me,' Sam said from the floor as Stanley jumped all over him.

'He's always been excitable. Every time I went around to Jessica's I came home with dog drool all over my clothes.' She closed her eyes tight and swallowed the emotion she could feel rising up inside her. She hadn't cried for Jessica yet. It was finally dawning on her that she was gone.

'How old is he?'

'Erm, I'm not sure. Let me think… Jessica had him about two years, I think. So maybe two-ish?'

'Well, if you ever need a dog walker, I don't have much to do in the daytime,' he said, standing up and going over to the sink to wash his hands.

'I'll hold you to that.'

'I love dogs. My parents have four golden retrievers and two Dalmatians back in Devon.'

'Wow. You must have a big house.'

'It's an old farm building. Plenty of land.'

'Do you miss it?'

'I miss the open space, the quiet. London is just… I don't know.'

'A wall of noise,' she finished his sentence for him.

'That's it.' He perched himself on the edge of a stool at the island, picked up a slice of pizza and took a huge bite. 'I did a double shift last week. I didn't leave the hospital until gone one o'clock in the morning. There was still plenty of traffic around. The city never switches off.'

'Welcome to London,' Olivia smiled.

'I don't know how you cope with it.'

'I grew up here. It's all I know.'

'I don't think I'll work in a city once I'm qualified. I'll try and find a nice country practice somewhere.'

'Sounds lovely.'

They fell silent while they ate pizza and drank their wine.

'So, the man who was leaving, is he your boyfriend?'

Olivia almost choked on her pizza. 'God, no. He's with the police. I'm doing some consulting work for them.'

'Interesting.'

'Well, it can be. I don't always feel like I'm appreciated in my work.'

'What? How can you say that? You've written four books. You lecture all over the world. Of course you're appreciated.'

'It's not always *my* insight they're after.'

'Whose would they be after?' He frowned.

Olivia mused over a reply then decided against giving one. She threw down the crust and wiped her hands. 'You know, I should probably be going to bed. It's been a very long day and I get the feeling tomorrow is going to be even longer. Thank you so much for the pizza, Sam. My treat next time.'

'I'd like that,' he smiled.

Olivia was about to show him out when a crash from the kitchen saw them both turn around. Stanley had jumped up at the bin and knocked it over.

'You deal with that. I'll see myself out.'

Sam watched from the kitchen doorway as Olivia dropped to her knees and began picking up the spilled litter from the bin. Stanley wasn't being helpful. He thought she was playing and he kept running in and out of the rubbish.

Sam smiled. He turned and headed down the corridor to the front door. He opened it and was about to step out into the night, when his eyes fell on a spare set of keys hanging up on a hook behind the door. He turned back; Olivia was still crouching down on the floor in the kitchen. He quickly snatched the keys and left, closing the door firmly behind him.

Chapter Twenty-Three

Wednesday 21st February 2024

'How the hell did you get him here on your scooter?' Sebastian asked as he and Olivia watched while Daisy sat on the floor fussing over Stanley.

'I'm not sure. It wasn't easy and I think I may have broken several laws in doing so.'

'You're going to need to buy a car,' he said with a menacing smile.

'I don't bloody think so. I've heard you moan about a twenty-minute journey taking almost double that time. I'll stick to my scooter.'

'And what about him?'

'I'll buy him a tiny helmet.' She smiled. She turned to go into the kitchen and flicked on the kettle.

'Have you seen the newspapers today?' Sebastian asked. His voice had taken on a serious tone.

'You know I don't bother with the papers.'

'Just as well, really. You're in them.'

'I am?' she asked, looking up.

On the large boardroom-style desk just outside of the kitchenette, a stack of newspapers was neatly arranged. Olivia pushed by Sebastian and picked up the first one. The headline news was something about property prices, which she had no interest in. She began flicking through the pages frantically.

'Page seven in that one, I believe,' Daisy said from the floor.

The picture had been taken using a long lens and showed Olivia with DI Foley walking into Sanderson Street Police Station. She ran her eyes quickly over the text for any mention of her father. Fortunately, the journalists hadn't made the connection.

'Most of the stories paint you in a very good light. I shouldn't worry,' Sebastian said as he set about making the coffee. 'They call you a world-renowned forensic psychologist. They mention your books and research. Even the BSA gets a mention. Briefly.'

'They also point out there's a serial killer in London,' Daisy said.

'They do?'

'Only one paper mentions that,' Sebastian stated. 'You know what papers are like; they say anything to sell copies.'

'They're not wrong, though,' Olivia said, closing the paper and sitting down at the table. 'I think I may have found another three victims last night. He's potentially killed six people, attempted another one, and he's growing in confidence. His crimes are getting much closer together.'

The phone on Daisy's desk rang.

'Here we go. I wondered when they'd start,' she said, trudging out of the office.

'That'll be the press wanting a statement,' Olivia said. 'They're going to be all over this. And all over me.'

'We can fend them off from this end,' Sebastian said, sitting opposite her. 'It's down to the police to release statements and answer questions, not us.'

'I'm just worried that they'll start digging and—'

'I know,' he said, squeezing her hand. 'Look, Daisy and I are the only ones who know who your dad is.'

'And Foley. And his team, probably.'

Sebastian shrugged. 'All I can do is shield you as best I can and try to stop the truth from coming out.'

She proffered a weak smile. 'Thank you. You're a good friend, Sebastian. Have you had any calls since Richard had his heart attack?'

He sighed. 'Many. I wrote the book on him, so they think I'm the go-to guy for when anything happens to him. I'm sure the press thinks we're best mates.'

'Have you heard how he is?' she asked, reluctantly.

'I know I shouldn't have, but I called a friend of mine in neurology who knows someone in A&E who is married to someone in ICU. Apparently, his condition is improving. He's stable, but weak.'

'He didn't seem weak when I was talking to him.' She shivered.

'I tell you what,' Sebastian said, taking Olivia by the shoulders. 'Why don't you come round for dinner tonight? Bring Stanley. The kids'll love him, and it'll give me an excuse to cook a decent meal for a change, instead of chips and burgers, which is all they ever want to eat.'

Olivia's smile was genuine. 'I'd like that.'

'Good.' He leaned forward and kissed her on the forehead. 'Now, you can either call a cab to the police station or I can put a blanket over your head and escort you out the back.'

'Don't worry, I've got my guard dog.' She nodded towards Stanley who was running around in circles trying to catch his tail.

Olivia stood at the front of the incident room and looked out at the sea of expectant faces staring at her. She would have loved to know what they were thinking. Did they expect her to magically come up with the name of the killer? If they did, they were in for a shock. What she was about to tell them would only add to their workload. She suddenly felt incredibly nervous.

She had asked Foley to get her a whiteboard so she could write information as she talked to the team – and because fiddling with the pen gave her shaking fingers something to do.

'Hello,' she began. Her mouth was dry, and she had to clear her throat a couple of times before being able to continue. She had been in maximum security prisons, alone in small interview rooms with mass murderers. She'd been attacked, spat at, groped and licked by serial killers all around the world, yet she was petrified of speaking to a room full of detectives.

'You currently have four victims: Sarah, Joanne, Phoebe and Jessica.' She wrote their names down the right-hand side of the board. When she looked at her shaky handwriting, she was almost ashamed. 'Looking at the victimology, the crime scene photographs and police reports, I was able to determine that the killer was a very confident man. There was no sign of forced entry, there was no overpowering of the victim as they answered the door, and nobody saw him enter or leave. From this, I came to the conclusion that he's worked his way up to this level by practising before. A person doesn't just wake up one morning and decide to kill and have the perfect way to get away with murder. It takes planning and effort to reach this stage. I was given the files of similar unsolved crimes by DS Holly Goodfellow and I believe I've found two other victims, and one attempted murder that may be connected.' She paused for effect and looked around the room. A few detectives adjusted themselves in their seats; some looked over to Foley. Holly was making notes while Leon Rippner had his eyes firmly fixed on Olivia. Not once did he look away.

Olivia continued: 'Neil Parker and Calvin Ashton.' She wrote their names down the left-hand side of the board. 'Neil was murdered on the fifth of November last year. A single stab wound during a fireworks display. Calvin was stabbed five times on the first of December during a Christmas lights switch-on. Very similar murders.'

'How do you know the same person committed these two?' a detective asked. 'They were outside while the four women were killed inside. Also, the victims are men.'

'I was getting to that.' Olivia felt her face flush. 'Your killer is a thrill killer; he likes the excitement, the adrenaline, the rush that killing gives him. On November the fifth, he was surrounded by hundreds of people, yet he wasn't able to spend time with his victim, which is why he only stabbed once. Afterwards, he will have struggled to remember anything about the kill – the feeling, the sense of power. People at this event will have been in groups of friends and family members, yet he will have been alone. The longer he was there, the more he would have stood out. However, he wanted to kill, so he did. He chose the first opportunity he could and struck. Then he fled. He will have been incredibly disappointed with himself.

'On the first of December, he waited until his victim moved away from the crowd. Calvin Ashton left his friends to go into some woods to relieve himself. The killer was either waiting in the woods or followed him there. He stabbed him five times. He had longer with the victim, but still had to leave in a hurry. Maybe someone else was heading for the woods to use it as a toilet, or someone had shouted for Calvin while looking for him. Either way, he had to leave, and quickly. Again, he was disappointed with his kill.

'For his third victim, he decided to change his MO. He liked the idea of having an unsuspecting audience – the crowds at the events – but that meant he couldn't spend much time with the victim. On the fifth of December, he stabbed Jamie Farr.' Olivia wrote Jamie's name in the centre of the board. 'It was one o'clock in the morning in the middle of a quiet street. Jamie was on his way home from a night shift at the petrol station where he worked. The killer stabbed him twice. Jamie fell against a car, the alarm started, and the killer was spooked and fled. He would need to change his MO once again.'

'How do you know all this?' asked the same detective.

'If you take all seven victims and line them up, as I have done here, you can see the natural progression of a serial killer increasing in confidence. As I've said, becoming a serial killer is an evolutionary process. He killed outside, amongst a crowd of people, thinking he'd be able to sink into the crowd afterwards. Although that was successful, the crowd also had the ability to unmask him. His third attempt would have been ideal if Jamie hadn't fallen against the car and set the alarm off. If he hadn't, who knows what horrors the neighbours would have woken up to the following morning. However, this failed attempt made the killer realise he would need to gain entry to his victim's home.'

'But there was no audience with the four women,' Holly pointed out.

'When Phoebe Harper and Jessica Sheffield were murdered, there were parties taking place very close by. While killing them, he could hear the music, the laughter, the chatter, but they had no idea what was going on. That was his thrill.'

'What about Sarah and Joanne?' Leon asked. His arms were folded. His face was unreadable.

'I admit I'm stumped there, but I'm working on it.'

'Why switch from men to women?' another detective asked.

'No offence to the women in the room, but killing them is easier. A killer will always go for someone weaker than himself; that's why the more vulnerable members of society are easy targets. In this case, he's killed two men and attempted a third, but hasn't experienced the thrill he anticipated. Yes, he wants an audience, but he also wants to see his victims scream and beg for their lives. A woman is more likely to do that than a man. Also, a woman alone in her house with a predator will believe she's going to be raped. Trust me, that's the worst feeling in the world. He will see the fear instantly and that's what will turn him on.'

'But you've said this isn't a sex crime?' Leon said.

'True. I should clear that up. Just because the victim isn't raped, we can't assume it's not a sex crime. Who knows what this killer does when he returns home? You've found no semen stains at the crime scenes, so we know he's not masturbating while there. Some people will say a man with a knife is a phallic symbol, and while I'm pretty sure the killer is getting a sexual thrill from these killings, his main enjoyment is seeing the fear.'

'How do you know this?' Holly asked.

'Looking at where Sarah and Joanne lived, they're surrounded by neighbours. At the end of such a highly emotive kill, the murderer will be buzzing on adrenaline. There's no hiding that. If he'd left the scenes straight away, someone would have noticed his erratic behaviour. I think he stays with his victims. He calms himself down until he feels safe enough to leave. When he does, he gets the confidence of being able to hide in plain sight. This is an incredibly intelligent man who is at the height of his powers.'

'So, what's our next step?' Foley asked.

'You need to bring Jamie Farr in for detailed questioning. His witness statement is very vague, but now that some time has elapsed, maybe he will have remembered more about his attacker. He's your best chance at identifying the killer.'

'I thought *you* were supposed to be our best chance,' Rippner said. There was a ripple of laughter from around the room.

'No. I analyse. You detect.'

Holly stifled a snigger.

'What can you tell us about the killer?' Rippner asked, folding his arms once again.

'I'm not a profiler.'

'But surely you've come up with something.'

'Leon,' Foley warned, giving his DS a dead stare.

'No. That's all right. I can tell you that you're looking for a white male, medium height and build, in his late twenties to mid thirties. He'll live alone, have a low-demanding job, and be socially confident. He's intelligent, clean living, and very good at blending into the background. Oh, and the job he has won't be regular hours. He'll work shifts.'

'How do you know that?' Leon asked again.

'He tried to kill Jamie Farr at one o'clock in the morning. Nobody with a regular nine-to-five job is out and about at the time. Also, he killed Sarah Millington in the late afternoon around four o'clock-ish. He's fitting his hobby in around his work.'

'A young white male who blends into the background; you've described practically eighty per cent of the people living in London,' Leon said, a smirk on his lips.

'I know this is frustrating for you all, especially as one of your colleagues is among the victims. However, I believe you already know who the killer is. This type of person is in it for the thrill, but the thrill of killing, no matter how elaborate his murders are, won't be enough. He'll have made himself known to the police and he'll have walked away with a huge grin on his face, knowing he's bested you. You, or someone on this team, have already interviewed him. Add that to the description I've given you, and it's narrowed your field considerably.'

'You sound very confident,' Leon said.

'I know how killers think.'

'Nobody should have to know that,' Holly said.

'True, but aren't you glad that I do?'

Chapter Twenty-Four

With the air of a man who felt he belonged there, Sam Halliday opened Olivia's front door, walked into her house, and closed it behind him. He waved the fob in front of the panel on the wall, which deactivated the alarm. The house was quiet. Sam leaned back against the solid storm door and inhaled. He could detect a hint of the fragrance Olivia had sprayed herself with after showering this morning before she left the house exactly fifty-seven minutes ago.

The first room he came to on the right was Olivia's bedroom. He pushed open the door and stepped inside. It was warm in here. The heat from the steam of the shower hung in the air and Sam imagined Olivia with a towel wrapped around her wet naked body. He sat on the edge of the bed and closed his eyes. A satisfying smile spread across his lips as he pictured her towelling herself dry, rubbing moisturiser into her soft skin and running a brush through her shiny hair.

He sat at her dressing table and looked at his reflection in the mirror. He opened the first drawer and took out a make-up bag. He unzipped it and removed a dark-red lipstick. He knew this was the one she used, as he stared intently at her lips whenever

The Mind of a Murderer

she spoke. He couldn't take his eyes from her naturally full pout. He took off the cap and rolled up the red stick. He sniffed it but it didn't have any smell. He licked the tip. The next time Olivia applied lipstick, he would be on her lips and would linger all day, like the remnants of a passionate kiss between two lovers.

On the bedside table, Sam picked up a framed photograph of a woman and a young girl. It was obviously a picture taken many years ago. The photo was slightly yellowed and the outfits the people were wearing were dated. He wondered if this was a young Olivia with her mother.

There was a well-thumbed paperback copy of *Little Women* next to the bedside lamp. Judging by the state of it, it was a book Olivia had read many times. He'd never read it himself, but he'd make a point of buying it so he could get a snapshot of the kind of things Olivia enjoyed.

In the top drawer of the solid oak chest he ran his fingers over Olivia's delicate underwear. He pressed them against his face, breathing in the clean smell from her knickers and bras. He took a pair of pants from the bottom of the drawer – white, lacy with a pink trim – and stuffed them into the pocket of his jeans.

Sam looked back at the bed. He could picture himself and Olivia curled up underneath the duvet together, their naked bodies pressed against each other, legs entwined, his hands all over her, her head on his chest, him listening to the sound of her steady breathing as she slept. He'd inhale the scent from her hair and warm skin. He'd caress her gently and hold her close. He wondered what he would have to do to win over someone as special as Olivia. Would she even consider a trainee doctor? He didn't have much to offer. In fact, he had nothing to offer. He was twenty-three years old and all he had to his name was a damp basement flat, which took most of his student loan money in extortionate rent, and three maxed-out credit cards. Someone of Olivia's class wouldn't look twice at him. He'd need to offer her something no other man could.

Walking through the rest of the ground floor, Sam ran his fingers along the spines of hardback books in the living room, most of which he hadn't heard of. He read the titles of the DVDs and Blu-rays on the shelves on the back wall. Most were foreign-language films and the odd box set of an Icelandic crime drama he'd seen on BBC4 and abandoned without a clue what was going on. Olivia was way out of his league, but he could change for her. He'd watched the original Swedish Millennium trilogy on DVD and enjoyed that. He could get used to subtitles.

He took the first flight of stairs slowly, listening for any creaks. The seventh and eighth steps groaned under his weight. He made a mental note, just in case he decided to enter the house at night while Olivia was sleeping. He'd hate to wake her up.

The only room on the first floor was Olivia's office. From the back window, he looked out over the stunning view of her back garden and the concrete city beyond. He quickly turned away. He hated London; just the sight of its landmarks filled him with loathing.

The large table in the centre of the room was neat and tidy. Her desk in the corner had files and folders neatly arranged. There was another framed photograph of the same woman and girl but on a beach this time. He stood back and looked at the notes Olivia had written on the whiteboards. She had clear handwriting, and he loved the way she drew her zeros with a slanting line through them.

He wanted to sit in her chair at the desk and imagine what it would be like to be her at work, but it was too close to the front window and he worried he might be spotted by the nosy neighbours opposite. On the other hand, he'd yet to speak to any of the neighbours and he'd been living in the cul-de-sac for over a year. London was a world away from rural Devon.

Sam sat down in Olivia's chair. He was incredibly lonely. The people he worked with at the hospital were fine for a quick chat whenever they had a spare few minutes or happened to be grabbing a coffee at the same time, but they had their own lives, their own issues, their own friends and family. They didn't have space for someone new in their circle.

Sam knew he didn't have a sparkling personality. He wasn't a great conversational whizz. He didn't have a quick sense of humour and he found it difficult to make eye contact when talking. This often made him come across as aloof and goofy, but he couldn't help how he was. He was painfully shy, and he had no idea how to change that. He was sure that it would take just one person to unlock his inner confidence, someone warm, caring, kind and gentle, someone like Olivia, to break down the walls of isolation he'd built up around himself.

Whenever he thought of Olivia and any potential life they could have together, he felt a warm feeling develop inside him. He didn't care about the age gap. It was the fact they would have each other's heart and soul that would make it work.

Sam sat and daydreamed for a while. It was only when his gaze landed on the doorway and he saw the stairs leading up to the top floor that he wondered what was up there. When he'd moved into his basement flat, his landlady had delighted in explaining the layout of the four floors, as if rubbing his nose in how plentiful the space was that they had and how he'd never be able to afford something so luxurious. Fortunately, she worked away a lot and he never had to see her. Cow. But why did Olivia choose such an expansive house when she lived on her own? What did she do with all the empty rooms?

He ascended the stairs and felt the air get cooler the further he went. He shuddered. The door was locked but Olivia had left the key in the lock. Strange. It was stiff to turn, and he heard the mechanism echo as if the room was empty. He pushed the door carefully open and stepped into a room with nothing in it except for a leather sofa and a glass-topped coffee table.

The walls were painted a light grey and the plush carpet was a shade or two darker. It smelt new and looked as if it was hardly walked on. He remained in the doorway and looked at the large expanse of empty space. He frowned. There was an en suite bathroom to the left but nothing else.

He stepped inside and something caught his eye. He turned to look at the wall behind him and frowned as he tried to make sense of what he was looking at.

The wall had been turned into a giant notice board. A map of London covered most of it and various photographs of women were tacked around the side with pins and lines of red thread leading to different areas of the capital. He counted six women in total and at the top left was a photograph he recognised. It was a copy of the one in Olivia's bedroom – the woman and small child. Their line of red cotton pointed to a pin in Kingston Upon Thames. The same place where Olivia had told him she was from.

At the very top of the map was the photo of a man who looked vaguely familiar, but he couldn't think where from. He found the whole set-up bizarre in the extreme. It was like the set of a crime drama where the detectives are trying to hunt a serial killer by pinpointing the location of his victims. Is that what this was? But if this was Olivia's work, surely all this information would have been in her office downstairs.

On the low coffee table were several piles of files. He picked one up and read the label: *13th April 1999. Diane Hobbs*. He opened it and saw the face of a brown-haired woman with creases around her eyes, a small nose and a smile that lit up her face. Sam looked back at the wall and saw the same photo looking down at him. He flicked through the file, glancing at news stories printed from the internet telling of how she'd been reported missing then eventually found murdered on the bank of the Thames. There were copies of crime scene photos which turned Sam's stomach and he quickly moved away from them. A copy of a post-mortem report told him Diane had been stabbed eleven times and her left breast had been severed. He quickly closed the file. The others all belonged to the people on the board.

Next to the files were six copies of the same paperback book, *The Riverside Killer: The Double Life of Richard Button*, written by someone called Sebastian Lister. The cover showed what appeared to be a dead body lying at the side of a dirty river, her blood-spattered arm floating on top of the water.

Sam flicked through the book and focused on the glossy pages of photographs. The picture of Richard Button looked like the one on the wall at the top. But why was Olivia interested in him and his victims, when he'd already been caught and jailed?

He vaguely knew the story of Richard Button. He was a serial killer in the 1990s who'd murdered eight people, two of whom were his wife and daughter, but he was in prison; the case was closed. It made no sense for Olivia to seem to give this top priority over everything else in her work.

He sat down on the sofa and began reading the book. He skimmed over the page giving information about the author but stopped at the dedication. It simply read *To Olivia*. So, Sebastian had written this book and dedicated it to Olivia. Why would he do that? Is it a compliment to have a book about a notorious serial killer who mutilated eight women dedicated to you?

Sam sat back, made himself comfortable, and began reading.

It wasn't long before everything fell into place. Richard Button was the perfect family man. He lived a safe, normal existence, with a high-paid job as an accountant at a family brewery in the south of London. He was married to Geraldine and had two lovely daughters, Olivia and Claire. Flicking to the photographs again, Sam noticed the wife and daughter of the killer were up on the board, but there was no picture of Olivia. Why was that? Because she was still very much alive. Olivia Winter was Olivia Button, daughter of serial killer Richard Button.

This changed everything.

Sam decided it was time to leave. He was due at the Royal Free Hospital in an hour. There was a spring in his step as he descended both sets of stairs, and it was only when he reached the front door that he realised he was still holding a copy of *The Riverside Killer*.

A woman like Olivia, the sole survivor of a serial murderer, the daughter of a man who had killed her own mother and sister, was going to be a nervous woman. Yes, she was intelligent, but, he guessed, as a person, she'd be a complete basket case. He doubted she saw a therapist; she didn't seem the type to open herself up to a stranger. He imagined she bottled everything up and threw herself into her work. That was why she wasn't married. That was why she didn't have any children. She'd withdrawn from the world and society. How would he be able to win over someone as fragile as Olivia? By making her need him, of course.

He tiptoed back into the bedroom and placed the paperback on top of Olivia's bedtime reading, *Little Women*. Tonight, when she snuggled under the duvet and reached out to read a couple of chapters, she'd stop and wonder who had placed it there. Soon, she'd be knocking Sam's door down asking for his support, and he'd be there with open arms.

Chapter Twenty-Five

Detectives believe that witnesses should be interviewed straight after an event, before they forget what they've seen. Memory experts recommend that at least seventy-two hours should be left after the incident before a person is interviewed, so they can process what they have witnessed.

Olivia had first-hand experience that waiting to interview a witness is the best option. While she was recovering in hospital from her stab wounds at the age of nine, she had detectives bombarding her with questions about what her father had done. She had been able to answer them, but her answers had been garbled, and she had missed out key information. Three days later, still in hospital, and crying onto her grandmother's shoulder, she remembered everything, from coming home from Jessica's house full of excitement, to the final stab wound when she was plunged into unconsciousness. It was as if she was watching a recording of it in her head.

The attack on Jamie Farr took place on the fifth of December last year. His witness statement had been taken less than two hours after he was stabbed, and he hadn't been questioned about it since. Although more than two months had passed, Olivia knew he would be able to add more information this time around.

Jamie was led into the interview room. He seemed to be of average height, of slim to medium build and had cropped dark-blond hair. He was pale and held himself rigid. He was wearing a dark-green hooded sweater that looked a size too big for him and baggy blue jeans. He hadn't shaved in several days and sported a patchy beard which, along with his oversized clothes, gave him a shaggy appearance. Aged twenty-four, he lived in Ruislip Manor with family and worked shifts at a petrol station which was a ten-minute walk from his home.

He sat down carefully in the hard plastic seat. He showed no signs of his injuries causing any lingering discomfort, but, judging by his body language, he was incredibly uncomfortable being in a police station. Olivia guessed that was only natural. He would probably want to try and put the whole incident behind him. She certainly had when she was stabbed.

He declined an offer of a drink from DS Goodfellow, and DS Rippner started the recording, explaining for the benefit of the tape that this was an informal interview.

As a civilian, Olivia was not allowed to interview him. She was sitting in a cramped viewing room behind a one-way mirror beside DI Foley. They were so close they were almost touching. Olivia could smell the cheap deodorant he was wearing and the stale coffee on his breath. She could even hear his stomach rumbling. Knowing all this made her self-conscious about what he could detect about her.

On the desk in front of her was a notepad and pen. She hoped she'd be able to glean some information from the potential murder victim of a serial killer to help Foley and his team catch the man responsible.

'Jamie,' Holly began. She leaned forward in her chair. She didn't fold her arms and had made a point of taking her jacket off. She was showing Jamie that she was open, sympathetic, and she could be trusted. She reminded Olivia of a politician who rolls his sleeves up around election time to come across as one of the people. 'We need to know everything about what happened to you on the night of the fifth of December.'

'I've been through all this before.'

'I know, but new information has come to light, and what happened to you might have happened to someone else. We need to check and double check.'

'Someone else has been stabbed?' he asked, his eyes widened.

'Yes.'

'Are they all right?'

She turned to Leon who picked up the mantle. 'Jamie, what can you tell us about the man who attacked you?'

'Nothing. It was dark.' His head was bowed, his voice barely above a whisper and he was playing with his fingers.

'There must be something you recall,' Leon said. He was getting agitated already and the interview had only just begun.

'Let's take it one step at a time,' Holly said. 'We'll work down from head to toe. Now, was his head covered?'

'Have you been coaching her?' Foley leaned in and whispered loudly to Olivia.

'I gave her a few pointers,' she smiled.

'Yes. He had a hood up.'

'OK. What colour was the hood?'

'Dark. Black, I think.'

'Could you see any of his hair?'

Jamie thought for a moment. 'No.'

'Was his face covered?'

'No.'

'Did he have a scarf or a mask covering his face?'

'No.'

'What colour was his skin?'

'He was white.'

'Pale? Dark?'

'Pale. I think.'

'Did he have a beard, moustache or stubble?'

'No. He was clean shaven.'

'Did you see his eyes?'

'No.'

'Was he wearing glasses or sunglasses?'

'No. His hood was pulled down low.'

'So how do you know he wasn't wearing glasses?'

'I saw enough of his face to know he wasn't wearing glasses but not enough to see the colour of his eyes.'

'OK. Did anything stand out about his face? Did he have any scars or tattoos? Any birthmarks? Any acne scars or wrinkles?'

'No. He had a smooth complexion.'

'Would you say he was young in appearance?'

'Yes.'

'How young? Younger than you?'

'I don't know. Maybe the same age.'

'OK. You're doing very well, Jamie.' Olivia had told Holly about the importance of rewards. It was like giving a puppy a treat when it was learning to sit. 'What can you tell me about his clothes?'

'They were dark. I think he was wearing black jeans.'

'What about up top? Was he wearing a coat?'

'Yes.'

'What kind?'

'It was kind of padded but not like a bomber jacket or anything.'

'Did you see any logos?'

'No. Wait, yes, there was something on the sleeve, a little rectangular thing. It shone under the streetlamp.'

'Could you see what it was?'

'No. It was only small.'

'Hang on a minute,' Leon said. He stood up and left the room.

'You're doing very well, Jamie. Are you all right to continue?'

'Yes. I'm fine.' He gave her a small smile.

'How are your injuries?'

'They're fine. All healed up. Just a couple of scars.'

Leon re-entered the interview room within seconds of leaving. He was carrying a dark-blue jacket which he placed on the table. 'Is this similar to the jacket your attacker was wearing?'

Jamie examined the coat. He looked at the little logo on the left sleeve. 'Yes. This is it. This is definitely the coat,' he said, the most animated he had been since he arrived at the station. 'But it was black rather than blue.'

'For the benefit of the tape, I have shown Jamie Farr my own jacket which is a Barbour coat.' Leon took the jacket back from Jamie and draped it over the back of the chair.

'What about his footwear, Jamie? What can you tell me about them?' Holly asked.

'They were black. They were like walking shoes. They didn't make a sound when he walked so they weren't big and heavy. They didn't have a heel on them, but they certainly weren't trainers.'

'How can you be so sure?' Leon asked.

'When he stabbed me, I bent over, and I got a good look at them.'

'Did you see any markings, logos or brandings on them?'

'No. They didn't look expensive, and they were quite worn.'

'Did he speak to you at all?'

'No.'

'Did he make any sound?'

'No.'

'What about smell?' Holly asked. 'Was he wearing a fragrance or a particularly strong deodorant?'

'Not that I can remember. He didn't smell of sweat or anything. He smelled... I don't know, sort of clean, maybe?'

'Could you smell alcohol or tobacco on him?'

'No,' he replied firmly.

'OK. One more thing; tell me about his height and build.'

'He was a bit taller than me, but not much, and he was sort of average build. I'm sorry, I know that's not helpful, but he wasn't thin and he wasn't fat; he was kind of... regular.'

'This is futile,' Foley said, rolling his chair back and hitting the wall.

'No it isn't.'

'Of course it is. All he's told us is that he's an average bloke wearing walking shoes and a designer jacket. Do you have any idea how many outlets sell Barbour? Then there are online stores, charity shops and eBay.'

'You know he's white. You know he's clean-shaven and looks after his appearance. You know he's slim to medium build. Look around you at how many people are classed as overweight or obese. Look how many men have designer stubble. You can narrow your search down dramatically by his description.'

'And we'll still be left with several million suspects.'

'You're thinking negatively here, Amyas.' She'd only known him for a few days but knew calling him by his first name would elicit a look of daggers. It got his attention, however, and that was all Olivia wanted. 'Your killer is highly intelligent. He's killed six people so far and you have very little to go on. He's an expert at covering his tracks. However, he messed up with Jamie Farr in there. He didn't kill him so you need to use what he can give you.'

Foley gave a deflated sigh. 'You're right.'

'I know I am.' She smiled.

Olivia decided against going back into the murder rooms. She had work of her own to go back to in George Street.

She left the police station and was buttoning up her coat when she looked up and saw Jamie Farr leaving the building by another door. She watched as he zipped up his jacket, plunged his hands into his pockets and, with his head down, headed quickly out of the car park.

Olivia decided to follow him. He must be going through hell right now. He'd survived a knife attack. Maybe he thought it was an attempted mugging gone wrong. That was bad enough, but when the news was made public that there was a serial killer operating in London and that he had come within a hair's breadth of being one of his victims, the emotional turmoil would be massive. Already his world would have been turned upside down as he tried to make sense of living as a victim, but street muggings happen all the time, especially in major cities. Contact with serial killers was rare. He would not be ready for this. Olivia knew that life all too well.

'Mr Farr?' Olivia called out.

Jamie stopped dead in his tracks and looked around him. His eyes were wide with fear.

'I'm sorry. I didn't mean to startle you. My name's Olivia Winter. I'm a forensic psychologist working with the police. I witnessed your interview just now.'

'Oh,' he said, head down, staring at his shoes.

'It must have been a frightening time for you, getting attacked like that.'

'It was,' he replied in a soft voice.

'How are you coping?'

He took a deep breath. 'I don't know. I'm taking each day as it comes.'

'That's good. Are you seeing anyone? A counsellor, maybe?'

'No. I did think about it, but my mum said I'd get over it soon enough.'

'You're not, though, are you?'

Jamie didn't reply. He looked like he was on the verge of tears.

'If you find you're suffering, mentally, having nightmares, or struggling to cope, you may be suffering from post-traumatic stress disorder. There are people you can talk to who can help.'

'I just want to try and forget about it and get back to how I was before all this happened.'

'It's not easy, though, is it?'

He shook his head. His bottom lip wobbled.

'Here.' Olivia fished around in her handbag and brought out a business card. 'I'm not a counsellor, but I can put you in touch with some good people. Or... I don't know, if you think of anything, give me a call.'

Gingerly, he took the card and put it in his pocket without looking at it. 'Thanks. I'd better be going,' he said, turning on his heel and taking large strides.

Olivia was only nine when she was attacked – still a child. All she had wanted was for someone she knew to ask her if she wanted to talk about what happened, to try and make sense of it. She'd had her grandparents, but they'd been of the old school that believed things were better left unsaid, as Jamie Farr's mother seemed to be. Olivia hoped that her offer of the opportunity to talk would be enough for Jamie to move on in his life.

Olivia turned and went in the opposite direction to try and find a taxi. It was twenty-five years later for her and she was still trying to find a way to move on. Jamie needed help right now.

Chapter Twenty-Six

It had been Olivia's intention to go home, have a quick shower and change into something less formal, then scoot over to Sebastian's in time for dinner. She pushed open the front door and had to wait until Stanley finished walking all over the mail before she could pick it up. Amongst the brown envelopes and medical journals she subscribed to, she found a folded-up piece of notepaper. She opened it and saw this message in untidy capitals:

DIDN'T YOU LIKE MY FLOWERS?

In the hallway, Olivia looked up. The house suddenly felt different, as if she wasn't safe here. She called to Stanley who had been trotting around the kitchen, his nails echoing on the tiles. He came bounding towards her. She quickly scooped him up in her arms and left the house, slamming the door hard behind her. Why was her father taunting her like this? She'd had nothing to do with him for twenty-five years. He'd murdered her mother and sister. Wasn't that enough to live with, without the added torture of his constant reminders that he was still able to get to her?

Sebastian Lister lived on Alexandra Grove, within throwing distance of Finsbury Park, in a three-storey town house. He lived with his daughter Tilly, eighteen, who was studying for her A Levels, twelve-year-old Alistair and six-year-old twins Robert and Catherine. His wife, Rosemary, had died almost two years ago from breast cancer. It had hit the whole family hard. She had been diagnosed in April and was dead by July, so rapidly had the cancer coursed through her body. Since then, Sebastian had cut back on work to make the children his number-one priority. Tilly helped out as much as she could, but he was cognisant of her studies and her need for a life of her own. He refused to let her sacrifice herself for the sake of her younger brothers and sister. As far as Olivia was aware, he was coping relatively well, despite the lack of care he took in his own appearance.

On the way over, she stopped at an off-licence and bought a couple of bottles of wine and a few bars of chocolate for his kids. The twins would probably be in bed, but they could have them another time. The stop also allowed Stanley a few minutes to stretch his tiny legs. She would have to think of another way of transporting the little dog around London with her. It was only a matter of time before the police pulled her over for having a sausage dog balanced precariously on her lap. Maybe there was a special backpack for dogs to go in that she could buy. She doubted Stanley would be too much weight on her shoulders. She had a feeling this tiny dog was going to end up being quite high maintenance.

Olivia managed to find a parking space not far from Sebastian's house and rang the doorbell. She looked up; most lights in the house were on and she could hear the tell-tale sound of tiny feet pounding the stairs.

'If I have to come up there one more time, your Gruffalo's

going in the bin,' she heard Sebastian say before the door was opened.

'Problems?' she asked with a smile.

'Nothing that putting a pair of twins on eBay wouldn't solve. Come on in.'

'I thought they'd be asleep by now,' she said, stepping into the warmth of the house.

'They normally would be but they went around to a friend's house for dinner and the mother loaded them up on sweets and chocolate. They're bouncing off the walls up there.'

'Oh dear.'

'Go on through. I won't be a minute.'

'Am I all right to bring him in?' Olivia nodded to Stanley.

'Of course you are,' he said, scratching the little dog's head.

Sebastian stormed up the stairs while Olivia made her way into the living room. She pushed open the door and was hit with the heat from the wood burner and the soothing glow from the lamps dotted around the room. This was a proper family living room: a large television, bookcases jammed with colourful spines and DVDs, toys strewn about the floor, a comfortable sofa and magazines on the coffee table. This room was lived in. She plumped up the cushion on the sofa and sat down, feeling herself relaxing straight away. The house had atmosphere. It felt warm and safe, cosy and happy. She found herself smiling as she cast her eyes around the room, taking in family photographs and framed child paintings.

'Hello. Dad said you were popping over.' Tilly – tall, slim, with a shock of dyed black hair – entered the room. She wore a tight black vest top which advertised a band Olivia had never heard of. Her wrists were covered in charity bands and colourful braided bracelets and she wore silver rings on every finger. 'Oh my God, he's so cute,' she said, crouching to the floor as soon as she set eyes on Stanley. He bounded over to her and began jumping up at her and licking her hand. 'I didn't know you had a dog.'

'Neither did I until recently. He belonged to a friend who died.'

'I'm sorry,' Tilly said, standing up with the dog in her arms.

'Thanks. I like your hair,' Olivia said, eager to change the subject.

Tilly ran her fingers through her roughly cropped dyed black hair. 'I fancied a change.'

'It suits you. Are you still going out with… sorry, can't remember his name, the artist?'

She frowned as she thought. 'Rafael? God, no. I ended that months ago. He was a creep. Listen,' she said, sitting on the sofa next to her. 'Can I ask your advice?'

'Sure.' Olivia was taken aback. She had never been asked for advice by an eighteen-year-old. She hoped Tilly wasn't going to ask something personal.

'There's this programme that's come up at college offering me the chance of studying in America for three months. I've signed up but there is a limited number of spaces, so I may not get accepted. The thing is, if I am accepted, do you think I should go?'

'Definitely,' Olivia replied without having to think about it. 'It would be a wonderful opportunity for you. You'll learn more in those three months than you would in a whole year at home.'

'But what about Dad? I can't leave him with three kids on his own.' Her face wrinkled with worry lines on her forehead.

Olivia leaned forward and took Tilly's slender hand in her own. 'Tilly, you can't stop doing things just because your dad may need a babysitter. He'll tell you himself to go when he finds out. Besides, work is very flexible, and he can do more work from home. And Doctor Penhaligan has been itching to join our office for years. We could take him on part-time and he and your father can job-share. There's always a solution, Tilly.'

'I just don't want him to think I'm abandoning him,' she said. There was a catch in her voice.

'You're not abandoning him. You're starting your life. This is what you're supposed to do.'

Sebastian entered the room. 'I've finally got them to settle down, but I've had to promise them a pizza night at the weekend. They're not going around there again for a meal. She knows what Catherine's like on too much sugar, and Robert just eggs her on.' He slumped down on the sofa and let out a loud sigh. 'Anyway, what are you two talking about?'

Olivia and Tilly exchanged glances before Olivia bent down and pulled out two bottles of wine from her bag. 'We were debating which one to open first.'

Olivia watched Tilly pour herself a glass of wine before going upstairs to keep an eye on the twins and help Alistair with his maths homework. She asked if she could take Stanley with her. Within moments the sounds of cooing and laughter were heard. Olivia and Sebastian took their glasses, the rest of the bottle and the chocolate (which he said the kids were definitely not having) into the dining room.

'She's growing up,' Olivia remarked.

'Tilly? Yes. She's not a child anymore.'

'She's doing well at college, she was telling me.'

'Oh yes. They're all pleased with her.'

'You must be very proud.'

'I am. It's not been easy. I mean, she could easily have gone off the rails after Rosemary died, but she didn't.' He put his head in his hand. He looked up and his eyes were red with tears. 'It hits me out of nowhere sometimes. I know she's gone, but I loved her so much. I still do, and the thought of never seeing her again is like a punch to the stomach.'

Olivia went around and put her arms around him, resting her

head on his shoulder. 'I know. It's not something you get over, but something you learn to live with.'

'I know.'

'You're doing really well, Sebastian. I don't think I'd have been able to cope with four kids single-handedly. You should be incredibly proud of yourself.'

'I am. It's just… it's a struggle, you know? Every time the kids come home from school they've got a letter about some trip or project and they want more money from me. I had to pay the advance back to the publishers for that book about Danny Lee Grimes because I missed the deadline, then abandoned the book completely because I didn't have time to write it.' He lowered his voice. 'I'm worried I'm going to have to sell this place.'

'Really?'

'The mortgage payments are insane. I'd make a decent enough profit if I sold, but we'd have to move to a cheaper area.'

'I didn't know things were that bad.'

'They're not at the moment, but it won't be long before I get through our savings.'

'Sebastian, I'm sorry. Is there anything I can do?'

'No. I'm sorry. I shouldn't be burdening you with all this.'

'You're not. Look, I know you wouldn't take money as a gift, but how about a loan?'

'No,' he replied firmly. 'I appreciate you offering, and thank you, but I could never borrow money from a friend. It wouldn't be right.'

'Look, I've no intention of having kids, and my father put paid to the possibility of having nephews and nieces to leave anything to. I've done pretty well out of these books; the money is just sitting in my account. Let me help.'

Sebastian stood up and headed for the kitchen. Olivia followed. She stood in the doorway while he lifted the lid from a large pan and stirred the contents. Whatever was cooking smelled delicious.

'I'm sorry. I've embarrassed you,' Olivia eventually said.

'No. It was kind of you to offer. I just... I couldn't,' he said without turning to look at her.

'OK. I won't bring it up again, but any time you change your mind, let me know.'

Once they'd eaten – homemade soup and bread to begin with, then grilled seabass and new potatoes with vegetables – they spread Olivia's notes out on the dining table.

'Bloody hell. Do you really think he's killed six people?'

Olivia nodded, taking a piece of chocolate.

'The media are going to love this.'

'I know.'

'So, what do you want from me?'

'DI Foley and his team are asking me to profile this guy. They want me to be more specific than saying he's a white male in his late twenties to mid thirties, but that's not what I do,' Olivia said, sinking into her seat and looking fatigued. 'I can't just give them a name and address and tell them to go and arrest their killer.'

Sebastian looked down at the map where Olivia had marked the areas where the victims were murdered. 'Three victims in Brent, the others in Ealing, Hillingdon, Hackney and the City. We're talking central, north to north-west London. It's strange how his first and his most recent victims are close to each other, whereas all the others are out to the west.'

'What does that mean?'

'I don't know. When were the first and latest ones killed?'

Olivia opened her notebook. 'First victim was Neil Parker. He was killed on the fifth of November last year. The most recent one was Jessica Sheffield on the fifteenth of February.'

'So, three months between the two, more or less,' he said.

'Significant?'

'Well, as you know, crime isn't random. It's either planned or opportunistic. There's a theory that states a crime occurs when a victim's activity space intersects with the murderer's activity space.'

'What do you mean by "activity space"?'

'Well.' He took a sip of the strong coffee and picked up a Mars bar from the pile Olivia had dumped on the table. 'We all have our own activity spaces which are our homes, places of work, places we go to on a regular basis like the gym, the supermarket, the park et cetera. Now, to get to and from these places we travel on personal paths. So, if you picture in your mind a map of where your home is, the office is, the swimming pool is, and draw lines between them, they're the personal paths getting you to and from your activity spaces.'

'OK. Go on.'

'Now, you're not the only person who uses those activity spaces and personal paths. Other people use the swimming pool and I use the same office as you, so everyone's map will look different. We all intersect with each other from time to time. It's these events that lead to crimes being committed.'

'So, say I'm at the pool and so are a couple of dozen other people, there is a higher likelihood of a crime taking place because of the number of people there compared to when I'm at home?'

'Yes. Take in other factors too, like the car park. Loads of cars are parked there, and I'm guessing it's not very well lit, as they never are, so car thieves will purposely target that area because it's easy pickings.'

'I'm with you,' she said, nodding while making notes.

'Say our killer had a particular victim in mind – tall and blonde, for example. That's his trigger. He's been to work, and he decides to go for a swim. He parks in the car park, gets out and spots a tall blonde woman heading for the building. Something in his mind snaps that she's going to be his next victim. She's crossed into his activity space and, unknowingly, made herself a victim.'

'She's in the wrong place at the wrong time.'

'I hate that saying,' he said. 'We live in a democracy. We have freedom of movement. Unless you're trespassing on private land, there's no such thing as being in the wrong place at the wrong time. We're free to go anywhere we want, when we want.'

'I'd not thought of it like that,' Olivia said. 'So, he could have just been passing any of these locations and seen someone that triggered something that made him want to kill them?'

'Not necessarily. The three in Brent are interesting,' Sebastian said, picking up the map again. 'One thing we can say for certain is that he knows the borough of Brent well. He's killed there three times. He's comfortable, he knows the layout and he's confident he can kill without detection.'

'But that doesn't mean he lives in Brent, does it?'

'No. Maybe he lived there a couple of years ago, maybe he works in the area, maybe he has a partner who lives there, maybe his parents live there. We move about now more than we used to, so all we can say at the moment is that he's very familiar with Brent. There is one area of geographical profiling that interests me.'

'What's that?'

'We all have areas that we know and feel safe in; we call them our comfort zones. That's usually where our home is. The killer will want to stay local as he knows the area, but he won't want to kill on his own doorstep, so there needs to be a buffer zone.'

'Sort of like a safe area between the two.'

'Exactly. So, you've got this cluster of three in Brent,' Sebastian said, pointing at the map. 'And then two others close-ish in Hackney and the City. In the middle, you have—' He stopped and looked up at Olivia.

'What? What's in the middle?'

He swallowed hard. 'Camden.'

'That's where I live.'

Despite efforts from Sebastian to get Olivia to stay the night, she and Stanley braved the darkened London streets and headed back to Modbury Gardens. She paid the traffic very little heed and stopped at red lights and stop signs by rote rather than paying particular attention. Her mind was working overtime. Surely this wasn't about her. There was no way the killer would have guessed she'd end up working with the police in this case. But maybe she wasn't a target in the personal sense of the term, maybe she was simply in a list of potential targets. She ticked all of the boxes on the killer's list of requirements for his victims. She was a single female who lived alone, and she would definitely fight back if confronted. As much as she hated to think it, Olivia was a prime candidate to be a victim.

They pulled up outside her house. She looked at the building and saw it was in darkness. Nothing unusual in that, but the long shadows created by the yellow sodium of the streetlights gave an eerie sense of foreboding. She looked around her. Most of her neighbours' houses were dark. They were all safely tucked up in bed, snoring gently, while she was petrified on her own doorstep, fearful of what else might have been put through her letterbox while she was out.

She unlocked the front door and entered, swiped her fob over the alarm and closed the door behind her. She reactivated the alarm, so should any doors or windows be tampered with, the whole cul-de-sac would hear about it. She put Stanley on the floor. He trotted into the kitchen and she followed, turning on all the lights.

Nothing else had been posted through her door and there was no sign of anyone trying to gain entry. She silently berated herself for her paranoid thinking. If this was what working on an active investigation did to her, then this would be her first and final one. It was bad enough having serial murderers safely locked in prison cells sending her messages and asking for her used underwear, but a killer on the loose was unpredictable, and despite having an expensive security system, concealed cameras and alarmed windows and doors, Olivia still felt her safety was compromised somehow.

Stanley emptied his water bowl. He'd eaten some leftover seabass at Sebastian's and Olivia made a mental note to pop to a pet shop tomorrow to get him everything he needed. For the time being, she decided he could sleep on her bed. He'd be no substitute for a German shepherd should anyone break in, but he was company. She couldn't help but smile when she looked down at his adorable face.

In her bedroom she quickly changed into tartan pyjamas and pulled back the duvet. Stanley had struggled to jump up to the bed, so she'd given him a helping hand. She sat on the edge of the bed, applied hand cream and swung her legs up. She snuggled down and reached over to turn off the bedside lamp when her eyes landed on the copy of Sebastian's book about her father.

Who had done this, and why? There was no way someone could have been in her home without her knowing. Her security system informed her through an app on her phone if there was any interference when the house was alarmed, and she hadn't received any such alert.

She sat up and grabbed her iPhone. She logged on to the security app, checked notifications and the history. The only person who had activated and deactivated the alarm had been herself when she'd left for work and come home again. She threw back the duvet and jumped out of bed. She went into the hallway and looked at the display on the wall to see if there were any error messages displayed that the app hadn't picked up, and that's when she noticed the missing spare set of keys from the hook.

The only people who had been in her house recently were Jessica, Amyas, Sam from next door and... Ethan. Had he taken the keys while she'd been crying on the floor of her en suite bathroom after their disastrous sex session? If so, why? What did he want from her? Or was it whoever her dad had sent round with the flowers? Had they, somehow, managed to get the keys? Unless Ethan had been sent by her father…

'Jesus Christ!' she chastised herself aloud. 'You're taking paranoid to the next level. Just change the fucking locks.'

There was a simple solution. There always was. Yes, it would be an inconvenience to change the locks and alter the override code on the alarm system, but if it was something she had to do in order to feel safe, she'd do it.

Olivia looked at the front door as she went back to her bedroom. The door was locked with a Yale and a Chubb. There were two bolts at the top and bottom of the door and the security chain was on. If someone tried to break in, they'd have to make a hell of a lot of noise and Olivia would have plenty of time to call the police and arm herself.

She went back to bed. Stanley must have sensed her anxiety because he padded up the bed and curled up on the pillow next to her.

'I hope Jessica taught you Krav Maga,' she said to him.

Chapter Twenty-Seven

Sam Halliday sat on the edge of his bed. The room was in darkness and the curtains were wide open. The light from the streetlamps outside cast long shadows in the room. He looked at his reflection in the mirror on the wall and hated what he saw.

Sam was naked, except for the underpants he'd stolen from Olivia's bedroom. They were a tight fit, but comfortable. His body was slim and small, nothing impressive. He leaned forward and turned his head, looking at himself from all angles, noting his dull eyes that were too close together, his thin lips, his weak jawline. There was nothing striking about him, nothing enviable or fanciable. People didn't look at Sam and wink or flirt or swoon. He was a bland, uninteresting lump of emptiness.

'Why would Olivia fancy you?' he asked himself. His voice was low, a heavy whisper. 'Look at the state of you. You've got nothing to offer her.' He jumped up and pulled the underpants down and looked himself up and down. 'Do you think she'll be impressed with that?' he spat, grabbing himself in the crotch. 'You've seen the men she likes: older, rugged, someone with a past, with life experience, like that copper or that leather biker bloke. You're pathetic compared to them.'

'I'm not,' he immediately replied to himself. 'I'm intelligent. I'm kind. I'm caring. Anyone would be lucky to have me in their lives.'

'Is that what your mum told you?'

'Fucking shut up!' he screamed.

He threw himself onto the bed, grabbed the pillow and pulled it over his head. He couldn't block out the thoughts running around his mind and he continued to curse himself.

The muffled sound of a siren, a car horn and a door slamming made him sit up. He looked at the clock. It was well after midnight and the noises from outside still intruded.

Why was it so noisy in London? Didn't people ever sleep, for crying out loud?

He pulled his legs up to his chest and hugged himself tight against the cold. He had tears in his eyes. He hated London with a passion.

When living in Devon with his parents, he had found the silence deafening. He had been surrounded by openness and space and he'd felt like it was killing him. He'd wanted to be out in the world, to experience what life had to offer beyond the farm. When that dream became a reality, he had discovered how much he preferred the solitude, the birdsong, the stars in the sky, the sounds of nature.

London was a place of violence. Sirens could be heard twenty-four hours a day. The air stank of petrol fumes. It lingered and stuck to the insides of his nostrils and the back of his throat. He felt dirty just riding to the hospital on his bike. His hair always seemed to feel greasy. How could people survive here? Nobody spoke. Nobody said hello or smiled or made eye contact. Buses were silent of chatter but full of the tinny noise of music coming from headphones. Everyone looked so defeated, sad, depressed, angry.

Even his fellow junior doctors didn't chat. There was no camaraderie, no banter, no drinks in the pub at the end of the week, or if there were, they didn't invite him. Why? Was the problem with him or with them?

He'd been in London for a year and only one person had been kind to him, and that was Olivia. She had taken him in after the attempted mugging. She'd tended to his injuries, fed him, gave him succour when she obviously had issues of her own. She smiled at him. It was the first smile he'd received in a year and it had lit up his heart. Olivia was beautiful. He needed her in his life. She would make everything right. He could enjoy life, he would learn to like London, if he had Olivia.

Chapter Twenty-Eight

Thursday 22nd February 2024

Olivia barely slept. After checking all the windows and locks to make sure they hadn't been tampered with, she went into her office and opened her laptop. There were concealed cameras above both entrances to her house, front and back, and footage was saved for seven days before being deleted. If someone had entered her home yesterday while she wasn't here and left a copy of the book about her serial killer father on her bedside table, she'd know who it was.

She had no idea what time the intruder had entered so had to watch from early morning when she'd left for work. As usual, she'd locked the door with both locks, tried the handle several times to make sure it was secure and given a quick glance up to where the camera was situated before trotting off down the steps with Stanley under her arms. She'd mounted her scooter and set off for work.

Her eyes grew heavy as she glared at the monotony of nothing happening on the screen. Half an hour later, a delivery man pulled up outside. He knocked loudly on the door and waited a few moments before knocking again. It was a clear picture and Olivia could easily make out his features. He had dark curly hair beneath his brown baseball cap. He went back down the steps and up to the house next door to see if they would take her package. A minute or two later, he was back at Olivia's door, putting a card through her letterbox. Within moments of him reversing down the cul-de-sac, Olivia nodded off, slumped over her desk.

She had woken fitfully throughout the night. She had jumped awake from a disturbing dream she couldn't remember, looked back at the laptop, which had slipped into sleep mode, and decided to join it.

Years ago, when her father had first been arrested and Olivia moved in with her grandparents in Tower Hamlets, she'd had terrible nightmares about what had happened to her mother and sister. She'd wake up screaming, dripping with sweat, to find her grandmother at the side of her bed holding her hand. When the nightmares stopped, the sleepwalking began. On many occasions her grandfather told her that he'd found her at the bottom of the garden, trying to climb over the fence while she was asleep, just like she had done to escape her murderous father.

Had the sleepwalking returned? She'd thought she was stronger now. If she could survive the murder of her family, the constant bullying and name-calling from her fellow pupils at school, the long, slow, agonising death of her grandmother from lung cancer and the decline of her grandfather's mental health before he eventually succumbed to Alzheimer's disease, surely she could cope with visiting a man she had banished from her life a quarter of a century ago. Obviously not. Had she been up to the top floor, picked up the book and brought it back to her bedroom with her while still asleep? It was possible. In fact, as none of the locks, doors and windows had been tampered with, it was probable. Maybe it was time to book an appointment with a therapist again.

Olivia was woken at six o'clock by Stanley yapping. He needed to go outside. She padded down the stairs, grabbed her dressing gown from her bedroom and went into the kitchen where she unlocked the back door and let him out into the dark morning. She stood in the doorway beneath the sensor light above and shivered.

Back in the kitchen, she set about making breakfast. She couldn't stomach anything too heavy so plumped for a slice of toast and coffee so strong it could beat her in an arm-wrestling contest. It tasted foul, but it woke her up. She had a feeling today was going to be a long and difficult day.

A cold shower set the blood running to every part of her body and once she'd brushed her teeth and dressed in black trousers, a cream sweater and black Doc Martens, she felt ready to leave the house. She looked at Stanley who had set up home on the fluffy throw on the Chesterfield in the living room. He looked back at her with his big brown eyes.

'I promise I'll pop to the pet shop today and get you a proper bed,' she said to him.

There was a knock on the door.

Stanley got there before her. She picked him up and pulled open the door to find Sam Halliday on the doorstep holding a cardboard box.

'This was delivered yesterday. I thought I'd bring it round,' he said with a smile. He looked younger dressed in casual clothing: jeans, a hooded sweater and scuffed Converse trainers. Olivia was about to thank him when he spotted Stanley. 'Good morning, Stanley,' he said, scratching under the young dog's chin. 'I think he likes me,' he said as the dog licked his hand. 'My mum always

The Mind of a Murderer

says, never trust a person who doesn't like dogs, but always trust a dog who doesn't like a person.'

'Wise woman. Sorry, come in.' She stepped back and made room for Sam to enter. Once the door was closed, she placed Stanley on the floor. He ran straight for Sam who sat on the floor and began playing with him.

'They're great companions, aren't they? You're never lonely if you have a dog.'

'So I've been told. Unfortunately, it's not practical trying to balance him on my scooter.'

'You take him to work?'

'I can't leave him here on his own all day. Poor thing.'

'Well, I'm on nights at the moment. I can take him out for walks during the day, if you like.'

'I couldn't ask you to do that.'

'You haven't. I've offered. It would get me out of my basement for some fresh air and allow this little guy to stretch his legs.'

'Are you sure?'

'Yes. I'd love it.'

'I'd really appreciate that, Sam. Thank you.' It would make sense for someone to come in and walk him while she was at work until she could make her mind up on how she could transport Stanley to and from work. The only problem was, Sam would need a key. Nobody had ever had a key to her house. Could she trust Sam? That was Olivia's problem, she didn't trust anyone apart from Sebastian. She couldn't live a life permanently on edge and thinking everyone was a potential killer. She needed to open herself up more if she was going to have any kind of a normal life.

She remembered the missing set of keys and her mind immediately went into overdrive. She was in the midst of a personal crisis where she didn't know if she was capable of walking up to the top floor to retrieve a book without realising. If she'd done that, could she have moved her keys, somehow?

'Hang on,' she said to Sam, going into the kitchen and

grabbing a single front-door key from a drawer. When she had high-security locks fitted, she chose a top-of-the-range system that needed a card with an identity number attached, should she require more copies. The missing one would cost a fortune to replace. She felt reluctant to give the key to Sam.

She looked him in the eye and gave him a quick assessment. He was a young man, a junior doctor, living in a world that didn't make sense to him. He was nervous, scared, frightened of his own shadow and in need of a friend. She could be the one to help him settle in London. She wanted to help him. 'I'd better talk you through the alarm,' she said.

'I've only got one key for the front door,' she said, handing it to him. 'I can't find a full set at the moment. This fob is for the alarm. Just wave it in front of the panel when you come in and leave, and it automatically sets everything. You don't have to press any buttons.'

Sam smiled as he took the key from her. Their fingers touched briefly.

'I'll look after him. You have nothing to worry about.'

Olivia had only been sitting at her desk in her office for five minutes when Daisy called to say DI Foley was here to see her. As she heard him pounding up the stairs, she looked at her reflection in the computer screen and neatened up her hair. There was a gentle knock on the door and it opened without her giving permission.

'Good morning,' he said as he entered the room. He was wearing a dark-grey suit and matching tie. His once white shirt had dulled due to over-washing and his shoes were in urgent need of a polish. He looked shattered. Olivia wondered if he'd had as bad a night's sleep as she'd endured.

She offered a weak smile. 'Would you like a coffee?'

The Mind of a Murderer

'I've lost count of the number of coffees I've had since midnight. Any more and I'll be able to see through time.'

'Haven't you been to bed yet?'

'No. We've made an arrest,' he said as he slumped down into the seat opposite Olivia's desk. There was a satisfied smile on his lips.

'Really? Who?'

'Sean Fincher. He's twenty-three years old. He lives in a council flat on Rosemead Avenue. He's practically on the same page of the A-to-Z as Sarah, Phoebe and Joanne.'

'How did you come across him?' Olivia asked. Despite the relief in Foley's voice, she was keeping an open mind.

'A call from a neighbour said he'd been acting suspiciously lately. She said he'd always been quiet, but lately he'd started to frighten her. He's also been cleaning his car out on a regular basis too, almost every weekend. We ran his registration plate through the ANPR, and we've got him at three locations when the murders took place.'

'Which murders?'

'He was at the bonfire party and the Christmas tree light switch-on where Neil and Calvin were murdered. His car was also at Stilecroft Gardens on the day Joanne Douglas was killed.'

'Did he give a reason for being there?'

'He started to until his solicitor told him to keep quiet. We've been conducting a search on his flat and we're going to interview him again. Obviously, I can't let you sit in on the interview, but I was wondering if you'd like to observe?'

'I'll get my coat,' Olivia said, standing up, trying not to seem too eager. 'Did he resist arrest at all?' she asked as she put her coat on and began switching off her computer and desk lamp.

'No. He answered the door, our officers arrested him, and he walked calmly to the car. Why?' he asked when he noticed her frown.

'No reason.'

'Yes, there is. Why didn't he resist arrest?'

'There are a couple of reasons for that: maybe he's tired of killing and wants to get caught to stop himself from claiming another victim, or there's something else going on. You don't have any forensic evidence from the crime scenes – he'll know this, and he'll also know you'll have to release him without such evidence. You need to be careful, Amyas. If this guy is your killer, he's playing a game with you. A game he intends to win.'

Chapter Twenty-Nine

The interview with Sean Fincher was to be conducted by DI Foley and DS Rippner. DS Goodfellow led Olivia into the observation room, which was more like a cubby hole, it was so small.

In front of the large glass window was a small desk with two chairs and two microphones. They sat down with a bottle of water each and made themselves comfortable. Olivia took a notebook and pen out of her bag.

'The interview is going to be taped and videoed,' Holly began. 'Mr Fincher has been read his rights and is under caution. Both DI Foley and DS Rippner are wearing earpieces, and whatever you say into the microphone, they'll both be able to hear. They're not automatically switched on. You have to hold down the button to speak. When you let go, it cuts transmission.'

The door to the interview room opened and Sean Fincher was led in with his solicitor following. Olivia sank in her chair.

'Is anything wrong?' Holly asked.

'No.'

'Do you know him?'

'No.'

'Recognise him?'

'No. It's not that.'

'What is it?'

Olivia shook her head. She turned to Holly. 'He's not your killer.'

Sean Fincher stood at well over six feet tall. He was painfully thin, and had dyed black hair tied back in an untidy ponytail. He had piercings in both ears, in his nose and bottom lip, and a tattoo of a spider's web on his neck. The backs of his hands were tattooed to make them look skeletal. He was deathly pale with wide staring eyes. He wore black skinny jeans and black boots with the laces missing and a black hooded jumper a size too big for him. With his shoulders hunched and his head down, he headed for the far side of the table and took a seat. His solicitor pulled out a chair and sat next to him. She took out a folder from her briefcase and opened it, riffling through her notes while Foley and Rippner closed the door behind them and started proceedings.

'How do you know he's not the killer, just by looking at him?' Holly asked.

'The reason the killer has been able to escape from the murder scenes is because he blends in with the area. Don't you think this guy would have stood out on Spencer Road and Stilecroft Gardens?'

'But we know he didn't make his getaway in broad daylight. The killings took place in the late afternoon and early evening. He could have left in the middle of the night, for all we know.'

'But he's researched his victims. He's been in the neighbourhoods before he's made his kills. How else did he know which houses to target? He'll have visited at all different hours of the day, so he knows when to strike. He would have stood out a mile. You've read the house-to-house reports; have any neighbours mentioned a walking skeleton?'

'No.'

'Exactly. He is not your killer.'

'Shit. Foley is not going to be happy,' Holly said.

'Mr Fincher,' Foley began. 'Can you tell us where you were on the night of November the fifth last year?'

Olivia sighed. It was going to be a long interview.

Sean admitted to being at the fireworks display, the Christmas lights switch-on and Vale Farm Sports Ground on the dates when the three people had been murdered. He answered in a clear and concise voice. On tape, he would have sounded confident, but he kept fidgeting and playing with his fingers, evidence he was fearful of where this interview was going. The longer it went on, the more unstable he became.

'I'm showing Mr Fincher photographs labelled as ID one to seven,' Foley said as he laid out pictures of the victims in front of him. 'Do you recognise any of these people?'

Sean leaned forward and took a detailed look. 'I recognise that one, and that one,' he answered in a soft voice.

'For the benefit of the recording, Mr Fincher has identified Jessica Sheffield and Phoebe Harper. How do you know them?'

'I don't. I recognise them from the newspapers. They've been killed. I'm guessing they've all been killed.'

'Do you know anything about their deaths, Mr Fincher?'

'No.'

'In your flat, we found a series of weapons. I'm showing Mr Fincher photographs of some of the items which have been identified as the following: a zombie hammer, a trigger-assisted trench knife, a butterfly knife, and a machete. Can you tell us why you have these items?'

Olivia shook her head as she made a note of the weapons.

'They're props. They're for my work,' he said. His voice had increased an octave.

'What work is that?'

'I work for Zombie Battle UK. I have done for four years. People pay to be part of an end-of-the-world experience and I play a zombie,' he said, almost embarrassed.

Rippner and Foley exchanged glances. Rippner didn't even try to hide his snigger.

'He's not your killer, Foley,' Olivia said through the earpiece.

Foley glanced at the window for a split second before turning back to his notes.

'Mr Fincher,' Foley continued, ignoring Olivia, 'were you with anyone on the nights of November the fifth, December the first, and January the eighteenth?'

'No.'

'Why did you attend such public events alone?'

'Foley, he's not your killer. There's no reason to keep questioning him,' Olivia said, getting agitated.

'You don't have to answer that question,' Sean's solicitor instructed.

'I went because I wanted to be around people,' he replied, picking at the sleeve of his jumper.

'Aren't you around enough people at work when you're playing at zombies?' Leon asked, his question dripping with sarcasm.

'It's not the same,' Sean replied, his head down. 'I don't go out much. I don't... I don't like being outside. I'm trying to do things to help me get better at socialising.'

'You think having these weapons in your flat is going to help you make friends?' Leon sniggered.

'They're not real weapons. They're props.'

'They are offensive, illegal weapons which could cause serious damage. You should not be keeping them in your flat,' Foley said. 'Mr Fincher, are you single?'

'That question is irrelevant,' his solicitor said.

'Foley, for the last time, he is not your killer. Why are you questioning him like this?' Olivia almost shouted into the microphone. 'Are you sure this thing is switched on?' she asked Holly.

'Yes.'

'Yes. I'm single,' Sean said, a hint of sadness in his voice.

'I'm not surprised,' Leon muttered under his breath but loudly enough for all of them to hear.

'I need to talk to you right now,' Olivia said into the microphone. 'Right now, Amyas.' She knew using his first name would cause a reaction in him.

'Interview terminated at' – he looked at his watch – '11:07,' Foley said, standing up and leaving the room.

Olivia met him in the corridor.

'What the hell is going on in there?' she asked. 'Were you even listening to what I was saying? Sean Fincher is not your killer.'

'He was at three of the crime scenes—'

'No,' she interrupted. 'He was in three very public places along with hundreds of other people. In any case, Joanne Douglas wasn't killed at a public event. She was killed indoors. Yes, Sean Fincher was close by at the time of her death but you're making him fit what you perceive the killer will look like, and you're wrong.'

'I doubt one person was at all three events.'

'You don't know that. Besides, I've told you the kind of person you're looking for. The reason there are no witnesses to the killer leaving the scenes of the crimes is because he fits in with his surroundings. He belongs in those kinds of neighbourhoods. Do you think a tall, skinny bloke like Fincher with dyed black hair and pasty skin would blend in on Stilecroft Gardens and Dollis Hill? No, he wouldn't. He's not your killer, and you know it.'

Foley stepped away. He squeezed the bridge of his nose.

'And the way you're questioning him in there is pure character assassination. He's scared. He obviously has emotional and behavioural issues which he's working through and you're going to set him back years. Leon certainly is, with his unprofessional conduct.'

'Fuck.' Foley kicked the wall in anger.

Olivia walked up to him and placed her hand on his shoulder. 'I know you're desperate to catch the killer. I know you've got people on your back, but you've got the wrong man in there. You need to let him go.'

'I need to charge somebody,' he said quietly.

'I know you do. But not him.'

'If I charge him, it will keep the press off my back, and I can still keep looking.'

'What? You're not thinking straight. Do you have any idea what being held on remand will do to someone like Sean Fincher? It will destroy him.'

'He had weapons in his flat that scared even me,' Foley said. His tone had softened.

'And he's given you a valid reason why he has them. Confiscate them if they're illegal, slap him with a caution, but do not charge him with murder.'

Foley didn't say anything. His face was red with rage. He was a mass of pent-up frustration, itching to explode.

Olivia continued: 'You charge him, and his face will be on the front page of every newspaper tomorrow. The whole of the country will have him down as a serial killer. When you eventually release him, all charges dropped, the press will bury that news on page twenty-six and nobody will read it. Wherever he goes, whatever job he applies for, people will see him as a murderer. You'll ruin his life. Is that what you want?'

He turned away and headed back for the interview room.

'Where are you going?' Olivia asked.

'To continue the interview.'

'Then I'm not watching,' she said, heading down the corridor.

'What?'

'I refuse to be a party to this. I refuse to sit and watch you destroy an innocent man, just to buy yourself a few temporary brownie points with the press. You're on your own, Amyas. You want any more help, find yourself another psychologist.'

She took long strides, her shoes clacking loudly on the tiled floor. She didn't know DI Foley, but had at least thought him a man of integrity. Obviously not. She tore off her visitor's pass and tossed it onto the reception desk. She didn't want to work alongside a man who used underhand tactics or a police force that allowed such things to happen.

Stubborn detectives were another reason to add to the ever-growing list of why she would not work on active cases.

As she left the building and crossed the car park, she buttoned up her coat. Her mind was whirling and she wondered what would happen to Sean Fincher once Foley and Rippner had torn him apart. Poor guy.

She stopped at the entrance to the police station car park and looked around her. She had no idea which way would be the best way to go to get a taxi. She turned left and walked away, head high and shoulders back, completely oblivious that she was being watched by a man behind the wheel of a car in front of her. He had a long-lens camera pointed straight at her and took several photographs as she passed him on the other side of the road.

Chapter Thirty

STATION GROVE, WEMBLEY

Thursday 22nd February 2024, 2:15 p.m.

I knocked on the door, stood back and waited for it to be opened.

'Mrs Cheetham?'

'Yes,' she replied.

'Sorry to disturb you, love, but I've been doing some work for your neighbour on the roof, and I think I might have knocked your Sky dish. Do you want to check if it's working all right? If not, I'll pop back up and sort it out for you.'

'Oh. Fine: I'll just check. Come on in.'

And with that little exchange, I had my next victim.

It never fails to surprise me, the things people will believe. Because I'm standing on her doorstep wearing the identifiable uniform of a trade worker and have a set of ladders propped up against a white van, people assume I am who I say I am. Today, I'm a roofer. Tomorrow, if I wear a hi-vis jacket and carry a theodolite on a tripod, I could be planning where to erect a set of traffic lights.

Mrs Kerry Cheetham didn't even ask how I knew her name. There's no reason for me to know her name, I'm supposedly doing work on the house next door. Yet, she didn't question me at all. She just let me in. She's practically asking to be murdered.

Kerry walks away from the door and goes into the living room. I close the door behind me which locks with the Yale. I quietly push up the snib so it can't be opened quickly. If Kerry is a fighter and runs for the front door, she'll be slowed down by it being locked.

I've been watching Kerry for a while. I know she lives on her own. I know she isn't working at the moment, but I've followed her to the job centre, so I know she's looking. She gets visited every morning by her dad on his way to the Tube station just a flight of stairs away. They chat on the doorstep, have a bit of a laugh, he gives her a kiss on the cheek and on he goes to begin his day. Kerry watches him climb the steps until he's out of view before going back into the house. They do the same in reverse when he comes home from work at the end of the day.

She doesn't go out much. I'm guessing she's been out of work for a while and money is a little tight. She only seems to leave the house when the journey is necessary. She shops for essentials and rarely puts anything in her basket that could be counted as a luxury.

Kerry has an aura about her, and it's an unhappy one. She seems to be defeated by life. There's a mark on the third finger of her left hand, showing she's recently split from a husband. Her life isn't panning out the way she imagined. Nobody has a dream to live in an end-of-terrace house next to a noisy Tube station with no job, no friends to speak of and little expendable cash. I want to know just how much this diffident thirty-something actually values her life. How much of a struggle will she put up when she realises her time is up?

I follow her into the living room. It's cold in here. The radiators aren't on, and neither is the electric fire. She's wearing thick jogging bottoms, comfortable slippers, and a heavy hooded jumper. She's obviously rationing when to put the heating on, so keeping warm by dressing in layers.

She picks up the remote, points it at the television in the corner of the room and turns it on. She begins flicking through the channels. At this time of the afternoon, there's very little worth watching. I can understand why she'd rather sit in silence and read. I tilt my head to see the well-thumbed library book on the sofa – something brightly coloured by Sophie Kinsella. It looks like pure escapism. Not something I'd read.

'Everything seems to be working perfectly,' she says, turning off the television.

'That's good. Do you want to check your internet connection, too, just in case?'

'Sure.'

She looks around the back of the television.

'Everything seems fine. The blue light is still on. Thanks for checking. It's very decent of you.'

'You're welcome.'

At this point, I'd turn and go back to the door, but I want to make Kerry feel awkward in her own home. This is supposed to be her place of safety, but I know I'll get excited when she gets scared, and by lingering in the doorway, I can already see the smile begin to fall from her lips and her eyes widen slightly. She's unnerved.

'Is there… is there anything else?'

I put my bag down on the floor, reach inside and take out my large, clean, sharp carving knife.

'I'd really like to see how many stabs it will take to kill you.'

Kerry's face changes within the blink of an eye. The tears come like a tap has been turned on and fall down her face. She doesn't wipe them away. She backs up until she hits the fireplace. She tries to speak, but the words won't come. She's visibly shaking. Fear has already gripped her, and I haven't even done anything yet.

'Please... don't hurt me,' she cries. 'I don't have much, but there's a few items of jewellery upstairs you can take.'

'I don't want to rob you, Kerry. That's not why I'm here,' I tell her, holding the knife up.

'Oh God. Please. Don't rape me. Please. I'm begging you.'

'I'm not going to rape you, Kerry. Calm the fuck down.'

She holds onto the fireplace, fearing her legs are about to give way. 'W-what do you want?'

'I've already said, I want to see how many stab wounds it will take to kill you.'

'No!' she cries. 'I don't want to die. I don't. Please. Don't kill me.'

'Surely you're not happy with how your life is going right now? I'd have thought death would be preferable to misery.'

'I do... I do want to live.'

'Really?'

'Yes,' she nods, sucking up her tears. 'Yes. Yes, I do. I want to live.'

'Oh,' I say, with mock surprise. I step away from the door and gesture towards it. 'You'd better make a run for it then.'

Kerry doesn't even wait to see if I'm joking or not. She pushes herself off the fireplace and heads for the door. She practically falls into the hallway, hurtles to the front door and tries to open it. She panics. With shaking fingers, she manages to flick the snib and open the door with the Yale. The light from outside and a cold breeze rush in. She's millimetres away from freedom. I slam the door closed from behind her. She looks up at me, fear etched on her face, tears streaming down her cheeks.

'Sorry, Kerry. My game, my rules.'

Her mouth falls open and a muffled cry comes out as I stab her in the stomach.

6 p.m.

Kerry's slumped on the floor of her bedroom. Her tracksuit bottoms are drenched in blood. Her jumper is torn where the knife sliced through it and is stained with her own blood. She's rapidly losing consciousness. When I picked her up from the living room floor and carried her upstairs, she looked me in the eye and asked me again not to rape her. I looked at her and winked. I had no intention of raping her, but that was obviously more terrifying to her than dying, so I let her think that was my plan all along.

I placed her on the floor leaning against the wall and went and sat on the end of the unmade double bed. I just sat there and watched her. Her hands were clasped against the deepest wound in her stomach. She was trying to stem the flow of blood, but it was no use. Her fingers were red where the blood had run out, and she had many other stab wounds where life was haemorrhaging from her.

Daylight is now fading and the small room is gradually darkening. I look at my watch. There's plenty of time left.

'My boyfriend will be home soon,' Kerry says. Her breathing has become more laboured.

I laugh. I know what she's trying to do.

'That would be the invisible man, would it?' I ask her. 'I've been watching this house for weeks. You live on your own. You get one visitor every morning and that's your dad on his way to the train station. He pops round for a few minutes to say good morning, and for a few minutes on his way home. You spend your days looking for a job. When you go out, it's only to the local shops for milk and bread. You daren't spend much because you're worried how long your savings are going to last. You refuse to meet with your friends. You don't have a boyfriend. You've been single since you changed your relationship status on Facebook last September.'

Kerry's eyes widen. 'How do you know all this?'

The Mind of a Murderer

'Research. I like to know everything I can about my victims.' I look at my watch again.

'You've done this before?'

'Oh yes.'

She winces as she tries to move. She's in a great deal of pain. 'Are you the man in the papers? The serial killer?'

I smile. She's the first of my victims to know who I am. I'm famous. I'm infamous.

I smile.

'You killed a detective?'

'I needed coverage.'

'Why are you keeping me alive?'

'I'm not. Don't worry, you'll be dead very soon,' I say nonchalantly.

Kerry cries. Tears fall down her face 'No, please. You don't have to kill me.'

'I do.'

'No. You don't. You can leave now. I promise, I won't identify you to the police. I'll say you wore a mask.'

'What would be the point of that? I need another victim. The more I kill, the harder the police will look for me, the more the people of London will be scared and the more chance I'll have of meeting the great Olivia Winter.'

'Who's she?'

How can she not know who Olivia Winter is? She's the best.

I get up from the bed and crouch down on my knees in front of her. She tries to back away from me, but there's nowhere for her to go.

'Oh, Olivia is the queen when it comes to serial killers. She's met them all. She's been around the world interviewing them in their cells, listening to their stories, writing about them, and people take notice of what she has to say. She'll write about me, too. But I'm different from all the others.'

'In what way?'

'Let me tell you something. When killers strike, people read about them in the news and they think they're just sadistic people who stab, shoot, whatever, then leave. I can't speak for all killers, obviously, but for me, that's not enough. I thought it was. That's what I did with my first couple of victims, but I wanted more. Do you know what I mean?'

She's struggling to hold in her emotions. Her bottom lip is quivering. She shakes her head.

'No. I don't suppose you do. You see, the thing for me is that I need the closeness. I need to watch you die. I need to listen to you scream. I need to hear the last breath leave your body. I need to be involved in all of it so that when I go home and think about this moment, I can relive everything from the second I saw the fear and terror in your eyes, to the blank look that will come once life has left you. That will hold a special place in my heart,' I say with a smile on my face and a hand on my chest.

I take an iPhone from my inside jacket pocket, open the camera, point it at Kerry's face and take a picture. The light from the flash lights up the whole room. Kerry recoils.

I look at my phone. 'You're beautiful when you cry. It gives you a look of childlike innocence. I'll take a few more when you've gone. I hope you don't mind.'

More tears fall. Kerry tries to stop them by biting her lip to stave off the emotion, but it doesn't work. I take two more photos of her.

'I don't have any photos of my first kills. I don't even remember them too clearly. When I went home after killing Calvin, I didn't feel anything. I was just... I don't know, void of emotion. Now, Sarah, she was my first proper victim. I spent the whole night with Sarah. I didn't do anything with her, nothing sexual, I just sat and watched her, and we chatted, like you and I are doing now. I explained everything to her, why and how I'd chosen her, how much she actually meant to me. I know she couldn't hear what I was saying, unlike you, but I like to think she knew and understood how important she was to me. As are you. You'll all be important to me.'

'This is wrong. What you're doing is wrong,' Kerry says, almost inaudible through her tears.

'Who's to say what's right and wrong anymore? Have you seen the world we're living in? It's all shit. It's all pointless. Governments don't give a fuck about us anymore. Billionaires are getting richer, and the hard workers are getting poorer. The planet is dying. We're killing it and nobody cares, so why not do what you enjoy while there's still time.'

'I care,' Kerry says.

'Sorry?'

'I said, I care. About the planet. About other people.'

'And look where that's got you, Kerry. If you'd been more selfish, more of a fighter, you might not have been made redundant. You might even have got that job in Lloyds you went for last month.'

'How—?'

I hold up a hand to silence her and listen intently to what is happening outside. In the distance, a train is beginning to pull into Wembley Central Station. I go over to the window and stand behind the curtain so I can't be seen.

I look at my watch. The train is bang on time for once. I look back at Kerry who is glaring at me with hopeful eyes. She's still clinging onto the notion she might still be able to survive this.

'Sorry, Kerry, your time is up.'

Kerry tries to move but her wounds won't allow it. While sitting down, she wasn't in pain, but when she attempts to stand up, the wounds open, the blood begins to seep out and the pain courses through her body like a shot of electricity.

I lunge for her. I grab her by the hair and pull her up. I slam her against the wall, hold the knife in one hand while the other is clamped tightly around her throat. She tries to scream but I press the cold steel blade against her lips.

'Sssh. Wait.'

The train at the station has come to a stop.

Kerry's house is the last one on the street before the concrete steps leading up to the station. I've often stood on the corner and watched the commuters entering and leaving the station by the concrete steps. I've even spotted Kerry glancing through the net curtains, waiting for her dad, the highlight of her dull day.

Kerry kicks me. I hadn't been expecting that. But good for her, for hanging on. I've been kicked in the knackers before. It's painful, even with the protection of a cricketer's box stuffed into my jeans. I'm more stunned by her bid for freedom than I am by the pain. She uses the split second while I keel over and grab my crotch to run to the window, to bang on the glass with her red hands and scream for help. This is hot. This is so fucking hot.

I grab her by the hair, wrap it around my fingers and pull her head back. She's screaming for help, but nobody can hear her. There are so many people just a few feet from her, but they're chatting among themselves or they have their headphones in.

'Thank you for fighting back,' I whisper into her ear as I slice her throat with the knife several times. Blood sprays on the window and walls. I keep slicing even after she's gone limp in my hand.

When it's over, I place her back on the floor, leaning against the wall. Her head is slumped on her chest. She's drenched in blood. The metallic smell fills the room. This has been amazing. Right now, right at this very moment, I fucking love Kerry Cheetham.

7:30 p.m.

From my bag, I take out a Thermos flask filled with a strong Columbian-blend coffee, pour myself a cup, sit back on Kerry's bed and savour the moment. Victim number seven. Wow. That's quite an achievement. I'm so happy right now.

Kerry's been dead for a little over an hour. Outside, it's completely dark now and the streetlights have come on. Her spilled blood looks black against the cream carpet. Her eyes lost their sparkle long ago, but they're still bewitching to look at. I stare into them. What am I looking for? Whatever it is, I don't find it. I never find it because there is nothing there to find. I don't believe in a soul or an afterlife. A person is just a body. Once the physical form has been destroyed, all that is left is a carcass.

I like this part of the kill. The adrenaline is still shooting through my veins. The comedown has yet to kick in as I'm still surrounded by the carnage. I can smell the drying blood. I can still hear Kerry's cries, pleas and screams ringing in my ears. I can feel her warm breath on me. I can feel her touch on my fingers. What I'd love to do is hold her. I'd love to have posed her in bed and got in beside her, snuggled her and felt her go stiff and cold beside me. But I can't risk doing that. I know all about Locard's Principle for transferring skin cells and single strands of hair. My DNA is most likely all over this house. I've tried to minimise it as best I can, but every contact leaves a trace. I'm not yet on the police database and the longer I can maintain that, the better.

I take another photo of Kerry. She's long since dead and rigor mortis is beginning to kick in. I look at the picture, pinch the screen and zoom in on her face.

'Do you know something, Kerry? I think you're better looking dead than alive. I also think you've been my favourite so far,' I say with a smile.

I should be going soon. It's a shame I can't stay for much longer, but her dad will be knocking on the door to ask how her dull day has gone and if she's applied for any more jobs. When she doesn't answer, he'll use his key or look up and see the blood spatter on the window. He'll find her tonight. I need to leave. I've thought of every eventuality and have a clean pair of overalls in my bag so I can get to my van unnoticed. I'll try to remember as much as I can for when I'm in bed tonight, but it won't be the same. It never is. Right now, I'm more content, relaxed and happier than I've ever been before in my whole life.

Chapter Thirty-One

On the way home, Olivia stopped off at a pet shop and bought a comfortable bed for Stanley, a new collar and a disc engraved with her contact details. After a conversation with an assistant, she bought several bags of food so she could try and figure out what the little dog enjoyed. Another Uber was summoned and she was home at a reasonable time for a change.

She asked the driver to drop her off at the bottom of the cul-de-sac as usual, and struggled with her shopping as she walked down the pavement, her eyes darting from one well-lit house to the next. It was dark and a fine drizzle was falling. This winter seemed never-ending. She went to work when it was dark and she arrived home when it was dark. It was the perfect cover if you didn't want to bump into anyone. It was also the perfect cover for committing a murder.

Olivia shuddered. She stopped in her tracks and looked around her. She was completely alone in the street. In the background she could hear the distant hum of traffic and the siren of a police car or ambulance. There was always a siren blaring in London. It was a little after six o'clock, early really, yet she felt vulnerable.

She unlocked the front door. It swung open and she was shocked to find the alarm didn't beep at her. Had Sam forgotten to set it before he left after walking Stanley? If he had, she'd annihilate him.

Olivia kicked the door closed behind her, locked it and was about to set the alarm when Sam stepped out of the living room, Stanley darting around his ankles.

'Oh. I didn't expect you to be here,' she said in the doorway.

'We've not been back long. I took Stanley into the park and he got a bit muddy, so I came in to give his paws a wash. I hope you don't mind.'

Olivia didn't move. 'Of course not. Thank you.'

'Here, let me take those from you.' Sam leaped to her aid and took the heavy shopping from her. 'We passed a shop on our walk that sold organic dog treats, so I bought a couple of packs. They're handmade, so not full of additives.'

'That's very generous of you, Sam, thank you.' She frowned, taking off her coat and hanging it up. 'How's he been?'

'Fine. Full of beans. You should have seen him running around the park. He loved it. He wasn't scared by the bigger dogs, either.'

Olivia entered the kitchen and saw Sam putting away the food she'd bought. How did he know where she wanted it to go? He seemed to be making himself very at home.

'Would you like me to make you a coffee or something?' he asked.

'No. I'll have a shower first. Aren't you on a night shift?' she asked, exaggerating looking at her watch.

'Not until seven.'

'Oh.'

Sam pulled out a stool at the island and sat down. Olivia remained in the doorway. She wasn't comfortable with this young man being so familiar in her home.

'Listen, I hope you don't mind, but, after I dried Stanley off, he went running around and disappeared into your bedroom,' Sam said, playing with his fingers and not making eye contact with Olivia.

'My bedroom?'

'Yes. I didn't know it was your bedroom and I followed him in. I mean, I don't know if you allow him to have the run of the house. Some people can be funny about where their dogs are allowed to go. Anyway, I saw that book on your bedside table… and…' he trailed off.

'And?' she asked, folding her arms tightly across her chest.

'I had no idea you were Olivia Button.'

'I'm not. I'm Olivia Winter.'

'No. I know. I mean, your father. I didn't realise it was… who he was,' he flustered.

'There's no reason for you to know.'

'No. It's just… you were so kind to me the other night after I'd been attacked and, with everything you've been through, well, it would have been understandable if you'd just left me out there.'

'That's not the kind of person I am,' she said. There was a defensiveness to her tone. Sam was making himself far too comfortable in her life. She knew why he was doing it. He didn't have anyone in London to be friendly with and had latched onto her. That wasn't her intention. She should really ask for her key back. Yes, it would hurt his feelings, but it would make her feel more comfortable.

'No. I can see that. You're kind. You want to help people. I'm the same. It's just, sometimes, when bad things happen, it's easy to look the other way. I'm not making myself very clear, am I?' he said, looking up for the first time.

'Sam,' Olivia began, fully entering the kitchen. 'We can't change what has happened to us in the past. We learn from it, adapt, and move on. That's what we do. We survive to the best of our ability. As you should do, too,' she said, not quite looking him in the eye. She was being subtle, but she hoped he'd take the hint that he was a survivor and should strive to make himself a life of his own. Do his own thing.

'That makes sense.'

'Good. Now, I'm sure you have a lot to do, and I do, too. You don't want to be hanging around here.' She wanted him to leave and tried to wrap up, asking him to go in as nice a way as possible.

Sam remained still, staring at Olivia a little too long for her liking. She'd made a mistake in helping Sam, in being the Good Samaritan. He was a lost soul, but he was clinging to her for support, and she couldn't provide it. She didn't want to provide it. She felt the cold fingers of fear grip her around the chest. His gaze was boring into her, almost as if he was undressing her with his eyes.

He eventually hopped off the stool. 'Would you like me to take Stanley out tomorrow?'

It was a while before Olivia answered. 'If you have other things planned, don't feel obliged. I can take him to work with me.'

'No. I enjoyed it. I'll come around mid-morning once I've had a nap.' As he passed Olivia, he gave her a hug. She didn't reciprocate. Her body tensed at his touch. 'Thank you.'

She remained motionless in the kitchen until she heard the front door close and then shuddered.

Stanley liked his new bed straight away. Within minutes he was curled up and snoring. Olivia had never thought about getting a pet, not even a self-reliant cat that could come and go as it pleased, but with Stanley in the house, the sound of his sleeping whimpers made her smile. It made the house seem warm and homely, less stilted. She set about making herself a quick meal – courgette spaghetti with grilled chicken and sesame seeds – before

The Mind of a Murderer

settling down with the *Evening Standard* she'd picked up on her way home.

Olivia rarely read the papers, but as she was working on an active hunt to catch a killer, she was interested to see how the case was represented in the media and what the mood of Londoners was.

There was nothing on the few first pages and Olivia read the headlines of several stories but didn't bother with the main text. When she turned to page seven she dropped her fork with a clatter, waking Stanley from his slumber. Seeing her face staring out at her made her jump.

The photograph had been taken earlier in the day as she was leaving Sanderson Street Police Station. Her face was thunderous – lips pursed, eyes wide – and she was taking long strides out of the car park. She hadn't noticed a photographer, but her mind had been on other things. POLICE CONSULT 'KILLER CATCHER' IN HUNT FOR LONDON MURDERER screamed the inaccurate headline.

The story was mostly filler. A spokesperson for the Metropolitan Police refused to comment but the prose was written in a way to stir up fear in the public. There was a serial killer stalking the streets of the capital and police were stymied to the point where a world-renowned 'serial killer catcher' had to be brought in to help. Mentioning Olivia by name, the story touched on her books and successful interviews with well-known murderers. Fortunately, they didn't seem to know who her father was. Long may that continue.

She was ready to turn the page when something caught her eye. In the corner of the picture of her was the name of the photographer: *Ethan Miller*. The name sounded familiar, but it took a moment or two for her to place it. When her memory cleared, her face reddened in anger. Ethan Miller, aka The Handsome Stranger.

She pushed the paper away, and her meal. She'd only taken a

few bites but felt sick at how naïve she had been to the charms of a good-looking stranger. Was there no one she could trust anymore?

Stanley barked in his sleep. She turned to look at the little dachshund. At least there was one man in her life who wouldn't betray her.

Chapter Thirty-Two

Olivia had trouble sleeping. She'd gone to bed at 11:30 as her eyes were heavy and she'd kept yawning while watching an old black-and-white film noir on Netflix. She dragged herself to her bedroom, undressed and slipped under the duvet. Even before she'd got comfortable, Stanley was whimpering in his sleep, lucky sod. An hour later and Olivia was still awake.

Her phone began to vibrate on the bedside table. She always turned the sound down at night. She reached over and looked at the display. Whoever was calling was not in her contacts, and she didn't recognise the number. Guessing that it would only be an emergency call at this time of night, she swiped to answer.

'Hello?' she said quietly.

'Is that... is that Olivia Winter?'

Olivia's heart sank. If this was a journalist, she was definitely putting in a complaint to someone.

'Speaking.'

'I don't know if you remember me. It's Jamie Farr? You came up to see me at the police station the other day?'

Olivia sat up in bed, suddenly interested. 'Yes, of course. How are you?'

'I'm not doing too good. Sorry, I've only just realised what time it is. I've just finished a shift at work. Is it OK to call you back in the morning?'

'No. I mean, it's fine. I was awake.'

'Are you sure?'

'Is there something you want to talk about? Have you remembered something?'

'I wish I had,' he said, sounding genuinely sad. 'It's... have you seen the newspapers?'

'No. I try to avoid them.'

'I read them all. There's a lot of empty time during a night shift. In *The Sun* yesterday there was a profile of all the victims of this killer the police said I was attacked by. I'm guessing you know them.'

'Yes. I do.'

'Phoebe Harper was a nurse. She was doing good with her life. According to her mother, during the Covid pandemic, she practically lived at the hospital so she could look after the sick. That young man, Calvin, he was at university. He was going to be a sports psychologist. He was an excellent long-distance runner, too. They were good people,' Jamie said, tears evident in his voice. 'Why them, Olivia?'

'I don't know,' she said, giving an honest answer.

'And why did I survive? I work in a petrol station, for fuck's sake. I'm not saving lives. I'm not contributing to society. Why did I survive when they didn't?'

Olivia turned on her bedside light, which lit up the framed photo of her mum and sister. Jamie's question was one she'd asked herself on many occasions when she was growing up. Why had she survived when they hadn't?

'Jamie, I'm really not qualified to help you, but to me it sounds like you're suffering from survivor's guilt, which is perfectly normal and understandable. I can put you in touch with some people to talk to about this but, please, don't beat yourself up because you survived when others didn't. You could actually use this as an opportunity to turn your life around. You've survived for a reason; so that your perspective on life has changed and you can do something laudable in the face of adversity.'

There was a silence and for a while Olivia wondered if Jamie had ended the call.

'Do you mean from, like, a higher power?'

Olivia smiled to herself. 'No, nothing like that. I just mean, maybe you could go back to college and retrain, or join a charity or an organisation and do good work in the community. Help others. You could say that you've been given a second chance at life. Use it to make a mark on the world.'

'Make a mark?'

'Yes.'

'Maybe I could do something so that Phoebe and Calvin and the others are remembered.'

'I think that's a good idea. I do think you should speak to someone, though. A professional. Can I give you a call in the morning with some numbers?'

'You mean a therapist?' He sounded uncertain.

'There's nothing wrong with seeking help. We all struggle with things at various points in our lives, and there are people who can advise us on ways to cope. We shouldn't bottle things up.'

'No. You're right. I'd like that. Thank you, Olivia. I really am sorry for calling so late.'

'That's fine. Look, Jamie, if you need to talk again, or if you think of anything more about the man who attacked you, please, let me know.'

'I will. I… I do keep trying to remember.'

'Thank you. Goodnight.'

'Goodnight.'

Olivia ended the call and leaned back in bed. She felt sorry for Jamie Farr and was suddenly transported back to how she felt in the immediate aftermath of her father's attack on her. The guilt was consuming. She spent night after night crying, and not just because she missed her mum and sister so much, but because she hadn't died with them. It was years before she had a full night's sleep without waking in a cold sweat to find her grandmother by her side, holding her, telling her she'd been screaming in her sleep again.

She saw a child therapist, but he hadn't been much use. He'd used dolls, one in each hand, called Timothy and Rosie. He'd spoken through them in a childish voice. She'd felt silly talking to squinty-eyed puppets and refused to go back after three sessions.

When she was in her early twenties, Olivia had plucked up the courage to see a psychotherapist. She'd known that the career path she was starting down was a mistake. She should be putting everything behind her and forging a life for herself, but she'd wanted to know just how attached to her past she really was.

She'd liked her therapist, Geraint Hughes. He had a lovely smooth Welsh accent and his eyes twinkled when he spoke. He'd told her that understanding the past was important in order to shape the future, but that we shouldn't live in the past, we should just visit it from time to time. Olivia had said that by trying to understand serial killers and discover why they committed the acts they did, she was doing more than visiting the past; she was buying a holiday home there. Geraint had smiled at that comment and said that as long as she didn't get her post redirected, it was fine. They'd both laughed and the mood had been lightened.

Basically, Olivia was trying to do what she'd told Jamie Farr to do. Her mother and sister had been killed in the most violent of ways and taken from her when she'd needed them the most. She was honouring their lives, and their deaths, by (hopefully) helping to understand these people in order to stop the serial killers of the future and to prevent their potential victims going through the agony that she, and now Jamie, was going through.

She heard a deep sigh, glanced down, and saw Stanley looking up at her.

'Sorry, you're going through it as well, aren't you?' she said to him.

His tail beat a couple of times against the duvet.

'You're really missing Jessica, aren't you?'

He stood up, padded over to her and curled up next to her.

'I wish you could talk. I bet you had a bloody good look at the man who killed her, didn't you?'

Stanley didn't say anything. Of course he didn't.

Olivia reached across for the lamp and turned out the light, plunging the room into darkness.

Chapter Thirty-Three

Friday 23rd February 2024

Olivia was woken the next morning by her mobile ringing on her bedside table. She tried to ignore it, but Stanley's yapping added to the noise. She flicked on the lamp and reached for her phone. She didn't look at the display.

'Sorry to call so early. Any chance I can come round?' It was DI Foley. After seeing the papers, she had wondered how long it would be before he'd ring. Was he going to offer an apology? Surely it could have waited until regular office hours.

Olivia cleared her throat. 'Erm... yes... I suppose,' she sounded hoarse.

Her doorbell rang.

'That's me,' he said.

'What? You're already here?'

'Yes. I thought you'd be up.'

Olivia flung the duvet back and shivered. She was shattered. She'd barely had three hours' sleep. She slipped her bare feet into carpet slippers, grabbed her dressing gown from the back of her door and went out into the hallway. She swiped the fob over the sensor and unlocked the door.

'Why would you think I'd be up at' – she looked at her watch – 'six o'clock in the morning?'

'I don't know. I just assumed you didn't sleep much.' Foley looked shattered. He was wearing a padded waterproof jacket over a dark-red jumper and black trousers.

'I usually sleep very well, thank you. Well, when I'm allowed to. I suppose you'll want to come in.' She stepped to one side.

'Any chance there's a coffee going?'

She rolled her eyes and showed him into the kitchen.

The strip lighting blinded her. She hated being woken so abruptly.

'I'm assuming you have a reason for calling so early.'

'I wanted to apologise for yesterday,' he said quietly as he sat himself down at the island.

She turned to look at him. 'Have you been worrying about this all night?'

'I've been worrying about it since you left yesterday. I haven't been to bed yet.'

'Why not?' she asked as she set about making coffee for them both.

'We've found another victim.'

'Oh my God.'

'You were right about Sean Fincher. I let him go almost as soon as you'd left. No charges. Although I've told him to buy a decent storage locker for his weapons. Well, the ones we've allowed him to keep.'

Olivia handed him a coffee and sat next to him. 'Tell me about this new victim.'

Foley closed his eyes and shook his head. 'Kerry Cheetham. She was thirty-six years old and lived alone in Wembley.'

'Who found her?'

'Her father. He has to pass her house on his way to and from work every day. He always calls for a few minutes to say hello. When she didn't answer the door, he thought something was wrong so used his spare key to let himself in. He found her in the bedroom stabbed to death.' Foley was finding it difficult to talk.

Olivia placed a comforting hand on his arm. 'I'm sorry. Are you all right?'

'No. He's laughing at us, Olivia. He's fucking laughing at us. How do I catch him?'

'Tell me more about the scene. What was happening close by? Was there a party or a football match?'

'No. Nothing.'

'Really? It might not be the same killer. He likes an audience. He likes the excitement that someone could catch him but he knows they won't.'

'She lived on Station Grove, right next to Wembley Central Station. Her house is the last one before the entrance to the station. Commuters have to go down some steps once they've got off the train.'

'Do you know an estimated time of death?'

'Early evening.'

'To coincide with rush hour,' she said, almost to herself.

'What?'

'He waited until people were coming back from work during rush hour. There would have been so many people walking past the house less than a few feet away as he was butchering this poor woman. He'll have heard them chatting, laughing, and it will have driven him to stab her over and over again.'

'The bedroom window was slightly ajar.'

'Perfect. He'd have been able to hear them clearly. How many times was she stabbed?'

'The pathologist came out to the crime scene. He tried to count the stab wounds but there were too many. We'll know more after the post-mortem.'

'Jesus. He's escalating.'

'He's cocky.'

'He's confident. He's getting away with it. He's beating you at a game you're supposed to be a champion at, and he's loving it.'

'Olivia,' Foley said, looking up at her. 'I really am sorry for yesterday.' She waved away his apology. 'I need your help more than ever. How do I catch him? How do I stop him from killing again?'

Olivia turned away. Her eyes fell on the open copy of the *Evening Standard* she'd pushed away last night. An idea came to her.

'You set a trap.'

'How do I do that?'

'You offer him something he wants.'

'What does he want?'

'Me.'

Chapter Thirty-Four

'How do you know he wants you?'

'Sorry?' Olivia asked, placing a couple of slices of bread into the toaster.

'I said, how do you know he wants you?'

'He's a psychopath and a narcissist. He's loving the fact he has an unwitting audience to his murders. He has potentially hundreds of eyewitnesses but not one of them saw a thing. Someone like him knows that he will be caught one day and when he is and he's sentenced to life in prison, the press will soon grow bored of him and move on to the next headliner. However, he'll want to remain in the limelight for as long as possible, and the best way for that to happen is for someone like me to interview him and write a book about him.'

'So, what do we do, put you in the middle of Trafalgar Square with a sign around your neck and wait for him to snatch you?'

Olivia chuckled. 'Nothing quite so subtle. Do you read the *Evening Standard*?'

'No. My ex used to work for them.'

'Well, I was in it last night. Someone took a photo of me leaving Sanderson Street yesterday and surmised I was helping the police. Now, if we set up an interview, maybe you and I have our picture taken together and mention we're some kind of crack partnership working to find this killer, it may just point him in my direction.'

'What?' Foley looked aghast. 'You want to set yourself up as a potential victim?'

'Obviously not, but if he knows I'm definitely working on the case he may try and contact me in some way.'

'No. Absolutely not. I'm not risking losing you like I lost Jessica.'

'You won't lose me. You can put a tap on my phone, you can put an armed guard outside my house – or inside if you like; I've got enough room.'

'No. Less than five minutes ago you were calling him a psychopath and a narcissist. Is that the kind of person you want coming after you?'

'No, but my picture has already been in the paper. He's a highly intelligent guy. He'll have put two and two together and worked out that I'm helping you. At least this way he comes for me with us being prepared.'

Foley hung his head low. Olivia watched as his neck reddened slightly. His eyes were darting left and right as he thought. His left leg jiggled involuntarily – his tell-tale sign of being uncomfortable. He'd never worked a serial investigation before, and his reputation would take a hammering if more victims were discovered or the killer went to ground and was never caught.

'Have forensics found anything at the scene of Kerry's murder? Any hairs, fibres, fingerprints?' Olivia said after a long silence.

'Nothing useful. We found a couple of skin cells under Kerry's fingernails, but this bloke isn't on the DNA database,' he said.

'What about the neighbours? Did they see or hear anything?'

'They were all at work.'

'Is there anyone else who could possibly have killed her? An ex-husband, a disgruntled boyfriend?'

'No. She'd been single for a while, according to her father. She was married and we've tracked her husband down to a villa in Spain with his new wife, so he's in the clear. She'd been made redundant from her job at a bank and spent most of her days scouring the internet for jobs. She rarely went out as she was trying to spend as little money as possible.'

'What about social media sites? Dating sites?'

'She was on Facebook and Instagram. No threats, no trolling. Everything was perfectly innocent.'

'So this is our guy. He's a perfect stranger to her and he's left nothing of himself behind. He's cool. He's cunning. He's vicious. He's evil and he has no intention of stopping unless he's lured out into the open.'

'My boss will never go for it – putting a civilian in harm's way.'

Olivia smiled to herself. Foley was obviously warming to the idea.

'OK. So we don't tell him. We do the interview with the newspaper as some kind of PR piece and let the chips fall where they may.'

He looked across at her. 'You're seriously willing to risk your life to catch him?'

'I don't consider my life to be at risk. If you have the manpower to keep an eye on my home and keep me safe, then we have absolutely nothing to worry about.'

'I'll move in myself if I have to.'

'Does that mean you'll do it?'

He took a deep breath. 'Is there any other way?'

'None that I can think of.'

'It doesn't look like I have much choice then, do I?'

Chapter Thirty-Five

The atmosphere was heavy in the CID room at Sanderson Street. Another victim, seven in total – eight if you included the attempted murder of Jamie Farr. As Olivia made her way through the melee towards Foley's office, she glanced at the whiteboard. Her eyes landed on the smiling face of Jessica Sheffield. If there were any doubts before about her using a fake interview to lure the killer out, the reminder of the murder of one of her few friends put paid to them. She knew she was doing the right thing. Jessica had been a young, ambitious DI. She had been pregnant and would have made a fantastic mother. She'd had her life and happiness torn away from her, as had the other victims. The killer had to pay and to Olivia, it didn't matter what the cost.

While Foley contacted a journalist he knew at the *Evening Standard*, Olivia dug out the dog-eared business card Ethan Miller had left on her scooter after their failed rendezvous at the swimming pool. She was fuming at his deceit as she entered his number in her phone.

'Ethan Miller,' he answered straight away. His voice was deep and strong. Olivia remembered the disgusting things he'd whispered to her as he'd fucked her hard and deep. It was what she'd wanted – needed – at the time. She'd hated herself afterwards, as she always did.

'It's Olivia Winter.' She tried to sound icy and disdainful, but the truth was, Ethan was an incredibly good-looking man and she was attracted to him. She had no interest in a long-term relationship, but he was the kind of man she wanted to make her *feel* again. It didn't matter that they were negative emotions.

His voice softened. 'Hey. I haven't seen you at the pool lately. How are you?'

'Pissed off, actually.'

'Oh?'

'Yes. You never told me you worked for the *Evening Standard*.'

'Ah.'

'Indeed.'

'I don't actually work for them. If I could earn enough money taking photos of wildlife and landscapes, that's what I'd spend my days doing, but I need to pay the bills and doing the odd bit for the press helps towards trips to Africa and the Arctic.'

My God, he's the perfect man, Olivia thought. *Good-looking. Fit. A filthy lover and in touch with nature.*

She felt herself thawing towards him. 'Be that as it may, you had no right to take my photograph without asking my permission, let alone sell it to a newspaper.'

'I know. I'm sorry.' He sounded sincere.

Olivia looked out of Foley's office into the open-plan CID suite. Holly looked up from her desk and smiled at her. Olivia turned away.

'OK. Apology accepted, providing you do something for me in return to make up for it.'

'Sure. Anything.'

'As you and now the rest of London know, I'm working with the police to try and catch this serial killer. We need to flush him out and we're hoping to appeal to his narcissism. To do that, we need a feature in the *Evening Standard* along with a couple of photographs of me and the DI.'

'I can do that. Make it a double-page feature and I'll earn more money,' he said with the hint of a smile in his voice.

'Maybe you can take me out to dinner on the proceeds,' she said playfully.

'Anytime.'

Olivia caught herself just in time. She hated the fact that she was becoming smitten with this man and bit her bottom lip hard to ruin the moment and put a stop to the flirting.

'Can you be at Sanderson Street in an hour?'

DETECTIVES CALL IN KILLER EXPERT TO CATCH BUTCHER OF LONDON

By Daphne Bytheway

Since November last year, seven people have been murdered by a serial killer stalking the streets of London. The killer leaves no forensic evidence at the scene and there have been very few witnesses. On the day that the seventh victim has been identified as 36-year-old Kerry Cheetham, police reveal they are now working with world-renowned forensic psychologist and serial murderer expert Olivia Winter to catch the killer before he claims an eighth victim.

Doctor Winter, 34, has interviewed more than one hundred serial killers around the world. Her aim has always been to discover why they committed their crimes in the hope of identifying the killers of the future before they are able to kill. She is the author of four bestselling books including The Secrets of a Serial Killer and My Life with a Knife, the story of Joseph Lansbury, known as the Seattle Slasher.

Ms Winter has been asked to consult on active cases by police forces around the world on many occasions but has always turned down their offers. Is the fact a serial killer is operating in her home city what lured her to join forces with the Metropolitan Police?

'I am not a profiler,' Ms Winter repeated more than once during the interview. 'I am a forensic psychologist. One of the victims of this killer was a very good friend of mine, Detective Inspector Jessica Sheffield. The police are grieving the loss of one of their own and I am grieving the loss of a friend. I know we can catch this man.'

Detective Inspector Amyas Foley, 43, is leading a team of murder squad detectives. 'This killer is highly intelligent. He is organised and knows how to stage a crime scene. We are in a fortunate position that we don't get many serial killers in this country. Our clear-up rate of murders is high, but when it comes to catching a serial murderer, we need someone with psychological insight to point us in the right direction.'

'It is the psychology of the murderer that interests me,' Ms Winter continued. 'I want to know why he is committing these crimes. What satisfaction is he getting out of killing?'

How sure are Ms Winter and the police that the killer is male?

'Serial murderers are more likely to be male than female,' Ms Winter explained. 'Studying the victims and the way they were killed has pointed out a number of factors that can identify who the police should be looking for.'

So why hasn't the killer been caught? Why has he been allowed to claim a seventh victim?

'Victimology is the study of a person after a crime has been committed for traits that give clues as to why that person has been targeted. From that I can estimate what kind of personality the police should be looking for. If I could narrow that down to a name, I'd be a very in-demand woman,' Ms Winter said with a smile.

Olivia Winter is one of the world's foremost experts on serial killers and walked us through the process of a psychological profile with ease. As the interview came to a close, I asked how confident she was the killer would be caught.

'Extremely confident. As DI Foley has said, this killer is very intelligent. He believes himself to be untouchable. However, nobody is that smart. I'm not waiting for him to become complacent and make a

mistake. I believe I can help catch him before that. I know exactly what kind of person he is. I just need to find him.'

The determination of Olivia Winter, DI Foley and his dedicated team of officers is admirable. The people of London, although frightened at the thought of a serial killer walking amongst them, should take comfort they are being protected by such gallant men and women.

Chapter Thirty-Six

In his hospital bed, Richard Button was sitting up, a mound of pillows behind him to keep him comfortable. He'd eaten his first full meal since being admitted to hospital and was on the road to recovery. It wouldn't be long before he was back in his cell in Belmarsh. The hospital food was much better, but he missed his own bed. It was comfortable. It was home.

A nurse was removing his dressings and apologised when he winced as the tape tore at his chest hairs.

'You'd think with all this technology that by now someone would have invented something to protect the wound by not ripping out hairs,' she said, smiling. Her fingers were shaking. She was obviously nervous about being so close to a serial killer.

'You'll be giving me a bald patch,' Richard replied.

'I could cut around the tape, if you want?' She looked back at the tray she'd wheeled in. 'I'm sure I put some scissors on here. I'll just go and grab a pair.'

'You couldn't bring me in a paper, could you? There's bugger all on TV.'

'I'll grab you one from the staffroom.'

As soon as the door was closed, Richard eased the stolen pair of scissors down his sleeve and slipped them under the mattress. He had no use for them at the moment, but he knew they'd come in handy at some point.

Once his dressing had been changed and he was comfortable in bed again, he sat back with the well-thumbed edition of the *Evening Standard*.

His eyes opened wide as he turned to pages four and five. It was a double-page feature about the hunt for the serial killer currently scaring the people of London. He remembered that feeling well and it made him smile.

The three pictures that went with the text warmed his heart. There was his little girl, his Livvy, all grown up, sitting at a desk with Detective Inspector Amyas Foley – what kind of a name was that? – looking deep in thought as they leaned over a file. In another shot, Olivia was standing at a whiteboard, a blur of detectives in front of her as she spoke to them. She looked authoritative, confident, determined. She looked just like her mother.

The third photo was posed – Olivia standing outside the police station in front of the Sanderson Street sign. Her hair was lifted by a breeze and she smiled into the camera. She didn't look happy in this picture. She obviously hated posing. Why? She had a beautiful smile, but the eyes told the full story. She looked sad, brittle, pained.

The story didn't mention Olivia's true identity as the only surviving daughter of serial killer Richard Button, but it didn't matter. He knew her secret. He knew what torment was hidden behind those big brown eyes.

Richard spent a long time staring at the photographs as he read the feature over and over. Daphne Bytheway or Ethan Miller would be interested to hear from him, he was sure.

Sam Halliday was out walking Stanley. Stanley was panting after running around in the park for almost an hour while he watched and shivered. On the way back to Modbury Gardens he passed a newspaper stand. He saw the banner headline mention a serial killer so took a free copy of the *Evening Standard* proffered by an elderly man wrapped up against the elements.

He let himself into Olivia's house and closed the door firmly behind him.

'Hi, I'm home. Have you had a good day, love?' he said, smiling to himself. He knew Olivia wouldn't be in yet, but it was fun to pretend.

While Stanley lapped at the water in his bowl, Sam flicked on the kettle and sat on a stool. He opened the paper and smiled when he saw Olivia staring out at him. He took in her face, the smile, the cute wrinkles at the sides of her eyes, the button nose, the thin lips, the pale, smooth skin. He'd love to reach into the photograph and stroke her face.

The kettle boiled. He made a black coffee and returned to read the story. He couldn't decide if Olivia's job was dangerous or not. He'd been reading her books in his free time since he'd met her. Usually she only interviewed killers once they were caught and safely behind bars, so this was new territory for her. He wanted to protect her, look after her. He didn't like the idea of a serial murderer using his brief encounter with Olivia for his masturbatory fantasies. The thought made his blood run cold. No, Olivia should not be doing this kind of work. However, it was work she loved; work she was good at. He'd need to show her that she was safer in an office, behind a desk, with him taking care of her.

It was strange how the feature didn't mention who her father was. Surely they knew. Would it affect her career if the truth that her father was an infamous serial killer was revealed?

Sebastian Lister was loading the dishwasher while the twins played nosily in the living room. Why didn't children come with a volume button? He'd had a long, hard day trying to pacify several professors from universities around the world about what questions they wanted to ask in their serial killer survey. There were only so many questions they could ask, but they all wanted their input for the money they were providing, and time difference and an intermittent internet connection added to the frustration.

He had picked the twins up from school and found a letter in Robert's book bag informing Sebastian his son had been bullying a girl in his class. They had a talk in the car while stuck in traffic, but the slow-moving cars, his short temper and his son laughing had caused Sebastian to explode with anger, which had resulted in both children crying. He had tried to apologise but the damage was done. Rosemary would have handled things a lot differently. He wasn't coping too well as a single parent.

They arrived home to find twelve-year-old Alistair needing new rugby boots and there was a class trip to Reykjavik next winter he'd love to go on to see the Northern Lights. Every time that child opened his mouth it ended up costing Sebastian.

When he eventually found a few minutes of alone time to open the post that had been piling up in the last few days, he noticed his bank account was rapidly emptying and his bills were rising. The last letter was a royalties statement from the publisher of the two books he'd written: *The Riverside Killer* and *The Perfect Killer*, the story of Sheffield serial killer Stuart Mills. Last month's sales had given him a paltry £180.57. That wouldn't even make a dent in his monthly bills. Last month's electricity bill alone was more than that.

'Have you seen this?' Tilly asked, entering the kitchen.

'What?'

'Olivia's in the paper.'

'Really?' Sebastian stood up from loading the dishwasher. 'Why?'

'She's helping the police track down that killer. It's a full two-page spread.' She handed the paper to her father. 'She looks pretty in that bottom photo, don't you think?'

'Yes,' he said absently as he read the story. 'She didn't say she was doing this.'

'Well, she doesn't have to run everything by you, does she? Can I have this éclair in the fridge?'

'It's not like her,' he said, going over to the kitchen table and sitting down. 'She hates all this publicity stuff. She's always worried the press will find out who her father is.'

'It doesn't matter who her father is, surely. It's not her fault.'

'No, but the press would have a field day.'

'I bet you'd sell more of your books if they found out,' Tilly said. She slapped him playfully on the arm and left the kitchen.

Sebastian frowned. It *would* be advantageous to him if the truth of Olivia's parentage was known by the press. Not only would his book sales increase but his publishers might ask him to write an updated version. It would be tastefully written, naturally. He wouldn't go into any gory details about Olivia's distress at having a killer for a father. He was sure she'd understand his need to provide for his children.

'Did they have to use my first name?' Foley asked.

'You've no reason to worry. Look at this photo of me,' Olivia said. 'I look like I've just escaped from somewhere.'

Olivia and Amyas were in Foley's office. They each had a copy of the *Evening Standard* and wanted to see if Daphne Bytheway had done what she promised to do and written an article that would tempt the killer into contacting the police, or Olivia, in some way while at the same time appeasing the frightened members of the public. She seemed to have struck the right tone and while they were happy with the text, they were not too happy with the publicity shots.

'I like it. You look very authoritarian in the others. The one outside the station gives you a softer, welcoming look.'

'Do you think?' Olivia asked, a hint of a smile on her face.

'Yes. You look approachable.'

'I don't like the thought of that. I don't want random people approaching me.'

'Apart from the killer.'

'Well, yes.'

'I'm still not sure about this,' Foley said, closing the paper.

'A bit late for that now. About half a million of these things are now being read around London.'

'We should have waited until tomorrow. We've had no time at all to set up extra security at your house.'

'I don't need extra security. All I need is for someone to be parked close by in case something happens. You've seen my house. I'm alarmed up to my eyeballs.'

'You've signed all the forms, haven't you? About us tapping your phone lines?'

'Yes.'

'Good.'

'I wish they'd gone into more detail about the type of killer we're looking for,' Olivia said, going back to the article.

'In what way?'

'Daphne seemed interested when we talked about the thrill killer and what he'd be getting out of his murders. She hasn't mentioned any of that.'

'Maybe she's waiting until you've caught him.'

'Maybe. Well, I think I'll call it a day. I'm neglecting my other work. We're starting one of the biggest studies ever into the early lives of serial killers and I want to be in at the very start of this. It's not fair leaving Sebastian to do all the legwork. He'll probably be sticking pins into a little doll of me.'

As she left, Olivia continued to wonder why Daphne hadn't included more details about the killer they were hunting. Olivia had been vague when questioned about his personality. She had tried to answer as fully as possible, but the truth was, Olivia hadn't come into contact with many thrill killers. Most murderers had a motive for their crimes – manipulation, domination, sexual gratification – but homicidal mania wasn't something she knew much about, especially with killers in England.

Her father had been a thrill killer. He'd had no real motive apart from the buzz and rush of adrenaline it gave him. If Olivia really wanted to understand this killer, and catch him, she would have to understand what fully drove him, and there was only one way to find that out. She stopped in her tracks. Many times, over the years, Sebastian had brought up the prospect of her interviewing her father, not only for research purposes, but for her to understand him as well, to silence the demons. She'd flatly refused. Now, she was changing her mind, and she didn't like it. She felt sick every time she thought of her father and what he had done, what he had robbed her of, but she needed to understand this killer, and, as much as she was loath to admit it, she needed to understand her father, too.

If she went to see him, and it was a huge if, how would she feel afterwards? Sick, dirty, violated, tortured. They were feelings she felt on a regular basis, especially when she touched her scars in the shower, or when she was dressing and caught a glimpse of them in the mirror, or when a man put his hand on them while they were having sex. She was full of rage, angst and self-hatred; a little more wouldn't hurt.

Chapter Thirty-Seven

Why were hospitals always so hot?

Olivia was in the lift on her own. She was nervous as she looked up and watched the numbers of each floor light up as she rose further up the building. Whenever she entered a prison, anywhere in the world, there was a sense of trepidation. She had a rough idea of what to expect from the serial killers she would be interviewing, but they always surprised her at some point. That's what made her so fascinated. This one, however, was different. She was related to this one, and it didn't matter how much she tried to tell herself Richard Button was simply just another murderer, the fact he was her father continued to itch at her brain. She didn't need to see her father ever again. After what he'd done, he'd given up the right to call himself a dad. He'd murdered her mother and sister. That was unforgivable. However, she could honour their memory by trying to understand what happened. Their deaths should not be in vain. Olivia refused for her mum and Claire to be victims. As the lift pinged and the doors juddered open, she stepped out into the corridor with its sick-coloured tiles and off-white walls scuffed with marks from passing trolleys, and the feeling of self-loathing grew.

It seemed quiet, as if the hospital had been abandoned for some reason. She looked left and right but there didn't seem to be any staff around. She set off for the intensive care unit, her shoes clacking loudly on the cracked tiles and echoing off the walls.

She pulled open the door marked ICU and saw her father's room straight ahead. There was no armed guard standing outside. She wondered if he'd been moved.

Behind the reception desk, a tired-looking nurse was eating an apple with one hand and typing frantically on a keyboard with the other.

'Excuse me,' Olivia said quietly. 'I'm looking for Richard Button. He was in room three the other day.'

She nodded. 'He's still in there,' she said with a mouth full of Granny Smith.

'Where's the armed guard?'

'Are you a relative?'

Olivia thought long before answering. She swallowed her scratchy dry throat. 'I'm his daughter.' Those words tasted disgusting.

The nurse looked her up and down. 'Oh. Apparently the police removed the guard. There's a prison officer in there with him.'

'Am I all right to go in?'

'He's your dad,' she smiled.

Don't rub it in, Olivia thought.

Olivia turned from the reception desk and headed for her father's room. The nurse's words were ringing in her ears. *Dad* was a more personal word than *father*. In her opinion, any man on earth could be a father, but it took a special someone to be a dad. Richard Button was her father, unfortunately. She didn't have a dad.

She pushed the handle of the door down slowly, and carefully opened the door. If it was possible, it was even hotter in the small, dark room. She peeped around the door and saw Richard sitting up in bed playing cards with a vastly overweight man wearing shiny black trousers and a blue sweater stretched tightly over his enormous gut. They were laughing and joking like two old friends.

Richard looked up. His eyes met Olivia and the laughing stopped.

'Livvy, you came back! I knew you would. Gordon, this is my daughter.'

The chair Gordon was sitting on strained under his weight as he turned to look at the visitor.

'The famous Olivia. Nice to meet you,' he said in a deep, hoarse voice.

Olivia gave him a simple nod of greeting.

'Gordon, you couldn't give us some privacy, could you?'

'It's past my dinner time anyway.'

Olivia had to step further into the room to make space for Gordon to squeeze past her. He closed the door firmly behind him.

'You wouldn't think to look at him that he was a prison officer, would you? He can hardly climb a flight of stairs without wheezing.'

Olivia watched her father as he stacked the playing cards and put them neatly away back in their box. He was chatting and making small talk as if he were simply a harmless old man in a hospital bed rather than a convicted serial killer.

'Come and sit down,' he said with a toothy smile.

She hesitated. In the lift she'd told herself to take the upper hand and show her father she had no feelings for him whatsoever. He was another killer in a long line of killers she had interviewed. Unfortunately, all that bravado went out of the window when she saw him again. Two decades' worth of pent-up anger and emotion at what he'd done came flooding back to the surface. She hoped she was a good enough actor to pull off the professionalism she didn't feel.

She pulled the chair Gordon had vacated away from the bed

and sat down. She didn't want to be too close to him.

A silence grew between them.

'So,' Richard eventually began. 'How've you been?'

Olivia looked at him with incredulous eyes. 'Are we really going to do small talk?'

'It's not small talk. I'm showing an interest.'

'Why?'

'Because you're my daughter. I care about you.'

She wanted to laugh in his face. Care! What did he know about caring? 'Really? Is that why you tried to kill me?'

'I did that to protect you.'

Her eyes widened in shock. 'I didn't realise that particular lesson was in the parenting handbooks.'

'I'm sorry.'

His empty apology rang hollow in her ears.

'For what? Murdering eight people or failing to make me number nine?' She so wanted to be the professional serial killer interviewer but her lust for answers was too great.

He looked down and began playing with a corner of the tape holding his canula in place that had come unstuck. 'I never meant to hurt any of you. I loved your mum and Claire with all my heart.'

'We had a good life, the four of us. At least, I thought we did.'

'We did.'

'So why did you have to go and ruin it?'

'Because a good life wasn't enough,' he said, looking up at her. 'There was always something missing. At the back of my mind, I knew life wasn't complete. I had a wife, two daughters – two beautiful daughters—' He looked at her with smiling eyes that made Olivia inwardly shudder. 'We had a nice house, I had a good job, a decent car, money in the bank. It's what everybody wanted, but... it wasn't enough for me. I thought I was having a mid-life crisis; can you believe that? I even contemplated having an affair,' he half laughed.

'Then why didn't you?'

'I couldn't hurt your mother like that.'

'And you didn't think she'd be hurt, knowing you'd killed six women?'

'To be perfectly honest with you, I never even thought of your mother when I was killing. I didn't think of anything. That part of me was completely separate. I remember one evening, me and your mum were curled up on the sofa together – you and Claire were in bed – and the news came on about Isobel Atkinson being found. She was—'

'I'm aware of who Isobel Atkinson was,' Olivia interrupted.

'Anyway, me and your mum were watching the news and it was like watching it all for the first time. On that sofa, I was Richard Button, husband and father. I wasn't Richard Button, killer. If I had been, your mum would have probably realised it was me straight away.'

Olivia frowned as she thought. 'So, you were able to swap between the two sides of your personality?'

'I never saw it as having more than one personality. It was more like two separate beings. Completely different lives.'

'So, as Richard Button the killer, you could have slept with another woman and you wouldn't have considered it as cheating on Mum?'

'Are you interviewing me, Livvy, or are you visiting your father?'

Olivia shuddered at the use of her nickname. 'I don't look at you and see a father.'

'What do you see?'

'Just a man.'

'Anything else?'

She shook her head. She could see a glint in his eye. He was enjoying this cold interaction. She didn't want to play him at his game.

'Bring your chair closer,' he said.

'I'm fine where I am.'

'No. Come closer. You need to look deep into my eyes.'

'I don't,' she said, her voice a touch above a nervous whisper.

'Olivia, look at me.'

She found the courage from somewhere. She swallowed hard. Her throat was dry. She inhaled deeply, felt the prickle of sweat under her armpits and looked up at the man whom she had almost wet herself laughing at when he did the perfect voice for Mr Toad when he was reading her *Wind in the Willows*. She had no idea where that memory suddenly came from.

'What do you see when you look in my eyes?' he asked.

She shook her head again. 'Nothing. There's nothing there.'

'I think there is. You see yourself. You see Claire. I'm your dad, Livvy.'

Olivia bit her bottom lip hard. She was struggling to hold onto her emotions. She refused to allow him to see her cry.

'I don't see anything,' she eventually said.

He adjusted himself in his bed. He brought himself closer to the edge. If he wanted to, he could reach out and touch her. 'You still haven't answered my question: what are you doing here?'

'I don't know. I thought I did, but I don't.'

He leaned forward. 'I do,' he whispered.

She doubted it. 'Go on.'

'I've written to you on a regular basis from the first day I set foot in prison. I've sent you cards for your birthday and Christmas, and I've lit candles in the prison chapel on the anniversary of your mum and sister's deaths. You've always been in my heart. I may not have seen you grow up, but I've shown an interest. I wrote to your grandparents asking for updates, but they never replied. However, once you left university and started getting your work and research published, I was able to watch you from afar. I've read all your books and your papers in specialist journals. I'm incredibly proud of you,' he said with the smile of a beaming father.

The Mind of a Murderer

'We both know there are four types of serial killers: the visionary, the mission-orientated, the hedonist and the dominant ones. There are also those who are influenced by media, but we'll not count those. Now, in your entire career, you've interviewed them all, but you've been itching to speak to someone under a specific hedonistic subheading.'

Olivia didn't comment. She was uncomfortable in the hard plastic seat but didn't dare move. Her gaze was fixed firmly on her father.

'There are three types of hedonistic killer: thrill, lust and comfort. You've interviewed more lust killers than you care to remember, and comfort killers are ten-a-penny. But you've rarely come across a thrill killer, have you? Why is that?'

'I'm not sure,' she said quietly.

'You had the opportunity to interview Robert Hansen in 2012 but turned it down. Any other person in your position would have jumped at the chance. Why didn't you?'

'I couldn't get funding to go to Alaska.'

'That's bollocks and you know it. You've used your own money on many occasions to interview a killer. Your grandparents left you very well off and your books sell in their millions around the world. Why didn't you interview Robert Hansen?'

Richard had control of the conversation and Olivia had allowed him to take it. When had that happened? With anyone else she always kept her guard up and never allowed the gruesome details to get under her skin. Here, there was a little voice in her head that kept screaming at her that he was her father, and that hurt more than anything else. Olivia was sweating so much she could smell herself. She felt sick. Was it the stuffy room, her empty stomach, or the fact that her serial-killing father was gaining the upper hand and clearly enjoying himself?

'I honestly can't remember,' she lied.

'Then let me tell you. You didn't interview him because he reminded you of me, didn't he?'

'No.'

'Robert Hansen murdered at least seventeen women in Anchorage, Alaska between 1980 and when he was caught in 1983. He captured his victims and took them to a secluded area where he would release them and hunt them, killing them for fun. He was a thrill killer. I am a thrill killer. You didn't want to interview him because, despite telling yourself you've always wanted to know why I killed, you actually don't want to know at all, do you?'

'That's not true.'

'So, you do want to know why?'

'You've already told me why.' She shivered and turned away.

'But you can't accept that as a reason, can you? You can't imagine a person taking the life of another person simply for pleasure. It goes against everything you believe in.'

'Of course it does,' she almost snapped. 'It should go against everyone's reasoning. Killing is not a natural state.'

'OK,' he said, calmly sitting back in his bed. 'You want the truth? God's honest truth?'

Olivia swallowed. Her mouth was dry. 'Yes.'

Richard slowly leaned forward. He lowered his voice. 'I killed them because I fucking loved it,' he smiled. 'I killed them because I knew I could get away with it. And why? Because your mother gave me the perfect alibi.'

Olivia frowned. 'What are you talking about?'

'Who was my first victim?'

'Diane Hobbs,' Olivia replied without hesitation.

'Date?'

'Thirteenth of April 1995.'

'And what's the significance of that date?'

Olivia thought. It wasn't her birthday, or Claire's. It wasn't her mother's either. 'I don't know.'

'Come on, it's in Sebastian's book.'

'I haven't read it.'

'Are you sure about that?'

'I don't need to read it.'

'You really should have read it.'

'Why?'

'The thirteenth of April is mine and your mum's wedding anniversary.'

Olivia's mouth fell open. Of course it was. How had she forgotten that? Maybe she hadn't wanted to remember any of the good times, as she knew her father's true identity sullied the happy memories.

'I killed Diane in the late afternoon. I went home and there was nobody there. I showered, put my clothes in the washer, had another shower, and cleaned the house as a little treat for your mum. Then I went out, bought a couple of dozen bunches of roses and scattered them about our bedroom. When she came home at four, she was so surprised and happy. If I had appeared on the police's radar when the body was found your mother would have covered for me. I couldn't have been out killing as it was our wedding anniversary and we had the best day ever,' he grinned.

'You used your own wife to cover up for your crimes?' Olivia asked, incredulously.

'Second victim.'

Olivia was dumbstruck. She couldn't speak. She couldn't think. Richard really was pure evil.

'Second victim, Olivia,' Richard said, louder, with more force.

She jumped. 'Julie Wainwright.'

'Date?'

'Sixteenth of August 1995.'

'Now, you might have trouble with this one, and it wasn't mentioned in Sebastian's book either, even though I did tell him. What happened on that specific date?'

She shook her head hard. She really didn't want to play this game.

'To be more accurate, it happened the next day. On the

seventeenth of August we all got up very early because we had to be at the airport for five o'clock as we were flying to Portugal to spend two weeks at my mum and dad's villa in Lagos. Remember now?'

Again, Olivia's eyes widened at the memory. She nodded. She remembered her and Claire getting into the car half asleep while her mum and dad loaded the boot with cases. She'd been so nervous when the plane took off that her father held her hand and read to her from *Peter Pan* until the plane levelled out.

'The day before, on my way home from work, I killed Julie Wainwright. It took me ages driving around trying to find the right victim. It was such a warm, sunny evening, everyone seemed to be out in couples or groups. I found Julie on her own, walking home with a bag of shopping in each hand. I pulled over and asked for directions – no satnav in those days. She looked at my A-to-Z and I elbowed her in the face. She fell backwards. She was more stunned than anything else. I jumped out of the car, grabbed her, threw her in the back and we drove away, leaving the shopping by the roadside. They found that before they found her. Third victim.'

'I'm not doing this,' Olivia said. 'I have very few happy memories to cling onto – I will not have you ruin them.'

'Ah, but you see, the seed is in your head now, Livvy. You know each date was significant for us as a family. All of you were my perfect cover. I used all of you to get away with my crimes.'

Olivia stole a glance at him and saw the twinkle in his eyes; the pleasure and sparkle had brightened his whole face. He was enjoying himself. She stood up.

'Are you leaving?'

'It was a mistake for me to come here.'

'You didn't need to come here. I told Sebastian everything. It's all in his book. Well, most of it. You could have read it any time. I think you wanted to visit. I think you wanted to see me.'

'No. I really didn't.' She headed for the door.

'You may not want to believe it, but it really is the truth. I, Richard Button, your father, whose DNA is inside you, enjoyed ending the life of another human being.'

'How can you enjoy killing someone?' she asked, looking at him with venom.

'It's the ultimate act. Anyone can climb a mountain, travel the length of America on a bike or swim the English Channel. But it takes a special someone to look death in the face and shake his hand. I've looked into people's eyes, seen an expression I cannot even describe, as I've drained them of their life, and I have never felt a feeling of pure contentment anywhere else. That power has been like a nuclear explosion. It's made even greater by knowing very few people walking the earth have experienced anything close to it.'

'You're sick,' she uttered as tears filled her eyes.

'I'm not. I'm really not. To label me as sick is saying that I wasn't in control of my actions, and that couldn't have been further from the truth. I knew exactly what I was doing. I found those women, I followed them, I learned their routines, I hunted and stalked them and knew when the best time to strike was. Sometimes just for a day, sometimes for an hour, sometimes for much longer. I watched Diane Hobbs for six weeks. Can you believe that? For six whole weeks she went about her life unaware that I was right behind her.'

'But why kill her? If the thrill was in the hunt, why end it? Why not go on following her?'

'What's the point of that? Does a lion follow a zebra around all its life just to let it know who's boss? No. It stalks, it puts the fear of God into it, then it obliterates it from the face of the earth. Job done.'

'Oh my God.' Olivia turned away.

'And that's why you've come here today, isn't it? This killer that's on the loose, he's a thrill killer and you haven't got the first idea how to catch him, so you've come to see me for a few tips. I'm right, aren't I?'

Olivia didn't reply.

'Aren't I, Livvy?'

'Yes,' she almost snapped. She was pressed firmly into a corner of the room. The handle on the door was right there for her to reach out, open and leave, but she couldn't tear herself away. It was like passing a car crash on the motorway; you always had to look.

He smiled. 'Tell me, why are you working with the police on this? You've had police forces from all over the world ask you to help them in the past and you've turned them down. Why now?'

'Because…'

'Go on.'

'Because one of the victims was a friend of mine.'

'The detective?'

Olivia nodded.

'He struck lucky, there. I often wish I'd offed someone high up, but, to be honest, I didn't think about the victims until they were named in the press. He won't have known she was a detective when he killed her. All he was interested in was the chase, the hunt, the thrill and putting the fear of God into her. Once she was dead, he'd have stepped over the body and started thinking about the next one. Trust me, Livvy, as much as you build up the kill in your mind, the feeling is over very quickly. You soon realise that it's all about the chase.'

The image of Jessica, her best friend, popped into her mind. Did she know she was pregnant and was trying to get her head around it herself before sharing the news with her, or did she really not know? Either way, those final few minutes of her life were lived in terror. Olivia had walked the crime scene. She'd seen the horror inflicted upon her. She must have been so scared. How can anyone get enjoyment out of doing something so despicable?

Olivia couldn't stay any longer in this room with this…

creature. She pushed down the handle on the door and pulled it open. In the corridor, she heard the normal sounds of the hospital, machines beeping, trolley wheels scraping on floors, people chatting. Everything was normal outside of this room.

'Close the door, Livvy,' her father said, calmly.

She really didn't want to, but her professionalism took over. She'd come this far. She'd endured so much. What else could he tell her that might help her catch this killer?

Reluctantly, she closed the door, though she remained squeezed into the corner of the room.

'There's one thing about the thrill killer you may have overlooked. I doubt he's thought about it much either, but it will be there, at the back of his mind.'

'Go on,' she prompted.

'What he wants, more than anything, is to commit the perfect murder. It's what we all want. He'll want to get away with it for as long as possible and the more he kills, the more he'll think he's doing so. He'll start getting cocky. He'll make mistakes. He'll taunt the police, or even you, now he's seen the great serial killer biographer is looking for him. He won't be able to help himself getting in touch. That'll be his first mistake.'

'The police are getting calls all the time. A great many of them are cranks. How will I know it's him?'

'He'll tell you, and you'll believe him.'

Olivia looked at her father, studied his face. He was no longer smiling as he spoke but looked like he was in deep contemplation.

'How did you feel after you'd been caught?'

'I'm sorry?'

'Well, you say a thrill killer wants to commit the perfect murder, but that means getting away with it. You didn't. Surely that must have been a blow to your ego.'

Richard leaned forward again. The smile was back. 'Olivia, I was convicted of killing eight people. I never said I'd only killed eight.' He winked at her.

Chapter Thirty-Eight

Olivia sat in the back of the taxi on the way home in a state of shock. Her father had confessed to killing more people than the eight he had been convicted for. Could she believe him? She knew what killers were like. They were manipulative; they liked to shock and control people. A killer in prison had been stripped of the power and mind games they were able to hold over their victims. However, when an opportunity presented itself to regain some of that influence, they grabbed it with both hands. Was this what her father was doing? Was he manipulating his own daughter into thinking he was a more prolific killer than originally thought? Was he trying to impress her or scare her? She should have thought of all this before she'd gone in to see him, but, foolishly, she didn't think her father would be so calculating to his own daughter.

As usual, Olivia asked the driver to drop her at the bottom of the cul-de-sac. She stumbled out of the cab and dragged her feet to her front door. She felt physically and mentally drained after spending an hour in her father's company. She held onto the cold iron railings and pulled herself up the steps, where she stopped dead in her tracks at the bunch of yellow roses waiting for her on the doormat. How the fuck had he been able to arrange a delivery of flowers so quickly?

Olivia wanted to cry. She wanted to scream, but she was all spent of emotion. She picked up the flowers, opened the wheelie bin, dumped them inside and slammed the lid shut. She entered the house, making sure she set the alarm as soon as the door was closed.

Her home had always been her place of safety. It didn't matter who she interviewed, the killers she came into contact with, or the distressing gory details they revelled in telling her – she had always known that nothing could penetrate the safety of home. Now, thanks to her father, the horrors and dangers of her everyday life were literally right outside her front door. If she had been thinking clearly, she would have opened her laptop, logged on to the security system and seen exactly who had placed the flowers on her doorstep, but as Olivia leaned against the front door and slowly slid down to the floor, she was thinking anything other than rationally. She wanted to crawl into a bottle of vodka and drown. She wanted to open her mouth and scream until every window in the cul-de-sac shattered. She wanted to phone Ethan Miller, ask him to come round and fuck the living daylights out of her.

One sound managed to break through the miasma of black thoughts running around her mind. It was a tiny tip-tap sound. She opened her eyes and saw Stanley standing less than a foot away from her, his head tilted to one side, his big brown eyes looking at her. She smiled and opened her arms. His tail wagged as he trotted towards her, jumped up and began to nuzzle into her.

'You know how to make me feel better, don't you, Stanley?' she said with a smile.

In the kitchen, Sam had left a detailed note explaining what he'd done today with Stanley. She screwed the note up and tossed it into the bin.

While drinking a glass of wine, she opened the cupboards to see what she could make for dinner. She was in the mood for something fattening, tasty and bad for her. All she had were bland, safe, healthy options – quinoa, chickpeas, wholemeal pasta and dried lentils. She pulled a face at her own lack of adventure and decided on a meat feast pizza from the local takeaway.

The doorbell rang. Stanley yapped and Olivia sighed. The last thing she wanted was a visitor.

Through the spyhole in the solid door she could see Sam standing on the doorstep, hooded sweater acting as shelter from the drizzle. He hopped from foot to foot to stave off the cold. Olivia had no intention of letting him in.

He rang the bell again and Stanley yapped. She wondered if he'd use his key. He shouldn't, not without her permission. She watched, one eye closed, the other firmly fixed on his distorted face. He too leaned into the spyhole even though he wouldn't be able to see in from his side. She held her breath. He was just a few inches away from her.

Eventually, he turned on his heel and went back down the steps. He paused at the bottom then returned to his flat. Olivia double-checked the door was securely locked and returned to the kitchen.

Less than an hour later she was in the living room she rarely used and her feet were up on the coffee table, the fire was roaring, and she was tucking into the twelve-inch pizza with extra cheese and extra pepperoni. A tray of chips was balanced on her lap which she'd liberally covered with salt and vinegar, plus a few she'd set aside for Stanley who was next to her, eyeing up her dinner.

'When I was little, Stanley, I always wanted a sausage dog. I've no idea why,' she said as she fed him a chip and she tore a bite out of her third slice of pizza. 'Actually, I do know why. Mrs Montague a few doors down had two. They were black and tan just like you are. What did she call them? Anyway, it doesn't matter. They were gorgeous little things; always pleased to see me when I went around. Then Jessica was given one just before... well, just before. I remember asking Dad to get me one. He kept saying no. He said we didn't have room for one, which was a lie. I mean, you don't take up much space, do you?'

Olivia leaned back into the sofa. 'Mrs Montague,' she said wistfully. 'She was a lovely old lady. She's probably dead now. I remember going back to the house after... well... after everything that happened to collect my things with my gran and grandad. She came to the house. She was in floods of tears. She hugged me tight for so long. She wanted to keep in touch and wrote her address and phone number down on a card and gave it to Gran, but we didn't bother writing to her or anything. Grandad said it was best to cut all ties with the area. He was probably right.'

The doorbell rang for a third time in less than an hour. Stanley jumped down from the sofa.

'If that's Sam again, I'm going to tell him to piss off.' Olivia stood up and staggered on her feet. She'd already had a bottle of wine which had obviously gone straight to her head.

At the door, she looked through the spyhole and saw DI Foley looking windswept and half-drowned.

She disarmed the alarm and pulled the door open, shivering as a gust of wind blew into the house.

'Amyas. Is everything all right?'

'Can I come in?'

'Of course you can.' She stood back to let him in and quickly closed the door on the bad weather. 'I hope you're hungry. I ordered too much pizza and I'm making a real pig of myself.'

'I'm starving.'

She opened a second bottle of wine and handed a glass to Foley, who sat on the armchair and helped himself to a couple of slices of pizza, garlic bread and a handful of chips.

'Has something happened? Have you found another body?' she asked, hoping she wasn't slurring her words.

'No. Nothing like that. Just... well, emotions are running high at the station. Leon says one thing, Holly says another and before you know it they're all kicking off.'

'Is this to do with Leon having a thing for Jessica?'

'He can't focus on the investigation. He's hell bent on finding out who got her pregnant. He's convinced himself the father of her baby is the killer.'

'Remove him from the case,' Olivia said.

'He's one of my best officers.'

'Not when he's acting like this, he's not. You're trying to find a serial killer who is one step ahead of you at every turn. You need every single detective one hundred per cent on their A-game. If he's got his own personal vendetta, he's a liability. More people will die, Amyas. You need him off this case.'

'We're falling apart,' he said, looking up at her with tears in his eyes.

Olivia went over to him, sat on the arm of the chair and put her arm tightly around his shoulders. 'You need a break. When was the last time you had a proper meal or a good night's sleep?'

He thought. 'I don't know,' he said.

'You're no good to anyone like this – to your team, to Jessica or to the other victims.'

'I just keep thinking about how frightened she must have been.' He wiped his eyes with his sleeves before the tears had chance to fall. 'We know what he's doing to them. She'll have known he was going to kill her, and he was playing with her. We're only surmising she didn't know she was pregnant because she didn't tell you, but what if she did know? What if she just hadn't got around to telling you yet?'

'Don't do this to yourself,' she said, even thought she'd done exactly the same thing to herself a couple of hours ago.

'She was having my child. I was going to be a father. We wouldn't have been a conventional family by any stretch of the imagination, but I'd have been there for her and the baby. I'd have done everything right for her.'

'I know you would.'

'And then some bastard comes along and destroys it all.'

Olivia went over to the coffee table, pulled a few tissues out of the box and went back to Foley. She knelt down on the floor and began dabbing his eyes and nose.

'You need to take a step back. If you continue like this, you'll end up having a breakdown.'

'I can't. I can't stop. I need to catch this man.'

Olivia took a breath. 'I went to visit my father this afternoon.'

Foley's eyes lit up. 'Really?'

'I needed to know some things.' She stood up and went over to the fire. She glanced down at the cooling pizza and felt sick. 'You said it yourself – who better to catch a killer than a killer?'

'I shouldn't have said that. I'm sorry. How do you feel?'

She thought for a moment. 'Numb. Empty. But then, I'm hardened. I'm pretty sure there's ice wrapped around my heart.'

'That's not true,' he said softly. 'Did he tell you?'

Olivia stared into the fire. 'He told me a few things. Did you know he killed his first victim on the day of his wedding anniversary?'

Foley nodded. 'I read that part in Sebastian's book last night.'

'I never knew. I never put the dates together. His second victim he killed the evening before we flew to Portugal for a holiday. He was using his family to give him alibis. He was able to switch off from killer to happy husband and father so easily. And Mum was excited about her anniversary and a holiday abroad, so she didn't notice any hint of a change in him. How cold is that?'

'What about the other victims? What events do they coincide with?' he asked.

'I don't know. I don't want to know. Not yet.'

They fell silent. Olivia could feel Foley's gaze burning into her.

'He's hurt you, hasn't he?'

'I don't have many happy memories from my childhood. The ones I do have were somewhat tainted when I thought about what he'd gone on to do. Now, I don't know what are genuinely happy memories and what were manufactured by him to give himself an alibi. He's fucking ruined everything, Amyas,' she said, crying.

He went over to her and placed his arm around her shoulders. She didn't even flinch at the touch.

'He's playing mind games,' Olivia continued. 'He's loving the fact that nine million people living in London are in fear for their lives.' She turned back to Foley and wiped her eyes with her sleeve. 'I think we may have made a mistake asking the *Evening Standard* to run that feature.'

'But you said it might flush him out. He'll love the fact that you're helping in the hunt for him.'

'I know. I was wrong. I'm sorry,' she said, struggling to hold onto her emotion as she wrapped her arms tightly around herself. 'He'll do exactly what my father did. He'll laugh. He'll love the fact you're bringing in an expert, that you're stopping at nothing to catch him, yet he's eluding you. It won't flush him out. It'll feed his ego.'

'So, what do we do now? Where do we go from here?'

'As I said before, I believe you already know who the killer is. You'll have already interviewed him. I also believe that in the next few days, I'll meet him for the first time, too.'

'How do you mean?'

'The feature in the paper will have told him I'm helping the police. He'll love that. But now he'll want to show himself to me to prove how clever he is.'

'You think he's just going to come up to you, hold out his hand and introduce himself?'

'No. But someone new will come into my life, and it will be him, because he will want to be close to me.'

'Jesus Christ, Olivia. What have we done?'

'I've put myself in his path. He'll come for me, and that's how we'll catch him.'

'He could kill you.'

'He won't. He'll want me to write a book about him. I can't do that if I'm dead.'

Foley took a deep breath. 'What if you're wrong?'

'Then you'll have to adopt Stanley,' Olivia said, with a nervous laugh.

Chapter Thirty-Nine

Foley stayed long enough to have a second glass of wine but decided to leave while he was still able to drive. Besides, he had his own dogs to walk and feed.

He promised Olivia he would protect her and made her promise that she would take care of herself. She showed him out and closed the door behind him. She was light-headed from the wine and fumbled with the security chain before giving up.

She let Stanley out into the back garden to do his business and finished off the second bottle of wine while waiting. Once he was back in the house, she locked the door and went straight to bed. She struggled out of her clothes and slipped under the duvet. Stanley needed help getting up and found a comfortable spot at the bottom of the bed.

Olivia was in a deep sleep within minutes. As was Stanley.

It was a little after one o'clock in the morning when the key turned in the lock and Olivia's front door was slowly pushed open. The wind had eased slightly but the rain continued to fall.

The hallway lit up with the white light from the streetlamps outside and wet leather shoes left footprints on the wooden floor as Sam Halliday crept into the house.

Earlier, he'd watched as Olivia had let the detective into the house, whereas *he'd* been ignored. He waited, counting the minutes, until the man left. He'd been in there over an hour. That rankled. Sam wouldn't have intruded. Sam would have been happy with ten minutes in Olivia's company. He was doing her a favour by walking her dog, yet she couldn't be bothered to invite him in for a quick chat or a cup of tea. No, she rejected him, but welcomed the detective in. That wasn't fair.

Sam had waited in his basement flat in a deathly silence while Olivia's house slipped into darkness. He'd had no idea how long it would take her to fall asleep and he had almost nodded off himself while waiting. He should have been at work, but a colleague had asked him to swap shifts. He was more than happy to do so. Despite enjoying helping Olivia with Stanley, he wasn't seeing her as she was out all day. He'd hoped to see her this evening, but that fucking detective had been let in instead.

In the hallway of Olivia's house, he stood quietly and inhaled. He could smell leftover takeaway and a hint of wet dog. The fragrance Olivia used had disappeared. He listened and caught the rhythmic sound of the deep breaths of someone in a relaxing sleep.

Carefully, he wrapped his hand around the doorknob, twisted and pushed the door open.

There was very little light in the bedroom. Fingers of brilliant white came from behind the curtains and cast lengthy shadows across the double bed.

Stanley, alert to any hint of a noise, woke and lifted his head up. He recognised Sam straight away and wagged his tail. Sam stepped into the room and patted the dog on the head.

He tiptoed over to Olivia's side of the bed and dropped to his haunches. She was lying on her side, facing him. He could just make out the flittering of her eyes behind the closed lids, evidence of her deep sleep.

He reached out and lifted the corner of the duvet slightly. He could see she was naked and had to bite his lip from gasping when his eyes fell on her small, firm breasts. He wanted nothing more than to place his hand inside and gently caress them as she slept. He was achingly close to experiencing a moment of perfection, but he was unable to touch her for fear of disturbing her.

Olivia's mouth was open slightly and the tip of her tongue stuck out. A droplet of drool caught the light. Sam reached out and captured it on his little finger, taking care not to touch her in case she woke. He brought his finger to his own lips and licked it before standing up and making his way out of the room. At the door, he paused and picked up the pair of knickers Olivia had been wearing and idly tossed aside as she undressed. He pocketed them before leaving.

Chapter Forty

Saturday 24th February 2024

Olivia slept through her alarm clock and woke with a throbbing head. A mixture of alcohol and the trauma of yesterday had resulted in a strange dream in which she felt she was being stalked and hounded, that her life was in danger. She woke with a start around three o'clock, causing Stanley to bark. She felt cold and exposed and put it down to having fallen asleep naked, something she never did, preferring the comfort of pyjamas.

After a shower and a meagre breakfast of plain yogurt and granola, she was ready to face the day. She couldn't remember where she had parked her scooter. It was either outside her office or at the police station. She didn't usually go into work at the weekends, but she'd missed so much with helping Foley that she needed to catch up. The thought of catching the Tube on a Saturday filled her with dread.

As she left the house and made sure the door was locked she turned and saw a marked police car leaving the cul-de-sac. Mrs Blackstock from the house opposite was standing at the bottom of the steps, her arms folded across her chest, a worried expression on her overly made-up face.

'Is everything all right?' Olivia called out.

Mrs Blackstock jumped and turned to Olivia. 'Oh, good morning. Yes. Fine.'

'There hasn't been a break-in or anything, has there?'

'No.' Dorothy Blackstock was a woman whose age it was incredibly difficult to estimate. She wore clothes that were far too young for her, dyed her hair and slathered herself in make-up to hide every wrinkle, mark and pore. She doused herself in a strong scent that Olivia could smell before Dorothy was even halfway across the road. 'We're having a party tonight. Nothing big. Rupert and I have been married for twenty years,' she said in a nondescript accent.

'Oh, congratulations,' Olivia said in the lengthy pause Dorothy left.

'Thank you.'

'Anyway, Elizabeth, the silly girl, posted it on Facebook and before you know it the whole of London is talking about the party. We've had threats of gatecrashers and everything. So that's Elizabeth grounded until she's twenty-one,' she said, rolling her eyes. She looked over her shoulder to make sure nobody was eavesdropping then lowered her voice. 'We've got a friend in the police force. I called him up and asked if he could send a uniformed officer round to have a chat to Elizabeth. She looked scared to death thinking she was going to be arrested. Serves her right, too. Anyway, they've said they'll increase patrols around here tonight, just in case, but now the post has been taken down, they doubt people will remember.'

'Fingers crossed.'

'Absolutely. By the way –' she edged closer and lowered her voice '– I haven't sent out invitations to the neighbours, especially after that business over the parking with the Cokers two doors down. However, you'd be more than welcome to join us. Rupert's brother's coming down from Stirling. He's in criminal law,' she said proudly.

'Oh. Well, thank you very much for the invite. I'm a bit behind with work, but if I get a chance, I might come across for a drink.'

'You'd be more than welcome. Anyway, must dash. I've a thousand and one things to do and you know what men are like.'

She trotted back across the road in ridiculously high heels.

Olivia lifted the collar on her coat and headed down the cul-de-sac. Out of the corner of her eye, she could see Sam standing at his kitchen window looking up at her. She pretended she hadn't seen him. She was grateful to him for helping with Stanley, but his overfamiliarity in her home was making her feel uncomfortable. She was aware he was finding it difficult to settle in London, but he was latching onto the first person who'd been pleasant to him, and that wasn't healthy. He needed to widen his circle. He needed friends in his own demographic. She wanted her key back and tried to come up with a way to ask without hurting his feelings. She didn't want to upset him, but she needed her privacy.

As she walked to the Tube station, Olivia's mind began to wander. A party had been advertised all over social media, and the killer stalking London loved an audience. If he had read the feature in the *Evening Standard* and was now watching her, he would know where she lived. The party was his perfect cover for committing a murder. This could be the breakthrough she was looking for.

Olivia needed to think. Instead of heading for the Tube station, she turned around and headed home. A smile appeared on her lips. If she played this right, she would be able to catch the killer tonight. There was only one problem: she would be revealing her true self to the world. Is that what she wanted? No. Would she give away her privacy to stop the killings? Yes.

Chapter Forty-One

Richard Button looked up at the nurse and smiled. They made eye contact, briefly, before she quickly looked away. She was nervous at being alone in such a small space with a convicted serial killer. Why did the prison guard think it necessary to leave the room whenever a nurse came to check his blood pressure and heart rate?

'How am I doing?' Richard asked.

'Fine,' she replied quickly, tearing off the blood pressure cuff.

'No lasting damage?'

'You're due another scan later. That'll show if there's been any serious damage, but your heart rate is spot on.'

'Excellent. I'll be able to go back home soon,' he said with a sly grin.

She smiled nervously before quickly leaving the room.

Richard chuckled to himself. He enjoyed making people feeling uncomfortable. Neither his fellow prisoners in Belmarsh nor the guards responded to his jibes and empty threats. Out there, in the real world, he might have been convicted of murdering eight people, but inside the prison he was just a number. That hurt. He didn't necessarily care about being feared, but he felt he was due some respect built on his history.

There was a knock on the door, and it opened slightly. A fresh-faced young man in jeans and a blue checked shirt popped his head around the door.

'Mr Button? I'm Ronald Nash.' He held up the lanyard around his neck, but from this distance, Richard couldn't see it. 'I'm a physiotherapist. I've come to talk you through your recovery and how you can improve your health when you go back...'

'Home?' Richard grinned.

'Well, quite,' Ronald said. He pushed the thick-rimmed glasses up his nose and stepped fully into the room, closing the door behind him. He grabbed the chair and sat closer to Richard than any other visitor had. 'How are you feeling?' he asked once he'd crossed his legs and took a notepad out of his folder.

'I'm fine.'

'You're not in any pain?'

'No.'

'And your breathing isn't laboured in any way?'

'No.'

'Have you been out of bed much?'

'Only to go for scans and X-rays. I tried to walk up a flight of stairs yesterday but had to stop halfway. I get tired easily.' He was genuinely unhappy about his state of health. In prison, Richard used the gym whenever he could. He walked miles around the exercise yard and on the treadmill. He lifted weights and, as much as was possible, didn't indulge in carbohydrates and fatty food. However, it was a prison, not a health resort, and there was only so much he could do before the cheap food clogged up his arteries and caused his heart to malfunction.

'Well, take it slowly. One day at a time. There's no point in rushing these things and ending up back in here,' Ronald said.

'I've got all the time in the world, mate,' Richard said with a smile.

Ronald looked up and returned the smile. 'I'm afraid I've exhausted the extent of my medical knowledge when it comes to rehabilitation.'

'I'm sorry?' Richard frowned.

'I'm here under false pretences, Richard. May I call you Richard?'

'Erm... I suppose.'

'You'll have read about me in the papers, I'm guessing.' He nodded to the two folded-up copies of the *Evening Standard* Richard had on his table. 'The Butcher of London isn't the most inventive of nicknames the press could have come up with, but it'll do for now.'

Richard's eyes widened. 'You're him?'

He held his arms out as if revealing himself. 'In the flesh.'

Richard beamed. 'And I'm guessing your name isn't Ronald Nash.'

'No. I'd like to keep that nugget of information to myself for the moment. I'm sure you understand.'

'Of course. Why have you come to see me?'

'I couldn't resist. When I read in the paper about the great Richard Button suffering a heart attack and being transferred out of prison for treatment, I knew I had to try and find a way to visit.'

A smile appeared on Richard's lips. He'd never met one of his admirers before. He'd received countless letters from around the world from people enamoured by him and his crimes, but to have one sitting within touching distance was like all his Christmases had come at once.

'You're a fan?'

'I'm a big fan. I was born the year after you were convicted—'

'Well, that makes me feel old.'

'Sorry, I didn't mean it to. I've read every book written about you. I feel like we have a special connection.'

'Oh. Why's that?'

'We grew up in Suffolk, me and my family. We moved to

London when I was three years old. My dad bought this house that hadn't been lived in for years. It was run-down and needed doing up. He bought it for a song, I believe the saying is. A lovely spacious family home on Elmbridge Avenue.'

Richard's eyes widened and a smile spread on his face.

'Your dad bought my house?'

Ronald nodded excitedly.

'The neighbours thought we were mad to be living in the house of a serial killer. When I was old enough and I told people at school where I lived they asked all sorts of questions. I was so popular. People wanted to know if there were any bloodstains, if it was haunted, if I heard strange noises in the night. I tell you, nobody dared knock on our door on Halloween.'

Richard threw his head back and laughed.

'It was years before the neighbours sent us a Christmas card. When I was young, I didn't fully understand, but then I found that book Sebastian Lister wrote. I've lost count of the number of times I've read it. I loved it. I grew up sleeping in your Olivia's bedroom. And now, here I am, sitting opposite the great man himself. You have no idea how amazing this is for me,' he said with a huge grin on his face.

'And you're following in my footsteps, it would seem?'

'Of course. Who wants to go to university and study for years to become a doctor or something when you can achieve worldwide infamy by becoming one of the great serial killers? And how good will it be when it's discovered that, by pure chance, I lived in your house? There are going to be so many books written about me. They'll start believing in some kind of... I don't know... ethereal being that's attached itself to the house. Our very own Amityville House of Horror.' Ronald's excitement was palpable. He couldn't sit still.

'How many have you...?' Richard asked, tailing off.

'Killed? Only seven up to now. One off your total.'

Richard raised an eyebrow. 'You plan to continue?'

'Of course. I couldn't stop if I wanted to. It's fucking amazing.' He beamed.

Richard looked at him, studied him.

'What?' Ronald asked when he noticed Richard's stare.

'You remind me so much of me when I was killing,' he said quietly. 'That thirst, that rush, that feeling like you're a god.'

'Do you miss it?'

Richard thought before answering. He gave a slight nod.

'I have so many questions I want to ask you, I don't know where to start. How old were you when you first decided to start killing? Did you always want to kill from when you were young? Or did it come later, after you were married and had kids?'

Richard looked bewildered as he was bombarded by questions. 'To be honest with you, *Roland*,' he said, purposely getting his name incorrect, 'I can't answer those questions. I don't actually know. I just... I just saw this woman one day and I had this urge build up inside me and I wanted to put my hands around her neck and squeeze the life out of her.'

'Did you?'

'No. The very thought shocked me. I was married. I had kids. I had a good job and a good life. I took a few days away from everything and thought about it. My life wasn't good at all. It was dull and boring. I was doing everything by rote and not enjoying life to its full potential.'

'And that potential was having another person's life in your hands.'

'Precisely.'

'Can I ask, though, that last kill of yours, Fiona Goddard. It was...' He struggled for the correct word.

'Sloppy,' Richard offered, though he didn't tell him Fiona Goddard wasn't his final kill before his wife and daughter. It was merely the final one he was convicted of.

'Why did you do it?' he asked, leaning forward, elbows on his knees, waiting for the answer.

'The more people you kill and the longer you go undetected, the more you crave it. Like I said, you feel like you're a god and there is no greater feeling in the world. You've killed so many people and nobody knows who you are. You begin to think you're invisible, infallible, and you start listening to that voice inside that tells you you're capable of absolutely anything.' There was a look of serenity on Richard's face as he was taken back to another life, one he obviously missed and longed for.

Ronald cleared his throat. 'There's a theory that you wanted to get caught.'

Richard turned his head sharply to look at him. His face showed anger. 'You've been researching.'

'I live in the age of information. It's all at my fingertips.'

'Too much information is not always a good thing. Don't believe everything you read. I did not want to get caught,' he said firmly. 'I wasn't finished. Not by a long shot.'

'But you can't continue.'

'No,' Richard said, relaxing into his pillow. 'I can't.' He turned to look at Ronald once again. He smiled. 'Tell me about your first kill.'

Ronald shook his head. 'My first couple of kills were pathetic. I'd rather forget about them, but they're part of my legacy. I was so nervous. You know, I actually pissed myself when I stabbed Neil Parker. A single stab wound, that's all it was, and I wet myself like a child. I didn't think I'd be able to do it anymore. I had to talk myself into killing again. I knew this was my path – I've been surrounded by murder and the myth of it for years, thanks to you – but I needed to grow, to become someone different.'

'What did you do?' Richard asked. He watched Ronald Marsh with wide-eyed expectation. He was enthralled by his story.

'I needed to boost my confidence. If I came across as nervous I'd fuck the whole thing up. I knocked on a few doors, tried to worm my way into some poor old dear's house. I pretended to be from one of those energy watchdogs where they ask you to change suppliers to save money. It's all bollocks and nobody really knows what it's all about, especially the elderly, so I was able to take advantage. I nicked something from every house I went in. It didn't matter what it was, I wasn't going for anything valuable, I just wanted to feed my confidence. I took remote controls, fridge magnets, pens, a packet of biscuits. They're not going to call the cops and say they've lost their remote, are they? By the time I stabbed that Calvin lad, I knew I had it in me.'

'But it wasn't enough, was it?'

'No,' Ronald said, looking down. 'I couldn't spend any time with him. That's what I wanted. I saw the look in his eyes when I put the knife in, and that feeling was electric. That was a fucking multiple orgasm, but it was a public place. I had to leave or I'd have been caught.'

'So you changed your MO?'

'I *evolved*,' he said with a crude smile. 'I was a master at getting into people's houses. If I found the right woman, I'd be able to terrorise her until I wanted to go in for the kill. I could spend hours with them if I wanted to.'

'And do you?'

'Oh yes,' he almost salivated. 'That first woman, Sarah Millington, I spent the whole night with her. I chased her around the house. I terrified the bitch. She was crying, begging and pleading with me to leave her alone. A shallow stab here, a deep stab there, I had her in the palm of my hand. I was rock hard too. I couldn't believe the adrenaline rush. Why hadn't I started doing this years ago?' His face lit up in the retelling.

'You've found your niche.'

'I found what I was born to become.'

'You're a serial killer,' Richard smiled.

'I'm a fucking serial killer,' Ronald agreed.

Richard held out his right hand. Ronald couldn't hide his

excitement. He reached out, took the older man's hand in his and shook it hard.

'Welcome to the club,' Richard said.

'Thank you, sir.'

'Why did you really come here?' Richard asked.

'What do you mean?' Ronald asked, pulling his hand away.

'I'm a convicted killer in a public hospital. You must have known I'd be surrounded by prison officers. You've taken a hell of a risk coming here.'

'I wanted to see you.'

'You've lived with me in your head for years, haven't you?'

Ronald nodded.

'You're disappointed, though, aren't you? They always say never meet your heroes, as it'll ruin the mystique you've built up about them. You'll go away, relive this conversation over and over, and you'll feel flat.'

Ronald's face dropped.

'I should probably go.' Ronald stood to leave. He took a tentative peek through the Venetian blinds out into the corridor.

'I've read about you in the newspapers. The police have drafted in Doctor Olivia Winter. You'll know all about her, I'm guessing.'

The smile appeared once again on Ronald's face. 'The great forensic psychologist. Of course I know about her. She's interviewed some of the greats. Though she's never interviewed you, I've noticed.'

'Do you want to know why that is?'

Ronald frowned.

'Come and sit back down.'

Ronald obliged.

'Would you do something for me?'

'Of course.'

'Obviously your next victim will put you on a par with me. I don't even mind if you eclipse my total, but how about we make your next victim a bit special.'

'What do you mean?'

'You've read about me, obviously. You know everything about me; that I killed my wife and daughter?'

'Yes,' he nodded excitedly.

'And that I had a second daughter.'

'Yes. I slept in her room for years.'

'Pass me that top paper.'

Ronald reached for the newspaper and handed it to him. Richard took his time as he flicked through it. He folded it back and handed it to Ronald.

'Olivia Winter. She was born Olivia Button.'

It took a moment for the penny to drop. 'No. Fucking. Way.'

'Yes. Fucking. Way.'

'Olivia Winter is your daughter?'

Richard nodded and smirked.

'That is fucking mental.'

'I want you to make her your eighth victim.'

Ronald's smile dropped. He looked from his hero to the smiling photo of Olivia in the newspaper then back up to his mentor.

'Why do you want me to kill your daughter?'

'Parents aren't supposed to have a favourite child, but I did. Livvy was my favourite. I knew the moment she was born she was going to do something special with her life,' he laughed to himself. 'I didn't think it was going to be something like this. However, when I knew the police were on to me, the first person I thought about was Livvy. It wasn't my wife; it was my Livvy. I couldn't have her be disappointed in me. That's why I went home to kill them all.

'It was easy killing Geraldine and Claire. I'd never really bonded with Claire. She was always her mother's child. But Livvy, she was my star. When it came to it, I couldn't kill her. I stabbed her four times, but none of them were deep enough to kill her. I just couldn't do it.'

'Why not?'

'I don't know,' he said, looking away.

'Did you and she... you know...?' he trailed off.

Richard looked at him. 'What?'

'Did you... did the love you had for Olivia go further... you know,' he said, clearly uncomfortable with asking if Richard sexually abused his oldest daughter.

Richard didn't say anything. He continued to stare at his visitor. Unblinkingly, he burned a hole in him with his gaze. The longer he looked, the more uncomfortable the situation became.

Ronald cleared his throat and looked away first. 'So why do you want me to do it?'

Richard let the silence grow. He was taking everything in about this young man in front of him. He'd learned so much more in that awkward silence than words would ever tell him. 'The so-called experts think they know everything there is to know about serial killers. Let's show them how wrong they are. You're The Butcher of London, and you hate that title, but you're my number-one fan, so why don't you turn yourself into The Riverside Killer? Pick up where I left off. Grab Olivia, take her to the bank of the Thames and take her heart out.'

Ronald's face paled. 'Take her heart out?'

Richard nodded. 'Take it out and deliver it to the detective in charge. DI Amyas Foley at Sanderson Street Police Station.'

Ronald thought for a moment. 'That's fucking sick.'

'A word of warning. Olivia is my daughter, remember. She's the daughter of a serial killer. She's going to put up a fight like you wouldn't believe.'

'I'm sure I can handle her.'

'Make me proud,' Richard said with a wink.

Chapter Forty-Two

SERIAL KILLER HUNTER IS SERIAL KILLER'S DAUGHTER

Renowned forensic psychologist, Olivia Winter, has been unmasked as the only surviving daughter of serial killer Richard Button.

Doctor Winter, 34, a leading forensic psychologist at the Behavioural Science Administration, has travelled the world interviewing some of the most notorious serial killers to glean insight into why they committed their appalling crimes and to get an understanding of the mindset of serial killers. Her one goal, she said in a newspaper interview in 2018, was to discover the reasoning behind the killings in the hope of identifying future serial killers before they strike.

The fact that Ms Winter, who lives in an exclusive Camden suburb, is the daughter of a man who murdered eight people, including his own wife and daughter, tells us as much about Olivia's own state of mind as it does the men and women she's been trying to understand for the past ten years.

Can a woman who was stabbed four times at the age of nine by her own father, and who witnessed the brutal murder of her family, remain impartial when she's writing award-winning books about criminal psychology, papers in trade journals, and lecturing students around the world on what turns a person into a multiple murderer?

The Metropolitan Police have drafted Ms Winter into their investigation to hunt The Butcher of London who has claimed seven victims. A police source said that despite Ms Winter working alongside Detective Inspector Foley, they are still no closer to a suspect or even a person of interest.

In interviews, Ms Winter has previously remained elusive and aloof when questioned about her personal life. How damaged must she still be by what she went through as a child, and how capable is she of tracking down a killer when her own judgement could possibly be impaired?

Professor Norman January of Liverpool University, an expert in victimology said: 'While it isn't impossible for a person to recover from unimaginable trauma as a child, they will be changed by what they have witnessed. Whether they were caught up in a terrorist attack, displaced by an act of war, or survived a rape or attempted murder, their whole life is shaped by that moment, whether consciously or unconsciously. Here we have a highly intelligent and respected woman like Olivia Winter generating theories about serial murderers, and now we see she is related to one of Britain's most notorious killers, we have to ask ourselves whether her conclusions aren't shaped by a subconscious desire to understand why her father killed her mother and sister in the first place. In fact, we have to ask what led Ms Winter to take up such a career at all.'

Olivia was not at her Westminster office yesterday and her colleague, Sebastian Lister, who wrote the bestselling book on Richard Button, declined to comment.

Olivia didn't read the article. She saw the headline on the newspaper's website and immediately ran to the downstairs toilet to vomit up the breakfast she'd just forced down. Who had done this? Why had they done this? What purpose lay behind exposing her secret? The fact she had been contemplating doing this very thing herself only made the treachery harder to stomach.

Her mobile began to ring. It sounded muffled while her head was down the toilet. She let it ring and soon the voicemail kicked in, only for it to start ringing again less than a minute later.

This was a nightmare. She'd changed her name when she'd been forced to change schools once again due to the constant bullying and name-calling. When she became Olivia Winter, she became a new person. Yes, she had entered the world of criminal psychology to try and find some answers as to why a seemingly loving father and husband would become such a vile and evil man, but that was not her main goal. She was interested in unlocking the door of what made a person take another person's life. Were people born murderers or were they shaped by their surroundings and upbringings to become killers?

Her mobile rang again.

Now, whenever anyone read a paper she published or a book she had written, they'd have her father at the back of their minds and wonder if she'd written it just so she could understand him rather than the real subject of the text.

She flushed the toilet and leaned back against the cold tiled wall. Tears were rolling down her face. She didn't know if they were from her secret being exposed or the physical retching.

Stanley trotted into the bathroom. He tilted his head as he looked at her before snuggling up next to her, sensing her need for comfort.

'Maybe I should just pack everything in and live in the middle of nowhere with you, Stanley. I could get another dog, maybe a dozen or so, and spend the rest of my days hiding from the world, living off-grid.'

The doorbell rang.

'Oh, fuck off,' she said through gritted teeth.

She hoped it wasn't Sam. She couldn't be doing with his non-problems this morning. If it was a journalist asking for a comment she had no idea how she'd react. She hated journalists. On every occasion in the past when she'd been interviewed they'd always question her private life: was she married, did she have any kids, was she seeing someone? They never asked a man the same questions. Sebastian was never quizzed about his personal life, so why was it deemed acceptable to question a woman in this way?

The doorbell rang again.

'Olivia, it's me, Foley. Are you in?' Foley shouted through the letterbox.

She struggled to stand up and made her way to the door. She welcomed a friendly face.

'I came over as soon as I saw,' he said, holding up the newspaper.

She let him into the house and closed the door behind him, locking it and activating the alarm.

'How are you feeling?' he asked as he made his way to the kitchen.

'Sick. I can't believe I've been betrayed like this.'

'I called the editor of the paper. She owes me a favour. I asked her to name her source and she said she couldn't. The story came through anonymously, but he had facts that checked out.'

'He?'

'Just a guess. So, who knows your real identity?' he asked as he sat down on the sofa next to where Stanley had curled up.

'You make it sound like I'm in the witness protection programme. Olivia Winter is my real identity. I just don't make it known who my family are. Coffee?'

'Please.'

'Jessica knew. I doubt she told anyone, though. She wasn't like that.' Olivia set about making the coffee. Her voice broke as she spoke about her only friend. 'Sebastian knows. That's how we met all those years ago.'

'Could he have phoned the papers?'

'Why would he do that now all of a sudden? He could have done it years ago.'

'Anyone else?'

'My grandparents. But they're both dead.'

'Would they have told anyone? Friends? Neighbours?'

'No. They were overprotective of me. It was them who suggested I take their surname so people wouldn't realise who I was. When I changed my name, I moved school and we moved to a new area, so nobody knew us.'

'Can you think of anyone else?'

'No. It's not like I— Ah.'

'What?'

'Sam.'

'Who's Sam?'

'He lives in the basement flat next door. He's been looking after Stanley for me whilst I've been at work. He found a copy of Sebastian's book on my bedside table.'

'What was he doing in your bedroom?'

'He went in after Stanley. He didn't think the dog was allowed to go in there. The thing is, the book shouldn't have been in there. I keep them hidden away on the top floor, but... I don't know. Maybe I had brought one down,' she said, looking confused as she ran her fingers through her knotted hair.

'Could Sam have been up to the top floor while you were out?'

'Why would he do that?'

'To be nosy.'

'I... I don't know. I don't really know him that well.'

'Yet you've given him a key.'

'I felt sorry for him. He's lonely. And he was attacked last week. I just... oh, I don't know.' She slumped against the island and put her head in her hands.

'Olivia.' He waited for her to look up. 'You said the killer will be keeping an eye on the investigation, which means he'll have known you were helping us, even more so after the article in the papers. Do you think it's possible he's been following you; that he knows who you really are and is playing with you?'

She thought for a long moment. 'I don't know,' she replied, barely above a whisper. 'This could ruin everything.'

'Why do you think that?'

'Because every time I'm mentioned in the papers or I have a new book out or I'm lecturing somewhere, all people are going to want to talk about is who my fucking father is. I'll never be rid of the man. I should never have agreed to help Jessica. I should have seen this coming. I *did* see this coming. Bloody newspapers! They're relentless. They love any kind of dirt and gossip. They—'

'Olivia, calm down.'

'Calm down? How do you expect me to be calm when I'm going to be all over the news, when I'm going to be stared at in the street, when people are going to have that look on their face that they're just itching to question me about how did I not know that my father had killed six women while living under the same roof.'

'You were nine years old, for crying out loud. How could you have possibly known?'

'My mother should have.'

'No.' Foley jumped up and went over to her. He held her by the shoulders. 'Don't do this to yourself, Olivia. Don't let him win and sully the memory of your mother. You know, more than anyone, what serial killers are like. They're manipulative, they're sneaky and they're secretive. Your mother had no idea what was going on, and nobody could have guessed how it was going to end. Do not let him taint your memories. That's what he wants.'

'I shouldn't have visited him,' she cried.

'I know. I apologise for that. I shouldn't have pushed you.'

'This is such a mess. I don't know what to do next.'

'Come here.' He pulled her to his shoulder and allowed her to sob on him.

Olivia felt herself soften. The last time a man had held her in his arms was in her bed dressed in biker leathers. Ethan's method of trying to help her forget was very different to Foley's. It hadn't worked. Maybe the soothing, friendly approach was needed.

She had known Foley for less than a week, but his hold was comforting. She leaned her head on his shoulder and breathed in his scent – coffee, deodorant and a strong hint of fabric conditioner. It was a smell that brought back happy memories of life with her grandparents. It didn't seem to matter how much she was bullied at school – the hurtful remarks, the taunts, the kicks – her grandfather had always known that one of his hugs would make things right. She'd sit on his lap, her head on his chest, breathing in his Brut fragrance and whatever her grandmother washed his clothes in. She could have stayed like that for ever.

Her angry tears had stopped. Olivia pushed herself out of Foley's embrace. He wiped her eyes with his thumbs and smiled.

'You're a good woman. You've survived so much. Don't let people who don't know you and who don't matter change who you are.'

'You're right,' she sniffled. 'Thank you.'

'You're welcome.'

They held eye contact a little too long. Amyas swallowed hard, and his pupils dilated. Olivia leaned forward, but stopped herself just in time.

'I'll go and have a word with this Sam character next door,' he said, clearing his throat and backing away. 'You have a shower, get dressed and, you know, just take a day off or something.' His words were lost as he made his way out of the kitchen to avoid any awkwardness.

Olivia turned to Stanley who was looking up at her from the sofa with wide brown eyes. 'I think he likes me,' she said with an innocent smile.

Chapter Forty-Three

Foley walked down the damp stone steps to Sam Halliday's basement flat. He took in the pristine bike and pressed the doorbell. It was a while before the door was opened and he was about to ring again when a sleepy-looking young man with bed hair and wearing a thick dressing gown answered.

'Sam Halliday?'

'Yes.'

'Detective Inspector Foley,' he said, showing his identification. 'Mind if I come in for a quick word?'

Foley made to enter but Sam filled the small space, blocking the view to the darkened flat behind him.

'What's it about?' He looked worried.

'Just a chat about your neighbour; nothing to worry about.' Foley gave him his most earnest smile.

'Which neighbour? What's happened?'

'Ms Winter. I believe you've been walking her dog for her.'

'Yes. Is anything wrong?'

'No. May I come in?'

'I'm not sure. The flat's a bit of a mess.'

'I've lived on my own for years and I still haven't got around to buying a mop and bucket. Nothing can shock me.' Foley's grin was so broad it was beginning to hurt.

Sam seemed to think for a while before pulling the door open wider and allowing his visitor in. 'Sorry, I'm a bit dazed. You woke me up.'

'Shift work?'

'Yes. I'm a doctor at the Royal Free.'

The basement flat was small and poorly lit and there was an underlying smell of damp and stale sweat. The door led straight into a living room which was spartan even for a student – one two-seater sofa and a coffee table with a laptop and several textbooks. Not a television in sight.

'Do you live here alone, Mr Halliday?'

'Yes. It's a one-bedroom flat.'

'The reason I'm here is because Ms Winter believes someone has been in her home while she was out. I understand she recently gave you a key so you could go in and collect the dog. Have you ever left a door or window open, perhaps?'

'No,' he replied, a frown of concern appearing on his face. 'Has she been burgled? Has anything been stolen?' He stood as far away from Foley as he could get while still being in the same room. His shoulders were hunched and his hands were plunged deep into the dressing-gown pockets.

'Not stolen, more... moved.'

'Oh. That seems strange.'

'Highly.'

'I'm very careful with the locks. I make sure the door is secure when I leave. I'm not in long, anyway. I clean Stanley's paws, make sure he has plenty of water and then leave.'

'Mind if I sit down?' Foley asked.

'Of course not. I'm sorry, I haven't asked if you'd like a drink.'

'I'll have a coffee if you're making one,' he smiled.

'I've only got instant.'

'That's fine.'

'Milk and sugar?'

'Just milk. Thank you.'

Reluctantly, Sam left the room. Foley remained in the lounge. Usually he'd take this opportunity to have a snoop around, but there was nowhere for him to snoop. There was no cabinet with drawers or TV unit to look behind. This blank space took minimalism to the next level. He picked up a few of the textbooks and flicked through the pages to see if anything had been hidden in there, but all he found were neatly pencilled notes.

Foley sat back on the sofa and sighed. The view from the window was uninspiring. A brick wall and the edge of the pavement at ground level above. He'd be able to see people walking past but nothing from the ankle upwards.

Sam returned with two mugs of coffee.

Foley made eye contact with the young student doctor as he took the mug. Sam quickly turned away and went over to the back of the room by the door leading to the rest of the flat.

'Have you lived here long, Mr Halliday?' Foley had no intention of drinking the coffee. The smell alone told him it was nasty.

'Just over a year.'

'You don't seem to have made this place a home.'

Sam chuckled. 'No. Well, I'm hardly ever here. If I'm not at the hospital then I'm studying in the library. This is just a place to shower and sleep, really.'

'How did you get to be on friendly terms with Ms Winter?'

'I've smiled, said hello, you know, and taken a parcel in for her occasionally. Last week, I fell off my bike. Olivia was coming out of her house and saw me coming home injured, and she patched me up.'

'That was kind of her.'

'Yes.' His face turned from one of worry into a beaming smile. 'She's lovely.'

'Attractive too.'

'Yes. Well, I mean, yes, she is, for an older woman,' he quickly back-pedalled.

'Are you seeing anyone romantically?'

'Seeing anyone? No. Look, I'm sorry, but what does this have to do with Olivia being burgled?' Sam asked, shuffling his feet, not able to stand still.

'I didn't say she'd been burgled.'

'No. Sorry, but you said something had been moved?'

'That's right.'

'And you think I did it?'

'I didn't say that.'

'Your tone is quite accusatory.'

'Is it? I apologise.' Foley placed his mug of coffee on the table and stood up. 'Sam, I'm here informally. I know Ms Winter professionally and she told me about something strange happening in her home. Now, only you and she have keys to the property.'

'Is she blaming me?'

'Nobody is blaming anyone. Someone has been in Ms Winter's home and it's spooked her a little. I'm sure you can understand.'

'Of course. I'd feel the same.'

'Is everything all right?' Foley asked, frowning.

'Yes. Why?'

'You seem a little nervous.'

Sam gave an exaggerated laugh. 'I've never been interrogated by the police before.'

'I'm not interrogating you.'

'No. I mean… it's just… Shit. Sorry. I…'

'Perhaps you should give her back her key.'

'What? Why?' he asked quickly.

'I've advised Ms Winter to increase her home security and to limit the people to whom she has given keys. I think it would be best if you gave me her key and I'll return it.' He held his hand out.

'But what about Stanley?' Sam asked after a long pause.

'That's not really your problem, is it? He's her dog. It's up to her to walk him.'

'I was only doing her a favour. I was being nice.'

'I know. And I'm sure she's very grateful. However, things have happened, and the arrangement has to change.' Foley held his hand out further.

'It's in my coat pocket in my bedroom. I'll go and fetch it,' he said. Sam left the room with his head down, looking hurt. When he returned, he was taking the key and alarm fob off his own keyring. He handed it to Foley, placing it, reluctantly, in his upturned palm.

'Thank you.' Foley headed for the door.

'Will you tell Olivia...?' he trailed off.

'Yes?'

'Tell her that I'll still walk Stanley for her any time she wants me to.'

Foley smiled. 'I'll tell her.'

He left the flat and Sam watched from the doorway as Foley made his way back up the steps before turning and going back inside.

Sam felt hurt. He felt sick and betrayed. If Olivia had wanted her key back, why didn't she ask for it herself? Why did she have to get the police involved? He liked her. He genuinely had feelings for her. He'd gone out of his way to look after Stanley for her. He'd changed to nightshifts – something he hated – so that she could go to work and not worry about that bloody dog, and how had she repaid that kindness? By making him feel like a criminal.

He went into his bedroom and closed the door. The room was clean and tidy. Clothes were freshly laundered, ironed, neatly folded and put away in their own designated space. Furniture was polished and the threadbare carpet vacuumed on a daily basis despite there being hardly any dust or crumbs. The en suite bathroom shone like it had never been used, yet he could still smell the damp coming from deep within the brickwork. There was nothing he could do about that, but it made him feel dirty. It made the flat feel grimy. It made him feel filthy.

He removed his dressing gown, placed it carefully on the hook behind the door, and climbed back into bed. He wouldn't be able to get back to sleep and his mind was whirling with Olivia's treacherous behaviour. One moment she was grateful for everything he was doing, the next she was sending a detective round to demand her key back. What was wrong with the bloody woman? She wasn't the only one who could play mind games. He opened the top drawer of his bedside cabinet and smiled. There was the bunch of keys he'd stolen with an alarm fob attached. It would take more than a mentally unstable forensic psychologist and a bully detective to out-fox him.

Chapter Forty-Four

Olivia had waited by her bedroom window for Foley to leave Sam's flat. It was almost half an hour before she saw the detective ascend the steps and head down the cul-de-sac to his car. Within seconds, her phone pinged an incoming text message. Foley told her he thought Sam had a crush on her and he'd managed to get her keys back. He'd give them to her later.

Although Olivia felt guilty asking for her key back, and hoped Sam wasn't too hurt, she relaxed at the thought of having her security back under control. She had never given her key to anyone before and wondered why she had offered Sam access to her home. She had let her guard down while being kindly and offering help. Past experience warned her she should always keep the barriers up. She was still wondering where that spare set had gone and made a mental note to check her drawers at work. She could have hidden them there for safe keeping before she went to America.

While waiting for Foley to come out of Sam's flat, Olivia's mind had been formulating a plan. The anniversary party tonight at the house opposite was the perfect camouflage for the killer to strike in the street, but did the killer know about it? Did the killer even know where she lived? There was no doubt in her mind he was keeping a very close eye on the investigation, and, hopefully, thanks to the double-page spread, and the cruel exposé about her being Richard Button's daughter, he'd know Olivia was helping the police. That being the case, she surmised the killer would know her every movement, and that meant knowing her address. He would also have checked out the perfect entry and escape routes from the cul-de-sac. Add into the mix a party that seemed to have gone viral, and the conditions were spot on for him to make himself known to her tonight. All she would need to do was wait for him to strike.

The doorbell rang, making her jump. She felt nervous. The news was out about her father. It was only a matter of time before the reporters descended on her doorstep. Was this the first of many?

She looked through the spyhole and found herself pleased to see Ethan Miller on the other side. She checked her appearance in the hall mirror. She hadn't showered yet. Her hair was sticking up in random directions and she had dark circles under her eyes. She smoothed down her hair as best she could and opened the door.

'Hello,' she said, looking him up and down, taking in the tight worn jeans, the heavy boots, the black leather biker jacket that sat perfectly on his broad shoulders. She could smell the intoxicating hint of peat, pollution and Ethan's own masculinity emanating from him. She almost forgave herself for giving in to her base urges the other night. The man oozed sexuality.

'Hi. I was in the area. Hope you don't mind me just popping round.'

'That depends.' She shivered from the cold.

'Can I come in?'

She stepped back and allowed him to enter. She closed the door firmly behind her and alarmed it.

'That's some security system.'

'Would you like a coffee?' she asked, ignoring his comment, and heading into the kitchen.

He followed. 'Please.'

Olivia busied herself with the coffee. She turned to him and saw him straddle a stool at the island. Stanley trotted in, tail wagging with excitement at a new face. Ethan picked him up with one hand and allowed the dachshund to nuzzle him and lick his face. If Olivia had found Ethan attractive before, she practically erupted seeing him go all soft with a dog.

'He's gorgeous,' Ethan beamed.

'Yes. Sorry, how do you take your coffee?'

'Black. Thanks.'

She should have guessed. He didn't seem the type to ask for a non-fat oat-milk latte. She placed the mug on the island for him and stood back, watching this hunk of a man go silly over a tiny dog. She couldn't help but smile.

Eventually, and reluctantly, he put Stanley back down on the floor.

'Sorry,' he said. 'I love dogs. When I was growing up, we always had three or four running around. They're great company, aren't they?'

'They really are. Great listeners, too,' she said. 'Ethan, why have you come here?'

He took a sip of his coffee. 'A couple of reasons, actually. I wanted to apologise, again, for taking your photo outside the police station. I was asked and I should have said no, but...'

'It's OK. It's your job,' she shrugged.

'That's no excuse. Also, I saw in the paper about you being Richard Button's daughter. That can't be easy.'

'You could say that.'

'I rang round a few people I know, tried to find out who the source of the story was. I don't know if you already know, or even if you want to know who gave the story to the press.'

She took a deep breath. 'Go on then. Which of my few friends betrayed me?'

'None. It was Richard Button himself.'

'Why am I not surprised? I was only saying this the other day. Killers, once they're caught and incarcerated, lose all their fame and mystique. They'll do anything to get back in the limelight. I should have known.'

'But wouldn't he want to be known as the source?'

'I'm sure he's saving that up for another time. Give it a couple of weeks and there'll be a whole feature on Richard Button and the daughter he tried to kill. I'm never going to be free of him, am I?'

'I'm really sorry.'

She looked up at him and smiled. 'That's OK. Thank you. I appreciate you telling me.'

'I also had another motive for coming round.'

'If you want me to give you an exclusive, you can think again.'

'No. Nothing like that. Listen, Olivia, I know we don't really know each other, even though we've been swimming next to each other for months, but you're a beautiful woman, and you're intelligent and have the cutest smile I think I've ever seen. Can I take you out to dinner one night?'

Inside, fireworks were flaring in all directions. Olivia decided to play it cool.

'Wow. Thank you for the compliments. Can we wait until all of this is over? My head is full of serial killers right now and that's not good when trying to have a meal with a...' she stopped herself '... friend.'

'Sure.' He gave her a simple smile, but his entire face lit up. 'I'd better be going. I'm taking publicity shots on the *EastEnders* set in an hour.'

'Oh. That sounds...'

'Boring?'

'It might not be. It could be fun, surrounded by famous people.'

'Trust me. It's not. Still, London Zoo tomorrow to photograph penguins. Give me animals over people any day.'

A man after my own heart, Olivia thought. She showed him out, struggling against the urge to grab him and throw him into her bedroom as they passed it to reach the front door.

Sam watched from the living room through the almost-closed venetian blinds as the hunk in the leather jacket left Olivia's house. *So, that's the kind of bloke she likes*, he thought. *Tall, broad shoulders, oozing masculinity. What a cliché.*

His mother used to tell him that girls liked a sensitive man who wasn't afraid to show his feelings and wear his heart on his sleeve. He wasn't tall, and no amount of working out at a gym would ever give him a rugby player's physique, but when he'd found out who Olivia really was and what she'd lived through, he'd thought she'd want someone loving, caring and sensitive to her needs, not some hulking Neanderthal who was all brawn and no brain matter.

Sam closed his eyes and shook his head. He could picture the two of them together in a haze of sweaty sexual excitement. She'd be screaming in ecstasy at the top of her voice as he ploughed her hard and rough. His back would be covered in scratches from where she'd clawed at him and her breasts would be covered in bite marks. He'd never been that kind of person. He'd never even rattled the headboard. His one and only girlfriend, Lauren Trench, from back home, had said he'd made love like he was building a house of cards: slowly and delicately, as if he was afraid she'd break. He'd found that humiliating.

He could feel his anger levels rising. What was wrong with

him? He was intelligent, loving, had a lot to offer. Surely any sensible woman would be lucky to have him fall in love with her.

Maybe women weren't sensible anymore. Maybe women didn't look for kindness and warmth from a man. He'd thought, in this day and age, women no longer looked for the cavemen to protect them and be rough and physical. He was obviously wrong. If Olivia wanted moody and dark with a hint of danger, then that was what she'd get.

Chapter Forty-Five

Olivia was putting the finishing touches to a lecture on the role of twenty-first-century culture in the creation of killers, when there was a knock on her office door. She'd been surprised when she turned up at the office to find Sebastian in the building along with the twins. He made an excuse about finishing off a paper he was writing, but she suspected he'd just needed to get out of the house. It hadn't felt the same for him since Rosemary died. Maybe he *should* consider moving. She was about to ask the person to come in when the door opened, and Sebastian charged into the room with an iPad in his hand. He looked worried.

'What's the matter?' Olivia asked, looking up.

'Look at all this,' he handed her the iPad. 'I've had so many emails asking me to comment on the piece about you being Richard Button's daughter and if I knew your true identity.'

As she looked down at the iPad, she saw more and more incoming emails popping up, all with the subject heading of 'Richard Button' or 'Richard Button's Daughter'. She handed it back to him without reading any of them. Journalists are blunt and straight to the point, but that kind of language often hurts.

'What are you going to do?' she asked.

'What do you want me to do?'

'They'll expect a reply.'

'I know. I don't want to say anything that will hurt you.'

'I think that ship sailed a long time ago.'

'How about I work on something that will sound like it's from the both of us? We'll release the one statement and draw a line under the whole thing.'

'You sound like someone who has never encountered the British press before.'

'I know. I'm trying to be positive.'

Olivia's computer pinged with an incoming email. She glanced at the screen, didn't recognise the name of the sender, but the subject heading 'Is Richard Button your father?' told her what to expect.

'They're starting on me now,' she said as she deleted the email, unread.

'I'll draft something together. Leave it with me. I'll take care of it,' he said in his best protective, big-brother tone.

'Thank you, Sebastian. I really appreciate it.'

'Do you want to come over for dinner again tonight? The kids loved seeing you the other night. They really loved Stanley, too.'

She smiled. She really enjoyed being in Sebastian's company and his kids, when not loaded on sugar, were a joy to be around. His house genuinely felt like a real home. But she, hopefully, had plans with a killer.

'Can we do it another time?'

'Sure. Open invitation. I'll leave you to it.'

Sebastian left Olivia's office. Another ping brought news of another email with her father's name in the subject bar. This was never going to go away. This was her life now.

Richard Button was tired. A genuine physiotherapist had had him walking the corridors to get his strength back up, but having open-heart surgery took a great deal of energy out of a person. With his ribs broken, it hurt when he breathed, coughed, sneezed, laughed and hiccoughed. He grew tired quickly and climbing a flight of stairs was no easy task. Following a twenty-minute walk, he was sweating profusely and eager to get back into bed.

In the corner of the room, the television was tuned into a brain-numbing antiques programme that Gordon White, his prison guard, seemed to be enjoying. He had one eye on the screen and the other on his mobile, while his free hand went from his mouth to a large packet of Hula Hoops and back again.

Despite Richard originally enjoying being away from his prison cell, the agony he was in and the not-so-rapturous company meant he was actually looking forward to being back in Belmarsh.

'Here, isn't this your daughter?' Gordon said with his mouth full. He held up the phone and showed Richard the screen.

'Yes. That's my Livvy,' he beamed.

'She's all over Twitter.'

'Is she? Why?'

'Dunno.' He shrugged and took another handful of crisps from the bag. He scrolled through his phone. 'Everyone seems to be talking about her being your daughter. Someone's leaked it to the press. Oh dear, there's some prof bloke in Liverpool who says her whole research should be called into question, as her ulterior motive for interviewing killers renders her insight suspect. Whatever that's supposed to mean,' he shrugged. He looked at Richard as he sat back in bed, arms folded across his chest, a smile on his lips. 'You look happy.'

'Do I?'

'Your daughter's trending on Twitter. She's being slated and you're smiling. Hang on a minute, did you do this? Did you tell them Olivia Winter is your daughter?'

Richard's smile grew.

'You could have ruined her career. Everything she does from now on is going to be scrutinised by the letter.'

Richard didn't say anything. He merely glowed in the prospect of what was to come for Olivia.

'How did you even contact the papers? You're rarely left on your own.'

'I did it through a third party,' he said with a wink.

'Who?'

'None of your business, Gordon,' Richard said, an icy tone to his voice. 'I don't have to fucking answer to you.'

'I think you'll find that you do. Me, prison officer. You, sick fuck.'

Richard raised an eyebrow. 'Well, if we're trading insults now, you're a fat cunt.'

'Listen, I can lose weight whenever I want to. You'll always be a sick fucker.'

'Are you allowed to talk to me like this?'

'There's no one around. I can talk to you however I like. And I'll tell you something else, when you keeled over in your cell, not one person ran to get help. It was that new kid that said we should get medical attention. Everyone else just stood there watching you die.'

From under the covers on his bed, Richard swiftly pulled out the scissors he'd been hiding. With his free hand, he quickly pressed them to Gordon's throat. The prison officer froze. Richard's breathing was laboured. It hurt to move too much, and he'd overstretched himself. Still, life without a little pain, had no meaning.

'I'd stab you but there's that much flesh the blade would be blunt long before I hit an artery. I know what I've done. I know who I am. I know people don't exactly like me in prison, and, you know what? I don't fucking care,' he spat into his face. 'Now, you watch what you say about me, and my daughter, because I won't always be in this hospital bed and there's no way you can outrun me, you fat fuck.'

Gordon had paled. He held his hands up in surrender and nodded his head. Richard took the scissors away, slowly, from his throat, and replaced them under his covers.

Gordon took a deep breath. 'I'm going to need to take those scissors from you.'

Richard held up his hands. 'If you want them, come and fetch them.'

Gordon didn't attempt to move. The truth was, Richard Button scared the shit out of him. He turned his gaze back to the television, but he wasn't paying any attention to the programme. After a long silence, Gordon stood up and left the room, saying he was going to get more crisps. Richard smiled. He knew Gordon was going to report him, tell someone he had a concealed weapon. Fortunately for him, in Gordon's panic to leave, he left his mobile behind.

Chapter Forty-Six

Olivia opened the front door to find Foley with a serious expression on his face and his arms folded across his chest.

'I can't read you,' he said by way of a greeting.

'Good afternoon, Amyas, would you like to come in?' She stepped to one side.

He entered, but still he seemed to be fuming. 'There's a party happening across the road from you tonight.'

'I know. I've been invited.'

'Are you going?'

'No. I've got some reading to do.'

'So, there's a party right opposite your house. There's a killer who enjoys an audience, and he knows you're working with the police. Didn't you put those together and think you might be the perfect target for him tonight?'

Olivia looked away.

'You did, didn't you?'

'Amyas, calm down. That vein in your neck is going to explode in a minute and I had this hallway decorated last year. Let me get you a drink.'

She went into the kitchen, leaving him to follow her.

'I thought you were an intelligent woman,' Foley said as he went into the kitchen. He squatted to stroke Stanley. 'I thought you'd have mentioned this. I could have armed officers in several of these houses tonight. We could be lying in wait for him upstairs or something.'

Olivia opened the drawer to the dresser and picked out several items, slapping them onto the island. There was a taser, which was illegal in this country, as was the pepper spray. She also took out a monkey ball, which looked innocent enough, like something you'd tease your cat with – a ball of yarn on the end of a string. What any potential attacker didn't know was that the yarn was wrapped around a heavy steel ball. She also had a 'cat's ears' self-defence key chain which you wore on two fingers, and the spikes of the 'cat's ears' would stun any attacker. Finally, she had a stun gun disguised as a lipstick.

'I also have several baseball bats around the house, a sock with a snooker ball in it in my bedside cabinet, and I take Krav Maga lessons.'

'OK, first of all, the majority of those are illegal in this country.'

'I'm aware. But I will do whatever it takes to keep me alive if I'm being attacked.'

'Have you always been this paranoid in your own home?'

She turned back to the coffee machine to make Foley his drink. She didn't want to answer that question.

'You're not going to be here on your own tonight. I'll make sure you have officers in this house.'

'Well, even if the killer doesn't show up, Mrs Blackstock across the road will be happy with the presence,' she said, handing him his coffee.

'Why?'

'It doesn't matter. I was going to tell you, Amyas, I promise. I just... this is why I don't work active cases. I honestly have no idea who the killer is. Have I met him? Is he in my life already? If so, for how long has he been watching me? Is he watching me right now? He's going to see a whole troop of police officers coming into my house tonight. He's a killer like Richard is, and Richard told me he spent weeks watching some of his victims. If I am a victim, am I already being watched?'

Amyas sighed and nodded. He could see where she was coming from.

'I can understand that.'

'I wasn't purposely shutting you out. This case is being heavily reported on. It's all over the internet and on the news. Realistically, he knows his time is almost up. He'll want to make his next kill count, just in case it's his last one.'

'What do you want me to do?'

'Ideally, I'd like you to have the army and the navy in here tonight with the SAS on standby. But if he's watching me then he's going to know about it, and nothing will happen. Or worse, he'll go and kill someone else. I think the best scenario would be for me to be on my own here with all my illegal weapons, with you hiding discreetly around the corner, listening in.'

'I don't like that scenario.'

'Neither do I. But it's the best chance we have of catching him.'

'I can fit you up with a wire.'

'I think he's going to smell something's going on if he sees you go and come back again. I think it would be best if we just kept the phone lines open.'

Reluctantly, he nodded. 'I'll be right around the corner.'

'Not too close. And not too conspicuous.'

His eyes fell on the collection of weapons. 'I really should confiscate those.'

'I'll try not to use them.'

'After tonight, please get rid of them.'

She nodded. She didn't mean it.

'I really do not like this.'

'You should try standing in my shoes. I'm not thrilled either.'

'Olivia, promise me the moment you think you see anything or hear anything, you let me know so we can make an arrest.'

'Amyas, I pay my taxes. I intend to use the police to the full extent of what I pay for.'

'Any chance of a pay rise?' he asked, trying to make light of a tense situation.

Every room in the Blackstocks' house opposite was lit up and the dancing shadows and silhouettes of people moving frantically were testament to how much was still to be done in preparation for the party. Olivia watched from a distance. She didn't want to be seen as a nosy neighbour, or as if she was waiting for a killer to call. She took a deep breath and let it out slowly.

She leaned towards the window, looked over the railings and down to Sam's flat. It was in darkness. She hadn't seen him since Foley had gone round and asked for her keys back. She went out into the hallway, put Stanley's lead and collar on, picked up an expensive bottle of champagne from the rack beside the fridge and headed out.

It was pitch-dark despite it only being six o'clock. She trotted across the road, Stanley in tow, and climbed the steps to the Blackstocks' house. She rang the bell and stood back. Within a few moments, it was pulled open by Dorothy wearing a pink dressing gown, her hair and make-up perfectly done. The bright light from the house almost blinded Olivia.

'Hello, I won't be able to make it to your party this evening, but I thought I'd bring you this as an anniversary present.' Olivia held out the bottle of Veuve Clicquot which had been a present from her American publishers on the launch of her previous book. Wine and vodka she could drink alone, but champagne, in Olivia's opinion, was a drink that needed company.

'Oh, wow!' Dorothy looked genuinely pleased with the gift.

'This is amazing, thank you. Are you sure you won't be able to pop over for a little while?'

'I can't. I'm way behind with the revisions for my next book. I think I'm just going to get my head down and spend the weekend at my desk.'

'Well, we'll try and keep the noise down.'

'Don't be silly. That's what noise-cancelling headphones are for.' She smiled. 'You enjoy yourself.'

'Thank you. I really do appreciate this.'

'You're welcome. Well, better get Stanley walked. I don't want his feet freezing to the ground. Have a good night.'

Olivia turned away and headed down the steps with Stanley alongside her. She didn't take him far, although it probably seemed far to his short legs. There was a patch of green a few blocks away where he had a good sniff, and she was back home within twenty minutes.

The front and back doors were securely locked. The windows were locked, and the alarm was active. She went into the kitchen to make something to eat, but doubted she could stomach anything, she was that nervous. A glass of wine helped calm her nerves, but she couldn't help thinking that tonight might be her last, if everything didn't go to plan.

'Why couldn't you have been a German shepherd?' she asked Stanley, who was curled up chewing on a dental stick that was bigger than he was.

Olivia's house was as silent as the grave. No television, no radio. The only sounds came from the ticking clocks in the living room and hallway and the distant hum of the fridge in the kitchen. Occasionally, Stanley stood up to adjust his position on his bed, but he remained quiet and content.

As much as Olivia tried to relax with a magazine, she kept

stealing glances out of the window and watching guests arrive for the party. Taxis came and went. Some guests arrived on foot carrying bottles or gifts, all dressed smartly in casual suits and tight dresses. The house was filling up nicely.

'I spy with my little eye, something beginning with B,' Foley's voice came from her iPhone on the coffee table in front of her.

She laughed. 'You can't see boredom,' she said.

'I could be crude and say "bollocks". I think mine have dropped off, it's so cold.'

'I should have made you a flask of soup or something.'

'I'd have preferred a whisky.'

'I really don't think we should be chatting,' she said.

'Probably not. It was "bus", by the way, if you were wondering.'

'I wasn't. But thank you.'

Despite having the heating on, Olivia's nervousness was making her cold. She changed to a thicker jumper. Her palms were clammy, and her mouth was dry. How long was she going to have to wait before the killer made his entrance? Or had he guessed her plan? He could be on the other side of London right now killing someone else. It's hardly likely the Blackstocks were the only people in the capital having a party tonight.

She heard a noise coming from upstairs. She went out into the hallway and looked up into the darkness. There was nothing there. There was nobody in her house, but it didn't stop her mind working overtime, conjuring up all kinds of scenarios. It was probably just the house settling.

By ten o'clock, Olivia was growing tired. Sitting waiting for a killer who might or might not turn up was exhausting. In the living room, she'd tried to relax. Several times she'd read the same page of a historical novel Daisy had recommended, and hadn't taken anything in. She'd flicked through the television channels and quickly turned it off.

'I was enjoying that,' Foley said through the phone.

'Do you even know what it was?'

'No. But it sounded interesting.'

'You're a fan of property programmes, are you?'

'The people on those programmes always annoy me. I just like looking around the houses.'

'I enjoy that part, too. This was a beautiful barn conversion in Norfolk.'

'High ceilings?'

'Yes. Master bedroom had a dressing room, too.'

'I heard that mentioned. Hot tub in the garden, did I hear correctly?'

'You did. Stunning views, as well. A snip at £1.5 million.'

'Just out of my price range,' he said with laughter in his voice. 'Anything else on?'

'I'm afraid not.'

'Typical.'

Olivia stood up, peeled back the living-room curtains and looked out at the expanse of back garden. It looked wild due to the harsh winter and it would take a skilled gardener to do something with it once spring arrived. Fingers of wispy clouds blew across the night sky, blocking out the moon. Under the cover of darkness, Olivia couldn't even see the end of her lawn. Somebody could be at the bottom of the garden, standing by the oak tree, watching the house, and she wouldn't know it. Hopefully, when they stepped forward and made their move, the sensor would kick in and the garden would light up like an alien invasion.

The Mind of a Murderer

'Olivia, are you still there?' Foley called out. He sounded urgent.

'Yes. I'm here,' she said, picking up the phone. 'Has something happened?'

'I've just heard from Holly. There's been another murder. A woman found stabbed to death in Cricklewood. A neighbour heard screaming. She looked out of her window to see a man walking out of the victim's house.'

'Shit!' Olivia exclaimed. 'We were wrong. We were so wrong.'

'I need to go. Look, lock your doors, keep the alarm on and a baseball bat handy, just in case. I'll come and see you in the morning.'

'Take care, Amyas.'

The call ended, plunging Olivia into silence.

She went over to the sofa and slumped into it. Stanley came over to her and sat on her lap.

'What the fuck have I done, Stanley? Have I assumed I'm so important to the killer that he's going to come after me, when really he's just going to carry on as he's always done? Why would he change now to come for someone connected to the case, when he knows we haven't a clue who he is? Jesus! I've really ballsed up here, Stanley. I think I should probably go to bed, don't you? Look at this tomorrow with fresh eyes.'

Olivia got up and went into her bedroom. Stanley followed and she lifted him up onto the bed. As she sat on the edge and began taking off her jumper she saw the book about her father on the bedside table. Who the hell had put it there? Had she done it in some kind of daze?

'You can go right back to where you came from.' She snatched it up and headed for the top floor of the house.

It was cold up there. The heating was never on, as she rarely came up into the attic. The odd occasion she did was when she felt melancholy about her childhood, when she missed her mother and sister, when she wanted answers she knew she'd never get from her father.

She looked at the picture of her father at the top of the map. He looked completely different to the person she'd visited the other day in hospital, but the eyes never changed. People grew older and greyer, some put on weight, some lost weight; everybody gained wrinkles and the neck sagged, but the eyes were a constant. She looked deep into her father's eyes and saw pure evil looking back at her, just as she had in the hospital.

She heard a creaking noise from downstairs. She placed the paperback on the table and edged to the door. She looked down but couldn't see any movement. Had Stanley jumped off the bed and started walking around, wondering where she'd gone? There it was again. A creak like someone treading on stairs. Stanley didn't make that kind of noise; he wasn't big enough. There was somebody in her house. There was somebody coming up the stairs.

DI Foley pulled up in Ashford Road in Cricklewood. Crime scene tape already cordoned off the murder house and white-suited scene of crime officers were entering the property. Nosy neighbours were on the doorstep, shivering in their dressing gowns.

He got out of the car and headed for the tape. He flashed his warrant card to the uniformed officer and dipped underneath to enter the scene. His mobile vibrated in his coat pocket. He fished it out, looked at the number he didn't recognise and ignored it.

'Holly, what have we got?' he asked his DS.

'Mrs Granger across the road called, as she heard screaming, and when she looked out of the window, she saw the torn curtain of the upstairs window.'

They both looked up and, from this angle, they could see a bloodied handprint on the glass.

Holly continued. 'She saw a man leaving the house but said Rose Abbot lived alone since splitting with her husband last year. Uniform came, saw the door ajar and found who we believe to be Rose Abbot in bed. She's been stabbed multiple times.'

'Any sign of a break-in?'

'No.'

'Sir?'

Foley turned at the sound. Leon Rippner approached up the garden path.

'Uniform have picked up a man a few streets away. He's covered in blood and got a knife with him. He's incoherent. His driving licence says he's Jeremy Abbot.'

Foley's phone vibrated again. He looked at the screen. It was the same number. He rejected it.

'The ex-husband?' Holly asked.

'Not The Butcher of London then,' Leon said.

'Leon, don't lower yourself to the level of the press and use the tabloid nickname. Tell uniform to take him back to the station and get the duty doctor to look over him. Interview him tonight if you can.'

'Will do.'

Foley's phone vibrated again. 'Who the bloody hell keeps ringing me?' He moved away from the murder house and swiped to answer. 'DI Foley.'

'Detective Inspector Foley, I have some information for you.'

'Who is this?' he asked.

'We have a mutual acquaintance. Olivia Winter. Although I know her as Olivia Button.'

Foley's eyes widened. 'Richard Button?'

'Who else?' he said with a smile in his voice.

'How... erm, what do you want?' he asked, thrown by receiving such a call.

'I just want to give you a little heads-up, really. I know how closely you and my Livvy have been working lately. I'd hate you to ruin a crime scene by vomiting all over Livvy's hallway.'

He frowned. He looked up and saw Holly talking to the pathologist who was just leaving the murder house.

'What are you talking about?'

'Olivia is going to join her mummy and her sister tonight.'

'What? How…? I don't understand,' he stammered.

'Then let me explain. The killer came to visit me in hospital. It turns out he's quite a fan of my work. He was looking for tips.'

'WHAT?' Foley exploded.

'I had a similar reaction. As if I'm going to help a pathetic copycat get away with murder and eclipse my work.'

'Who is he? What does he look like? Do you know his name?' Foley asked, his questions tripping over each other.

'Calm down, Amyas. If you listen carefully, I'll tell you exactly what's about to happen. Now, do you have access to a fast car?'

'Why?'

'Because you're going to need one. You see, I gave the killer Olivia's address. I told him to pop round tonight and pay her a little visit.'

'You set up your own daughter?'

'Amyas, I'm The Riverside Killer. I'm the most prolific serial killer in modern-day Britain, and I intend to stay that way. If anyone's going to continue my work and kill Livvy, it's going to be me.'

Chapter Forty-Seven

Olivia had always believed she was a strong individual. Sebastian often invited her to spend Christmas, birthdays and New Year with him and his children, but Olivia always turned him down. She didn't get lonely. She didn't feel sad. She enjoyed her own company. Celebrations were for families, and she hadn't belonged to a proper family for a long time. However, facing the reality of a killer inside her house frightened her to the very core. She was scared. She was vulnerable. Is this what Jessica felt in her final moments?

She edged her way down the stairs, taking care to tread lightly on each step so as not to make the floorboards creak. She had no weapon to hand and her iPhone was still in the living room. She tried to remember the moves she'd learnt at her Krav Maga classes but her mind was blank. Everything she knew about self-defence had melted away.

At the bottom of the top flight of stairs she stopped and listened. There was definite movement coming from the upper ground floor. But why hadn't Stanley yapped? She hoped he hadn't come to harm. She stood in the doorway of her office and looked around the darkened room for something she could use as a weapon, should she need one. There was nothing there. She wouldn't be able to do much damage with a stapler, a packet of envelopes and a pen pot.

Olivia leaned forward over the banister, head angled to one side, and listened intently for any other sounds that suggested someone might be in her home. In the background, she could hear the Blackstocks' party in full swing. The music was loud, and the laughter was even louder. How many people were there across the road? Had anyone gatecrashed the party? Fingers crossed, the police were patrolling, as promised. That's if they could hear her scream over the din of Olly Murs.

She heard the creak of a floorboard. It sounded like it was coming from her kitchen. There was now no doubt in Olivia's mind that someone had broken into her home.

She leaned against the wall and slowly glided down the stairs. She kept squatting to look through the gaps in the spindles, but she was too far up the stairs to see anything. Once at the bottom, she would be close to the front door. She could run out and go across the road to the Blackstocks' and call for help.

Olivia's breathing grew heavier, the closer she edged to the ground floor. Her heart was pounding. She had always thought of her house as her place of refuge where she felt safe against whatever was happening in the world, but now, if someone could penetrate her fortress, what did that leave her with?

She squatted and peered through the spindles. She saw a shadow of a shape cast on the open door of the kitchen. It turned and she saw a face. She gasped, slapped a hand to her mouth and pushed herself back against the wall. With her eyes tightly shut, she didn't dare move a muscle. All she could hear was her heart beating loudly inside her chest. Every move she'd learnt in every self-defence class she had ever attended was suddenly forgotten. She was frozen. She was nine years old, scared, horrified and in fear of her life.

'Olivia? I was beginning to think there was no one home. Why don't you come down?'

It was a voice she had heard many times before, but it sounded different now, somehow. There was power, confidence behind the words.

DI Foley drove through the busy streets of London. The roads were full of taxis taking people for a Saturday night out at a restaurant or a nightclub. They double parked while people alighted and turned their hazard lights on, as if that made up for their disregard of other road users.

He ignored the speed limits and the red traffic lights. He was sworn at and beeped at, but he blocked them out. He needed to get to Olivia's house. Why had Richard Button set his own daughter up to be murdered? He knew the man was sick, but this was beyond evil.

Foley took one eye off the road while he fumbled with his mobile phone. There was no point in calling Olivia and frightening her. She had excellent security. He'd fill her in once he got there. He scrolled through the contacts to the incident room at Sanderson Street Police Station and pressed call.

'This is DI Foley,' he said as soon as it was answered. 'I need an armed response unit to go to Modbury Gardens. I've reason to believe the killer is going for Olivia Winter.'

'I don't have anything in the vicinity, sir. Armed response are currently dealing with a stand-off at a petrol station in Marylebone. The nearest unit is a good twenty minutes away.'

'Fuck!' Foley screamed, partly at the delay and partly at the pillock in the Audi who had just tried to cut him up. 'Is there anyone nearby?'

'I've put a call out. We've got a uniform patrol unit with an ETA of four minutes.'

'Jesus Christ! Look, get all available units to Modbury Gardens right fucking now!' He ended the call, turned left and went the wrong way down a one-way street.

Olivia opened her eyes, which released a tear from her left eye. She should have known from the beginning that he was the killer. It all made sense. The so-called attack on his way home from the hospital when he was pushed off his bike was an obvious cover-up for him having just murdered Jessica Sheffield. Why hadn't she seen it before now?

'Olivia?' Sam called out to her again. 'Come on down. Let's have a chat.'

He sounded calm, controlled… but then most killers were.

She took a deep breath and went down the stairs, holding onto the banister for fear of collapsing.

In the hallway, she stood with her back to the door and faced Sam Halliday. He was dressed in dark-blue jeans, Converse trainers and a black hooded top. He was nondescript. He wouldn't stand out anywhere, hence why he had got away with killing seven people so far.

'Why are you doing this, Sam?' Olivia asked. She tried to sound strong and confident, but her nerves were betraying her.

'I really like you, Olivia. When I first moved in, I saw you in the window of your office upstairs. You were cleaning the inside of the window. I thought you were beautiful. I tried everything I could to get your attention, but what would someone as attractive as you see in someone like me, eh?'

'Sam, I…'

'Don't say it. I know what you're going to say. You'll say the age difference is too great. But it's not.' He took a step forward and Olivia took one back. 'There's only ten years between us – that's nothing. I know I'm only a junior doctor now, but I won't be one for ever. A few more years and I'll be a qualified surgeon.' His eyes were wide and staring and he had a huge, hungry smile on his face. 'And besides, when you're eighty and I'm seventy, the age difference won't matter at all, will it? I really like you, Olivia. I want you to like me too. I want you to notice me.'

'Oh, I've noticed you.'

'You have?' His smile grew wider. 'Do you like me, Olivia?'

'Yes. Of course I do,' she lied. Tears were filling her eyes.

The smiled dropped. 'Then why did you throw my flowers away?'

'Your flowers?'

'The ones I sent you. The roses. They were a thank-you for helping me after I was attacked, and you just threw them away. I saw them in your bin.' His face was angry.

'They were from you?'

'Of course they were from me. Who else would they be from?'

'I didn't know.'

'Don't be thick. There was a card with a message and my name on them.'

'There wasn't a card,' she said, frowning.

'There was!' he said, almost shouting. He took another step forward. Olivia was pressed against the wall of the hallway. She had nowhere else to go.

'Honestly, Sam,' she began, holding her hands up in defence. 'There was no card on those flowers. Maybe it blew away. I wouldn't have thrown them away if I'd known they were from you.'

He stepped forward again. He was so close, she could feel his breath on her face. He was studying her.

'I don't believe you. You just think I'm a child, don't you? I've seen you with that bloke on the motorbike, all tall and muscular with broad shoulders. I heard you that night you brought him back here. You practically screamed the block down. What do you see when you look at me, eh? A short, skinny runt, is that it?'

'No, that's not it at all.'

'It is. I know what women are like. I've heard you all talking and sniggering. They see someone who's thin and small and they think he can't be much of a man. "I feel sorry for the poor cow who ends up with him."'

'No, Sam, you're being too hard on yourself. Look, I think you're a lovely guy. You're smart, intelligent, handsome.'

'You're lying!' he screamed in her face. 'Stop lying to me! You threw my flowers away.' Tears fell from his eyes. 'They cost a fucking fortune and you just threw them away.'

'Sam, I genuinely didn't realise—'

'Don't lie to me.'

'I'm not lying. I thought they were from my father. He sends me cards and letters. I thought this was just another of his ways of taunting me,' she said quickly, her words tripping over each other.

Sam took a step back. He frowned as he looked at her.

'You're hurting, aren't you?' he said, softly. 'You've been hurting all these years, living in the shadow of what that man did to you. You deserve so much better.' He reached out and placed a warm hand on her face.

Olivia closed her eyes at his touch. She felt her skin crawl as his clammy fingers stroked her cheek.

'I'd look after you, Olivia. I promise to take care of you. I wouldn't let anyone hurt you. It will just be you and me.' He pulled her into an embrace and held her gently. 'I love you, Olivia. I'll always love you.'

Over his shoulder, Olivia could see the front door. She noticed it was closed and locked. 'Sam, how did you get in here?'

'I used my key.'

'But you gave it back to DI Foley.'

'I took a set you had hanging on the hook.'

'You *stole* them?' Her entire body tensed. 'Sam, please, let me go,' she said.

He pushed her away but still held her firmly by the arms and looked deep into her eyes. 'Let you go? What are you talking about?'

'You've gone too far. I can see your motive behind it all. I understand why you thought I might be impressed, but you're an intelligent man. You must have known it would never end well.'

'I have no idea what you're going on about,' he said, looking genuinely perplexed.

'The night you said you were attacked and fell off your bike was just an excuse, wasn't it? I didn't know at the time, but looking back, I should have seen the signs. It was the night Jessica Sheffield was murdered. The night you killed her. You were covered in scratches and blood from the scene and you had to invent a lie when I saw you coming home.'

'What? You I think I killed that detective?'

'You may as well admit it. The… the police are on their way.' She hoped he wouldn't see through her lie.

'Oh my God. You think I'm that killer, don't you? You think I murdered all those people. Is that what you think I'm capable of?' he asked, his anger growing. 'I haven't killed anyone. I love you, Olivia. I want to make you happy. That's all. And all along you've thought I've been stalking and killing… Jesus fucking Christ.'

He stepped away and Olivia made a move towards the kitchen. He grabbed her by the shoulder and spun her around.

'You're warped, do you know that, Olivia? You spend so long with killers and rapists that you see murder in everyone. How could I have fallen for someone as sick and twisted as you?' he spat in her face.

'Sam, please,' she cried. 'You're hurting me.'

'Hurt? You don't know the meaning of the word. Hurt is being ignored. Hurt is having everyone you care about turn their back on you. Hurt is having your heart broken. I love you and you won't even look at me.'

'You don't love me.'

The sound of Stanley yapping from the kitchen made Olivia turn around. She saw the small dog through the glass in the door.

Sam shook her hard and she turned back to look at him.

'I've done everything for you! I've bought you flowers. I've walked your fucking dog. I've put your bins out. I've cleaned your kitchen. Have you even noticed? No.'

'I'm sorry,' she said through tears.

'No, you're not. Don't lie to me. You—' He froze as a phone started ringing.

Their eyes locked together. It was Olivia's mobile ringing.

'Where is it?' he asked calmly. She shrugged.

He looked over her shoulder and into the kitchen. He nudged her to one side and took large strides. He pushed open the kitchen door. Stanley was yapping and jumping. With one swift kick from Sam, the little dog was sent flying across the kitchen. He yelped.

Olivia barged past him and went to the dachshund's aid. He quickly jumped up to his little feet but Olivia picked him up to check he was OK. He didn't seem injured, but it showed Olivia the mental state Sam was in. They were both in danger.

'Who's Sebastian?'

She looked up and saw Sam holding her phone aloft.

'Who is he? Is he the leather-jacketed hunk you've been fucking?'

'No. He's a colleague.'

'Really?' He didn't believe her. 'Are you shagging him, too?'

'No. He's a good friend. I've known him for years. Look, Sam, I think you should leave before you do something you're going to regret.' She had Stanley in her arms and was stroking him gently.

He put the phone down on the island and let it continue ringing.

'I don't believe you. I bet you're a slut really, aren't you? I bet you sleep with men left, right and centre. I bet you handed it out on a plate on your American tour. How many students did you fuck out there? And you won't even look twice at me.'

'Sam, I want you to leave. Right now,' she said, finding the strength to sound forceful from somewhere.

'I'm not going anywhere.'

'Fine.' She turned on her heels and headed for the front door.

'Where are you going?' he asked, running after her.

'I'm going across the road to call the police from the Blackstocks'. I will not have you terrorise me in my own home.'

She reached the door, but Sam grabbed her by the hair and pulled her back. She dropped Stanley who squealed and then started barking.

Olivia regained her balance and kicked Sam hard between the legs. He let go of her hair and doubled up in pain. She shouted for Stanley and they both ran to the door but the security chain was on. She fumbled with shaking fingers but managed to take it off. The door wouldn't open. It was locked with the Yale as well as the mortise lock and her keys were in the living room. She was trapped.

Before she had time to run back into the house, Sam was up and on her once again. He grabbed her by the hair and pulled her down to the floor.

'I might not be very big, but once I'm riled, I'm as strong as any man,' he said through gritted teeth. 'I'm going to make you scream, Olivia. I'll make you scream louder than that leather bloke ever did.'

Olivia cried out and tried to break free.

Sam pulled her along the floor. He kicked open the door to her bedroom, dragged her to her feet then threw her onto the bed. He closed the door behind him, leaving Stanley out in the hallway barking.

Olivia lay on the bed. She could hear The Killers singing 'Mr Brightside' from the Blackstocks' house across the road. How loudly would she have to scream before someone heard her? Would Sebastian worry that she hadn't answered the phone and come to see if she was all right?

She looked up and saw Sam unbutton his jeans, dropping them to the floor and climbing onto the bed.

'See, I'm as a big as any man.'

Olivia tried to back away but there was nowhere for her to go. She edged her way to the head of the bed. She turned her gaze away and caught sight of the picture of her mother and sister that sat in a frame on the bedside table. She wasn't going to end up like them. She refused to be a victim again.

'Run!' her mother said.

She tried to knee him between the legs, but he must have sensed what she was about to do as he pushed her legs down and forced them open. He fumbled with the buttons on her jeans and began to roughly pull them down. Olivia looked left and right for something she could use as a weapon, but it was hopeless. All she had were her own hands.

With her left hand, she grabbed Sam's hair tight. With her right, she pressed her thumb hard into his left eye. He screamed and she heard a squelch as her thumb disappeared into his socket.

She pushed him to one side. He rolled off the bed and onto the floor. She scrambled to her feet and headed for the door. Sam stood up. Blood was dripping from his eye.

'You've blinded me!' he screamed. 'You've fucking blinded me!'

She ran out into the hallway and headed for the living room, desperate to find her keys. Stanley followed, barking the whole way. So did Sam.

She found them on the mantlepiece, but as she turned around she saw Sam lunging for her. She picked up a hardback textbook from the coffee table and swung it at his head. It hit him flat against the face and he fell to the floor. Olivia jumped over his body and ran for the door.

Fear and adrenaline were coursing through her body. With shaking fingers, she managed to open the first lock but the second took some effort. She didn't dare look back in case Sam was coming after her again.

She pulled the door open and was hit in the face with a blast of cold air and a wall of noise from the party opposite. She picked Stanley up and ran, barefoot, out into the winter night.

'Help me!' she screamed.

Nobody heard her.

She considered running to the Blackstocks' house, but it didn't seem far enough away from her own and she doubted they'd even hear her over the volume of the music. She turned right and headed down the cul-de-sac. Dorothy had said the police were going to increase patrols in case of gatecrashers; surely there would be a marked car somewhere close by.

As she turned the corner, running down the middle of the road, she ran straight into the path of an oncoming car. She heard the sound of the brakes being applied, and the scream of the tyres pierced the air. She fell onto the bonnet, almost dropping Stanley.

She looked up and there was Foley, standing next to her, his arm on her shoulder.

'Olivia. What's happened?'

'It's Sam. He tried to rape me,' she said through the tears.

'Are you hurt?'

'Yes.'

'Where?' he asked, looking her up and down.

'Every-fucking-where!'

Chapter Forty-Eight

Olivia Winter's house was a crime scene. By the time she had been checked out for any injuries in A&E and had given a statement to police, it was almost one o'clock in the morning. Foley said she was welcome to spend the night at his house. As much as she would have preferred a hotel, she felt obliged to accept, especially as Sam Halliday had fled and was nowhere to be found. She'd feel safer in the house of a detective inspector.

Upon seeing Foley's two German shepherds, Stanley had refused to get down from Olivia's arms. He, too, had been checked out by a vet following being kicked in the ribs, but he was fine; no internal injuries. Foley's dogs were interested in the miniature dachshund and kept approaching and sniffing him as he stayed firmly by Olivia's side on the sofa. Eventually, Stanley found the courage from somewhere to jump off the sofa. Once the initial curiosity was over, the two large dogs looked on Stanley as something to be protected and they all curled up in front of the fire together.

'Gentle giants,' Olivia said as Foley entered the room with a mug of coffee each.

'They have a mean bark on them, but they're soft. Besides, how can you be scared of something that runs away from a vacuum cleaner?'

'Why do you have two dogs when you have such a demanding job?'

'They're incredibly therapeutic,' he said, looking at them and smiling. 'They cheer me up when I'm down, calm me when I'm stressed and they're companionship when I'm lonely. And there's no better feeling than coming home to be welcomed by a huge bouncing dog who is genuinely happy to see you and wants nothing more in return than your presence, and maybe a Bonio.'

'I'm starting to see that,' she said, watching Stanley kick his legs as he slept. 'Thank you for letting me stay here.'

'My pleasure. Stay as long as you want. It's nothing special but it's home.'

'I like it,' she said, looking around the living room and taking in the large space with very little in it.

There was a large-screen TV on the wall above the fireplace and shelves of DVDs and Blu-rays either side. Apart from the two comfortable-looking sofas and a coffee table, that was it. No pictures on the walls, no ornaments, nothing personal.

'I'm sure you've gathered I don't spend much time at home.'

'You work a great deal.'

'So do you, but your house is cosy.'

'It's more than a house. It's a fortress.' She took a sip of the coffee. It tasted good. 'Oh, the other murder you were called out to…'

'A domestic. An estranged couple. Husband couldn't accept the marriage was over and killed her. He confessed as soon as Leon got him into the interview room.'

'Violence against women, especially by people they know, is on the rise. People are blaming the pandemic and lockdowns. They always need something to blame.'

'Who was Sam blaming?'

'Sam isn't the killer.'

'He tried to rape you in your own home. If you hadn't managed to escape, who knows what else he would have done to you. He could have killed you tonight, Olivia.'

'I know, but he's not who we're looking for. Sam is… well, he's sad. He's incredibly lonely and he fixated on me. I showed him kindness and he mistook it for something more. In the cold light of day, he's going to be full of regret.'

'It sounds like you feel sorry for him.'

Olivia took a deep breath. 'In a way, I sort of do. The world is a scary place for someone as fragile as Sam. Obviously, he needs arresting and charging, but he also needs help.'

'And, let me guess, you're the one to give it to him?'

'Absolutely not. I don't want to see him ever again. Like I said, he's sad. But he's not a killer.'

'Bugger.'

'Have you got any leads on his whereabouts yet?'

'Not so far. I've put an alert out to all hospitals. He's going to need that eye seeing to if you've caused as much damage as you say you have.'

Foley went into the kitchen and returned with a bottle of whisky and two glasses. He poured a large measure into one and handed it to Olivia.

'You're shaking. This'll settle you.'

'It's the adrenaline finding a way out. I'm fine.'

'So, tell me, as I'm just an ignorant detective—'

'You are not an ignorant detective, Amyas,' she interrupted.

'Tell me anyway; why are you so sure Sam isn't the killer when he tried to rape you?'

Olivia took a sip of the whisky and smiled as the rich golden liquid began to soothe her. 'First of all, when I accused him of murder, he genuinely didn't have a clue what I was talking about. Yes, he's obsessed, but only to the point of leaving flowers on my doorstep and going into my house. It's a big leap from that to committing murder. We can both agree that our killer is a sadist, someone strong and determined, yes?'

'Yes.'

'And that's not Sam. He's weak. He's passive. When he became angry with me he used the one thing a man can do to ruin a woman – he tried to rape me. Sexual conquest represents the ultimate power for a man, and a rapist is a weak man who *thinks* he has power and control. This killer doesn't need to fake it because he really is a psychopath. Sam, well, he just isn't. He's confused.'

'Wait, you're defending him now?'

'No, I'm not. I'm understanding him. It's my job to understand people. Charge him with breaking and entering, attempted rape, stalking, whatever you can make stick, but he is not your killer.'

'So, we're back to square one?'

'Not quite. Square five.'

'How do you mean?'

'Is there any chance of something to eat? My stomach thinks my throat has been cut.'

'I'm not much of a cook but I make a mean fry-up.'

'That sounds wonderful,' she said with a smile.

Foley led Olivia into the spartan kitchen. Despite it being the early hours of Sunday morning, they were both hungry and Foley set about frying eggs, mushrooms, bacon and sausages, while a saucepan of beans bubbled on the hob. Olivia sat at the table and buttered some white bread. This was the ultimate in comfort eating, and Olivia needed plenty of comfort right now.

The dogs had followed them into the kitchen and sat patiently next to the table, waiting for any leftovers. Judging by the sounds Olivia's stomach were making, there wouldn't be much left.

Foley brought two full plates of food to the table and they both tucked in as if it were their final meal on earth.

'I can't get my head around that business with your father,' Foley said with a mouthful of bacon.

'You need to show him a photo of Sam Halliday; see if it's the same person who went to see him. I doubt it will be, but, just in case.'

'Can we trust his answer, though?'

Olivia shrugged.

'I've put a guard outside his room again and we're interviewing the prison officer who's supposed to have been keeping an eye on him. I've no idea how he got hold of the mobile he used to call me. It's just… I mean, I know he's a killer, but he's still your father at the end of the day, yet he sent someone round to your house to kill you. Why would he do that?'

'Power. Control,' Olivia said. Her voice was calm. Despite the fact she was related to a serial killer, she tried to pigeon-hole him with all the others. He was a killer, not a member of her family. He was a man, not her dad. 'When a murderer is going about their business, they have power over their victims, and they get joy out of seeing others living in fear. When they get caught, they have the full attention of the nation's media and a court case to show off their expertise. When they're imprisoned, that's when it hits them. The papers are no longer interested. Nobody cares about them. They're locked up and left to rot. That's why you get killers confessing to old crimes they haven't committed. Briefly, they're back in the limelight and seem to have some kind of a hold over the police. That's the attention they crave. By sending a killer after me, Richard was back in control. He was having a second taste of what it was like being free to kill again.'

'But you're his daughter,' Foley said incredulously.

'He tried to kill me when I was nine,' she said, pulling her shirt open and showing Foley the scars. 'It doesn't matter that we're blood relatives. I'm still a potential victim to him.'

Foley shook his head. 'He is one sick, twisted individual.'

'Yes,' Olivia said, putting down her knife and fork. 'And I share half his DNA.'

Meal over, they were back in the living room and lounging on the sofas, and alcohol had been replaced with mugs of tea. Olivia was replete. She could have fallen asleep where she sat, but judging by the pensive look on Foley's face, he had more he wanted to say.

'Go on,' she said.

'What?'

'Your eyes have been going to that book Sebastian Lister wrote since I got here. You're itching to ask me some questions. While I'm in a receptive mood, now is the time to ask because when I'm on my A-game, I clam up,' she said with a smile.

'You don't have to answer anything.'

'I know I don't. And I won't if I don't like the question.'

Foley took a breath. 'Richard was named in the press as The Riverside Killer because he left his victims on the bank of the Thames. Why did he do that? Did the river hold some kind of special significance for him?'

Olivia thought for a moment. 'Not that I'm aware of. I don't think Richard has an aquaphilia.'

'What?'

'A sexual arousal from water or watery environments.'

'I didn't realise there was a name for it.'

'There's a name for all of them. He did like the river. He often took us out on the Thames on a boat whenever it was one of our birthdays or a bank holiday. Maybe he did have some kind of weird thing with water going on. You'd need to ask Sebastian that question.'

'How did you survive being stabbed?'

'Two police officers came to the house. I lowered myself

through the bathroom window – well, you know all that from the book. I was climbing over the back garden fence when the officers came into the garden. Richard lashed out at one and slashed him across his arm – fortunately, only a flesh wound. The other officer followed us over the fence and into the woods at the back of the house. He dragged my father off me, so I was told, punched him in the face and sat on him until back-up arrived.'

'Brave man.'

'Yes. I believe they both received commendations.'

'How can you talk about all this so calmly?'

'You think I'm calm?'

'That's how you come across.'

'Some days are better than others, obviously. The truth is, I'm actually a complete mess. One morning I can wake up and be focused and get through the day without giving what happened a single thought and I'm just a regular working woman. Another morning I wake up and wonder why I couldn't have died in my sleep to put an end to all the horror.'

'You're hurting?'

Olivia bit her bottom lip and nodded. 'I am. I loved my mum and my sister so much. I still do. I hate that they're no longer in my life. But I keep going for them. Is there anything else you'd like to ask me?'

'I do have one more question.' He leaned forward. 'This is quite a big, personal one, though.'

'Oh God. Go on.'

'Can I take you out sometime?'

Olivia raised her eyebrows. Two offers of dates in the space of a couple of days. Suddenly she was hot property.

'For a meal, obviously. I don't mean with a rifle or anything,' Foley added.

Olivia laughed. 'Do you mind if I wait until we've caught the killer before I answer that one?'

'Of course not.'

Chapter Forty-Nine

Sunday 25th February 2024

Olivia woke up in a strange bed in a strange room. It took her a few moments to remember where she was.

She'd finally gone to bed around three o'clock after she and Foley had had a long talk about the investigation, and about her past. She'd found herself answering Foley's personal questions with ease when before, whenever her father was brought up by Sebastian or Jessica, she'd felt the tears well up inside her. Had seeing Richard stricken in a hospital bed, aged and ill, made her realise he was no longer the monster she'd had living in her head for the past twenty-five years? Olivia no longer saw a therapist and preferred to keep her demons taunting her as a form of self-flagellation, but maybe she was turning a corner without realising. Surely that was a good thing.

Foley had given her his room. It was similar to the living room in that there was nothing personal in here – a solid oak wardrobe, a king-size bed and a single bedside table. Again, no pictures, no ornaments, nothing to suggest family or close friends in his life. The room was clean, neat and tidy. The bedding smelled fresh and

Olivia was asleep within minutes of her head touching the pillow. When she woke up, sunlight was creeping around the sides of the curtains. She could hear the sounds of a hectic London going about its business.

She pushed back the duvet and swung her legs out of bed. Obviously she hadn't brought anything with her so she'd slept in her underwear. She redressed and left the room. As she made her way to the stairs, she saw that the door to the spare bedroom was ajar. She looked inside. It was empty. Not even a bed. Where had Foley slept, then?

Downstairs was quiet. No Foley and no dogs, not even Stanley. She frowned and went into the kitchen. The dishwasher was humming away, and the kettle was warm to the touch. She flicked it on and set about making a coffee. She looked in the cupboards but couldn't see anything she fancied to eat. The fry-up from last night was lying heavily on her stomach. It would take more than a few laps of the swimming pool and a Krav Maga class to work that off.

The front door opened and slammed closed. All three dogs came trotting into the kitchen and headed for the water bowls. Foley followed, taking off his hat and coat.

'Good morning. Or should I say good afternoon,' he said.

'Afternoon?' Olivia asked, surprised.

He looked at his watch. 'Well, no, it's only just gone half eleven.'

'What? Have I been asleep all that time?'

'It was very late when we went to bed.'

'So how come you're up so early?'

'I'm always up early. Besides, these two never let me have a lie-in.'

'Where did you sleep? I didn't see a bed in the spare room. Would you like a coffee?'

'Please. I slept on the sofa.'

'You didn't need to do that. I could have slept there. I feel guilty now.'

'No need. I can sleep anywhere. I've nodded off at my desk at work many times and slept perfectly well.'

Olivia made them both a coffee and fussed over Stanley while it cooled.

'I had a call a couple of hours ago,' Foley said, sitting down at the kitchen table. 'Sam Halliday was picked up in the early hours.'

'Where?'

'He was in A&E at St George's Hospital in Tooting.'

'How is he?' Olivia asked without looking up from her coffee. Despite him trying to rape her, she felt guilty about the level of injury she'd inflicted upon him.

'I'm afraid he's lost his eye.'

'Oh my God.' Olivia was genuinely shocked. 'Am I going to face some kind of criminal charge?'

'No. You acted in self-defence and he's admitted attacking you.'

Olivia shook her head in shame.

'You feel sorry for him?'

'Yes, I do. He was confused. He told me he hates living in London. He hasn't fitted in at all. He has no friends. I think I was probably the first person who took an interest in him.'

'That's no reason for him to do what he did.'

'I'm not trying to excuse him. I'm trying to understand him. He was incredibly lonely and isolated. Maybe he was physically attracted to me. If he'd had friends and lived a normal life, he would have dealt with it better, but he went to the extreme because he wanted to hold onto our relationship,' she said with sympathy.

'Olivia, when we took him back to the station, we obviously needed to take his clothes. He was wearing... well, he was wearing... some underwear which we think might have belonged to you,' Foley said, uncomfortable at the nature of the topic.

Olivia looked up. Her eyes widened. 'I was missing a pair of knickers. I thought the washing machine had eaten them. It's had several socks over the years.' She gave a hint of a chuckle. 'What's going to happen to him?'

'He's been charged with trespass with the intent to commit a sexual offence. He'll be going to magistrates' court on Monday.'

'Will he be jailed?'

'That crime carries a sentence of three to five years.'

'Is there anything I can do to stop him from going to prison?'

'What? Why would you want to?'

'Because he didn't mean any of it. I know he didn't. He was lonely. He's mixed up. He's living in a world that makes absolutely no sense to him.'

'That doesn't give him the right to—'

'I know,' she interrupted. 'Look, I know all this. If he was a serial rapist I'd say he deserves everything that's coming to him. But the last place someone like Sam Halliday should be is prison. It's almost the same as when you thought Sean Fincher could be the killer. Prison for people like them would inflict further damage, especially if they don't need to be there.'

'And you think someone who attempted rape shouldn't go to prison?'

'You make him sound like a sexual predator.'

'Maybe he is.'

'He isn't. He's inexperienced and confused. I'll go to court with him. I'll give a victim impact statement and ask the judge for leniency. Hopefully, the fact I'm a forensic psychologist will work in my favour, too.'

'Olivia, you—'

Olivia stood up. 'Am I allowed to go home? I'd like a shower.'

'You can have a shower here.'

'I need to change my clothes as well.'

'Yes. Your house has been released.'

'Thank you.'

'I'll drive you back.' He looked down at the table, hurt. Olivia didn't know if that was because she was planning to get Sam a lighter sentence or because she was leaving to go back home.

She placed a hand on his shoulder. 'Thank you for everything. You're a good man and an excellent detective. And I'm very grateful for your company last night.' She left the room as Foley's phone began to ring.

Upstairs, she made the bed and neatened up the room. She pulled back the curtains and squinted at the bright day outside. The sky was a brilliant blue, not a cloud to be seen, but it looked bitterly cold, and people went about their business wrapped up in layers of warm, comfortable clothing.

Olivia loved days like this. She preferred the winter to summer as it meant she didn't look strange wearing a jacket to hide her scars, as she did during a heatwave. Cold, crisp days like today were perfect for going out in. She leaned her elbows on the windowsill and watched the world go by. The view from Foley's window wasn't inspiring but there were plenty of people around, each with a story to tell. That was what fascinated Olivia more than anything, although, the more she thought about it, it terrified her slightly, too. Who knew what was going through the mind of each individual? How many active killers were there in London alone?

'Olivia.'

She jumped at the sound of her name being called. She turned around to see Foley standing in the doorway to the bedroom.

'Blimey, you scared the life out of me!' she said with a hand on her chest. She noticed the grave look on his pale face. 'What is it? Has something happened?'

'I've just had a call from Holly.' He couldn't look at Olivia, his gaze fixed firmly on the floor. 'Sam Halliday hanged himself in his cell about an hour ago.'

Tears exploded from Olivia's eyes. She clamped a hand to her mouth to stop the scream from coming out and slid down the wall to the floor.

Chapter Fifty

Foley had wanted to stay with Olivia and Stanley when he dropped them back home, but she refused, saying she wanted to be alone. She wouldn't even allow him to accompany her into the house. He mentioned the fact the killer was still out there, that her father had told him to go to her house, but his words fell on deaf ears. Olivia wanted, needed, to be alone.

She avoided looking down at Sam's basement flat as she walked up the stairs to her front door and didn't turn back to wave at Foley. Once inside, she locked the door behind her, set the alarm and went straight into her bedroom. She crawled onto the bed, grabbed the blue dog her sister had taken everywhere with her and held it tight, crying loudly into the pillow. A man's life had ended. His family would be destroyed.

There was no denying what Sam had done was wrong. His clumsy attempts to get her attention had come at the wrong time and she'd misread them or hadn't even noticed them. In a hedonistic world, an inexperienced man had latched onto the one person who he thought could bring him out of himself and, in his eyes, she'd rejected him. He'd obviously seen Ethan and Amyas coming to her house and his mind had gone into overdrive. Faced with a prison sentence, a career ruined before it had even begun, and his family finding out he'd attempted to rape someone, Sam had obviously felt he had no other way to turn. He must have felt so lost.

Some people said that taking your own life was the easy way out, but Olivia didn't think so. Not in this case. Sam had taken control of his life for the first time and realised he couldn't fit into twenty-first-century living. He'd gone down the wrong path, but she knew he had not been a bad man at heart.

A yap from Stanley woke Olivia with a start. The dog was pacing up and down in the bedroom, heading to the door and back to the bed, a sign he needed to go outside.

Olivia dragged herself off the bed. She felt listless and her limbs felt heavy. She unlocked the back door and Stanley charged out into the garden. She stood on the threshold, arms wrapped around her chest, and looked out at the darkening sky. She had no idea how long she'd been asleep. She didn't even know what time it was.

A thought entered her brain. Why hadn't the killer come last night? There had been the party opposite and her father had made contact with him and told him to come round. So, why hadn't he?

'Stanley, come on,' she called out to him with a sense of urgency in her voice. She needed to check something.

The little dog ran up the stairs and into the house. She was going to leave the kitchen when she saw him out of the corner of her eye, looking longingly into his food bowl.

'I'm sorry, sweetheart, I've been neglecting you lately, haven't I?' She poured a few biscuits into it and left him to his meal while she charged upstairs to her office.

It seemed like an age since she'd sat down and done any work. It had only been just over a day. She turned on her laptop and logged in to the security system which was connected to the camera above her front door.

She had the option to watch live footage or choose a date and time in the last seven days before it was wiped. She tried to remember what time it was when she'd heard Sam in her house. It must have been after ten o'clock. She typed in 22:00 and watched the footage.

At the top of the screen, people were coming and going from the Blackstocks' house across the road. She ignored them and kept her eyes firmly on the steps leading up to her front door.

At 22:13, Sam appeared. She watched as the junior doctor walked slowly up the steps, keys in hand, oblivious to the people on the opposite pavement, as if he had every reason to be there. She paused the footage. A wave of sadness swept over her as she looked at his young face. He had his whole life ahead of him, a wonderful career in medicine, and it had all ended so suddenly.

Something didn't make sense. Why hadn't she seen him on the footage when she was looking to see who had delivered the flowers? She looked away from the screen and frowned as she thought, chewing on the inside of her cheeks. She went downstairs and unlocked the front door. She stepped out and looked up at her house and the one next door. Of course. It was obvious. Sam had known about the camera above her door and not wanted her to see him leaving them, so had stood on next door's front step and thrown them over the railings, which was when the card had become detached and blown away. She smiled to herself. He really had been a shy young man. If he'd gone about it another way, told her how he'd felt, she could have let him down gently and maybe they could have remained friends. He would still be alive now.

Olivia went back into the house. Life was full of ifs and maybes. If only the police had driven faster to her house when she was younger, her father might not have had time to kill her mum and sister.

She went back upstairs to her office and let the footage continue. She watched as Sam unlocked the door and stepped inside. She went back to 22:13 and watched it again.

Something was odd about it. Something didn't make sense.

Back to 22:13 again, and this time, when Sam first appeared at the bottom of the steps she paused the footage and played it frame by frame until he disappeared inside her house. What was wrong? She watched it again, this time concentrating on what was happening in the background, and not Sam. People were entering the picture and going to the Blackstocks' house, knocking on the door and entering. Some were coming out, drink in hand, for a sneaky cigarette before going back in. A couple entered the screen from the right, hurriedly walking to the house, obviously late attendants, carrying a bottle of wine each. They ran up the steps and disappeared into the house. A taxi appeared and three people got out and went into the house. The taxi drove away. A man walked into view. He had his hands in his pockets. He stopped at the entrance of the party house, looked around, looked ahead at Olivia's house and remained there for a few minutes before turning on his heel and going back down the pavement, out of shot. He hadn't gone into Dorothy's house. He hadn't been a guest at the party. That was what had seemed so strange to Olivia. She watched it again, this time leaning closer into the screen.

Although the picture was of excellent quality, the main focus of the camera was on what was going on outside of Olivia's house and the road. It was impossible for her to zoom in on the action across the street. When the man entered the shot again, she waited until he stood still and turned towards Olivia's house. She paused the footage, took a screenshot and zoomed in on the face. Whoever he was, he was looking directly into Olivia's house.

He must have walked up the street to see if Olivia had gone to the party or not. When he saw Sam enter the house and realised that Olivia now had company, he had simply turned around and left. It was him. It was the killer. It had to be.

It took her a few moments to place him, but suddenly, everything dropped into place. She recognised the man standing opposite her house. His appearance was slightly different; he'd shaved and had a haircut, but it was definitely him. If she'd read the police files with a more open mind and not been so distracted by her father and her own worries, she would have identified the killer much sooner.

Something snapped in her mind. She opened Google and searched for *The Sun* newspaper. It took a few scrolls and clicks to find the article she was looking for, but then there it was.

'You sneaky little fucker,' she said to the screen.

Chapter Fifty-One

The sensible option would be to call Foley, to ask him to come round and view the footage, explain her theory and leave him to decide where to go next with the investigation. That would mean telling Foley she'd made an error of judgement, that her mind hadn't been one hundred per cent on the job and that through her incompetence, lives had been lost, including her friend's. Giving a job less than one hundred per cent was not an option for Olivia, it screamed of failure. She would have to put this right herself.

Scrambling through the files on her desk, she found the one she wanted and opened it. She bypassed crime scene photos and witness statements and found the single sheet of paper she was looking for, the one that detailed everything she needed to know about the victim: name, age, address, place of work, job description, financial status. Her eyes darted from left to right as she quickly took everything in.

Olivia ran downstairs, slipped into her shoes and put her coat on. She was almost out of the door when she heard a small yap behind her. She had completely forgotten about Stanley. He stood in the middle of the hallway with a wide-eyed look of loss on his face. She wondered what was going on in his mind.

She squatted down. He trotted up to her, jumped, and placed his front paws on her knees. She stroked him and allowed him to lick her hand.

'Right then, Stanley. I'm going out for a little while. I'm not sure how long I'll be, but you've plenty of water in your bowl and a comfortable sofa to sleep on. Tomorrow, I'll take you out for a long walk and we might even pop in to see Amyas and his dogs, too. Would you like that?'

She kissed the top of his head and found she had tears in her eyes, though she had no idea why.

Olivia parked the scooter around the corner from the petrol station in South Ruislip and walked the rest of the way. It was dark, and the wind had picked up. Looking up, there wasn't a cloud in the sky and there were no stars visible either, thanks to light pollution. She had no idea how this confrontation was going to play out. On the ride over, she tried to think of what to say, but nothing came. She'd never accused someone of murder to their face before. What would their reaction be and what would be her reaction to their reaction? She was out of her depth and knew it.

The petrol station was busy. Cars were parked at every pump, and the kiosk was lit up in a brilliant white. Standing on the pavement, she squinted as she tried to make out the features of the two staff members behind the counter. The nearest one to the window was a large woman with dyed purple hair. Olivia couldn't see her colleague well enough, as he was partially hidden by the chunky lottery machine. She'd need to go in. She approached and stopped in her tracks. There he was. The face of evil.

The young man came from around the back of the kiosk, an electric cigarette in hand. He'd been on an extended break and had taken the opportunity to get some fresh air; he'd clearly wanted a few drags on his e-cig and a scroll through Twitter to see if Londoners were still living in fear of him. He already had his next victim lined up. She was twenty-four and lived in Brent. He'd gone for a black woman this time. That would really screw with the police's theory of serial killers sticking to their own racial group. He looked up and saw Olivia. He almost stopped dead in his tracks, but doing that would have given him away. He'd learned how to think on the spot when he was practising his technique of getting into people's houses. He made a play of looking around him at what was going on, put his phone in his back pocket and went back into the petrol station.

As soon as his back was turned to Olivia, he frowned in thought. What was she actually doing here? He knew where she worked. He knew where she lived. There was no reason for her to use this petrol station on her journey from office to home, not even if she'd been to the police station in Sanderson Street. Also, she'd parked her shitty scooter nowhere near the petrol pumps, so this wasn't a random coincidence. So, again, why was she here? Unless…

'Fuck,' he said to himself under his breath.

She'd worked it out. She knew who he was. How? He knew she was good, but she couldn't be that good, surely.

His mind went into overdrive. He'd known it was risky going to the hospital and paying her father a visit. Had the great Richard Button lied to him? Told him what he wanted to hear, then called his daughter as soon as he was alone to reveal the identity of the killer and save his precious little girl?

He could feel the anger bubbling inside him. Richard Button had set him up. The sneaky bastard. He should have realised he was a manipulator. He'd killed six women then tried to murder his family; of course he shouldn't have trusted him. How could he have been so blind? Richard had even said to him never to meet your heroes. He'd been telling him that he was a sick, twisted, manipulative bastard.

He went straight into the back room for his coat and left. His supervisor, Cheryl, called out to him, but he ignored her. There was no coming back from this.

It was a shame it was going to end so soon. He was enjoying himself. Seven victims was a good tally. He would like to have reached double figures, but it didn't matter. Seven was an impressive number. Seven would see him remembered as a prolific serial killer.

He plunged his hands into his pockets and took out the card Olivia had given him the other day outside Sanderson Street Police Station.

Maybe reaching double figures wasn't such a long shot after all. Olivia would be victim number eight, and he was pretty sure he could take out a couple of detectives, too.

He looked up at the sky. He wished he could see the stars. He took in a lungful of cold winter air. This might be his final night of freedom. He wanted to savour it.

Olivia watched him go back into the petrol station. It was time to call Amyas. She suspected she knew who the killer was and had had her theory confirmed by his body language. It was only slightly, but the hesitation when he'd seen her spoke volumes. She went back to her scooter and took her mobile out of her pocket. It wasn't her job to confront someone and accuse them of murder. She dealt in the aftermath once they were locked behind bars. She was scrolling for Foley's number when her phone began to ring. The number had been withheld, but something inside her told her to answer it. She took off her helmet and swiped to answer.

'Hello?'

'Doctor Winter, hello.'

'Yes. Who is this?'

'You know exactly who I am.'

Olivia froze. Her entire body ran cold. 'Jamie Farr.' Her voice had started to shake.

She looked around her. Here she was, on a busy street in London, people around her going about their normal lives, and she was talking to someone who had murdered seven people.

'If you're looking for someone to help you, I wouldn't bother, if I were you.'

'You can see me?' She looked back towards the petrol station but couldn't see him.

'Oh, yes. You're surrounded by people yet not a single one can help you. Doesn't that make you feel lonely, Olivia?'

'Are you lonely?' Olivia asked.

'Reverse psychology? I thought you were better than that. Although I will answer your question. I used to feel lonely. However, once I started killing, the loneliness just drifted away. I'm on the front page of every single newspaper. People are talking about me on the Tube, the train, buses, in the queues in supermarkets. Suddenly, everyone knows me.'

'They don't, though, do they? They know *of* you, but they don't know your name.'

'They soon will.'

'But for them to know you, your game will be over. You'll be caught, thrown in a prison cell for the rest of your life and soon forgotten about. You'll be lonely again.'

'But everyone will know who I am.'

'They'll soon move on. We live in a very fickle world. People are selfish. Once you drop out of the newspapers, they'll forget about you. And do you honestly think your fellow prison inmates will be scared of you? They won't care who you are or what you've done.' The fear Olivia had felt when she realised she was talking to a killer had soon dissipated. He tried to come across as a formidable psychopath, but he wasn't. All he wanted was to be noticed, recognised. Why fear a narcissist who has so little brain power that his only reach for immortality is the most basic principle of murder?

'Oh, they'll care. Everyone will care.'

'They won't. Trust me on that. I've interviewed people like you before. You're nothing special. You don't stand out. You haven't covered any new ground. You're just a cheap copycat. You don't have the mettle to be different.' She remained still. If he could see her, he was obviously close. If he saw her looking around for someone, trying to get someone's attention for them to call the police, he would notice.

'You're trying to make me angry.'

'I doubt you have the capacity to be angry.'

'You want me to show my hand, lash out, reveal myself.'

'I don't need you to reveal yourself, Jamie. I know exactly who you are. As do the police. I think I've probably distracted you long enough for them to have searched your flat.' She was lying and hoped he couldn't detect it in her voice.

'You bitch! You're lying!' he spat down the phone.

Olivia tried to hide her smile. He was ticking all the boxes of a stereotypical killer. She increased the grip on her helmet. Hopefully, if he ran towards her, she could swing it and crack him over the head with it, stun him, then call Foley.

'It's over, Jamie. Admit it.'

'It's not over until I say it is. You think you're so smart, don't you, Olivia. You think, because of your work and your insider knowledge, you know everything about me. You're wrong. You want to catch me? You want to be the big killer hunter? You're going to have to come to me. Elmbridge Avenue. Quick as you can.'

Olivia felt like she'd been hit in the face. She opened her mouth to speak, but no words came out.

'That shocked you, didn't it? It's a long road, I know, but I think you'll know where I want you to be. I'll be waiting.'

The call ended.

Olivia looked at her phone. Her hand was shaking. She could feel her heart pounding in her chest. She took a few deep breaths to steady herself, but it didn't work. She felt sick.

Putting her helmet on, she started the scooter and joined the traffic without checking it was safe to do so. A car sounded its horn, but she ignored it. She needed help. There was no way she was going to Elmbridge Avenue on her own. The last time she'd been there was twenty-five years ago when her father had destroyed her childhood and her family. Why did Jamie want to go back to the beginning? What was this really all about?

Chapter Fifty-Two

Olivia drove through the busy streets of London. She zigzagged through cars and lorries, drove down bus lanes and skipped a red light. She was breaking the speed limit and she didn't care. Once she'd left the bright lights of the restaurants and clubs, the traffic began to thin out and Olivia was able to put her foot down harder. The cold air was blowing at her face, biting her cheeks. She was freezing but had to keep going.

When she turned into Foley's street, she slammed the brakes on when she saw him up ahead, a German shepherd at each side.

'Foley!' she called out. Her lips were so numb she barely heard it herself. She shouted again and the detective inspector turned around.

'Olivia! What are you doing here?'

'I know who the killer is. I've spoken to him on the phone.'

'Who is it?'

'It's Jamie Farr.'

Foley frowned. 'Farr? The bloke who was stabbed in the street in the early hours of—'

'Yes,' Olivia nodded. 'I don't know why I didn't see it before. All the other victims were killed when there was an audience, or the potential to be an audience with neighbours in close proximity, where the killer was practically sticking two fingers up at the police by showing off. Jamie's so-called attempted murder was on an empty street in the middle of the night with nobody to witness the attack. It was staged in order for him to insert himself into the investigation. It's what people like him do.'

'Fuck me. We've interviewed him several times. We've had him do an identikit and everything.'

'I know. And he'd have loved every moment of it.'

'You're sure about this?'

'He called me the other night. I gave him my card outside the police station and said if he needed to talk I could put him in touch with someone who could help. He... it reminded me of when I was attacked. I'd lost my mum and sister and was thinking, why had they been killed and I survived? He asked the same question. He told me he'd seen an article in the newspaper about the victims and he mentioned Calvin. I looked up the article he was talking about and Calvin and Neil were not mentioned. Just the women.'

'We held Calvin and Neil back from the press. We wanted to keep something up our sleeve.'

'If I read the papers, I'd have seen it sooner. He was telling me. He was fucking telling me he's the killer!' Olivia said, practically shouting.

'Jesus Christ!' Foley dug his mobile out of his pocket. 'I'll get on to Holly and ask her to—'

'I've just spoken to Jamie now.'

'You confronted him?'

'No. He called me. He asked me to meet him. I can't go on my own.'

'You need to leave this to us now, Olivia. I'll get someone to sit with you.'

'Amyas, wait,' she said, putting a hand on his arm. 'Where he asked me to meet him... it means he wants me involved in this.'

'Where?'

She took a deep breath. 'Elmbridge Avenue.'

'That sounds familiar. I can't place it, though.'

'It's in Kingston. Elmbridge Avenue was where I grew up. It was where my father killed my mum and sister.'

'How would Jamie know that?'

'He went to see Richard in hospital. My father has obviously given him chapter and verse. I think he wants to finish what my father tried to do but failed.'

'How do you mean?'

'He wants to kill me.'

Once they were in Foley's Toyota, he asked for exact directions. Olivia surprised herself by remembering her postcode from twenty-five years ago. He typed it into the satnav, and they were soon speeding towards Kingston.

As he drove, he kept looking over at Olivia, who was slumped in the front passenger seat. Her head was against the window and she was looking blankly out into the dark night.

'Why do you think he wants to kill you?' Foley eventually asked.

It was a while before Olivia answered. 'He's been in touch with Richard at the hospital. He's probably asked for tips on how he can be such a successful serial killer. He probably sees himself as the next Richard Button, continuing his work… and eclipsing it. In order to do that, he's got to kill the one victim Richard couldn't: me. And where better than where it all ended?'

'We need an armed response unit. Hey Siri,' he said, waking up his phone. 'Call Holly.'

'Calling Holly,' his phone said.

Olivia reached over and disconnected the call.

'What are you doing?' Foley asked.

'You can't,' she almost snapped. 'If he sees he's surrounded he'll do a runner. He'll go to ground and we'll lose him. He knows that we know who he is. He'll do everything in his power to avoid capture.'

'I'm not having you walking up to him so he can put a knife in your throat. We can place concealed armed officers at a safe distance from the house.'

'Look, he was watching me when he called. He's going to Kingston, just like we are. He'll see fleets of police vehicles pulling up and armed officers jumping out, whether they're camouflaged or not.'

'This is non-negotiable, Olivia.' He dialled and put the phone on speaker.

Olivia turned to look out of the window at a darkened London racing past her at fifty miles per hour. She'd always known her past would come back to haunt her one day, but she'd thought the exposure in the newspapers would have been it. She could live with the gossip, the taunts and the lingering looks in supermarkets. What she didn't expect was to be thrown back to where it all began. She heard her mum's voice in her head again telling her to run. She ran twenty-five years ago. She should run now.

'Olivia, are you listening?' Foley asked.

'Sorry? What?' Olivia's mind had been elsewhere.

'I said, I've sent Holly to the hospital to show Richard a photograph of Jamie Farr and see if he recognises him as the bloke who went to see him.'

'He'll deny it,' Olivia said, almost defeated.

'Then we'll ask the nurses, search through CCTV. I've got everyone looking for him just in case, and Holly is going to contact the station in Kingston. I've also got armed response going there too.'

'Do you get the feeling that this is going to end badly?' she asked, looking across at him.

'No,' he said after giving the question a thought. 'We're going to catch him. He'll be in custody before midnight.'

'I wish I shared your optimism.'

On a good day, it would take an hour and a half to get from Holloway to Kingston. They had already been driving for forty minutes and were making good progress. Olivia glanced at the speedometer and saw it creep past fifty and sixty miles per hour. It shouldn't be long before they were at Elmbridge Avenue. She had no idea how long it took armed response to scramble, but hopefully she and Foley would arrive before the team turned up with their weapons. She didn't want this to end in a bloodbath. Despite being personally involved in the investigation, she wanted him kept alive so she could interview him, discover how his mind worked, why he had become so fixated on her father's crimes and now, it seemed, on her.

'Do you think we should contact the people who live in my old house, tell them to lock all their doors until police can get there?' Olivia asked.

'Holly's taking care of it.'

'Although,' she began, thinking aloud, 'I don't think he'll want us to go to the house.'

'What are you talking about?'

'He wants to pick up where my dad left off. The last time I saw my dad was in those woods when he stabbed me.'

'I'm not having you go into the woods on your own in the dark with a fucking serial killer hiding behind a tree!' Foley exclaimed. He turned quickly to the right, throwing Olivia into the passenger door. He apologised.

'I have no intention of going in there on my own.'

'Good. I'll give Holly a call, see if armed response is close by,' he said, picking up his mobile.

'Can you tell them to hold back? I really want to talk to him. Obviously, if he tries anything, then do what you have to do, but

I'd rather get something out of this,' she said, looking through the window at the darkened exterior.

'Absolutely not! For a start, you're a civilian. Secondly, even if you weren't, you're not wired, and you're not wearing any protection under your clothes. There is no way I'm letting you go in there alone. Do you have any idea how many rules I'm breaking right now?'

Olivia smiled. 'One or two.'

'Try one or two dozen.'

'Whatever happens, I'll take the blame. I'll tell your bosses this was all my idea.'

'And what if you end up getting killed?'

'Would you like me to sign something now?'

'Don't be flippant.'

'I'm sorry. It's just… I've faced killers for years.'

'Yes, and they've all been behind bars.'

Olivia sighed. 'In 2013 I interviewed Carl Ray Baxter in Oregon over a six-week period. Do you remember him?'

'The name sounds familiar.'

'He raped and murdered four women he'd met on dating sites. The press called him The Cherub Killer because he had such a cute baby face. He really did, too. Blond curly hair, brilliant blue eyes and not a blemish on his skin. He was very popular with women, even before he became a killer. He had a string of girlfriends from when he was about twelve onwards. He lost his virginity when he was thirteen. He loved women. He loved sex and he loved the attention. I wanted to know why someone so popular, who seemed to have everything at his feet, became a multiple murderer, a brutal and vicious butcher of women.

'During our interviews, he flirted with me non-stop. He wrote me very graphic love letters and drew some incredibly detailed pictures. One of the last times we met, he stabbed a prison guard in the neck with a sharpened pencil and asked me to have sex with him.'

'Oh my God.'

'He didn't rape me. What he wanted was for us to make love. Obviously I said no, and I tried to help the guard, but there was nothing I could do. He choked on his own blood. But Carl Ray wouldn't take no for an answer. He broke a leg off one of the chairs and said he was going to force it into me if I didn't sleep with him.'

'What did you do?'

'I just stood there, my back against the wall. He came towards me slowly. He put his arm around my waist and started kissing my neck. His head was just at the right angle for me to lean down and bite his ear. He dropped the chair leg. I picked it up and hit him over the head with it.'

'Wow,' Foley said, impressed. He had a smile on his face.

'I have been in so many situations that I thought I couldn't get out of. And I obviously did because I'm in this car with you. I'm covered in scars and I'm probably so mentally fucked up that I shouldn't be working as a psychologist, but I've survived. I'm a winner. And I'm not going to let some pale copycat of my father kill me.'

Foley studied her. 'You're a remarkable woman, do you know that?'

'I do now,' she said, smiling back at him.

Chapter Fifty-Three

It was a little after eleven o'clock when they arrived in Kingston. Although Olivia had spent most of the journey with her head against the window watching the view blur by, she knew when she was back where she grew up. Surprisingly, it didn't seem to have changed much in the past twenty-five years. She recognised roads and landmarks, and all the old memories came flooding back. She remembered the friends she played with, the parks she went to at the weekends, the shops. She tried to find something to make her look back on her childhood and smile, but there was nothing. Richard had tainted it all.

'Pull over,' Olivia said to Foley.

'What's wrong?' he asked once he'd turned off the engine.

'Elmbridge Avenue is the next left,' she said quietly.

'OK.'

'You'll need to go down Raeburn Avenue to get to the woods around the back.'

Foley drove slowly down Raeburn Avenue. Olivia looked at each of the houses and the memories came flooding back. Jessica had lived in one of these. She'd had sleepovers at Olivia's house many times. They drove slowly past Jessica's childhood home. It looked completely different now. There was an extension and the garden had been turned into a driveway. The girls had planned to meet up in the Christmas holidays, but that obviously hadn't happened. Once Olivia was discharged from hospital, she was shipped straight off to Tower Hamlets. She never returned to Elmbridge Avenue, never spoke to any of her old friends. More than fifteen years had passed between the night she was nearly murdered and the first time she and Jessica met up again. They had both carried so much pain, but they had helped each other. Olivia wiped away a tear.

At the mini roundabout, Foley drove straight on and pulled up just before the bridge which ran over Hogsmill River. He turned off the engine and they remained in the car, listening to the sound of the cooling engine.

Olivia told herself she was prepared for whatever Jamie planned to throw at her, but the truth was, she wasn't. Taking a deep breath, she looked ahead at the sports ground she had played on many times as a child with her sister and friends, and at the woodland either side of the river where she and Claire had played hide and seek. Claire had always won. She had been a master at it. There was no turning back. Olivia took off her seatbelt.

'I'll be right beside you,' Foley said.

She looked across at him and proffered a nervous smile.

Olivia shivered when she stepped out of the car. She didn't know if that was due to nerves or the biting wind. She zipped up her jacket and pulled up the collar. They set off into the woods, taking confident strides.

She had no idea if Jamie Farr was already waiting for her, or if he was watching her from somewhere, but she didn't want him

The Mind of a Murderer

thinking she was scared. Inside, she was shaking like a leaf, her inner voice screaming at her to turn back and wait in the car until armed response arrived, but her legs continued to walk down the makeshift path. She had to see this through.

The temperature was a couple of degrees below freezing. A cloud of breath formed as she exhaled. In the sky above, there wasn't a cloud to be seen, and here, away from the main part of the capital, millions of stars twinkled. The further she went into the woods, the denser the trees became. She lost sight of houses and the sounds from the roads faded away.

She and Foley didn't speak. They kept glancing at each other and nodding that they were both fine, even though the expressions on their faces told the truth. They were walking into the unknown over uneven ground. He was here somewhere. He had to be.

Olivia heard a noise. She turned just in time to see Foley hit the ground. Jamie Farr was standing over him with a heavy branch in his hand.

'Amyas!' she screamed. She ran towards him, but Farr stopped her by pushing the branch into her chest.

'I knew you'd bring someone. I don't mind,' he said, tossing the branch to one side. 'But I'd prefer it to be just us two.'

Olivia's eyes were fixed on the stricken DI. He wasn't moving, but there was no blood coming from his head – not that she could see much in the darkness. She hoped he was just unconscious and not suffering any internal injuries. She'd never forgive herself if he died.

'So, have the memories come flooding back?' he asked in a playful voice. 'It's a nice area, isn't it? I bet you had some fun times with your sister in these woods. I know I did.'

'What are you talking about?'

'Come with me.'

He grabbed her by the elbow and dragged her along the rough terrain. She almost fell a few times, but he was stronger than he looked and pulled her up single-handedly. His other hand was deep in his coat pocket. Olivia dreaded to think what was in there.

Suddenly, he pushed her hard against a tree.

'I love this time of year, don't you?' Jamie said. 'All the leaves have fallen, and you can see through the trees for miles. We can see the back of the houses on Elmbridge Avenue from here. Can you see your house? Can you see your bedroom?'

Olivia wasn't looking.

'I can. It's that one right there.' He pointed. 'Olivia, you need to look.'

Reluctantly, she looked up.

'See where I'm pointing to? There's a light on. Pink curtains and I'm pretty sure that's a dream catcher hanging in the window. That was your room, wasn't it?'

Olivia was struggling to fight back the tears. Whenever she thought of this house, of a time before her family was destroyed, she tried to think of the happy times, the days when she and Claire were playing with dolls in her bedroom or drawing pictures. Claire had loved to draw horses. Her bedroom wall had been covered in pictures of horses, even though she'd never ridden one.

'How do you know?' Olivia asked, her voice quiet.

'Because that was my bedroom, too.'

Olivia looked up at Jamie, shock on her face. Jamie was grinning.

'We moved in when I was a child. I heard mutterings for years about how we could possibly stand to live in a murder house. Mum and Dad wouldn't tell me about it. They tried to protect me, so I had to do some research of my own. That house was where the great Richard Button tried to slaughter his family, and I was sleeping in the bed of the only survivor.

'I had no idea you were his daughter when you came up to me in the car park at the police station. I would never have guessed you'd have pursued this as a career.'

'So, this is all because you slept in my bedroom?'
'Partly.'
'Huh,' Olivia sighed.
'Something wrong?'
'All this time I thought I was looking for someone who attached deep psychological meaning to his actions, and it turns out you're just a cheap copycat.'
'I am not a copycat!' he said, raising his voice.
'You are.'
'I inveigled myself into the police investigation. I put myself amongst the team. You didn't pick up on that, did you?'
She looked him up and down. 'You stabbed yourself, didn't you?'
He unzipped his coat and lifted his jumper, revealing his pasty, skinny body and the two pale scars, neither of them an inch in length.
'I call them my war wounds. Injured in the line of duty,' he said with a smile.
'You're sick.'
'No, I'm not. You know I'm not. If I was sick I wouldn't be able to put so much planning and effort into all this. A sick person just goes mad with a gun or a machete. To be a successful serial killer, you need to be cool, calm, in control and have your wits about you. I'm as sane as you are. Although, that's not giving myself much credit, is it? Because you're FUCKING PSYCHOTIC!' he screamed. His voice echoed around the trees.
Olivia took a step back. Her eyes widened in fear.
'How many locks do you have on your door? Then there's the alarm system, the cameras and never taking the same route home from work. You're fucking paranoid. And what's with all the sex with random men? Do you hate yourself that much that you have to punish yourself with cheap sex to make you feel dirty? God forbid you meet a nice bloke and settle down. Your father really fucked you over, didn't he?' He laughed.

Olivia wiped away a tear.

'What did you do with the knife?' she asked quietly, her voice shaking. She wanted him off the subject of her. She wanted this over with so she could leave and get help for Foley.

'Sorry? What knife?'

'The one you stabbed yourself with.'

'Oh, that. That went down the drain at the side of the road. So simple.'

'So then why have you brought me here? What's your plan? If you're hoping for some kind of a reaction from me, think again,' Olivia said. 'I'm not here to play games, and I've no interest in listening to your shit, either. I've heard it all before.'

'Go on then, Doctor Button – sorry, I mean Doctor *Winter* – tell me, use your expertise. Who am I?'

'Simple. You're a no-hoper who has failed at life. Your parents are divorced. You were brought up by your mother who worked in a dead-end job to make ends meet. She resented having to look after you and failed to give you the love and attention you wanted. You grew up in a notorious house so latched onto the one thing that made you stand out from the crowd.'

'No. You're wrong,' he said without conviction.

'Am I?' Olivia stepped forward, getting closer and closer to him. 'I don't think I am. You wanted to see your father, but either he had no interest in seeing you or your mother refused. I'm guessing the latter. Your mother was quite dominating, wasn't she? She stifled you, shattered your dreams.'

'Stop. S-stop,' he stuttered.

'You failed at school and the only job you could get was working night shifts in a shitty petrol station. When you realised that was what your life was going to be like for the next seventy years, you decided to give yourself a bit of excitement. The only problem is, you're not clever enough to be a master criminal, so you had to become the simplest of them all: the killer. It doesn't take a great deal of brain power to become a killer. Anyone can stick a knife into someone, but a bank robber, a jewel thief, that all takes planning, thought, careful consideration, and you're just too stupid for that.'

'You don't have a fucking clue!' he spat as he backed into a tree.

'So, why a knife?' Olivia continued. She was so close now, she could almost smell his rancid breath. 'Symbolic, don't you think? Phallic, even. It gives you power and control that you can't get anywhere else. You don't have a girlfriend. I'm guessing you've never had a girlfriend, but you're not a virgin. Did you have to pay a prostitute to lose your virginity? Did women laugh at your small penis? Did your mother—'

'Don't mention my mother!' he screamed.

'Oh dear. Have I hit a raw nerve?' She smiled.

'No. But I have.' He lunged forward, taking Olivia by surprise. He produced a knife from behind his back and slammed it hard into Olivia's stomach. She fell back against a tree.

With the knife still inside her, Jamie leaned in close. Their noses were almost touching.

'You think you're so fucking clever, don't you? You're way off the mark, by the way. My mum and dad are happily married. They've recently celebrated their twentieth wedding anniversary and run a guesthouse in Blackpool. I received four A stars, three As and three Bs in my GCSEs, I have four A Levels and a degree in history. I've never been with a prostitute and I've fucked so many women I've met on Tinder that I've lost count. And the reason why I'm working in a shitty petrol station at night is because during the day I'm busy writing my thesis on war-torn Europe during the twentieth century. How does that fit into your psychological profile, Doctor Button?'

Olivia was in agony. Her breathing was rapid, and she tried to slow it down, but she couldn't. She could feel the knife inside her as Jamie turned the blade left and right. She felt sick. She could taste blood.

With his free hand, Jamie unzipped her coat and pulled back the shirt beneath. He ran his fingertip over the scars her father had made.

'Aren't they pathetic? You're very self-conscious about them, aren't you? I've seen you in the swimming pool in your ugly swimming costume that covers them up, drawing attention to yourself. Your father was a second-rate killer who didn't have the balls to finish off his own daughter. Now, why didn't he do it, do we think? Hmm, let's try and work it out, shall we? Four stab wounds to a nine-year-old should have been enough to see you join your mother and sister, so what happened? What was it you said about a knife? It's a phallic symbol? So, what can we deduce from that? He didn't rape his victims, but that doesn't necessarily mean he was impotent. I didn't rape mine and I have a full sex life. What could it be? Some daddies have a very special relationship with their first-born daughter. Were you daddy's little princess?' he asked in a sing-song voice as he stood over Olivia. 'Is that why he couldn't kill you? Because he loved you? But surely he loved your mother and sister, too, and he despatched them easily enough. Maybe his love for you ran a little deeper. Is that it? He didn't love you, did he? He was *in* love with you.'

Jamie looked into Olivia's eyes. Hers were full of tears; his were dancing in the moonlight.

He leaned in closer and whispered into her ear. 'Did he fuck you, Olivia? Did he come into your room at night to play a special game, a game that only daddies and their favourite child play?'

'You're sick,' she struggled to say.

'Am I? Or am I just more intelligent than you are? Do you want to know why I killed all those people? Because I wanted to. Because I thought it would be fun. Because it gave me a thrill to watch them die. There was no psychological cause behind it all. There was no childhood abuse or abandonment. I did it because I could. It really is as simple as that. How do you feel, Doctor Winter, knowing that your entire career has been for

The Mind of a Murderer

nothing? You've spent your life trying to find out the secret of why killers kill, and you've just been told there isn't one. You must be gutted. Still, you're not going to be alive much longer to worry.'

He pulled the knife out and plunged it back into her again.

'Can you taste blood? Does it hurt? What's going through your mind? Talk to me, Olivia. Describe to me what it's like to die.'

'Fuck you,' she spat.

'Oh dear. Do you really want those to be your last words?'

Again, he pulled out the knife and stabbed her a third time.

'Come on. Say something profound, something meaningful, something that will go down in history.'

She spat in his face, spraying him in blood. 'I said, fuck you.'

Olivia brought her knee swiftly up, which got him hard between the legs. Jamie recoiled, doubled over in pain. The knife was pulled, jaggedly, out of her body, making her scream. She clamped a hand over the wounds to stem the blood flow and ran for her life.

The trees surrounding her began to blur as the amount of blood she was losing made her light-headed and dizzy. Behind her, she could hear Jamie following. She had definitely caused some damage, judging by the sound she heard when her knee had made contact with his testicles. She hoped they were ruptured beyond repair.

She stumbled over tree stumps and struggled to stay on her feet. She was cast back in time twenty-five years when her father had chased her through the same woods. She didn't die that night, and she had no intention of dying tonight either.

She tripped, fell, and rolled down the embankment, landing with a splash in Hogsmill River. The water was freezing. She tried to climb out, but her hands could not gain any purchase on the bank, and she was rapidly losing consciousness.

'You're a fighter, I'll give you that.'

She looked up and saw Jamie standing over her.

She slumped, her head landing in the mud. She coughed and spat blood.

'Your choice now, Olivia. I can either finish you off quickly with a knife to the throat or you can drown.'

Olivia tried to stand up but the life was draining out of her. She could feel the cold from the water soaking through her clothes to her skin. She swallowed hard and tasted blood. She dug her fingers into the bank of the river and tried to pull herself up. She mumbled something, barely audible.

'What?'

She repeated it, but not loudly enough to be heard.

Jamie stooped down to her level and leaned in. 'You'll have to speak up.'

'I said, fuck you.' She headbutted him so hard that she heard a crack.

He cried out in pain and bent over. Olivia reached up, grabbed the collar of his jacket and pulled hard. He fell head first into the river. The splash caused a wave and Olivia hit the bank. With the last of her strength, she leapt forward and threw herself onto Jamie's back, holding him down under the water.

Chapter Fifty-Four

Monday 4th March 2024

DI Foley and DS Goodfellow had been to interview Richard Button in Belmarsh Prison for a third time. On the previous two visits, he'd given them no-comment answers to their questions. This visit was at his request.

'It was Jamie Farr who came to see me in hospital,' Richard said. 'He told me he lived in my house in Elmbridge Avenue when he was a child. He was obsessed with me and wanted to continue my work.'

There was a sense of pride in his voice, as if he was pleased his legacy was continuing.

'Why didn't you call the police and tell us?' Holly asked.

'Why should I? Let him have his fun.'

'People have died.'

Richard shrugged.

'Why did you send him to Olivia's house?' Foley asked.

'I knew Livvy would be able to take care of herself against someone like him.'

'He could have killed her.'

'But he didn't. Livvy is my little girl. She's very special to me. I wouldn't let a creep like Jamie kill her.' He leaned forward. 'I've said it before, and I'll say it again. If anyone is going to kill Livvy, it's going to be me.'

'You're serving a whole-life tariff. There's no way you're going to be able to get to Olivia,' Foley said.

'You need to be more lateral with your thinking, Amyas. I may not be the one who pushes in the knife, but I'll decide when Livvy dies, no one else.'

An icy chill ran through Foley. 'What are you talking about?'

Richard sat back and crossed his arms, a satisfied smile on his face.

'What are you planning?' Foley asked.

'No comment.'

'Bastard!' Foley spat as they walked out of the prison and headed for the car. 'I can't believe we agreed to come here. He'll do anything to get the upper hand.'

'What do you think he meant about him killing Olivia?' Holly asked with a frown. 'I mean, how can he do that?'

Foley was rummaging around in his pocket for his mobile phone. He'd turned it off while in the prison – those were the rules – and was waiting for it to switch back on.

'I have no idea, Holly.' He'd had a voicemail and listened. 'I will do my very best to get every privilege he's got in that prison taken away from him. That was Leon,' he said, looking back at his phone. 'Olivia's awake.'

Olivia was sitting up in bed nibbling at a slice of cold toast. It was the first time she'd eaten anything in six days. She was weak, hungry and tired.

Next to her bed, Sebastian was keeping a watchful eye over her.

'Is Stanley all right?' she asked, not for the first time. She slapped the limp toast onto the plate. She couldn't eat it.

'He's fine. The kids are loving having him around. You may have to fight to get him back.'

She gave a half-hearted smile.

'I can't believe you put yourself in that situation, Olivia,' Sebastian continued. 'You could have died.'

'Just a few more scars to add to the collection,' she answered flippantly.

'Olivia, there's something I need to tell you,' he said, hitching his chair closer to her bed. 'I've asked Foley and he doesn't know who leaked your true identity to the newspapers. We have to assume it was Jamie Farr.'

'It was Richard.'

'What?'

'Richard called the press. He told them. I don't know how.'

'Oh my God. He really is evil, isn't he?'

'And there are still people in the world who don't believe evil exists. All they have to do is look to Richard.'

'The thing is, I... I... for a brief moment, I did think of doing it myself. I know they would have paid a lot of money for the exclusive story and... I'm so sorry for even thinking it, Olivia,' he said, not even daring to make eye contact.

She reached out and took his hand. 'It's all right, Seb. You had a dark thought. You didn't act on it. That's the main thing.'

He looked up at her. Tears were falling down his face.

'I'm guessing your publisher has been on to you?'

He nodded. 'They want me to write an updated version of *The Riverside Killer* and write a book about Jamie Farr, too.'

'A two-book deal. How much are they offering?'

'A six-figure advance.'

'High six or low six?'

'Low six.'

'Hold out for high six, then accept.'

'What?'

'I'll even let you interview me and write about what it's like, being the daughter of a serial killer.'

'I couldn't do that to you.'

'They know anyway, thanks to Jamie and the tabloids. Once I'm home, I'm going to have journalists knocking at my door asking for the story. This way, I know it will be written sensitively and professionally.'

'I don't know what to say.'

She held his hand tighter. There was nothing else to say.

Amyas Foley walked down the corridor of the hospital. As he reached the ward Olivia was on, he spotted someone he recognised. The photographer, Ethan Miller, was heading towards him. Tall, strong, swathed in leather, he squeaked as he walked.

'Have you been to see Olivia?' Foley asked, having to look up at Ethan, who towered over him.

'They won't let me in. I'm not family.'

'Ah. Fingers crossed, my warrant card will allow me in,' he said with a smile. 'Would you like me to give her a message?'

Ethan thought for a long moment. 'No. It's fine. Just… just tell her I was asking after her.'

Foley's warrant card did allow him access. He pushed open the door to find Sebastian sitting beside Olivia's bed.

'Oh,' he said.

'I'll leave you to it,' Sebastian said, standing up. 'Don't keep her too long. She needs to rest,' he said to Foley. And to Olivia: 'I'll come in and see you tomorrow.'

Olivia smiled and waved him goodbye.

'I thought only family were allowed in,' Foley said once the door was closed.

'I don't have any family. Besides, he's listed as my next of kin.'

'Oh.' He sat down. 'How are you feeling?'

'Numb. These drugs are amazing.' She smiled. 'How are you?'

'I'm fine. An overnight stay in hospital and a bump on my head the size of a chocolate orange. People keep bringing branches and twigs into the office and leaving them on my desk. I work with such a sympathetic bunch of people.' He grimaced.

'Sebastian won't tell me. He's trying to protect me. Jamie Farr...?' She left the sentence open.

He nodded. 'Jamie Farr died in the river. He cracked his head on a rock.'

Olivia looked away.

'Don't even think about blaming yourself. The man was a serial killer. He'd have killed you that night, Olivia. You know it, and I know it.'

She couldn't turn back to him.

'We've searched his flat. You were right about his obsession with serial killers. I've never seen so many books outside of a branch of Waterstones. We've looked into his background, too. He tried to join the police five years ago. He was turned down.'

'Why?' she asked, turning to him.

'He was registered bankrupt in 2012 and has a lot of outstanding debts.'

'Everything I thought was wrong,' she said. 'I tried using victimology and psychology to understand the killer, and it was all because he grew up in my house and had some kind of obsession with Richard. You see, this is why I don't work on active cases. I prefer to know the results before I talk to these people.'

'You helped us catch our killer. You did your job, Olivia. We wouldn't have got him without you.'

Olivia yawned.

'I'll let you get some rest,' he said, making to stand up.

'Wait. What about Richard?'

'He's back in prison.' He didn't tell her anything about his recent interview with him.

She shook her head. 'I can't believe I'm related to that man.'

He held her hand firmly in his. 'Olivia, you are nothing like your father. He's a psychopathic narcissist. You are one of the most intelligent and admirable women I have ever met,' he said with a genuine smile in his eyes.

'Thank you,' she said through the tears.

'Now, I want you to concentrate on getting better, and when you're discharged and you've got your strength back, I'm taking you out for a meal somewhere posh.'

'Are you sure you want to be seen eating out with a killer?'

'You are not a killer, Olivia. You did what you had to do to survive. I don't want to see you beat yourself up over a man like that.' He leaned down and kissed her on the forehead. 'I'll come back and see you in a few days.'

Olivia watched him leave. She turned away from the door and looked out of the window. Her memory of what had happened in the woods was patchy but there was one thing that was crystal clear: when she had grabbed Jamie Farr and pulled him into the river, when she'd thrown herself on top of him so he couldn't get back up, she had been willing him, with every fibre of her being, to die.

Epilogue

Monday 18th March 2024

It didn't seem like the winter was ever going to end.

For the past three days, the temperature had stayed around zero and the previous evening, a light dusting of snow fell on the capital. As Olivia walked around the park with Stanley on his lead, she almost smiled at her surroundings. To her, London reminded her of murder and death. It was the city where her father had committed his crimes and where he had killed her mother and sister. She should leave. For her own sanity, she should move somewhere else. But her family were here. Generations of her relatives were buried in graveyards all over London. As the last surviving one, she wanted to join them, one day.

Stanley was enjoying frolicking in the snow. He needed the exercise. Sebastian's children had made a fuss over him and fed him all kinds of treats. He was now on a strict diet. Unfortunately, as he only had tiny legs, he soon tired, so they were heading for the warmth of home within half an hour of leaving it.

As she entered the cul-de-sac, she noticed something that hadn't been there when she had left. The basement flat Sam Halliday had been renting was back on the market. She had wondered whether to send flowers to his family back in Devon but decided not to. It was best to move on.

Once in the house, she closed and locked the front door and set the alarm, took Stanley's lead off and went into the kitchen. Sebastian was coming over for dinner and she was going to try her hand at making fresh pasta. She'd had the machine in a box for years. It was about time she dusted it off and used it.

She took the ingredients out of the cupboard and found the recipe on her iPad. She was mixing up the dough when the doorbell rang.

'Typical. Someone always calls when you're in the middle of something dirty,' she said to Stanley as she wiped her floured hands on a tea towel.

She looked through the spy hole in the door but there was nobody there. She took a deep breath and contemplated whether to open the door or leave it. She turned on her heel and headed back for the kitchen.

The doorbell rang again.

She took her phone out of her pocket, logged on to the security app and scrolled back to see who had been to her front door. It was a man in overalls carrying a bunch of flowers and leaving them on her doorstep. He'd got back into his van with the word *Interflora* on the side and driven away. A purely harmless delivery.

On the doorstep was a bunch of yellow roses with a card attached.

Olivia stepped out into the dying daylight and looked down the cul-de-sac. Surely they could only be from Richard this time. He would never stop taunting her. Foley had said he'd contact the prison and ask for his mail to be monitored, but someone so cold and calculating would always find a way.

She removed the card and kicked the flowers down the steps. Let them die in the freezing temperature tonight.

Back in the kitchen, she placed the envelope on the island and went back to making her pasta. She kept looking from the dough to the iPad to the card and back to the dough again. She couldn't concentrate. She needed to read what he'd said.

She dusted off her hands, took a large swig of the wine she'd poured herself and tore open the cheap envelope. There was no mistaking her father's handwriting. He always wrote in neat block capital letters. She wondered what a handwriting expert would make of that; something to do with dominance and control, no doubt.

OLIVIA,

FROM THE MOMENT JAMIE FARR CAME INTO MY HOSPITAL ROOM, TOLD ME WHO HE WAS AND REVEALED HIS PLANS FOR YOU, I KNEW IT WOULDN'T BE A FAIR CONTEST. YOU ARE A MUCH STRONGER PERSON THAN HE WAS BOTH MENTALLY AND PHYSICALLY. I KNEW YOU WOULD SURVIVE.

AS YOU KNOW, I'VE FOLLOWED YOUR CAREER FROM THE BEGINNING. I'VE READ YOUR BOOKS. I'VE WATCHED YOUR LECTURES ON THE INTERNET. I'VE READ YOUR PAPERS ONLINE. THEY'RE FASCINATING. YOU HAVE A WONDERFUL INSIGHT, BUT THERE HAS ALWAYS BEEN SOMETHING MISSING FROM THEM. YOU'VE NEVER QUITE GOT TO THE HEART AND SOUL OF WHAT MAKES SOMEONE A KILLER.

I EXPECT YOUR NEXT BOOK WILL BE SOMETHING DIFFERENT AS YOU USE YOUR NEW-FOUND KNOWLEDGE TO UNLOCK THE SECRETS OF WHY SOME PEOPLE KILL.

IN YOUR WORK YOU'VE ALWAYS STATED THAT IT TAKES A SURVIVOR TO UNDERSTAND A KILLER. YOU'RE WRONG. IT TAKES A KILLER TO UNDERSTAND A KILLER. NOW YOU ARE

ONE, YOU'LL BE THE BEST FORENSIC PSYCHOLOGIST IN THE WORLD. AND THAT MAKES ME INCREDIBLY PROUD OF YOU.

YOU'VE GOT THE KILLER GENE, JUST LIKE ME.

I'VE PASSED IT DOWN TO YOU.

WE'RE THE SAME, YOU AND I.

WELCOME TO THE CLUB, LIVVY.

Acknowledgments

Publishing something new after so long writing a series is frightening. Fortunately, I have the back-up of some amazing people who give me advice and support that encourages me to evolve as a writer and not be afraid to explore new and exciting ideas. I've said it before but although there is only one name on the front cover of this book, it takes a whole team of people to put it together. Without them, this book would not be in your hands. So, the following people should take a bow:

Jamie Cowen – my agent at the Ampersand Agency who is always available with friendly and professional advice and putting me on the right path when I want to go down another.

Jennie Rothwell – my editor at One More Chapter who allows me so much creative freedom to tell the stories I want to tell and is a staunch supporter of my work.

Philip Lumb – an eminent pathologist who selflessly shares his expert knowledge in all things to do with post mortems. I may turn green reading his emails, but I couldn't write crime fiction without his input.

Simon Browes – a very prominent figure within the NHS who helps me with medical advice and tells me what happens to the human body when it has a sharp knife stuck into it. It bleeds, apparently.

"Mr Tidd" – my police contact who supplies me with the answers to what I assume to him are basic and pathetic questions, but he always answers me with a smile in the name of accuracy.

Andrew Barrett – a Crime Scene Manager and a fellow crime

writer who goes above and the beyond the call of duty to help me write the crime scene chapters. He really knows his stuff.

Any technical errors found within this novel are all my fault. Do not blame the experts listed above. I often have to change things to make them fit the story, but I try to be as accurate as possible. However, this is a work of fiction and not a technical manual.

Behind the scenes at HarperCollins and One More Chapter, the following people worked incredibly hard to make this book a reality: Simon Fox (copy-editing), Tony Russell (proofreading), Lucy Bennett (cover design), Arsalan Isa (editorial assistant), Emma Petfield and Chloe Cummings (marketing), Charlotte Ledger (publisher). Thank you, thank you, thank you.

Ask any writer and they will tell you that it can get quite lonely sitting in front of a computer screen every day. It helps to have the strong support of friends, family and hangers-on around you for textual support and basically to have a giggle with from time to time. Mum, Chris Schofield, Kevin Embleton, Jonas Alexander, Chris Simmons, Tom Simpson – you've all made me laugh and supported me in some way during the course of writing this book. Thank you.

Finally, to the readers, the reviewers, the bloggers, and my fellow authors who read early drafts of this book, I really cannot thank you enough. Writing is hard work but when you get a message from someone saying how much they enjoyed your book, it makes it all worthwhile.

Olivia Winter will return in 2025 and I hope you'll all be with me as her journey continues.

Extract: Vengeance is Mine

Read on for an exclusive extract from *Vengeance is Mine*, Michael Wood's standalone thriller releasing in 2024.

Prologue

Sunday, 14 February 1999
Winlaton, Tyne and Wear

Stephanie White had been begging and pleading with her parents for months to buy her a pair of rollerblades for her birthday, and now she finally had them on, she realised she had no idea how to stay upright.

As she rolled carefully down the cul-de-sac where she lived, she could hear from the doorstep the faint sound of her parents stifling giggles. At the bottom of the road, she grabbed hold of a lamp-post, clung to it for dear life, turned back and waved at them with a huge grin on her face to show how pleased she was with the gift. They waved back.

Biting her lip and trying not to show how much pain her ankles were in, she pushed off from the lamp-post and headed for the shops. Her plan was to sit on a bench for half an hour or so before heading back home and saying how brilliant she was at rollerblading and how they were the best present ever.

Stephanie was thirteen years old today. Along with the rollerblades, her parents had surprised her with a Newcastle United home football shirt which had been signed on the shoulder by her favourite player – Alan Shearer. When she had unwrapped it, she burst into tears and threw herself into her father's arms. The surprises hadn't been over though, and she opened an envelope to find two tickets to the next home game with VIP treatment. This really was the best birthday.

It was a cold and misty February day, but Stephanie had refused to wear a coat as she left the house. She wanted the whole world to see she was wearing a brand-new home football shirt, signed by the living god, Alan Shearer.

There were very few people around, which Stephanie was secretly pleased about, now she realised how terrible she was at skating. The last thing she wanted was to be laughed at, and if her mother found out how unsteady she was, she'd be in for a lecture beginning with the dreaded line 'I told you so.'

She struggled along Church Street, holding onto every lamp-post she passed to keep herself stable. She managed to get across the road without any problems and came to rest at the railings outside the Co-op. She looked at her reflection staring back at her through the window. Her blonde hair, tied back in a ponytail, had come loose, and strands were sticking to her head. Her face was red, and sweat was dripping down her face. She wanted to call on Terry and show him the blades, but not when she looked like this.

Stephanie struggled on down the alley beside the Co-op and almost collided with a man.

Extract: Vengeance is Mine

'I'm so sorry.'

'That's all right,' he said, holding her up by the elbows. 'Are you okay?'

'Yes. I think so.'

'You were coming down there at quite a speed.'

'I know. Sorry. I can't get used to these rollerblades.'

'Practice makes perfect.'

'That's what my mum always says. She's a teacher.'

'She should know then.' He laughed. 'Are you sure you're all right? You look like you're in a bit of pain.'

'They're pinching my ankles. I think they might be a bit tight.'

'You should take them off. They might have broken the skin. My mum always puts Vaseline in new shoes to help loosen them up.'

'I'll see if Mum's got some. Thanks.'

Stephanie became aware the man was still holding her by the elbows, and she felt uncomfortable. He was very close to her, and she could feel his warm breath on her face as he spoke.

'Is that the new Newcastle home shirt?'

'Yes.' She smiled awkwardly. 'I got it this morning. My dad bought it for me as a birthday present. Alan Shearer signed it,' she said, showing him the signature.

'Wow. That's pretty cool. I'm a massive football fan.'

'Me too. We've got VIP tickets for the next home game too.'

'You're very lucky.'

A car drove past. Stephanie looked up and saw a young girl watching her from the back seat.

'I've got a programme signed by Alan Shearer,' the man said.

'Have you?'

'Yes. And Shay Given too. Would you like it?'

'Don't you want it?' She frowned.

He slowly looked her up and down. 'I think you're a bigger fan than I am. You should have it. Call it a birthday gift from me.'

'That's very kind of you, but Mum and Dad have always told me not to accept anything from strangers.'

'Very wise. Look, see that white van over there?' He pointed to a dirty white van parked in front of the hairdresser's a few car lengths away. 'That's mine. The programme is in there. I can give it to you now, and you can be on your way home.'

Stephanie hesitated.

'It'll probably end up getting torn and ruined and thrown in the bin, which is a shame when you think about it.' He smiled at her. 'It'll only take a couple of minutes. I've also got some cushioned plasters that might help your ankles as well.' He headed off towards the van. He stopped after a few steps and turned back. 'Are you coming?'

Stephanie frowned as she considered what to do. She really shouldn't, but a programme signed by Alan Shearer and Shay Given would be immense. Her father would love it.

'Okay,' she said and followed him.

Chapter 1

Monday, 7 January 2019
Ryton, Tyne and Wear

'Who the bloody hell is ringing me at this time of night?'

I turned on the bedside light and squinted. It was like having a searchlight shone in my face. I had no idea what time it was. All I knew was that it was still dark, and I should be in dreamland. I couldn't focus on the display of my phone, but it wasn't somebody's name, just a series of random numbers. If this was some knob from a call centre on the other side of the world, I would not be happy.

'Yes?' I answered. I'm not a morning person. Even when it's

Extract: Vengeance is Mine

actual morning and time to get up for work. I like my bed, and I like my sleep.

'Dawn Shepherd?'

Oh God, it *was* someone from a call centre. I could hear the sounds of an open-plan office in the background.

'Yes?'

'Do you know a woman by the name of Rita Shepherd?'

Okay, now they had my attention. Suddenly, I was wide awake.

'Yes, she's my mother. Who is this?'

'My name is Suzanne Hardy. I'm a constable with Northumbria Police.'

'Police? What's happened?' A phone call in the middle of the night is never good news. But when the call is from a police officer, it can only mean one thing. *Oh my God, please don't let Mum be dead. She's the only relative I've got left.*

'A woman was found attempting to break into a shop in the shopping precinct in Blaydon. We arrested her for drunk and disorderly. She gave us the name of Rita Shepherd and your contact details.'

'What? That can't be right. My mother doesn't drink. Are you sure it's my mum?'

'Five foot two inches tall, slim, about seven stone, dark brown shoulder-length hair, a tattoo on the inside of her left arm with a date, the fifth of November 1998.'

'That's my date of birth.'

'In that case, we have your mother in the station. Apparently, the shop she was trying to break into was her own,' said the police officer.

'Hollyhocks?'

'That's the one.'

'Shit.'

'I've spoken to your mother at length and, in between crying,

Extract: Vengeance is Mine

she's told me a rather distressing tale. Do you think you could come and collect her?'

'Erm… yes… of course. I'll be right down.'

This made no sense. My mum doesn't touch alcohol. Why was she trying to break into her own shop when she had a key, and why the hell was she drunk? She won't even have sherry trifle at Christmas.

I kicked off the duvet and immediately felt the chill of the cold winter night. I'm not the neatest person in the world, so I had to scramble around the floor trying to find something decent and warm to wear. I grabbed my keys from the chest of drawers and was just about to leave my bedroom when I caught sight of myself in the mirror. I could not leave the house with dried drool on my chin, a crease in my face and my hair all over the place.

I ran into the bathroom and splashed cold water on my face. That certainly woke me up. I couldn't do anything about the crease running down my cheek – hopefully it would have faded by the time I got to the station – but a beanie hat would hide the Russell Brand tragedy I call my hair.

There wasn't a cloud in the sky when I left the block of flats, just an infinite number of stars. It was bloody freezing, and frost sparkled on every surface under the sodium of the street lamps.

I drive a VW Golf which is almost as old as I am. I slammed the door once I was inside and the sound resounded around the quiet neighbourhood. A light went on across the street. *Oops. Never mind.* The engine started on the sixth attempt. By the time it came to life, more lights had come on in houses along the road. I didn't turn the heater on. My car couldn't cope with driving and warming up the people inside at the same time. It was one or the other. I'd have to remain cold.

As I entered the police station, I realised this was my first time inside one. I'd recently started a new job: I was on the cusp of becoming one of the great paralegals of the twenty-first century… Although, at present, my job was mostly filing, making coffee and

Extract: Vengeance is Mine

asking Sharon if she wanted any post taking to the box on the corner. Still, we all have to start somewhere.

The tired-looking bloke behind the desk took my name, and I sat down on the hard plastic chair, looking around me at all the crime prevention posters. There was a strong smell of disinfectant that was tickling my nostrils. I wanted to sneeze, but the desk sergeant looked like he was about to nod off, and I didn't want to disturb him.

The door to the main part of the station opened, and a short, stick-thin police officer stepped out. She looked younger than me, and her uniform seemed a size too big.

'Miss Shepherd?'

'Yes.'

'I'm PC Hardy. We spoke on the phone. Would you like to come through?'

There I was, five foot seven, twenty-one years old and, despite my mother's many reassurances that I'm big-boned and have childbearing hips, I prefer to speak plainly and call myself fat. Next to me was a teeny-tiny police officer, and we were walking down the corridor looking like a comedy double act. I felt like I was in a farce.

'What happened?' I asked. 'My mum doesn't drink. She doesn't like alcohol. She never has done.'

'Well, I'm afraid she's taken a taste to it now. In a big way.'

'And you say she was trying to break into her own shop?'

'She was kicking the bottom glass panel of the front door. It's going to need replacing, I'm afraid.'

'Are you charging her with anything?'

She stopped walking. I carried on until I couldn't hear her dinky feet catching up alongside me.

'I've had a chat with your mum. She's told me something quite distressing. Have you noticed a change in her behaviour lately?'

I thought for a moment. 'She's been a bit quieter than usual, I suppose.'

'And she hasn't said anything to you about... anything?'

'Like what?'

'Look.' PC Hardy placed a hand on my arm. It wasn't comforting at all. In fact, it was incredibly awkward. The only Hardy I want touching me is Tom, and in that scenario, we wouldn't be fully dressed in a police station. 'There's something your mother has been wrestling with, but I think she's ready to tell you now. I've had a word with my sergeant, and he's perfectly happy to issue your mother with a caution and let her go.'

'Oh my God. She's ill, isn't she? She's dying.' My eyes filled with tears. I felt sick. I could taste last night's disappointing korma.

'It's nothing like that, I assure you. It's just... you should prepare yourself for a bit of a shock.'

The first shock was seeing the state of my mother. Rita Shepherd is the complete opposite of me. She's petite, dainty, wee. She wears size eight clothes and size three shoes. She's always dressed smart, doesn't overdo the make-up and has her hair professionally touched up once every three weeks to hide the grey she's paranoid about. The wreck of a woman waiting for me in the charging suite of the local nick was nothing like the person I've called Mum for the last twenty-one years. The moment she looked up and saw me, the tears started to stream down her face. I took a deep breath. I wanted to cry too but knew I needed to be the strong one here. This wasn't going to be easy.

The drive back to Mum's house in Ryton was fraught with tension. I kept glancing at her as we drove quietly along the deserted roads. Every time we passed a lamp-post, and the bright yellow light entered the car, her face lit up. She was unrecognisable. Who was this woman sitting next to me? She was slumped in her seat, arms rigidly folded, a look of tiredness and embarrassment etched on her face. The car reeked of alcohol. I wanted to talk to her, to ask her what the hell was going on, but now wasn't the right time. I just needed to get her home. Besides, I had no idea where to begin. There were so many questions running around my mind, I didn't know which one to ask first.

Once inside the three-bedroom semi-detached house I'd grown up in, in the comfort of a warm living room, both of us holding mugs of hot, strong coffee, I couldn't hold my tongue any longer.

'You've got some explaining to do, apparently.' I felt like the mother here. This was a real reversal of roles, and I didn't like it.

Mum nodded.

'What is it? Are you ill?'

'No,' she said, her voice barely above a whisper.

'Money worries?'

'No.'

'What is it then?'

'Dawn, just let me tell you in my own way.'

'Go on then.'

My lips were pursed. I glared at my mum, my role model, my hero. I couldn't begin to fathom what was going on inside her head. We never kept secrets from each other. We prided ourselves on having a very open and honest relationship. I told my mum everything – from the big issues like getting a new job, to the embarrassing ones like the time I was caught having sex in a bus shelter with Mark Foster on the night I passed my driving test. Mum reciprocated. She told me about the time she found a lump in her breast (fortunately, it was only a cyst) and when her business was in trouble (now fully solvent again). There was nothing, as far as I was aware, that my mother could be keeping from me.

'I was hoping I'd never have to tell you,' Mum began. A tear escaped her left eye and ran down her cheek. 'I don't buy newspapers, as you know, but I went into Morrisons, and there it was on the front page of a couple of tabloids. I almost collapsed right there and then. I've been looking online ever since, and it looks like it's definitely happening.'

'Mum... I don't know what you're talking about.'

'It's about your dad,' Mum said, looking up at me for the first time.

'My dad?'

She took a deep breath to compose herself. 'I've been lying to you your whole life. I've always known who your father is. I've always known where he is.'

I could feel my eyes widening. So this was the shock the PC was talking about. When I had been old enough to understand, Mum had sat me down and told me that she hadn't known my dad, had just met him once at a party, and although it hadn't been planned, she had been over the moon when she discovered she was pregnant. She had known she didn't need a husband or a stepfather to raise me – she was more than capable of bringing me up single-handed, and that's what she had done. I was a credit to her, apparently. Everybody said so. I'm not one to blow my own trumpet, but ten GCSE passes, all As and Bs; three A-levels, two As and a B. And... Screw it, why not brag? A first from Newcastle University.

'Who is he? Where is he?' I asked, the words tripping over each other as I spoke.

My mum cried. The tears fell in a torrent. She couldn't speak. All my life I'd wanted to know who my dad was. It was hurting me seeing Mum so upset, but I needed her to explain.

From under the sofa cushion, she produced a copy of the *Evening Chronicle* and handed it to me.

The newspaper was a week old. The front-page headline was huge: STEPHANIE WHITE'S KILLER TO BE RELEASED. I remembered reading that story in my lunch-hour. Stephanie White was a teenage girl who disappeared on her thirteenth birthday in 1999. Her killer was due to be released early for some reason I couldn't remember; I had only skimmed the story. Why was she showing me this?

'I don't understand,' I said.

Extract: Vengeance is Mine

'Dominic Griffiths,' Mum said through the tears, 'the man who killed Stephanie White. He's your father.'

My stomach lurched, and I suddenly felt freezing cold. What was she saying to me? I couldn't bring myself to look back at the newspaper I was holding. I couldn't take my eyes off my mum, searching her face for answers. She nodded, confirming what she'd said. Eventually, I looked down at the paper on my lap and at the small photograph of a young Dominic Griffiths staring back at me. He had only been twenty years old when that picture was taken, when he'd butchered little Stephanie. He was tall and had broad shoulders, large brown eyes and dark, floppy hair. I remembered looking at this exact same photo when I read the story last week and thought he looked pretty hot for a murderer. I had no idea I'd been looking at my father.

Oh my God, I actually thought my father was hot. My father, the killer.

I heaved. I dropped the paper and lifted a hand to my mouth, but it didn't get there in time. I vomited all over myself.

Chapter 2

'Are you all right?' Mum asked.

I walked into the kitchen with a spare dressing gown wrapped around me. After being sick all over myself, I'd gone upstairs to the bathroom, peeled off my clothes and jumped straight into the shower. I was in there for ages, just letting the hot needles of water rain down on me, numbing the pain. Actually, I didn't know if I was in pain. I couldn't feel anything. I couldn't make sense of anything I'd just been told.

Less than five hours ago, I was eating a shitty curry and flicking through the channels for something decent to watch. I was living in blissful ignorance. Now, suddenly, I was the daughter of one of the most hated men in Britain.

All through my childhood, I'd asked about my dad. *Where's*

Extract: Vengeance is Mine

Daddy? Will Daddy be here for Christmas? Why do Charlotte and Jodie and Teresa have a daddy, and I don't? When I was old enough, Mum had told me what I always believed to be the truth. She had put on an Oscar-winning performance, and I'd fallen for it. I mean, who would lie about getting knocked up after a one-night stand at a party with a complete stranger?

By the time I'd stepped out of the shower, my skin was red from the heat of the water. I'd felt cleaner, but I didn't feel any better. I'd dried myself and plonked myself down on the toilet lid, still mulling over all the questions running around my mind, wondering which one to ask first. I'd grabbed the dressing gown from the back of the door of my old bedroom and had slowly gone down the stairs. To be honest, I was dreading having to look my mother in the eye.

Mum was standing at the sink, rinsing out the bucket of soapy water she'd used to mop up the sick in the living room. My clothes were whirring around in the washing machine. I hoped they would dry quickly; I wanted to go home.

Mum turned to look at me. Her eyes were wide and full of tears. She seemed to have aged a decade in the past half an hour.

'Are you all right?' she asked a second time, and I didn't answer or move from the doorway.

I shook my head.

'Is there anything I can do? Or say?'

'Everything,' I said, stepping into the kitchen. 'Have you got any wine?'

'No. I don't—'

'I didn't think you did. It turns out you're full of surprises, though,' I said, sitting down at the kitchen table with a heavy thud.

'Would you like me to make you another coffee?'

I nodded. 'Better make it a strong one.'

'I think I'll join you.'

As Mum set about making the coffee, I kept turning to steal

Extract: Vengeance is Mine

glances at her. I had so much respect and admiration for my mum. She'd been a single parent, struggling to run a business and bring up a daughter on her own. It hadn't been easy, but she'd succeeded. When I was young, all I had wanted was to grow up to be like the strong woman she was.

'Do you want something to eat?' Mum asked.

'Sorry?' I'd heard her speak but hadn't heard the words. She repeated the question. 'No. I don't think I could eat anything.' First time for everything.

Mum brought the mugs over to the table, followed by the full biscuit barrel. She sat down at the opposite end of the table and took a sip of the hot drink.

'Wow. That really is strong. Just what I need,' she said, giving me an uncomfortable smile. 'I'm going to have a headache tomorrow.'

I didn't comment. I looked down into my mug as if it had all the answers I was looking for. Usually when I had something to contemplate, I sought solace in a bottle of wine or three. I doubted coffee would have the same desired effect.

'Dawn, talk to me,' Mum pleaded.

It was a while before I looked up. 'I don't know where to start.'

'Tell me how you're feeling.'

'If I knew, I would.'

'Are you mad at me?'

'Yes, I think I am. Why did you lie to me, Mum? All these years. I can understand you not telling me when I was a child asking where my daddy was, but when I was old enough, you could have sat me down and explained.'

'I know,' she said. More tears ran down her cheeks. She grabbed a tissue from the box on the table and wiped them away. 'I've wrestled with this for so long. Every time I decided to tell you, a voice in my head said I shouldn't, that you were better off not knowing the truth. Whenever I started to think you had a right to know, the voice would speak louder and... I don't know.'

Extract: Vengeance is Mine

She blew her nose, wiped her eyes and took a deep breath. 'Ask me anything. It's time to reveal the truth now. Ask me anything you want, and I'll give you an honest answer straight from the heart.'

'Why didn't you tell me before?' I asked firmly.

'When you were a child, I wanted to protect you. There was a lot of ill feeling around here about what Dominic did. There still is. I thought if I told you and you told a friend at school... Kids can be so cruel. I didn't want you being bullied.'

I nodded. 'I can understand that.'

My mum's face softened.

'How did you meet him?' I asked.

'At a party. We didn't go to the same school. It was Lizzie Denham's eighteenth. I met Dominic, and we had a few drinks and a laugh and arranged to meet up that weekend for a date.'

I smiled as I saw the brightness return to my mum's eyes as she remembered a time that was obviously special to her.

I've often wondered why Mum never married or even had a boyfriend. She met the odd bloke, and a couple of them were incredibly odd, but nothing ever went beyond a few dates. She always said she'd been on her own too long and was used to doing her own thing. I can certainly understand that. I may only be twenty-one, but I've been on enough dates to know, more often than not, men can be complete tossers – mentioning no names, Neil Whitaker.

'How long did you go out together for?'

'About a year.'

'What was he like?'

It was a while before Mum answered. It looked like she was struggling to find the right words. 'He was... lovely.' She gave a painful smile.

'Lovely. Is that it?'

'No. He was... sweet and kind and funny, but... he could be a bit overbearing at times.'

'How do you mean?'

'Remember Melanie Pritchard? Had the shop next to me, sold all that crap jewellery?' I nodded. 'Remember her husband? He was always phoning her asking what time she was shutting, what time she'd be home, where she was going, who she was meeting. Well, Dominic was a bit like that. He was… clingy.'

'Maybe he really liked you?'

'Maybe.' She shrugged.

'Did Nan and Grandad meet him?'

'Yes. They got on well with him.'

'So, what happened?'

'We were only eighteen. I was about to go to university. He didn't know what he wanted to do. He wasn't very academic, if I remember correctly. Anyway, people kept telling me not to have a boyfriend when I went to uni, as it wouldn't last and one of us would end up getting hurt. Also, I was planning on going to Sheffield, and I know it's not far, but I didn't want to do the whole long-distance thing. So we decided to end it.'

'How did he take it?'

Mum took a deep breath. 'He cried. A lot. I cried too.'

'He cried?' I was surprised.

'Yes. He told me… he told me he loved me.'

'But you didn't feel the same way?'

'No.'

'Why not?'

'I can't believe I'm telling you this. He was my first boyfriend. I didn't know what love was. I liked him, obviously. But love? No. I didn't love him.'

'Had I already been conceived at that point?'

'No. He asked if we could have one last night together. He picked me up in his van, and we went out for a meal in town. It was a good night.'

'Then what happened?'

'Well, you can imagine the rest.'

Extract: Vengeance is Mine

'And then you got pregnant. I bet Nan and Grandad went mad.'

'Your nan cried buckets. Grandad went ballistic. It took me ages to build up the courage to tell them, and I'd already started showing by the time I did, but I'd come up with a plan. If they were willing to help me look after you, I'd defer uni for a year, apply to Newcastle and stay at home.'

'And Grandad was okay with that?' I asked. As much as I'd loved Pop-pop and Mee-maw, I knew that Grandad had been tough and old-fashioned. I would have hated to tell him I was pregnant at eighteen.

'Your nan won him over, eventually,' Mum said, with a smile.

'Did you tell Dominic you were pregnant?'

'I did. I thought he had a right to know.'

'What did he say?'

Mum looked away briefly in embarrassment. 'He asked me to marry him.'

'He proposed! I'm guessing you turned him down.' She nodded. 'Why?'

'Like I said, I didn't love him. He didn't have any direction. He had no plan for what he wanted to do with his life. I was eighteen, still living at home and pregnant, yet I knew I wanted to have my own business. I let him down very gently. I told him I wasn't completely shutting him out. I said he could have as much input in raising you as he wanted.'

'So, what happened?'

'His mother happened. The next day, she came over to the house, banging on the door, demanding to be let in. She was a frightening woman.'

'Had you never met her before?'

'No. Dominic always put me off meeting his parents. He said they were very set in their ways.'

'So she came round?'

'She called me every name under the sun. I was a slag, a slut, a bitch, a whore. I'd trapped her son by getting pregnant to force him to marry me. She was furious.'

'Bloody hell. What happened?'

'Your grandfather happened. He read her the riot act and practically threw her out of the house. She left but told us not to have any contact with her or Dominic ever again. I was in tears when she left.'

'Did you ever see Dominic again?'

'Not until about three months after you were born.'

'Did he come to see me?' I asked, with a smile.

'No. I didn't see him in person. I saw him on the news being led to the back of a police car in handcuffs.'

Vengeance is Mine will be available in paperback and ebook in 2024!

DCI Matilda Darke...

Have you discovered the DCI Matilda Darke Thrillers?

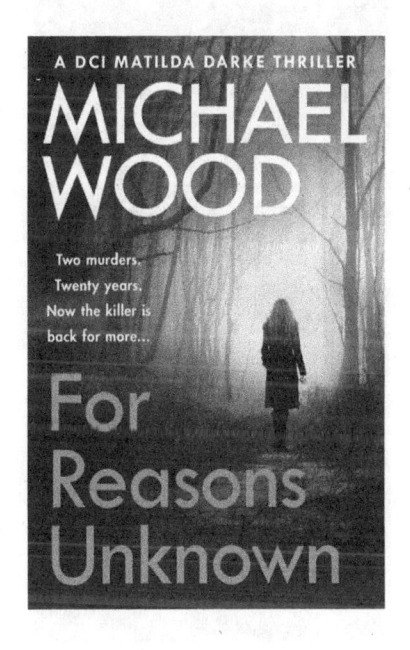

DCI Matilda Darke...

A DCI MATILDA DARKE THRILLER

MICHAEL WOOD

Two perfect families.
Two broken marriages.
And a killer who needs
to be stopped...

Outside Looking In

'She is the perfect heroine' ELLY GRIFFITHS

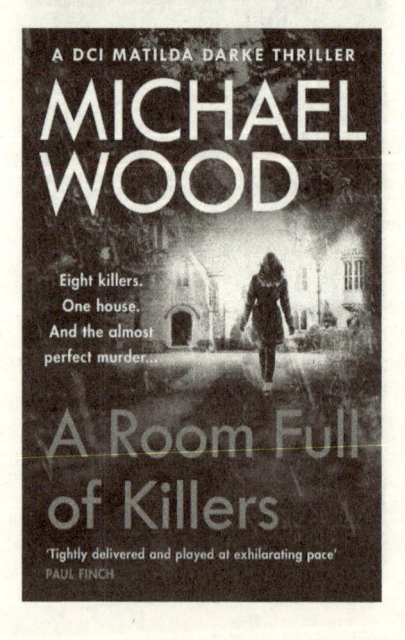

A DCI MATILDA DARKE THRILLER

MICHAEL WOOD

Eight killers.
One house.
And the almost
perfect murder...

A Room Full of Killers

'Tightly delivered and played at exhilarating pace'
PAUL FINCH

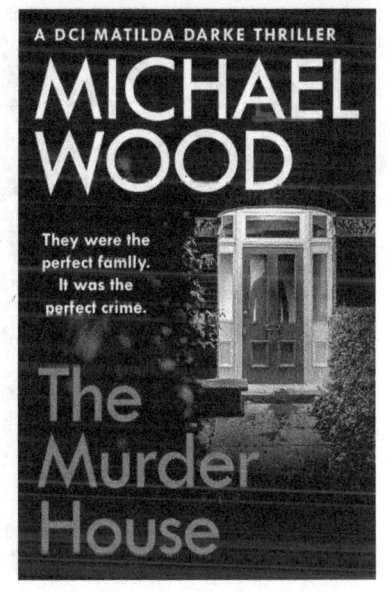

DCI Matilda Darke...

A DCI MATILDA DARKE THRILLER
MICHAEL WOOD
The Hangman's Hold
Your life is in his hands...
'Watch out for those twists – you won't see them coming!'
STEPHEN BOOTH

A DCI MATILDA DARKE THRILLER
MICHAEL WOOD
They were the perfect family. It was the perfect crime.
The Murder House

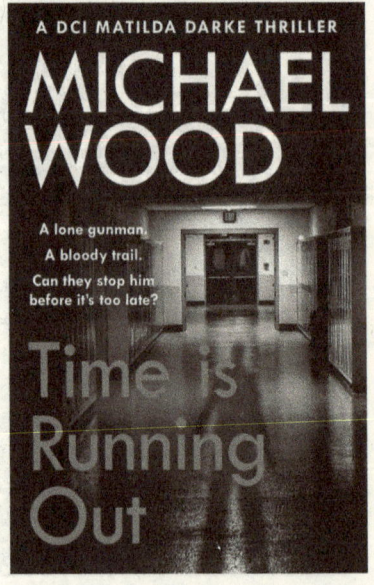

DCI Matilda Darke...

A DCI MATILDA DARKE THRILLER
MICHAEL WOOD
One Taken.
One Found.
Stolen Children

A DCI MATILDA DARKE THRILLER
MICHAEL WOOD
A lone gunman.
A bloody trail.
Can they stop him before it's too late?
Time is Running Out

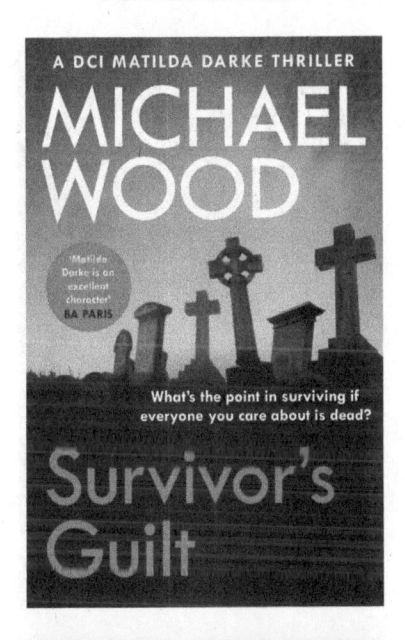

DCI Matilda Darke...

A DCI MATILDA DARKE THRILLER
MICHAEL WOOD

'Matilda Darke is an excellent character'
BA PARIS

What's the point in surviving if everyone you care about is dead?

Survivor's Guilt

A DCI MATILDA DARKE THRILLER
MICHAEL WOOD

The Lost Children

Twenty years of silence
Until now

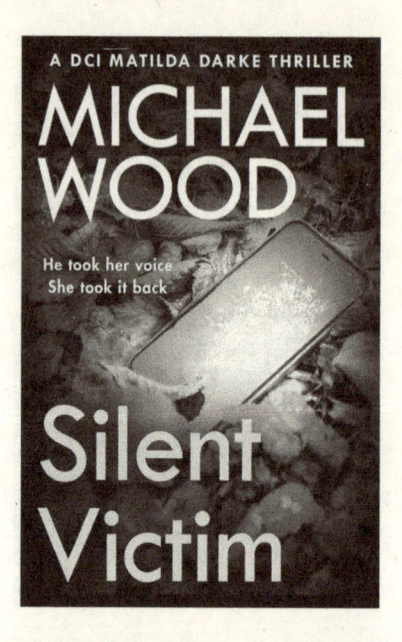

DCI Matilda Darke...

A DCI MATILDA DARKE THRILLER
MICHAEL WOOD

He took her voice
She took it back

Silent Victim

A DCI MATILDA DARKE SHORT STORY
MICHAEL WOOD

Making of a Murderer

DCI Matilda Darke…

A DCI MATILDA DARKE THRILLER

MICHAEL WOOD

The last place you
want to be found is…

Below
Ground

ONE MORE CHAPTER

YOUR NUMBER ONE STOP FOR PAGETURNING BOOKS

The author and One More Chapter would like to thank everyone who contributed to the publication of this story…

Analytics
Abigail Fryer
Maria Osa

Audio
Fionnuala Barrett
Ciara Briggs

Contracts
Georgina Hoffman
Florence Shepherd

Design
Lucy Bennett
Fiona Greenway
Holly Macdonald
Liane Payne
Dean Russell

Digital Sales
Lydia Grainge
Emily Scorer
Georgina Ugen

Editorial
Simon Fox
Arsalan Isa
Charlotte Ledger
Bonnie Macleod
Jennie Rothwell
Tony Russell
Kimberley Young

International Sales
Bethan Moore

Marketing & Publicity
Chloe Cummings
Emma Petfield

Operations
Melissa Okusanya
Hannah Stamp

Production
Emily Chan
Denis Manson
Francesca Tuzzeo

Rights
Lana Beckwith
Rachel McCarron
Agnes Rigou
Hany Sheikh Mohamed
Zoe Shine
Aisling Smyth

The HarperCollins Distribution Team

The HarperCollins Finance & Royalties Team

The HarperCollins Legal Team

The HarperCollins Technology Team

Trade Marketing
Ben Hurd
Eleanor Slater

UK Sales
Laura Carpenter
Isabel Coburn
Jay Cochrane
Tom Dunstan
Sabina Lewis
Holly Martin
Erin White
Harriet Williams
Leah Woods

And every other essential link in the chain from delivery drivers to booksellers to librarians and beyond!

ONE MORE CHAPTER

YOUR NUMBER ONE STOP FOR PAGETURNING BOOKS

One More Chapter is an award-winning global division of HarperCollins.

Sign up to our newsletter to get our latest eBook deals and stay up to date with our weekly Book Club!
[Subscribe here.](#)

Meet the team at
www.onemorechapter.com

Follow us!
🐦 @OneMoreChapter_
📘 @OneMoreChapter
📷 @onemorechapterhc

Do you write unputdownable fiction? We love to hear from new voices. Find out how to submit your novel at
www.onemorechapter.com/submissions